Marisa Mackle was born in Armagh, Northern Ireland. Educated at Mount Anville Senior School and University College Dublin, she now divides her time between Dublin and Marbella. She is the author of the number one bestseller *Mr Right for the Night*.

So Long Mr Wrong!

Marisa Mackle

DODDER

First published in Ireland and Great Britain
by Dodder Books Ltd, 2003.

Copyright © Marisa Mackle, 2003

Dodder Books Limited
9 Airfield Court
Dublin 4.

A CIP catalogue record for this book is available from the
British Library.

ISBN 0954491300

Cover design by Conánn FitzPatrick
Cover photo by Jim FitzPatrick
Typeset by Palimpsest Book Production Limited
Polmont, Stirlingshire.

Printed and bound in Great Britain
by Cox & Wyman Ltd, Reading, Berks.

Acknowledgements

Thanks to:

God, for making it all happen.

Sheila Collins for making my life so worthwhile.

Eamonn Mackle for organising my book tour and for being a wonderful father.

My sisters Tara and Naomi for all their support and my mum Daphne for patiently reading the manuscript as I wrote it.

My incredible friend Roxanne Parker.

Noelle O'Connor for setting up and managing my website.

My dear fellow writers: Catherine Barry, Cathy Kelly, Colette Caddle, Martina Devlin, Annie Sparrow, Dawn Cairns, Joan O'Neill, Tina Reilly, Julie Parsons, Catherine Dunne, Jacinta McDevitt, Mary Stanley, Shari Low, Niamh O'Connor, Marita Conlon McKenna, and Claire Dowling.

Also Sarah Webb who has done wonders for my social life and has been a fantastic friend, and Ethan Hawke for the kind words and for reading *Mr Right for the Night*.

Maeve Binchy for the encouragement at the beginning and also to Deirdre Purcell.

Everybody in Aer Lingus, especially Willie Walsh, Paula Pryor, Orla Kealy, Gráinne O' Malley, Lenora Naughton, Arthur Green, my former boss Colm Crowley and Tricia Dardis.

The wonderful Aer Lingus cabin crew, especially Sharon Ellis, Lisa Warren, Cara Minnock, Jane Curtin, Vanessa Landers, Barry Cunningham, Audrey Fennell, Nicola Keating, Suzanne Geoghan, Niamh Dunne, Karen O'Neill, Kara Long, Fiona Beare, Patrick Duffy, Tara Healy, Suzanne Gore, Louise Kane, Linda Dunne, Donna Murray, Ruth Connolly.

My friends: Barbara O' Donnell, Angela Jones, Jim FitzPatrick, Leah Feagan, Karen Walsh, Alma Curtis, Leisa Gafoor, Marjorie Parker, Eileen Jones, Michelle Quinn, Marian Flynn, Marie McAndrew, Niav Devine, Adrienne Leahy, Lorraine Shannon, Catherine Hickey.

Also Richard McNamara, Emer O'Reilly, Catherine Greenhalgh, Suzanne Tuthill, Etain Boyd, Larissa Nolan, Ken Finlay, Sue Leonard, Conánn FitzPatrick, Neassa Kiernan, Padraidh Hearns, Georgina Heffernan My editor Síne Quinn and to Ali O' Reilly for press and publicity.

My former English teacher Sr Íde ni Riain.

Eoin, David, Sally, Adrian and all the staff in Easons and also Andrew, Danny, Merlin and everyone in Hughes and Hughes and in Argosy as well as the staff in Dubray, Hodges Figgis, Waterstone's,

O'Mahony's, The Ennis Bookshop, Dublin Book-shop, Grafton Street, Hampton Books, Donnybrook and all the wonderful booksellers, especially Monica in Carroll's Dundalk, John and Mary in Easons Drogheda, Denise in Bookworld, Knocklyon S.C, Bláithin and the staff in Dundrum Books, Kenny's, Galway, Monica, Bernie, Anne and Jean of Easons, and The Open Book Co., Sutton for the wonderful window display.

The readers who turned up to the book signings and those who wrote such lovely letters.

Frank Coughlan, Dave Lawlor and David Diebold of the *Evening Herald*.

Joe Burns of Club Anabel.

Claire McKeon of Bliss Salon.

And finally and most importantly to St Jude and St Anthony for answered prayers.

www.marisamackle.com

To Sheila Collins with all my love.

Part One

Chapter One

Caroline's Richard was a man of his word.

He was also the 'marrying' kind.

A fact that pleased her family a lot.

And made some of her friends jealous.

Because *their* men were definitely *not* the marrying kind.

Caroline's Richard had decided he wanted to get married on his thirty-second birthday.

He'd always fancied a summer wedding.

A hot summer wedding preferably.

And thirty-two was a good age to get married.

He was going to be thirty-two next year.

An age when lots of fellows got married.

Before they completely lost their hair.

Yes, Caroline's Richard was definitely a man of his word. You certainly could never accuse him of being 'different'. Caroline should know. She'd been with him for nearly three years.

That's why everybody was surprised when Caroline's Richard finally popped the long awaited question.

To Sandra.
Caroline's best friend.

Chapter Two

The tube stank. It was a sticky sweaty sweltering summer. The heat was unbearable. A kind of filthy underground heat that made your hair disgustingly damp and make-up grubby and patchy. It wasn't sunny, just hot. Everybody was going on about the weather and *Big Brother*. Because nothing else was happening. And editors everywhere were ravenous for news. The World Cup was over; it was time to move on.

Caroline cared for neither the weather nor reality TV. Anyway she preferred the rain. At least when it rained you could hide under your umbrella. That way you didn't have to catch people's eyes and smile. At the moment there was no reason for her to be cheerful.

Things were different over here. People didn't know each other. Nor want to. It wasn't like Dundalk where Caroline was born. Dundalk was a big town near the border of Northern Ireland where everybody knew everybody. A town where there were lots of pubs and where people worried about the effects of Sellafield.

Not that people in Dundalk were particularly smiley. If you were walking down Park Street, people didn't stop to hug you or anything. But in her hometown, Caroline felt she was somebody. Not so in London.

Of course that's why she had come here: to escape. She felt she belonged in London. Very few strangers could claim that. They thought it was difficult to fit in. That's why people commuted so much. Back and forth on crowded weekend trains. But Caroline thought London was perfect, the way you could just blend into the background, with you knowing nobody and nobody knowing you.

The thin man opposite her was staring. Intrusively. Making her uncomfortable. Caroline loathed that. She wasn't a peep show. Normally she just pretended to read. But today there was nothing to read.

People who stared on the tube should be fined, she thought. At least back home in Ireland when people gawked at you on the train, you could pretend to look out the window. At the sea or something. You couldn't do that on the tube. You'd get a headache looking out the window. At the blackness. The nothingness. Apart from your own reflection. Caroline decided that today she wasn't going to examine her fingernails or pretend to stare at the ceiling map like a bewildered tourist. So she eyeballed the man – a lanky, bearded sallow-skinned youth – and raised an eyebrow.

The man exited at Arsenal to Caroline's relief.

She hadn't relished the thought of avoiding eye contact with him all the way to Knightsbridge. A slightly built woman with a tank top and a nose ring took his seat. She was reading a bridal magazine. A smug model graced the front cover. Smirking beneath her tiara. Caroline tried to ignore the image.

Why did magazines use models anyway?

Wouldn't a photo of a wedding cake do?

And why were there so many bridal magazines?

What about single people? Especially newly single people. Or people who had been unceremoniously dumped. Why weren't there articles such as 'Fun for one' or 'What to wear on a night in front of the telly' or 'How to make yourself laugh when everybody else is out?'

There should be more *normal* magazines for sale. Without those 'How to please your man' tips or advice on how to achieve the perfect orgasm. It was embarrassing reading things like that in public with people on the tube looking over your shoulder thinking you were smut.

Caroline arrived into work at 30 seconds to 9:00. She stepped into the lift with its plush red carpet and mirrors that made people look more attractive than they actually were. Her place of employment was a record company where employees were image-conscious. In the darkened mirror Caroline's fair skin looked almost sallow. Her highlights looked subtly blonde.

She exited at level three. If you were fortunate

enough not to work at M-City Music, if you were just a visitor, you'd be forgiven for thinking this might be a cool place to work. Low lighting, polished wooden floors and funky music playing in the background. But Caroline knew the reality. It wasn't great working here. But anything was better than going home to Ireland. Back to her old workplace where people would be pointing and muttering 'there goes that poor Caroline, you know, the one who was dumped.' She wasn't going back there. Not now. Not ever.

At least in London she didn't have to put up with work colleagues pretending to be sympathetic. Nobody ever asked, 'Are you coping all right?'

Her work colleagues weren't bad people or anything; just not as friendly as people were back home. Nobody ever asked what anyone was doing for the weekend. It had been different in her old job. People in Tele-Fone sometimes organised trips to the countryside and that, or if it were somebody's birthday say, everybody would go out for a meal. Caroline had once asked Diane from Telesales how she was planning to spend her weekend. Her colleague had just shrugged and said 'Oh you know . . .'

But Caroline didn't know. That was the point. She'd presumed when she'd got the job in London that she'd make lots of new friends through work and they'd all go out in a big gang. But no, it was nothing like that. Sometimes, if someone was leaving, a few people would go to the nearest pub for one but then they'd all split up and go their separate ways.

They were music heads – trendy people – who hung out in places like Browns, Chinawhite and Sugar Reef. And sometimes, if one of the 'stars' on the M-City Music books was in town, someone would get to accompany them to the Met Bar. That was a highlight. Josh usually got to do it because he worked in Press and Promotions. And he'd always sigh and say he wished he didn't have to go. But nobody believed him because he never let anyone else go instead. And he'd come in the next day, hungover, and give out that the Met wasn't really that good; it was tiny really and overrated. And he'd withhold any interesting gossip.

Everybody in the company said he was a pain in the bum.

And Caroline thought it was funny. Because even though the others bitched about him, they secretly wanted to be him. Out mixing with the stars. Fame by association. That kind of thing. Only . . . it wasn't really like that. Most of it was in their heads. These people dreamed of fame. Craved it. And dreamed of making money one day. They were just too busy making a living now to do anything about it.

Caroline's boss Andy, was always slagging off bands. Even bands he'd signed himself. He said that modern pop bands were overrated. Ten a penny. And couldn't stand the arrogance of their managers. Especially managers of Irish bands, who

thought by throwing in a bit of didley-eye into their
bland songs, that America would love them. But
America didn't love them. That's what Andy said
anyway. He said that the UK might tolerate them.
But not America. America didn't welcome them
with open arms. America sent them home.

'But why do they think Americans would buy
anything?' Caroline asked him one day after he'd
slammed the phone down on yet another whinging
band manager.

'They've watched too much *Jerry Springer* love,'
Andy took his cup of coffee from her. 'But America's
a hard sell. Capped teeth and waxed chests don't cut
too much cloth over there. You're either exceptionally talented – or not.'

Andy maintained that these bands should just give
up after a single attempt trying to 'crack America'.
Like America was an egg. Record companies were
no longer prepared to throw good money after bad.
Jumped up managers who boasted that their bands
were HUGE in Japan or Germany made him sick.
He'd given Caroline a list of names on her first day
and said, 'Even if I'm doing nothing but scratching
my arse Caroline, I'm not talking to these tossers,
understood?'

It was all a bit of a let down really. Working
in the music business. Even the celebrity bashes
were torturous. At least any of the ones Caroline
had attended. At first she'd been impressed. And
excited. Imagine her, a nobody from a town near

Northern Ireland, mingling with exciting international stars! She could barely believe how far she'd come! Just wait 'til Richard saw her in *OK* and *Hello!* magazine, pictured in between *Eminem* and *Jennifer Lopez*!

But it wasn't like that at all.

The first thing that had struck Caroline about these pop stars was how unbelievably tiny they were. And very demanding. Insisting that the air-conditioning be turned down, or moaning that the Guinness hadn't been pulled properly. And sometimes they'd complain about all the 'begrudgers' back home and people being jealous of them.

Caroline had got such a shock when she'd discovered what these people were really like. She'd said so to Diane. 'Oh you get used to it,' the other girl had laughed as they sat in the smoke-filled break room.

'I remember thinking it'd be dead exciting to work in the music industry too. But I've no interest in meeting the stars anymore. Ignorant is their middle and last name. Not that *I* ever get talking to the "stars" in person or anything.'

'But don't you ever meet them on the nights out?' Caroline was amazed. She was under the impression that Diane mingled with them all.

'Oh that's not what this game's about Caroline,' Diane puffed on a Marlboro light. 'You have to know your rung on the VIP ladder.'

'How do you mean?'

'Well, it's like this: the "stars" would never want

to talk to you or me. Ever. They always want to meet other "stars". To boost their own celebrity status. They're not there to waste time. They could have met someone like us before they were famous, do you know what I mean?'

'I suppose so.'

'They're not interested in us,' Diane had continued matter-of-factly. 'We're insignificant in their eyes. Even if we do work for their record company . . . it means nothing to them. Two minutes making small talk with us, means losing two minutes promoting their latest album or making another useful contact. See what I mean?'

Caroline was beginning to see. Clearly.

'And that's career suicide these days when A-listers become B-listers and B-listers become nobodies faster than it takes to make *Big Brother*.'

One celebrity party Caroline was at (and only because someone else couldn't make it), the guests were told that champagne was on the house but you had to pay for the 'coke'. Naively she'd wondered why there'd been a charge for soft drinks instead of the other way round.

But she was hardening up to the whole scene. London chewed up naïve young Irish women like her for breakfast and spat them out before lunch.

Still you had to look on the bright side – it was better than hanging around Ireland where people pretended to be the friendliest people on earth but often weren't.

And it was better than working at Tele-Fone where she'd spent the last three years of her life. When being Richard's girlfriend was the most important thing in her life; work, family and friends coming an insignificant second. She still felt ill when she thought about the time and energy she'd invested in trying to make Richard love her.

She hadn't socialised much in Tele-Fone. People had thought she was boring because she hadn't got legless at the annual Christmas party or slept with any of her male colleagues.

They'd christened her Celibate Caroline after the last Christmas party. That's what she'd been told anyway, by Julie Mutte.

She'd been very upset about the rumour. At the time. But a colleague of hers, Fiona, had told her to take no notice.

'Don't mind that one Julie. She's just the office bike,' Fiona had said.

'I think that's a horrible thing to be called though. Celibate Caroline.'

'Well, it's better than Mutte the Slut,' Fiona pointed out. 'Being considered celibate in a place like Tele-Fone is almost a compliment.'

Caroline shuddered just thinking about it. She didn't really miss the Tele-Fone crowd at all.

Wasting away the hours, days, years in the canteen.

The canteen crowd. They were a unique breed really.

Muttering in the corners of the dreary little basement with its ancient coffee machine and brown, plastic cups. Damning 'them'.

If they think they can . . . they can f . . .

Who were they anyway? The infamous 'they' who took the blame for everything? Who were those awful people known as 'they'?

Caroline sighed. She definitely didn't miss that place. She switched on her trendy laptop. In M-City Music everyone possessed laptops, not like in Tele-Fone where the PCs were the size of old black and white TVs.

Andy wasn't in yet. He wasn't a morning person. A blessing in disguise really. It meant you could enjoy a bit of peace and quiet before he swaggered in, reeking of BO, his black hair greased back into a ponytail. Everyone called him Bandy Andy. Caroline wasn't sure why, maybe it was because he worked with bands, or because he wore the waistband of his trousers up around his ears! Andy's hands were incidentally huge and had a horribly annoying habit of resting on Caroline's shoulders as he dictated letters, usually non-business orientated.

He was supposed to be single. Or divorced rather. But Caroline knew of a lady called Miss Smyth who regularly accompanied Andy on business trips. At least that was the name Caroline was told to put on airline tickets.

Miss Smyth. Hmmm. Original.

Caroline wondered what she was like. After all,

anyone that could share a bed with Bandy Andy and not pass out from the smell of BO must be extraordinary.

The phone rang. Caroline answered promptly. 'Good morning M-City Music?'

Her ear was assaulted by the chorus of Elvis's *A little less conversation*. Caroline patiently waited for the man on the other end of the phone to stop crooning. A typical M-City Music incident. He wasn't the first person to violate her eardrum.

'I'm afraid, our A&R manager is on his holidays,' Caroline explained to the Elvis wannabe. 'But if you'd like to send in a demo CD you're more than welcome.'

'But what did ya fink?' the crooner demanded.

'It doesn't really matter what I think,' Caroline explained wearily. She'd said this so many times over the phone she was beginning to sound like a broken record. 'I'm not the A&R manager.'

'But ya've ears doncha?'

'Have you got our address?' Caroline enquired in a deadpan voice. She didn't want to hurt the guy, who'd probably more chance of being run over by a bus than getting signed. 'Because as I said, you'll just have to send in your demo and take your chances.'

'But they don't listen to them demos, do they? It's just another demo in the bin innit?'

Caroline repeated herself again. Finally the 'future' Elvis seemed to get the message.

This job was really the pits, she thought as she put

down the phone to deal with a courier who didn't know whom he was picking from, never mind who he was delivering to.

Bandy Andy sailed in at about 10:30. He dropped 3 pound coins on Caroline's desk. 'I want you to get me two bananas and a Diet Coke,' he said, 'and when you come back, pop into my office – I've a job for you today my love.'

Surprise, surprise, Caroline thought. Andy had a little job for her every day. And it usually had nothing to do with the music business. Just the other day she'd spent the whole afternoon ringing the small ads. Andy had wanted to know the price of every second-hand red five series Beamer in London. Caroline often wondered what the M-City Music bosses, New York, would think of Andy and his unique time wasting skills?

Chapter Three

Emily-Ann's stomach was grumbling; loud thunder-storm grumbles, in between stabs of lightning hunger pangs. She felt fragile from the lack of food. Weak. But she was being extra good today. So disciplined. Slicing carrots and celery sticks with her teeth all afternoon. Tasteless sticks that made her feel sick. And sugar free gum, for a treat between the sticks. But God she was looking forward to going home. To lie down. To get out of this tedious Baggot Street office. With its claustrophobic walls. Walls that imprisoned her daily between the hours of 9:00 and 5:00.

She was looking forward to escaping and eating a huge plate of juicy cherry tomatoes and red onions sprinkled with freshly ground pepper. She was going to add a sprig of fresh basil and a bit of . . . wait for it . . . cheese. Just a little sliver, mind. But still . . . it was going to be heaven.

Emily-Ann went to the bathroom. Again. She hated having to drink gallons of boring water to fill herself up. The zip on her jeans was about to bust.

Still, it wasn't easy being a stick. Everybody knew that. Even celebrities starved.

When she re-emerged from the Ladies, the sight of a chocolate cake accosted her. Somebody, *somebody* very *cruelly* had produced a chocolate birthday cake for jolly old Tess. Twenty ton Tess who worked at reception. Somebody else had produced paper plates and plastic forks. Emily-Ann was horrified. How was she going to avoid all this without making a scene? Everybody was singing Happy Birthday and Tess was cutting huge slices of chocolate cake.

'For you', she beamed at Emily-Ann handing her the first plate. Emily-Ann stared at her. She felt sick. What kind of a nasty joke was this? Everybody was scrutinising her. Willing her to put on weight. She stuck the plastic fork reluctantly into the cake. 'Go on,' Tess urged. *Get fat. Be like all of us. Go on.*

Tess was smiling inanely. All four chins wobbling as she laughed. Emily-Ann felt dizzy. Slowly she brought the fork to her lips. And opened her mouth. She could feel all eyes of her colleagues on her. Women who'd never be able to put a leg into size 12 trousers. She could read their thoughts. Unkind thoughts. She closed her mouth on the fork, her tongue tasting the soft chocolaty crumbs. Her colleagues kept smiling. And staring. Why couldn't they just fuck off? After all these were the women who spent hour upon hour in the canteen discussing the latest cabbage soup diet! These were the women who absolutely refused to eat anything over four and a half points on the Weight Watchers chart. So why the hell were they guzzling into chocolate cake? Eh?

'Well?' Samantha asked.

'Oh it's divine,' Emily-Ann practically spat, 'You should have a huge piece yourself. I've only one complaint though, there's not enough cream on it, definitely not enough cream. I'll go into the kitchen and get some more.'

She ran into the tiny staff kitchen and scraped her piece of cake into the bin. After counting to ten, she re-emerged with the bowl of cream and a wooden spoon. 'Now,' she said, 'who'd like some?'

After the dreadful ordeal, Emily-Ann sat down at her computer. Relieved that it was all over. Until the next birthday. How many birthdays did the occupants of one poxy little office have anyway? She could still feel the sweet taste of chocolate in her mouth. She tried desperately to work out how many calories were in a mouthful of cake. If a whole slice was, say 350 calories, that meant that in just one mouthful you'd have at least 100. Emily-Ann sighed. That meant one thing – she'd have to forgo her slice of cheese tonight. In fact she wasn't going to eat anything for three days. And she was going to do a five-mile walk after work. And do 200 press-ups. Then again, maybe she'd just do 100. She hated press-ups. Passionately.

She wondered if she should invest in those pads you saw on TV. The ones that stuck to your stomach and did all the work for you. They looked great didn't they? And the ads always had really fantastic looking people in them. So they must *really* work.

Anyway if she could just lose a bit more weight her life would be so much better. Imagine. People would discuss her fab figure. Just like they talked about those 'skinny' celebrities. Journalists were always criticising them for being too thin. Too thin? Ha! They looked amazing, Emily-Ann thought. Those razor cheekbones, sunken faces and concave mid riffs. They were to die for.

Emily-Ann looked at her watch. Almost 5:00 thank God. This place was just so mind-numbingly boring. She wasn't *supposed* to be here. No. She, Emily-Ann, was going to be a star. A massive star. She'd always known that. She'd been different to the other kids in school. They'd spent their time fretting about the leaving cert. Biology: who cared how many legs a cockroach had? Geography: how many fjords were there in Norway? Emily-Ann didn't give a tinker's curse. It was all going to be irrelevant to her anyway. Once she became famous.

She wanted it all. The whole lark. She'd take the good with the bad. Even tolerate the paparazzi hanging from trees. Trying to snap her without make-up. She'd put up with them. And stalkers too. And extended family members eager to sell their stories. As long as none of them tried to hamper her route to fame.

Emily-Ann didn't believe people who pretended to

hate fame. Those who whinged about press intrusion. She knew from working in a PR office just how bloody difficult it was to get press coverage. Her boss Aidan was forever pushing her to ring editors and send out press releases about artists. Half the time you'd never get a reply. Papers were inundated with damn press releases. PR people were at the bottom of the editor's priority list. There was too much competition out there. Artists were prepared to sell their souls to get coverage; deliberately frequenting celebrity infested haunts and surrounding themselves with hangers-on, whilst desperately looking around, trying to be recognised.

Emily-Ann didn't feel one bit sorry for the 'stars'. If you didn't want the paparazzi after you, then you simply wouldn't court them in the first place, would you? You wouldn't do stupid things. Like jogging in a busy park with a mask on your face. Or bringing ten bodyguards to a nightclub. Or checking in for a flight wearing a pair of oversized sunglasses.

After all, if you just went along to your local pub night after night you'd be left alone wouldn't you? Of course you would. Because a photo of a person sitting in his local night after night was not a great photo opportunity, was it?

Anyway the pros of fame seemed to outweigh the cons. And Emily-Ann was looking forward to her share of the spotlight. Just thinking about it made her feel dizzy. Imagine! Her posters would line the walls of pre-pubescent boys. Bodyguards would surround her. Seats in VIP bars would be reserved for her use only. With little pieces of red rope to shield her from the general public. God, it was going to be so fantastic.

At the age of twelve Emily-Ann knew pretty much all of this. Even if nobody else did. Her dowdy career guidance teacher at school had recommended that Emily-Ann do a typing course.

'A typing course?' Emily-Ann had wrinkled her pretty little nose in disgust. 'A typing course? So that I can be locked away in a basement doing boring work for some bald old git? No way. Absolutely no way.'

'Emily-Ann, if you live your life looking for fame and fortune, you'll be very disappointed.'

But Emily-Ann had taken precious little notice of the unkempt looking career guidance teacher with her wild bushy grey hair. Huh? If she were such an expert, why didn't she have a brilliant career herself?

At home Emily-Ann took a good look at herself in her huge bathroom mirror. Her henna highlights looked positively stunning in her thick chestnut-coloured hair. And she was sure she'd lost a bit of weight since yesterday. Her eyes looked larger, her lips fuller. She gave herself a satisfied smile. She looked hot. Hot as you got.

It was high time she figured out what she was going to be famous for. Yes, she'd have to think carefully about it and make her mind up once and for all. After all, there were people in Ireland who were simply famous for hanging around. And getting snapped at one envelope opening after another. Or latching onto someone that was already famous. But Emily-Ann didn't want to be one of those people. God no. Those people were as stale as the smoke that hung about them in nightclubs.

She was getting ready to go along to some garden centre opening. Unfortunately, it was one of her duties of the boring PR job her dad had got for her. But this job was only a stepping-stone. It wasn't for the rest of her life. Oh no. This was just one of those nasty little press calls that had to be suffered. Once she'd done a few of these and became a familiar face, she could start demanding better terms for herself. It just took a little time, that was all. Just a bit of time.

Emily-Ann parked her mum's brand new navy BMW in Sandyford Industrial Estate. She wondered if this was the right building. The sign outside the office block read *Great Gardeners of Ireland*. This must be it.

She checked herself once again in the car mirror. She still looked pretty, she thought. But if she lost just one more stone, just one more miserable stone, she'd be absolutely stunning.

Emily-Ann sighed and got out of the car. It was ridiculous that she had to come to this heap of crap. Why couldn't someone else have come along?

There was just so much else she could be doing. She wanted to be out. In town maybe. It was the end of August, the evenings were still mild and there'd be lots of people out and about.

She'd been given 100 mini thistles in a big green box to give out to guests.

She'd also been handed a list of instructions (did they think she was thick or something?). Apparently she had to ensure the photographers snapped the right people. Oh, yawn, yawn, yawn. Who were the important people anyway? As if anyone *remotely* important was going to turn up to a non-event like this! God it was the pits being a pseudo PR woman!

It was such a pity *The Happiest Couple in Ireland* television show had been scrapped. Herself and Graham would have *definitely* won it. They'd had no competition at all. God, life was so unfair, wasn't it? Imagine if they'd won that magnificent villa near Puerto Banus in Marbella, with its pool and private bar and ensuite jacuzzi. Why were the best things in life always scrapped? Apparently the TV company had run out of money and the whole thing had been called off. It was infuriating.

She'd have walked the competition with Graham.

At first Graham had been reluctant to enter. He said he didn't want to be appearing in a stupid show like that. But Emily-Ann had managed to twist his arm. It hadn't been too difficult. There wasn't anything Emily-Ann didn't know about her next-door neighbour. So when Graham started complaining that a show like this would do nothing for his street-cred, Emily-Ann gently reminded him that if his rugby-obsessed property tycoon father ever discovered he was gay, he might be written out of the family will. Graham had never thought about this. But it was true. Graham's mother and father would die if they discovered the truth; pillars of high society they were always hoping that Graham would start dating Emily-Ann or one of her wealthy friends.

So he had thrown himself into the filming of the show.

And nobody but nobody had guessed that Graham actually batted for the wrong team.

Oh well you just had to be positive in life, Emily-Ann tried convincing herself. She was still only twenty and something else would come up sooner or later. Then she could leave PR once and for all. Emily-Ann wasn't really cut out for kissing other people's asses. Let them kiss *my* ass, she thought as she pricked her thumb for the hundredth time on a mini thistle.

'Are you the girl from O'Donovan PR? You're late you know,' a dour middle-aged, grey-faced, bespectacled woman barked the minute she arrived, dragging in the box of thistles.

'Are they the thistles? Have you the press release handy? Give me a quick look. I can never trust you PR types to get things right.'

Emily-Ann gave her a watery smile. *Nice to meet you too you plain old cow.*

It was 6:30. The guests should be arriving at 6:45. Hopefully they wouldn't stay long. The sooner she could escape the better. She was wasted in this dull job with people looking down their noses. Like she was a piece of dirt. Emily-Ann was sick of her dad pointing out that he'd moved mountains to get her this job. She hadn't asked for his damn help. If he thought the job was so great, why didn't he do it himself?

Yes, it really was such a pity things hadn't worked out on that TV show. How cool would it have been to win a house and become famous into the bargain? Appearing on chat shows, doing radio interviews and constantly getting your photo taken. Dammit. Why did things always have to go wrong?

The photographers did a double take when they spotted the tall striking-looking brunette. Christ where had *she* appeared from? They got their cameras ready to flash. What an absolute stunner. Emily-Ann saw them eyeing her up. And flashed her appreciation with a smile. She hadn't expected to see anyone normal at this thing. But these photographers were young, male and seemed to be on the right side of thirty. Well, well, well . . . maybe the evening wouldn't turn out to be so dreary after all.

On Wednesday morning Emily-Ann was laughing.

Her face beamed from the front pages of several dailies.

The director, Arnold, was ecstatic. How had Emily-Ann managed to pull this off?

God, she was a bit of a dark horse, wasn't she?

'THISTLE DO' screamed the headline of Ireland's most popular tabloid.

Emily-Ann could hardly contain her joy.

Her star had only just begun to shine.

Chapter Four

If you bought two bottles of shampoo you got a FREE deodorant.

Nina Dwyer stood in Roches Stores carefully considering the offer. The deodorant was a good-sized can. But she didn't really need the shampoo. Her flatmate was an airhostess who brought home lots of those little bottles from hotels. They lasted ages. Especially when you added some warm water to the bottles and shook them.

Dorianne let her have all the little bottles. She never used them; she said they wrecked her hair. She said hotel shampoo was like washing-up liquid. Nina disagreed. When she'd been a student she'd often used washing up liquid. It had made her hair awfully dry. The hotel shampoo was much better.

She stood blocking the aisles in Roches Stores, peering at the promotional ad. It wasn't the shampoo at all, but the big free deodorant can, that was tempting. Nina was sure if she splashed out, the can would last all year. Then again, she didn't really need any shampoo and Dorianne always kept a family size can of deodorant in the bathroom in case anybody was stuck.

She decided to pass. All these special offers were a gimmick anyway. Just another well thought out ploy to get customers to part with hard earned cash.

Nina allowed herself a tight little smile. And moved on up the aisle. You'd have to be up early in the morning to catch Nina Dwyer out that was for sure. She'd better just stick to her list. The basics:

1. Three tins of beans.
2. Small loaf of bread.
3. Two tins of tomatoes.
4. One medium onion.
5. Packet of ginger snaps (for visitors).

Well now, that was about it, she thought happily. This lot would keep her going for the next day or two. It was handy living with Dorianne. She was so organised. And always kept a generous stock of supplies like sugar and salt, tea and coffee, toilet paper and light bulbs, black plastic sacks and bleach. It was very handy indeed living with such a well-organised person. Not like the last fella she'd lived with. He'd been a bit lazy really, always watching TV and not doing his share of the washing-up. And if Nina was totally truthful, he'd been . . . well, a bit mean.

Now that the grocery shopping was done, it was time to have some real fun. She loved coming into town on a day off. And not having to go into Tele-Fone. There was really so much to do in the city.

As she was in Henry Street anyway, she thought she'd pay a visit to Arnotts. It was her favourite store. Such a lovely selection of clothes. She made her way up to the Benetton section. The autumn/winter stock was just in and Nina tried on a few garments. The helpful shop girl offered Nina some assistance. Nina thought she was a lovely girl and made sure to ask for sizes in everything to keep her busy. Nina often felt sorry for shop assistants. Some women would bark, 'I'm just looking thanks.' Not Nina. No. She always made sure to have a few words with them. A little chat about the weather or whatever.

After a while she became a little hot. It was always a little tiring trying on clothes. She handed a neat pile back to the shop assistant and thanked her for her time. Nina was not one of those rude women who opened lots of beautifully folded shirts only to throw them on the floor of the dressing room after she was finished. No. Nina prided herself on being one of the few remaining polite customers in Dublin.

Next stop was HMV. Nina loved HMV. You could go in and listen to your favourite album on a set of headphones. It was great. You could listen to the same song over and over again if you really liked it. Today she listened to an album one of the women in work had recommended. It was great. Really funky. She jotted down the name of the song she liked best. She was going to listen to the Top 30 hits later on the radio and make sure she taped it. She hoped there was space left on that blank tape of hers.

Eventually she came out of the shop and headed towards O' Connell Street. She half thought of stopping in Moore Street for a few apples from the women with the prams but then thought better of it. Those women were divils for throwing in a few rotten apples, thinking that you wouldn't notice. But Nina always noticed, she thought, walking past contentedly. Yes, Nina never missed a trick.

She was nearing the end of the street when a young lad appeared out of nowhere. 'Do you mind if I talk to you for a moment?'

'I'm sorry, I'm in a terrible rush,' she told him with a smile. She'd been caught out by his type once before. You see, people like that were never looking for a bit of chit-chat. No. It was a tried and tested sales technique. You'd stop for a second and before you knew it, they'd produce a scratch card or something. And try and persuade you to part with cash. But Nina didn't see the point in being rude to these people. A lot of people would just stare straight ahead as if they were deaf but Nina would always smile and pretend she was in a hurry; that way nobody got offended. After all these people were only trying to do their job.

She took a right turn at the corner, heading for Easons. It was a wonderful bookshop. They stocked books on every subject under the sun. All the latest titles. Best of all, they provided little stools at the back of the shop where you could sit and read your favourite book for nothing. Nina headed towards the back of the shop. She knew where to find the book she was reading, a hilarious comedy on trying to find a man. She was on page 141 at the moment. She reckoned within a couple of weeks she'd have the novel read.

She was going home to Mullingar soon, for her annual week's summer holiday. She wanted to find another good book to read at home, similar to the one she was reading now. A book with lots of characters that was value for money. One with lots of action and dialogue. Not one that spent two or three pages describing a cup and a saucer. Nina was pretty fussy when it came to her reading material. She loved books by Shari Low, Jane Green, Cathy Kelly and Sarah Webb. Robyn Sisman was also pretty fantastic. Nina's eyes wandered over the rows and rows of brightly-coloured covers. She was determined to pick something she really liked. Without a good book at home she'd die of boredom. She searched through the titles of newly-released bestsellers and picked up a pretty interesting looking one. Ah yes, this one definitely looked worth reading. She jotted down the title carefully. She'd ring her mam from work in the morning and get her to order it in the local library.

Coming out of Easons, Nina noticed the clouds. Her heart sank. If it rained, it meant she'd end up having to get the bus home. And Nina didn't really like buses. They were full of foreigners shouting things at each other. Not that she had anything *against* foreigners in general – she just wished they could be a bit quieter. She headed in the direction of Drumcondra. If she walked very fast she just might miss the rain. And anyway she needed the bit of fresh air – all that shopping made you exhausted and the exercise would do her good. Dorianne was always on to her about not doing enough exercise. A fitness freak, her flatmate was a member of an exclusive gym. Nina had thought it sounded lovely – all jacuzzis and saunas and everything but had nearly died of shock when she'd heard the price. Sure you'd almost get a deposit on a house for that! And anyway, she thought as she walked past the Gate theatre, glancing at the poster ads with interest, wasn't it much healthier just doing the bit of walking in the fresh air?

Nina made it home in 20 minutes. And let herself into the big Georgian house she called home for the moment. It was a lovely old house, especially in the summer. It had a little garden out the back where tenants could sunbathe if they wished. Not that anybody did really – there wasn't much sun in Drumcondra. So nobody bothered. Still it was handy for putting washing on the line.

In winter, however, it got bitterly cold when Dorianne would be off in New York or Boston or wherever – and Nina would be in the little flat by herself shivering, even with three jumpers on.

She wondered if Donal was downstairs in his flat. Donal wasn't really talking to her at the moment. He maintained that she'd just used him to try and win *The Happiest Couple in Ireland*. Nina had been hurt by his accusations. After all she hadn't *completely* used him. Sure if they'd won, he'd have got half the price of the house too, wouldn't he? But he hadn't seen it that way. Not at all. He said he hadn't entered the competition to win the house. That he'd *genuinely* been in love with her. And that she'd unceremoniously dumped him when the TV show was scrapped.

All the accusations had annoyed Nina. She thought he was making a big drama out of nothing. She hadn't just callously dumped him for no reason. But she was only twenty-six and too young to be thinking of settling down properly.

She wouldn't contemplate it. No. Not with someone in his twenties anyway. Twenty-something men were forever pontificating. Speaking in the future tense. Like when they were *going* to be partners in huge firms. And *going* to be worth millions. And *going* to be running the country. Nina preferred to keep quiet and let them talk. She'd seen too many women fall for this kind of nonsense, marry these ambitious young men . . . only for their dreams to inevitably fall apart . . .

Nina would not consider marriage with a man under thirty.

No.

A man in his thirties had either made it.

Or hadn't.

Chapter Five

On Caroline's lunch break she bought a badge that read, 'If you can send one man to the moon why can't you send them all?' She pinned it to her cardigan, bought a cheese and coleslaw wrap in a nearby deli and took it to Hyde Park.

She found herself a space of grass far away from anyone and took off her cardigan. She flicked through *Heat* magazine and wondered if you could get any sort of a tan in 20 minutes. The sun was scorching. She also wondered how much longer she'd stay in London. Renting in Finsbury Park, in an area where you wouldn't be comfortable walking about on your own after dark.

London was wearing her out. Endless time-wasting on the tube. Countless unrecognisable faces. Sharing a red-brick house with a couple of page three girls and their many many boyfriends. She was too old for all of this.

She'd done the whole adventure thing after school. Travelling around Europe on trains and buses. But she didn't have that kind of energy left. She was supposed to be getting married now for God's sake.

Married and living a nice sensible life.

That's what Richard had promised her.

A life with a house and garden and a rightful place among the ordinary Irish middle-class people. Where neighbours kept an eye on their house when they took their annual trip to Majorca. Where life revolved around bridge evenings and parent/teacher meetings. Nothing too hectic. Just something stable and safe. Not this.

God no.

Not this.

Not in a million years.

She closed her eyes and tilted her face towards the sun. Hyde Park was heaven in the sunshine. So vast and lovely. You could be anywhere here. Anywhere in the world. It was such a treat just to hear the birds singing. It reminded her a bit of Stephen's Green in Dublin. Richard and herself had often strolled around Stephen's Green. At the beginning. Towards the end he would have found it boring. Towards the end of their relationship everything had begun to bore Richard.

When they'd first met everything had been so different. He'd treated her a lot better then, though if she were to be completely honest, the relationship had always been a bit one-sided. She'd chased him. She'd won him over. But boy had she paid for it in the end.

Initially she'd met him in a Leeson Street club.

On a night out with Sandra, she'd spotted him across the bar. His gorgeous looks had made him look unattainable. He was so tall and handsome. A bit too good looking for her probably. But she hadn't been able to take her eyes off him all night. He hadn't noticed her at all but there was nothing unusual about that. Caroline rarely got attention from males in clubs. It wasn't that she was ugly or anything. But the fact that she wore glasses and was slightly overweight didn't help really. And although people always told her 'It's what's inside that counts', Caroline knew that men in clubs rarely took the trouble to explore people's insides. Once the lights had come on, Richard had been ushered out by the bouncers who were not taking any chances. He'd been very drunk and had fallen outside on the ground. Only wearing a rugby shirt, Caroline had been extremely concerned about him. She found a cloakroom-ticket in his pocket and had persuaded the bouncer to let her back into the club so she could fetch his coat.

When she came back out Sandra was pretty fed up. She was shivering and said there was no point talking to this guy because he was so drunk. She'd wanted to leave him there all by himself.

Caroline had been adamant that they couldn't leave him there alone; he could be attacked or some-thing and he didn't seem to have any money on him.

Sandra said he wasn't their responsibility. Where were his friends?

But Caroline eventually persuaded her to help her drag Richard back to her cousin Colin's penthouse around the corner from Leeson Street.

Her cousin had been working in New York for nine months and Caroline had been looking after his place, feeding his terrier Mitch, and driving his SLK whenever she needed it.

When Richard got back to Colin's place, Caroline poured some strong coffee into him as Sandra sat, still shaking her head in disapproval. Richard seemed to sober up then and kept saying things like 'Wicked pad you've got here' or 'Man, this place is bloody amazing.'

Caroline hadn't bothered to explain that the place wasn't really hers; she was too busy admiring his fit build, dark hair and green eyes under impossibly long lashes. In fact she couldn't believe that she'd managed to end up drinking coffee with such a handsome guy and wanted the moment to last forever. She was terrified that when he sobered up, he might just thank her for her hospitality, leave and never set eyes on her again.

That night he had slept in Caroline's bed and she had slept in Colin's room with Sandra. In the morning she rose early and popped her head into her bedroom to see that Richard was still there. She smiled to see him with her dressing gown wrapped around his shoulders. But apart from that he looked perfect. She filled a pint of iced water for him and left it beside the bedside table, then put on full make-up, her nicest cashmere jumper, tan-coloured skirt and black knee-high boots and drove to the nearest bakery for warm fresh rolls and croissants.

When Richard awoke, he didn't know where he was. He just knew he was hungover. And lying in a huge double bed in the trendiest gaff he'd ever seen. How the hell had he ended up here? This was the kind of place you could imagine 007 waking up in. But there was no bird in the bed. That was funny. What was going on?

Sandra had said afterwards that Caroline had taken a terrible chance bringing a stranger back to Colin's apartment like that. After all what if he had made off with the wide screen TV and Colin's Bang and Olufsen CD player? But Caroline had ignored her. Sometimes you just had to go for things in life. Things just didn't happen to people. And anyway her chance had paid off. Later on that morning, at Richard's parents' house, he'd got out of Colin's SLK and asked Caroline for her number. And had phoned the following evening. And the evening after that. So who said chances weren't there for the taking?

But now she was single again. And wondered sometimes how her life would have worked out if she hadn't rescued Richard from the cold Leeson Street steps that night.

Would she have met somebody else? Would she be married to them by now? And have started a family even? Would she still be working in Tele-Fone?

Instead of a place in London where most of the staff didn't even know her name. And cared less.

Caroline sighed and looked at her watch. It was time to go back. She stood up and brushed the crumbs off her cream trousers. This wasn't how she'd thought London would be. No. She'd expected things to be different over here. The thoughts of working for a record company had conjured up all different kinds of images. Rock 'n' roll. Shopping with the Sloanes. Enough champagne to choke on.

Her new life in London was supposed to have been so different to the one she'd left behind. A life of parties and paparazzi. Grooving with the movers and shakers in places like Browns and Abigail's Party.

Well not quite. She wasn't *that* unrealistic. She wasn't foolish enough to think she'd be living *that* high a life. Not at all. As an outsider, it was difficult to break into the London scene.

Especially an Irish outsider with no money.

What was the alternative though? Go back to Ireland? Head bowed? Apologising for herself? Back to her old job sitting alongside Luke, the oldest member of staff in Tele-Fone? Wasting away the hours? Dodging Richard and his friends on a regular basis? No, she couldn't do that. She'd never do that. And she had certainly no desire to look at Luke's glum expression on a daily basis ever again.

She'd shared her Tele-Fone office with Luke and another woman, Maureen, who came into the office in the mornings. A dour scornful woman in her mid-twenties, she never said anything to anyone and nobody said anything to her so half the time you'd forget she even worked there.

Luke had another three years to go until his pension. He talked about nothing else.

He did so little work that when he was actually asked to do something he practically sobbed. Passed over for promotion no less than seven times, his main aim in life was how to screw Tele-Fone in as many ways as was possible.

And to do absolutely nothing that could be identified as work.

'It's the same old thing every day you know,' Caroline had overheard him telling someone on the phone one day. 'Same old thing every day. But,' he added, his voice rising optimistically, 'There's no pressure and that's the main thing.'

Caroline couldn't understand him at all. Surely that couldn't possibly be the main thing in someone's life. Why would anyone's ambition be to do as little as possible and hope nobody would ever notice?

Because people did notice.

You couldn't not notice someone who stuck to a timetable like Luke's.

10:00	Drift in to work
10:30	Stare out window. Comment on the weekend not being long enough. Try to get scandal on someone

	who worked in the build-ing. Complain that it's rain-ing/cold in the office/only Monday or all the above
10:30-11:30	Morning coffee
11:30-12:15	Read office newspapers (then hide them under desk in case anyone else might want to take a look)
12:15-12:30	Toilet break
12:30-14:00	Lunch
14:00-15:00	Listen to radio
15:00-15:30	Ring relatives in Australia using office phone
15:30-16:00	Afternoon tea
16:00-16:30	Trawl the Internet
16:30	Home (taking newspapers with him!)

Caroline shuddered. Imagine going back there? Never. That would be like taking ten giant leaps backwards. Tele-Fone was a painful place to work in. A place where the general ethos was to dodge anything that could be classified as work. Where people's priorities were to arrive first at the canteen at lunch break, and leave last.

Life in a low-paid London job might not be a barrel of fun but it was better ... *anything* was better than the life she'd left behind ...

Chapter Six

APRIL

*R U THE HAPPIEST COUPLE IN IRELAND? DO U
WANNA BECOME RICH AND FAMOUS? R U READY
TO TAKE THE WORLD BY STORM AND WIN A
VILLA WORTH 1,000,000 EURO??? 14 LUCKY FINAL-
ISTS WILL ENJOY AN ALL EXPENSES PAID WEEK-
END IN MARBELLA, COMPETING FOR VOTES
FROM THE PUBLIC. FORGET POPSTARS. FORGET
BLIND DATE. THE HAPPIEST COUPLE IN IRELAND
TV SHOW IS GOING TO BE THE MOST TALKED
ABOUT SHOW THIS YEAR!!! IF U R IN LOVE AND
READY TO LET THE WORLD KNOW ABOUT IT,
TURN UP TO CLUB ANABEL AT THE BURLINGTON
HOTEL THIS SATURDAY.*

  CAN U AFFORD NOT TO?

Richard read the ad in the Evening Herald. *Imagine
that, he thought. A house in Marbella worth a
million euro! Wow. He read the ad again. And
again. Just to make sure the ad was authentic.*

After all it did seem too good to be true. He thought about it carefully. Himself and Caroline would have no trouble at all winning a show like that. And even if they didn't win, at least they'd get a free holiday in Marbella if they got to the finals. Excellent stuff. He only hoped Caroline would agree and not make a big fuss about it. Caroline could be very difficult sometimes and had never expressed much interest in fame. Then again, who in their right mind wouldn't want to be a TV star these days? It opened so many doors for people.

The queue ran all the way down the side of the big Dublin hotel. Caroline was dismayed. Just how many couples had turned up? Five or six hundred at least!!! The bucketing rain failed to deter the cameramen however. They were out in force. Like greyhounds chasing bewildered pairs of hares. The rain was incessant. Caroline's straightened hair was now going to end up looking like wet spaghetti. 'Oh God this isn't any fun,' she complained as the rain spilled onto her head. She held up her handbag as protection.

'Put that down,' ordered Richard, a tone of panic in his voice.

'Why?'

'Because the cameras won't be able to see us.'

'But it's lashing,' Caroline protested.

'Chin up,' Richard growled, 'Think of the house in Marbella. It's got its own private bar and a

swimming pool. I've always fancied a private pool – with no gobshites playing volleyball in it or lager louts lounging around listening to their stereos.

'Oh God,' Caroline winced as she felt her hands turning to ice, 'the house does look divine. At least it looked divine in the pictures in the papers. But do you really think we've a chance? There's millions of couples here.'

'Ah come on Caro, be positive, don't blow this for us before we've even started.'

The cameras were approaching. Richard noticed the fella in front taking off his rain mac and putting it over his girlfriend's shoulders. Feck it anyway. That was going to make him look really bad. He gave Caroline a weary look. She was doing a great job of looking like she was standing in the North Pole. Why was she doing this? Was she doing it on purpose? Didn't she want the house as much as him? He hoped she wasn't going to go and ruin everything. He'd kill her if she started any of her antics.

Reluctantly he removed his good cashmere blazer and wrapped it around Caroline's shaking shoulders. She looked up at him in surprise. 'Just smile,' Richard almost growled, 'Remember we're the happiest couple in Ireland.'

The cameras were on them.

Suddenly.

Right in their faces.

One of the cameramen recognised Richard.

He'd worked with him on various TV shows. He gave him a knowing wink, but pretended not to let on.

'Hi I'm Mikey Mark,' a smarmy looking interviewer with a long thin red pony tail introduced himself and thrust a microphone at them, 'You're here braving the Irish weather with many of Ireland's couples. You must really want this prize, a villa in sunny Spain.'

Richard beamed and squeezed Caroline's hand so hard he almost broke it. 'When you're in love, you don't really notice what the weather's like,' he said.

There, he thought, if that didn't impress them, nothing would.

But the interviewer wasn't letting him off that easily. This was the world of entertainment after all.

'What do you think of the other couples so far?'

'We haven't had a chance to . . .' Caroline began.

'They all seem lovely,' Richard interrupted, 'We can't wait to meet the rest of them inside.'

'Yes, its going to be so much fun, we're really looking forward to it,' Caroline said suddenly. She was catching on.

'Right,' the interviewer looked fairly put out. It wasn't fun talking to people who weren't making complete fools of themselves. It just didn't make good television. But give them time. They'd slip up eventually. All of them would.

He and his cameraman moved down the line. They stopped suddenly.

'Hello girls, what's all this about then?'

'Whadya mean?' the more butch of the two girls snapped at him, 'I don't remember reading anything about couples having to have different bits of equipment.'

'So are you happy then?' Mikey Mark didn't bat an eyelid.

'We're the happiest bleedin' couple in Ireland,' she said, sticking her middle finger up to the camera.

Nina held Donal's hand tightly. She knew he wasn't that comfortable about being here. She knew he was only here for her sake. Because she'd asked him. And he was only wearing a suit because she'd asked him. She'd told him that appearances were more important than anything you said.

'What should I say then?' he'd asked, bewildered.

'Not too much,' she'd advised quietly. 'Remember that saying? "It's best to be silent and thought a fool, than to speak and leave no doubt".'

'So what did your parents think about us coming along here?' Emily-Ann tossed her hair and looked around to make sure the cameras didn't catch her off-guard.

Graham shrugged. 'Dad was pleased and told me to go for it . . . and I dunno . . . I suppose my mum seemed kind of encouraging but I'm not sure if she fell for the story about us suddenly falling in love and all that.'

'Why not?' Emily-Ann arched an eyebrow. 'Does she not think I'm good enough?'

Graham looked shocked. 'Don't be so tetchy Em . . . she's my mum. Mothers just know things.'

Chapter Seven

There was something about working in town, Nina thought. Yeah. There was a real buzz about it. With people rushing around in suits. Looking important. The moneymen.

Handsome young men.

Working in the city centre was much better than working out in one of the industrial estates. It wouldn't be nice to be stuck out there. In the sticks. Miles from anywhere. Where there was nothing to do during your lunch break.

Nina wouldn't like that. She loved sitting in Stephen's Green watching the men in suits. She liked to figure out what they did for a living. It was a little game she played. She took particular note of their shoes while making judgement. You could always tell a lot about somebody by what they wore on their feet. Nina loved shiny leather shoes. And suits.

Nina always wore a suit. And a good pair of shoes. Because it made her feel like one of *them*. One of the important people. Somebody worth knowing:

People treated you better when you were in a suit too, she reckoned. They served you faster in shops. And were more respectful. Nina's mother had never worn a suit. Her father had an old grey one, which was a bit short on the leg. It was grand for funerals but God, if she ever got married she couldn't have him turning up in that thing. Her brothers had a couple of suits each. But then again they had got grants and gone to college and knew all about the importance of creating impressions. Nina had never gone to university. No. She'd done a secretarial course instead.

Of course a new suit didn't have to cost an arm and a leg. She'd picked up her navy one in the January sales for half nothing. It had had a little stain on the sleeve. As if some grubby kid had pawed it. So Nina had asked for a discount. And got it. No problem. But nobody knew that. It was better when people didn't know too much about you.

The Tele-Fone offices were close to the park, which was great. At lunchtime you could go and sit there with a book. And eat your own sandwiches in peace. Without people giving you funny looks. In the canteen, if you ate your own packed sandwiches, people stared. As if there was something wrong with you. Very ignorant people – hadn't their mothers ever told them it was rude to stare?

But in general Nina loved working in the big Tele-Fone building. There were so many people working there – like her uncle Luke. He'd got her the job in the first place. He'd known a man who knew a man who worked in personnel. Luke had been in the company for years. There was nothing about anybody that he didn't know.

Not everybody in Tele-Fone was as old as Luke though. No. Lots of them were young, which meant if you worked in the company, you'd automatic access to a whole new social life. A work-related social life. If you were into that kind of thing. Nina wasn't particularly. She didn't tend to meet the work crowd in the pub every Friday. It was always too smoky and too crowded. You had to get down early to get a seat. Besides, Dublin pub prices were a rip-off – probably twice the prices of back home. And you often got roped into rounds. And that's when things got messy.

But now and again, the management team at Tele-Fone organised get-togethers for the staff. Which were a lot of fun. Well Nina thought they were anyway. Get-togethers in the canteen. Pizza and white wine in plastic cups. You know, nothing too fancy. But the Tele-Fone employees usually laughed at the management's efforts. They weren't a bit grateful. No. They stood around, muttering under their breath about the management. Calling them cheapskates. And giving out that the white wine was warm. Not Nina. She thought it was pretty generous of the managers. After all they didn't have to do anything for the staff did they? Her uncle Luke obviously enjoyed the get-togethers too – he never missed one. In fact, at the Christmas party last year Luke had enjoyed the wine so much, he'd passed out and Nina had had to ring Auntie Noreen to give them both a lift home.

Noreen hadn't been too pleased to be woken up in the middle of the night. In fact she'd been furious. But still, as Uncle Luke had rightly pointed out, it was useless trying to get a taxi home at Christmas time. You wouldn't be able to hail one for love nor money.

Not everybody in Tele-Fone liked Luke, Nina had to admit. He wasn't everybody's cup of tea. There'd been times, when she'd heard him described as a 'first out of the taxi, last to the bar' type of man. Nina didn't think this was completely fair. There was a lot of internal politics going on in Tele-Fone. And people were very bitter. That was the reason why they hadn't promoted her uncle. They'd been afraid he'd 'shake things up a bit'. That's what Luke had told her anyway. She kind of felt sorry for him. It wasn't fun sharing an office with two women who were a lot younger and seemed to have no respect for him whatsoever. One of the girls, Caroline, was off on a career break at the moment apparently. Nina remembered her from *The Happiest Couple in Ireland* show.

It was such a pity the TV show had been scrapped, Nina thought. Her folks back home had been very excited about seeing her on TV. There'd been some very interesting characters on the show too, like the loud Australians who used the word 'mate' after every sentence. And the couple from Cork who were trying to get a record deal. Then there'd been that stunning girl Emily-Ann, with a figure to die for, although she was almost *positive* she'd heard Emily-Ann make herself sick in the bathroom on one occasion. But maybe she'd imagined it. After all why would anybody want to make themselves sick? And anyway the brilliant thing about the TV show was the fact you'd a constant supply of yummy chocolate biscuits all day. And as much tea and coffee as you wanted. Maybe that's why Emily-Ann had been sick. Perhaps she'd eaten too many of the biscuits.

Nina lazed on the grass. She could see the St. Stephen's Green shopping centre through the trees. The park really was an oasis in the middle of the city. She closed her eyes, enjoying the rays of sunshine dance on her face.

Her salty sandwich made her feel thirsty. She thought about going to the corner shop on Leeson Street and getting a can of coke but the queues would probably be too long. Anyway once she got back to the office she'd be able to get herself a glass of water from one of the water coolers.

It was a pity it was Friday. Friday nights were boring. She didn't like sitting in watching TV by herself, but Dublin was just so expensive. If only somebody was having a barbecue or something. Within walking distance of her house. Now, that'd be ideal wouldn't it? But unfortunately nothing was happening this weekend. Even Dorianne was going off on a three-night trip to Los Angeles.

Nina hoped there'd be something good on the telly tonight. Something other than *Big Brother*. She hated that. It was like looking at a mental asylum. Her dad had told her that long ago families would go to asylums on a Sunday, and peer at the inmates. For a bit of entertainment. *Big Brother* reminded her of that a bit. Legal entertainment. For Peeping Toms.

Nina's family in Mullingar had had their own Peeping Tom once. He'd nicked underwear off the line and once or twice they'd found him lurking in the bushes. The local guard had assured them there was nothing to worry about. Poor old Paddy had a bit of a drink problem and had been disowned by his own family. The guard had given him a warning however. And Nina's family hadn't had any trouble since.

No doubt he was glued to *Big Brother* now.

Nina reminded herself to check the telly listings on the Internet before she went home. It was always so frustrating when you didn't know what was on. Of course Donal would have a copy of the *Evening Herald* lying around. But she wasn't really talking to him anymore. At least he wasn't talking to her.

He said that he'd split up with another girl to go out with Nina. And maintained the TV show had cost him another relationship. But Nina didn't believe him for a minute. She'd never seen another girl near Donal's flat. Ever.

Chapter Eight

1. Conor from College
2. Gunter from Germany
3. Walter from work
4. Gary from Gran Canaria
5. Lenny from Leeson Street
6. Friend of Jim's – can't
   remember name
7. John (married)
8. Fred
9. Richard (engaged)
10. Rory

'What's all this then?' Leila picked up the scrap of paper from the sitting room table and squinted at it.

Caroline sighed. 'Oh it's nothing really. I went to a fortune-teller this afternoon, who said I'd meet someone from my past. I nearly died, thinking she might have been talking about Richard so I just wrote out a list of men from my past, to see if it could be any of them.'

'Were those married guys married when you were with them?'

Caroline was shocked. 'No, of course not.'

Leila looked at her quizzically. 'Haven't you slept with a married man then?'

'Definitely not,' Caroline said adamantly. 'Er why . . . why have you?'

'Not all the time . . . only if they were nice . . . I mean if they had a nice personality.'

Caroline lowered the remote control. She wasn't really watching *Big Brother* anyway. They'd been filming the chickens for the last 20 minutes. 'Well, they've hardly nice personalities if they're cheating on their wives,' she countered.

Leila reached for a mini Mars from the bumper pack on the table. 'I s'pose,' she said. 'I never really thought about it like that.'

Well that figures, Caroline thought. Leila rarely thought about anything except the size of her pneumatic chest. That and whatever new nightclub premier league footballers happened to be frequenting. Beyond that however . . .

Suzie was just as bad.

When she wasn't posing for some downmarket motorcycle magazine, she was off at motor shows handing out her phone number to one of her three 'fans', or pouring over the *Sunday Sport* and various tabloids to see which of her page three rivals were getting themselves coverage. Caroline was mortified every time Suzie stuck a picture of an enormous pair of tits under her nose and demanded, 'What do you think of her then?'

Of course Caroline always told her, the other girl wasn't that good looking. If she said anything otherwise Suzie would launch into a massive sulk and start damning every other page three girl in Britain accusing them all of having had boob jobs and being sluts. Caroline was very careful never ever to praise Suzie's competition in the world of 'glamour modelling'.

'I once wrote a list,' Leila said suddenly.

'Of your exes?'

'Nah,' she chuckled. 'Of all the famous men I'd like to bed.'

'Right.'

'I scored three of them.'

'Really? What about the others?' Caroline was intrigued.

'The others? Oh you mean the others on the list? Well, they're not famous anymore, you know. I wrote the list about two years ago. I s'pose I'd better make another list.'

'I see.' Caroline didn't bother asking who the famous men were. No doubt Leila would let her know before the night was out.

'So you don't think you'll get back with Richard then?' Leila said after a long pause.

Caroline turned to her in surprise. Where had *that* come from? It was unusual for Leila to remember anybody's name . . . unless it was a footballer's name or that of a soap star or maybe the name of a semi-famous DJ who could get her free into clubs.

Her flatmate noticed her obvious surprise. 'It's just . . . I forgot to tell you sorry . . . he phoned for you earlier on.'

'You're joking,' Caroline paled. But Leila's face remained expressionless as she fiddled with her white-blonde hair. 'Aren't you?'

'No,' Leila shrugged nonchalantly, turning up the volume on the TV again. 'No I'm not. So, you see that's why I thought it all might be back on again.'

Chapter Nine

Inside the hotel you took a number. Richard and Caroline were couple number 258. Couples from every walk of life were squashed into the conference room. Old couples. Middle-aged couples.

A couple wearing matching sarongs à la David Beckham stood out. As did a really young couple in tracksuits (the girl was about four months pregnant). Caroline even recognised Luke's annoying niece Nina from Tele-Fone there. She made a point of avoiding her. Caroline didn't want everyone in Tele-Fone knowing her business. God, it looked like the world, his wife and their belongings had turned up to this thing.

You could help yourself to tea and biscuits over the other side of the room but Richard thought it best not to be caught sipping tea on TV. 'It just doesn't look cool,' he said.

'They're looking for Ireland's answer to Posh and Becks here, not some old couple resembling characters from Emmerdale.'

Caroline was starving. Her stomach was rumbling.

And now she couldn't even help herself to a biscuit because it wouldn't look 'right'. God, this wasn't any fun.

She looked up at Richard. Tall, dark and built like a rugby player, Caroline admired his appearance. There was something irresistibly attractive about him. She wondered for the millionth time how somebody like herself had ended up with such a good-looking man. She was proud to be seen with him. Really. If only though . . . if only he could treat her with a little more respect. It wasn't asking too much, was it?

Still, she shouldn't be complaining too much. Who wanted a few biscuits anyway? They only made you feel sluggish and Richard had always been very vocal about his disregard for overweight women. According to him, they were a turn-off. And it was always very interesting to get a male point of view. Anyway she could have a snack when she got home.

Richard had always told her that nothing tasted as nice as being slim. He'd learned that piece of wisdom from his last girlfriend. And he'd thought it was a great attitude for any woman to have. Camille was the name of his ex. She'd been a top model from Switzerland and infuriatingly, Richard would often refer to her wonderful figure.

Caroline had Richard to thank for her own incredible weight loss. Their first Christmas together, he'd enrolled her into the same gym as himself. He said it would be a great opportunity to spend a bit more time together. He always suggested she ate salads when they were out and he never ever bought her chocolate. Dating Richard did wonders for her figure and the more he complimented her on her weight loss, the more encouraged she was to lose a bit more. Soon she'd got her waist back and looked as good as she had as a teenager.

Richard had also brought her to the opticians to get three months' worth of disposable contact lenses. Of course, he'd nothing against anyone wearing glasses, he'd assured her; but she'd such beautiful big blue eyes, it was criminal not to show them off.

Soon after she'd begun dating Richard, Caroline noticed men staring at her on the street. Her new figure encouraged her to wear more revealing clothes and she even got a few highlights in her hair. Everyone in Tele-Fone had started complimenting her on her new look.

All thanks to Richard.

When your number was called, you had to stand up in front of everyone. And tell the crowd your name, where you came from, how long you'd been in love with your partner and why you wanted to win the dream house.

Caroline wasn't looking forward to it. Not that she was shy about speaking in public or anything. She wasn't. It's just the whole set up here ... was a bit naff.

She spotted Luke's niece Nina sticking a few

biscuits in her bag when she thought nobody was looking. Caroline wasn't terribly surprised. Luke would have done exactly the same.

'Listen Caro,' Richard gave her a little hug, 'this is your chance to put your acting talents to the test.'

'But this isn't acting,' Caroline argued. 'Any fool can get up and make a laughing stock out of themselves.'

'Now listen,' Richard continued as if he hadn't heard her, 'you're to remember to tell them we met on holidays in northern Australia, up in Queensland. In a place called Mackay.'

'But we met in Leeson Street,' Caroline reminded him. 'Don't you remember? You'd fallen on the ground and couldn't remember your own name, never mind where you lived.'

'Ok Caroline,' Richard sighed, and spoke to her very slowly as if she was a small child being taught the ABC. 'This is why it's so important for us to communicate. If we can't even get our stories right we'll be thrown right out of here. So think very carefully now. Where did we meet again?'

'Australia? Queensland?' Caroline looked baffled.

'Of course we did,' Richard grinned.

'So how did we meet?' Emily-Ann nudged Graham who was eyeing up the young Spanish looking waiter pouring the tea. 'Come on, think of something quick.'

'On the dance floor? In a pub? I dunno. You choose Babes.'

'No, no, hang on a minute,' Emily-Ann shook her head adamantly. 'We can't say something boring like that. Everyone meets in a pub. It's so ten years ago darling.'

'We can say we met on the Internet?'

'Very clever,' Emily-Ann scowled, 'and then people will find out that our parents live next door to each other. What a coincidence.'

'Well why don't we tell them the truth?' Graham whispered, 'that we just happen to live next door to each other.'

Emily-Ann frowned. 'Do you not think that's too dull?'

'It's how you tell it.' Graham grinned. 'Listen, I have an idea. Let's tell them that I fancied you since we were kids but I never told you. You know like in the song 'Living next door to Alice'.'

Emily-Ann's eyes lit up. 'You mean, one day you saw me getting into my car . . .'

'. . . and I ran out and begged you not to go, that I was in love with you and we lived happily ever after and all that crap.'

'Graham, sweetie you're a genius. With your brains and my looks we're going to sweep the floorboards of this TV show.'

'I'm worried,' Nina confided in Donal as they took their number: 313. 'Everyone else here has a great *story about how they met. Fireworks, champagne, sunset beaches, you name it. They're not going to think much of our story.'*

Donal looked at her with an air of surprise. 'But it's a true story,' he said.

'I know it is,' Nina said unhappily. 'But when I tell them we met when I got locked out and that you broke down the door of my flat, it's not exactly going to bring tears to their eyes, is it?'

'If they don't like it, well so be it,' Donal said quietly. 'If we don't win, then it just wasn't meant to be.'

Chapter Ten

Richard parked his car outside Atlantic Homecare in Sandyford Industrial Estate.

'You'd better wait there,' he instructed his new fiancée Sandra. 'I shouldn't be too long.'

He left the keys in the car and disappeared.

Sandra sighed. She was getting tired of this Sunday afternoon ritual.

Atlantic Homecare today. Last week it had been Tile Market. The week before had been Des Kelly Carpets, or was it Navan Carpets?

It didn't matter now though.

They'd decided not to go with carpets.

At least Richard had decided.

After viewing hundreds upon hundreds of carpets in every shade and colour, he'd said it would be more practical to opt for wooden flooring.

He could hire a sander for half price from a friend. And varnish the floors himself.

Sandra was only just discovering Richard's secret DIY obsession. Men usually didn't let you know their annoying habits until it was too late.

She'd only discovered his obsession on their second 'date' – a visit to Power City.

They'd been having a massive sale.

But still, Richard hadn't found the *exact* power drill he'd been after. The one that he'd seen in the brochure. Richard was very exact when it came to stuff he was looking for.

He liked to think of himself as being 'thorough'. Thoroughly boring, more like, Sandra was beginning to think. She wondered if Caroline had spent all these years being ferried from garden centres to electrical stores and back again.

If she had she'd kept it very quiet.

No wonder.

Richard's uncle had left him a bit of money a few years ago and he had waited and waited for house prices to come down. But they hadn't. Unfortunately. And Richard's job as a TV researcher didn't pay enough for him to get a decent mortgage. It was a sore point. Richard's dream was to be a homeowner. He never stopped talking about property. And didn't like the fact that they were simply being allowed to live in Sandra's parents' property.

It seemed to Sandra that Caroline had kept most of Richard's annoying little quirks to herself. Had she noticed or simply turned a blind eye to them? It was hard to know why Caroline had worshipped Richard.

Then again, Caroline's self-esteem hadn't been exactly high when she'd met Richard. Her social life had been less than hectic. Richard had opened her eyes to a brand new world, bringing her to parties and whisking her off on weekends away. No wonder the girl had been sucked in by it all. God, she'd even lost weight, ditched the glasses and started colouring her hair. All for Richard.

Sandra flicked through her copy of *Image* magazine, trying to see did she recognise anyone. The magazine was full of pictures of ultra glam people out and about having fun. Sandra sighed. She wished she could get dolled up and head out on the town some night. And get absolutely trollied. Why did she never feel like she was having fun anymore? Everybody else was. Or so it seemed. You just had to look around you.

Other couples seemed happy. Strolling past the car, heading for the store. Those women seemed happy with their men, didn't they? They obviously didn't have a problem spending weekends DIY shopping. Maybe there was just something wrong with her? Maybe she was different. Why was she just so much happier sitting in the car? Instead of traipsing around Atlantic Homecare, with Richard bombarding the staff with a million different questions.

Eventually her fiancé returned to the car park with a big cardboard box and opened the boot. Sandra turned around. 'That's not a Dyson.'

'I know,' he answered snappily. 'It's an electric blanket,' he slammed the boot door shut.

'But we already have an electric blanket,' said Sandra as he got into the car. 'Unless,' she added, 'You're planning to sleep in a separate bed from now on.'

'Did I say it was for us?' Richard backed out of the car park, 'Jesus would you look at the traffic? Whatever happened to Sunday being a day of rest in this country?'

Whatever happened indeed? Sandra thought.

'Well, not wanting to sound stupid or anything,' Sandra said testily, 'but if the blanket is not for us, then why did you buy it?

'The wedding next Saturday. Stephen and Deirdre are getting married, remember? I thought this would be ideal for them?'

'Stephen and Deirdre? But I have a beautiful Waterford Crystal bowl for them.' Sandra exclaimed.

'I was thinking about that,' Richard tried to ease out into the line of traffic, 'get out of the way, you mad bitch you . . .'

'Sorry?'

'I was thinking that we could give that to Mr Byrne for his fiftieth and give the blanket to Stephen and Deirdre.'

'Mr Byrne?' Sandra sounded surprised. 'Mr Byrne as in your boss? B . . . but why?'

'We're invited to his fiftieth in his house Sandra. Don't you know what an honour that is for us? Birthday party today – big promo tomorrow. That's what I reckon anyway. Do you see where I'm at? Anyway I think Mr Byrne would appreciate it.'

'I think Deirdre would appreciate it,' Sandra said, 'that's why I went to the trouble of picking it out for her.'

'The blanket is totally respectable and will do Deirdre fine,' Richard said.

Sandra shut her eyes and said nothing more. Richard was just being difficult. He was often like this on a Sunday. It was probably because he'd such a stressful job as a TV researcher.

She hoped to God he was right about this big promotion he thought Mr Byrne was going to offer him.

This had all better be worth it.

Richard was always going on about how successful he was going to be.

In the meantime he was busy making contacts and trying to befriend rich people.

'But just because you cultivate rich people, doesn't mean you're going to make money yourself,' Sandra had pointed out to him. 'After all rich people don't sell their assets and hand half the profits to their new friends.'

Richard paid no attention.

In fact most of the time he didn't seem to hear her at all.

She was beginning to wonder how she'd ever ended up engaged to this man she barely knew.

After all, she'd given an awful lot up to be with him.

She'd lost her best friend Caroline.

Probably forever.

And that hurt. More than the break up of a relationship. She'd never get over the guilt she felt betraying her best friend. They'd shared so many secrets, comforted each other through the rough times and even gone on holidays together.

Sandra knew she'd never have a friend like that again.

Friendships like that weren't just made over night.

She'd lost quite a few of her friends actually. And given up her job as a buyer for an exclusive boutique. She'd probably never get it back now. Maybe she should have just taken a career break.

But no, she'd been too quick to resign. She'd panicked. The thought of being a single mother had been too much. Of course unmarried mothers weren't looked down on now, as much as, say, a few years ago. But the people she socialised with were different. They'd think she was a loose tart. Because her baby was the result of a one-night stand. A one-night stand with the fiancé of her best friend. Everyone in Dublin would have talked. And pointed in the street.

So she'd handed in her notice.

Along with her independence. And in some ways . . . her life.

At least in her old job, she'd maintained a pretty good social life. A successful fashion buyer, Sandra had had invitations to every party in town. Now she was stuck at home. Alone.

And slowly but surely, was going out of her mind.

She opened her eyes. The car seemed to be heading towards Foxrock.

'Where are we going?' she was curious.

'My parents,' Richard said. 'I have to collect the lawnmower and get cracking on the lawn before it gets dark.'

Sandra groaned. Richard's parents were an absolute nightmare. He drove up to the front door of the family home. 'Are you right?' he looked questioningly at Sandra.

'I don't have to come in, do I?' Sandra was horrified.

'You bloody do,' he said.

'We can only stay a minute,' Richard gave his mother a quick kiss. Sandra wondered should she give her a kiss too. But then didn't.

'We're only in from Mass,' his mother gave her a strange smile and switched on the kettle.

Richard went out to the garage to talk to his Dad.

'I see,' Sandra sat down.

'Have you gone yet?'

'Er . . . we'll probably go to evening Mass in Merrion,' Sandra said.

'I think it's best to go in the morning,' Mrs Staunton fetched three china cups and placed them on saucers on the table. She also emptied a pack of fig rolls onto a plate. 'Then you have the rest of the day to relax.'

'I agree,' Sandra said frigidly.

'Caroline used to go to 9:30 Mass in the morning,' Richard's mother's stare bore into her, 'so that she could meet us for Sunday tennis at 11:00.'

'Oh,'

'Do you play tennis?'

'Well, I played in school but I don't anymore,' Sandra said.

What the hell was keeping Richard? She bit into a fig roll even though biscuits were the last things she wanted to eat at the moment. She'd recently started craving avocados and Heinz baked beans for some bizarre reason.

The doctor had confirmed the foetus as being three months old. She wasn't to exert herself or do any strenuous exercise. She'd tried yoga but had given up after the second class. It just didn't seem right stretching to all that annoying whale music while Richard was out having fun.

Finally Richard came into the kitchen.

'The lawnmower's in the boot. Listen Mum I won't stay for a cup of tea. I want to get the lawn mowed before it gets dark. God knows when we'll have another dry Sunday this side of Christmas.' He looked at Sandra, 'But you can stay if you like. I'll be back later to leave back the lawnmower and I could pick you up then?'

'Oh no,' Sandra practically shouted, 'I'm not feeling that great, I need to lie down.'

'Sure you can call again, next Sunday,' Mrs Staunton said, 'I'll show you how to make Richard's favourite apple tart.'

Richard caught Sandra's eye. He knew as well as she did, that Sandra had absolutely no intention of learning any such recipe.

Mr Staunton didn't even bother coming in to say hello.

Apparently himself and 'Sweet Caroline' had got on like a house on fire. Caroline knew all about rugby and sailing boats and motor racing and that.

But it was easy for her.

She had three brothers to fill her in.

'I think your mother knows,' Sandra confided on the way home.

'About what?'

'About the baby . . . the reason we got engaged . . . the hurry . . . the whole thing . . . she's not a stupid woman, you know.'

'I know that,' Richard practically barked at her. He looked incredibly tense as his hands gripped the wheel. 'But do you really think she's guessed?' he asked, almost anxiously. As if he'd suddenly just thought of it.

'I think a lot of people must be wondering Richard,' Sandra warned him, 'When are we going to tell people?'

'Not yet,' Richard said flatly, 'We'll have to think of something. We'll have to think carefully about what we're going to tell people.'

'But aren't we going to tell them the truth?'

Richard looked at Sandra as if she'd just started to grow horns. 'The truth?' he looked aghast. 'Why on earth would we tell anyone that?'

'But why not?'

'Because nobody else does,' he snapped as though she'd suggested the most ridiculous thing in the world. 'Nobody ever does.'

Chapter Eleven

You were supposed to bond with the other girls.

Apparently.

So Caroline heard herself being told. By a hard-faced PR type trying (and managing very well) to look completely condescending. Caroline found herself being herded along with the other female contestants into the hotel's conference room.

It was insane! How were you supposed to bond with people when you were all competing for the same thing? The same dream? The same magnificent villa with its own pool and tennis court. It was mad. Like going to the auction of your dream house and befriending all the other bidders. It was all so false. So staged.

If only Richard wasn't so hell-bent on winning the show. If only he hadn't his heart set on living down in Marbella, hob-nobbing with the jet setters. But he was sick to death of living with his folks. Caroline wondered why there wasn't an easier way? Why were Irish people so hell bent on having their own place anyway? Ensuring that property prices were pushed higher and higher. Why couldn't the Irish be like the French and rent?

Realistically Caroline knew she couldn't stay in her cousin Colin's apartment forever. It was all very worrying. Suppose herself and Richard didn't win the competition? Suppose they didn't win and simply ended up making total fools of themselves on national TV? What then?

What would her family think? And all her ex-boyfriends and old school friends? She didn't want to give them the chance to sneer. And what about all the people in Tele-Fone? People like Luke? And Maureen. And all the people back in Dundalk. What would they say about her behind her back? They'd have a field day, so they would.

Richard said it didn't really matter. That they'd both get enough exposure to guarantee them a lifetime of television presenting. Then they could buy any house they wanted, in Marbella or else-where.

Caroline wasn't so confident. What about all those Big Brother contestants? What ever happened to them? She could barely remember any of their names. And anyway Caroline never wanted to be a TV presenter. That was Richard's thing. That was what he wanted to do.

'Caroline,' Mikey Mark was in front of her. The cameraman was in her face. And this time Richard was not there to 'supervise' her. 'Have you met many of the other girls? Tell us what you think of them and *why you think you make a better half of a couple than them?'*

God. Caroline could feel all the muscles in her body tense up. What kind of a question was that?

'I can't really say what they're like as couples since I'm probably never going to be romantically involved with any of them as a couple.'

Mikey Mark gave a raucous big laugh. 'Oooh you saucy thing you. Tell me, have you managed to bond with any of the girls yet?'

'I've only just arrived,' Caroline sounded surprised. 'Making best friends with someone in a few minutes is not what you'd call bonding, is it?'

'We'll have to cut that bit,' Mikey Mark said moving away. He sounded anything but pleased.

Oh God, that's it, I've blown it, Caroline felt a rush of horror. She could have kicked herself. Where on earth had that outburst come from? Why couldn't she just have been polite and just said nice things about the other people? The name of this game seemed to be to lie through your teeth. Richard was going to murder her.

Suddenly a tall girl with long chestnut-coloured hair was standing beside her. The cameramen suddenly swooped on her. She was tossing her hair over her shoulder and preening like a peacock. Her name, it turned out, was Emily-Ann.

'All the girls are getting on so well,' Emily-Ann

purred into the camera, her fingers deliberately play-ing with her long hair. 'They are all so sweet and not competitive at all. Backstage bitching? Don't be daft. Oh God no, where did you hear that? We're all like sisters here.'

Caroline slunk away before she had to hear any more. What was that girl Emily-Ann like? Sisters? Huh? The next minute she'd start talking about wanting world peace.

Chapter Twelve

'How much is a Diet Coke?' Nina asked the man behind the bar.

'Ha?' he shouted back, 'A Diet Coke, is it?'

'Let me buy you a Diet Coke,' a small man appeared at her side. He was stout and sallow-skinned. Not too bad looking except for his moustache. Nina reckoned he was from one of those faraway countries. Not Spain or France but even further away. Maybe one of those countries where men didn't respect women very much. Nina decided to decline his offer. She didn't want to be stuck with him for the night!

She handed a €5 note to the barman and waited patiently for her change.

She looked around for Sheena, her young seventeen-year-old cousin who'd disappeared off somewhere. Sheena had come to Dublin to buy a dress for her debs dance. Having persuaded Nina to let her stay the night, she'd then insisted on hitting the town. Nina had suggested Fagan's, around the corner. They'd had a drink or two there before heading to The Cat & Cage for another. It was best to drink locally, Nina thought. After all, they didn't want to be going too far and having the bother of looking for taxis and that.

But Sheena had other plans. After a few drinks she'd become very merry. And insisted on going out clubbing. Nina was in a tizzy. Where on earth was she going to take her? It was too early for Leeson Street, which was a pity – Leeson Street was very handy as you could dance there all night for nothing as long as you didn't sit down. If you sat down, one of the waitresses would always run up to you with a wine menu and that got embarrassing.

In the end Nina vaguely remembered the name of a club in Temple Bar where ladies got in free before midnight. So they'd ended up there.

Sheena, wildly excited at the prospect of actually being in Temple Bar for the first time, had hit the dance floor with gusto. Now she was boogying to *Destiny's Child*, with Beyoncé's moves perfected.

Nina stood at the side of the dance floor keeping an eye on her. Suddenly she felt somebody standing very close. Too close for comfort actually. She moved slightly away.

'Excuse me,' a voice said.

Nina turned around, ready to tell the owner of the voice that she was spoken for. That usually got rid of unwanted attention fast. But turning around she noticed the owner had a nice face, dark, curly hair and lightly tanned freckled arms. He was tall too, which was a pleasant surprise. Normally the guys that chatted Nina up, only reached her chest.

'Yes?' Nina gave him a polite smile.

'Would you like to dance?'

'Oh no, thank you,' she felt herself blushing. 'I'm just waiting for my . . . er, friend,' she added.

'Rightio,' the guy shrugged.

Nina breathed a short sigh of relief. Thank God he hadn't made a fuss. She hated when guys asked you to dance in clubs. The last time she'd refused to dance with a fella, he'd shouted, 'I didn't want to dance with you anyway, I was only being charitable.'

There was something different about this one though. He was nicely dressed, wearing a blue cotton shirt. Respectable. Suddenly she was afraid if she ignored him he'd just walk off and maybe chat to somebody else.

'I can't find her anywhere,' she called out to him. It was very loud in the club. You had to shout.

'Sorry?' he looked at her blankly.

'My friend, I don't know where she's disappeared to.'

'Maybe she got lucky,' the guy joked.

Nina didn't find that very funny, 'She's only seventeen,' she said, 'She's up from the country.'

'The country girls are the ones you've got to watch. I'm Aidan by the way,' the guy laughed, 'what's your name?'

'Nina,' she shook his hand.

'Where are you from?'

'Mullingar.'

'What do you do?'

'I work for Tele-Fone and yourself?'

'I'm a dentist,' he said.

Nina swallowed. Had she heard right? She thought he'd said he was a dentist but maybe she'd heard wrong. She'd never met a dentist before. Perhaps he'd said he was an apprentice.

'Excuse me?' she enquired, just to be sure.

'I'm a dentist,' he smiled showing even white teeth.

Good God. Nina thought. Well, wasn't this a stroke of luck altogether? Imagine meeting a dentist in a place like this! Gosh. Wouldn't her mother be thrilled if she ended up with a dentist? And everyone in Mullingar would be fierce jealous.

'What are you drinking?' he asked.

'A vodka and Diet Coke,' she answered like lightning. She didn't want to tell him she wasn't drinking. When you said that, people always presumed you were driving. When they found out you weren't driving they presumed you were an ex-alcoholic or something.

Nina didn't like to point out that the price of alcohol in nightclubs these days was scandalous. Sure, you could buy half a litre of vodka in the off licence for the price of the miserable measure they gave you in a club. But Nina had learned from experience that it was best not to get into that kind of a debate with strangers.

She waited for the dentist to return with her

drink. She glanced around the room. The talent was disappointing. It looked like she'd stumbled on the only decent male in the place. Wasn't it so lucky he had appeared? She noticed her cousin on the dance floor, shaking her bottom stupidly, trying to emulate Kylie Minogue. She looked awfully daft so she did. Nina hoped she wasn't going to be up half the night getting sick.

'Do you see her?'

Aidan was back.

'Yes, she's somewhere about,' Nina said uncomfortably. She didn't want to point Sheena out to him. In case he was disgusted and thought her family were tinkers or something. Sheena was now gyrating in front of some shaven-head freak. She was going to kill her for this later, she really was.

Nina sipped her vodka and Diet Coke. It was nice and cool. Aidan was from Mayo, it turned out, but had been living in Dublin for a while now. He'd recently bought a house in Dublin. Nina's ears pricked up. A house? He'd bought a house all by himself? Well now, he must be rolling in it. Dublin houses cost a fortune. Nina gave him an extra big smile. She hoped she wasn't looking too bad. She hadn't dressed up or anything 'cos she hadn't planned on going clubbing. She was wearing jeans and a black polo neck she'd bought in Dunnes. Her curly brown hair was pulled back off her face and tied in a scrunchie. She wasn't wearing much make-up but what harm; they said men preferred the more natural look.

Aidan was very interesting. He'd travelled to places like the Far East and Australia. Nina told him she hadn't travelled much. She didn't like to tell him that every Christmas she went into Budget Travel to have a look at the holiday brochures . . . just in case . . . but sure Ireland was so beautiful you'd be mad to go anywhere else. And anyway those foreign countries were notorious for ripping tourists off. Anybody could tell you that.

'I was supposed to go to Spain,' she told him, 'to a place near Puerto Banus in Marbella but the trip was cancelled.'

'Oh really?' he exclaimed, 'What a pity, Puerto Banus is supposed to be great fun. Whereabouts were you going to stay?'

'Oh in a villa,' Nina boasted, 'with its own pool and jacuzzi and everything.'

'Wow,' Aidan seemed genuinely impressed. 'Sound's fantastic, you're obviously one of those jet setters you sometimes read about in the back of magazines.'

Nina felt herself flush. Now, what had she got herself into?

'Why did you decide not to go in the end?' Aidan enquired.

Nina's mind raced. What was she going to tell him? Should she tell him that she'd entered a show called *The Happiest Couple in Ireland*? And that the trip to Marbella had been cancelled? No. He'd never ask her out then. He'd think she was a fruitcake. Or worse he'd think she'd been in love with Donal.

'Work commitments,' Nina said uncomfortably, 'I was snowed under with work.'

'You must be very committed,' Aidan seemed impressed, 'but all work and no play . . .'

'Sounds dull, I know,' Nina sighed, 'but I've decided to loosen up a bit now and learn not to take life too seriously.'

With that, harsh lights lit up the club.

'Is that it?' Aidan looked at his watch.

'Must be,' Nina said, scouring the room for her drunken cousin. Eventually she spotted her. Wrapped around the skinhead. Making a show of herself.

'Er . . . I'd better go and rescue my friend,' she told Aidan. She didn't want him to think she was related to Sheena.

'Will I wait here?' Aidan enquired politely.

'Er . . . yes . . . yes that would be great,' Nina told him.

She made her way over to where her young cousin and 'acquaintance' were chewing the faces off each other.

She tapped Sheena on the shoulder. Eventually her cousin prised herself away from the skinhead.

'What is it Nina?' she asked. Real cheekily, Nina thought.

'The disco's over we'd better go home.'

'Is it alright if Anto comes back for a coffee?'

'I don't think it's a good idea.' Nina said firmly. She hated being put in this situation. It made her look like she was a jealous old spinster. But her aunt had

made her promise that she'd look after her cousin.
She was too young to leave in a nightclub all by
herself.

'Why not?' asked Sheena, in a deliberate drunken
tone.

'Listen,' Nina said in a definite tone, 'Anto can
take your number and call you again if he wishes,
but we're not having strangers back to the flat.'

'I should've known a night out with you would be
no fun at all,' Sheena sulked.

Nina ignored her. There was no point having a
stupid conversation in a nightclub with her drunken
country cousin who knew nothing about anything.
Dublin wasn't like Mullingar. You couldn't just go
around picking up strange men in the capital.

Eventually Nina got her to leave the nightclub.
Aidan offered them a lift home. And Sheena remained
silent in the back of Aidan's Renault Laguna all the
way home. Nina hoped she wasn't going to pass out
or anything.

'I'm not going to ask myself in for a coffee,' Aidan
joked as he stopped the car outside the house in
Drumcondra.

'Thash good,' Sheena slurred from the back seat,
'cosh you weren't being invited in anyway.'

'Don't mind her,' Nina gave an awkward laugh.
'She's just tipsy, that's all. She's only seventeen.'

Sheena opened the back door and staggered out
without saying goodbye.

Nina was mortified. She hoped Aidan wouldn't

think little of her, keeping company with such a rude person.

'Listen, is it okay if I ring you?' he looked at her hopefully.

Nina's face broke into a nervous smile. 'That'd be fine,' she said, retrieving a half-chewed pen from her bag and scribbling her number on the back of an old bus ticket.

She said goodbye. Aidan tooted his horn and drove off.

Nina turned towards the house.

There was no sign of Sheena. She'd obviously let herself in. That was funny though, Nina thought, staring at the shut door. She hadn't given Sheena a spare key. Good God she must have pressed the bell and woken up one of the tenants. What a nightmare. She put the key in the door and let herself in. The light was on in Donal's flat. And she could hear voices. A woman's voice. Laughter.

Nina paused outside his door. The sound of laughter made her feel strange. So Donal had a new woman. Hmm. It hadn't taken him too long to get over her so, had it? Men, you couldn't trust them an inch. All talk, but not much action to back up the big words. She headed upstairs to her own flat and let herself in. The flat was dark and quiet. Sheena must have passed out on the sofa or something.

She tiptoed in switching on the light. No sign of Sheena. Maybe she was in Nina's bedroom.

But no. No sign of her there either. God, where

was she? Maybe she'd gone in to Dorianne's room by mistake. Nina sighed. She'd have to get her out of there. Sheena was very very drunk. Imagine if she got sick all over the sheets or something?

Sheena was not in Dorianne's bedroom or in the bathroom either. Nina felt her blood run cold. Where the hell was she? Oh God, what if she hadn't come into the house at all? Suppose she'd run away when Nina was giving her number to the dentist. How on earth could she explain that to Auntie May? Nina began to panic.

She ran downstairs. Perhaps Donal had seen her come in or out. Nina didn't like to knock on his door. Suppose himself and his er . . . company were in bed or something. He'd think Nina was checking up on him or something.

She heard the sound of laughter again. They must be sitting in the sitting room, she thought. Where *she'd* always sat. Laughing at his jokes. Before the whole *Happiest Couple in Ireland* fiasco.

She gave the door a quiet knock. But nobody answered. The sound of laughter rose. Nina hoped they weren't laughing at her. She took a deep breath and knocked again. A good hard knock this time.

The door answered slowly. Donal's eyes were bloodshot and he seemed to be having difficulty trying to stand straight. 'Nina, we were just talking about you.' He was speaking very slowly, very deliberately, the sign of somebody who's had way too much to drink.

She gave him a terse don't-touch-me smile. Her

blood was beginning to boil. She hadn't come down here for a bit of chit-chat with her ex-boyfriend. And his new bit on the side.

'Tell her to go away,' came the female voice.

Nina stood rooted to the spot, stunned. 'Is Sheena in there?' she barked suddenly.

'Yep,' Donal shrugged. 'She said you were outside getting stuck into some fella so she came in here for a bit of company.'

Nina barged past him into the flat. Sheena was lying on the couch, a can of beer balancing on her belly.

'Sheena come on, it's time to go to bed.'

Her young cousin closed her eyes and ignored her.

'Did you hear me Sheena?'

'Go to bed yourshelf if you want, jush leave me alone.'

Nina was fuming but she was determined not to let Sheena make a fool out of the two of them in front of Donal.

'Right then,' she said, trying to maintain her composure, 'I'm off to bed now, come up whenever you want.'

She went to leave the room. Donal grabbed her arm as she left, 'Sorry about this,' he said, 'I'll make sure to send her up after you.'

'Thank you,' she told him coolly.

Sure enough, as Nina was making up her hot water bottle, Sheena burst into the flat.

'I hope you're happy now, you've ruined my night,'

she shouted, 'Even Donal wanted nothing to do with me when he realised I wash related to you.'

Nina could feel her pulse rise. She took a deep breath. 'The reason he probably didn't want to get involved,' she began, 'is that (a) he realises that you're only seventeen and (b) that you've had a lot to drink and should be asleep.'

Sheena leaned against the kitchen table. Her eyes filled with tears. Drunken tears. 'I shouldn't have bothered coming,' she wailed. 'Sinéad shaid I was mad to come, she shaid I wouldn't have any fun, she shaid you were a mean old thing, so mean you turned off the heat in her room last time she shtayed and she nearly got pneumonia after, she shaid . . .'

But Nina never got to find out what else her cousin Sinéad had said about her. She'd walked out of the kitchen, slamming the door on Sheena's ramblings.

Chapter Thirteen

'Are we at a table of couples?' Sandra asked her friend Deirdre over the phone.

'Of course you are,' Deirdre said. 'Well you are part of a couple too, remember? Don't tell me Richard and yourself have split up already?'

'I know I'm part of a couple now. It's just that deep down I still feel like a singleton really. I'm such an uncouply person you know. I hate the word 'attached'. It freaks me out. And anyway, I'm no good talking about tablecloths, property and the price of gas-fire heating.'

'Not all couples discuss fuel prices when they're out together,' Deirdre laughed.

'I know, I know, it's just that I really don't want to be at a table of couples,' Sandra pleaded, 'I don't think I could stick it. Can't you just put us at a singles table – a fun table?'

'I think you were single for too long Sandra,' Deirdre giggled. 'Didn't you realise what you'd have to give up? A lot of freedom is foregone when you become half a couple.'

'Don't say that,' Sandra cried down the phone. 'It sounds so rotten and I'm feeling bad enough as it is.'

'It's your hormones,' Deirdre sympathised. She was a Holles Street nurse and one of the very few people who knew about Sandra's pregnancy.

'So tell me, are you looking forward to married life?' Sandra asked.

'Marriage is what you make of it,' Deirdre said practically. 'Just like everything I suppose. But I'm not expecting the rest of my life to be a fairytale. I've been with Stephen for eight years. I know when I walk up that aisle, that he will be waiting for me, not some handsome prince. Not that I'd trade him for a handsome prince. I wouldn't trade his little toe for an entire Brad Pitt.'

'That's sweet,' Sandra said, not believing it for a minute.

She tried to imagine someone giving her a choice between Richard and Brad Pitt.

Would she trade them? Would she what? Oh God, why was she feeling so miserable?

Why was she feeling so unloved? Why wasn't she happy to be engaged and expecting?

Because she didn't feel happy. Not one bit. But what was the definition of happiness anyway? What could you measure it against?

Recently Sandra was beginning to think she was living a lie. A nasty little lie. Nothing felt right. It was as if she'd mistakenly entered a chapter of somebody else's storybook. Richard wasn't her dream man. Of course he wasn't totally awful. And he was good looking. But there had to be more to life than that.

She'd never considered Richard in a ... in a romantic way. God no. But then again people didn't usually go around lusting after guys their best friends referred to as 'soulmates'.

Did they?

You wouldn't deliberately do that, would you?

It wouldn't even occur to you.

No.

Richard had never featured in her dreams.

He had been Caroline's dream, she thought almost guiltily.

Caroline's dream.

Poor trusting Caroline.

And she'd snatched it away from her.

God forgive her.

Because Caroline wouldn't be doing any forgiving.

And it was hard not to blame her.

Sandra sighed.

If only she hadn't been a silly twit.

If only she hadn't gone to Richard's stag.

If only she hadn't started doing shots with the lads in the nightclub.

If only she hadn't gone back to his place afterwards.

But it was all very well to look back and say 'if only'.

What happened that night happened.

There was no going back wishing it hadn't.

There was absolutely no point.

Ironically enough Caroline had been the one to insist.

'Go on,' she had urged, 'Richard would love you to go. You know he's as fond of you as any of the lads. He'd be insulted if you didn't show up. And besides,' she'd added with a wink, 'I know if you're there, he'll behave himself.'

He'll behave himself.

Those words would haunt Sandra for the rest of her life.

Chapter Fourteen

Nina woke to the sound of Sheena retching in the bathroom. She tried to block out the sound and go back to sleep. But couldn't. She was too upset. How much of Sheena's allegations were true? Had Sinéad really been bitching about her behind her back? It was hurtful to think about it. Sinéad was the same age as Nina and they'd always been friends. Nina had always loved playing with her cousin's toys as a child. Sinéad had always had so many of them. And later in life, when Sinéad got a job in Galway, Nina had visited her and stayed a full three and a half weeks. Now, you wouldn't stay that long with someone you didn't get on with, would you?

Having said that, she had noticed a lack of phone calls from Sinéad in recent months. Nina hadn't thought about it too much. She'd just put it down to the fact that Sinéad had a boyfriend now. Some women were funny like that when a man arrived on the scene. They just dropped all their female friends immediately.

Eventually she got up. What was she going to say

to Sheena? Should she just act like nothing had been said? Or should she confront her young cousin? And demand the exact meaning of her outburst. She made her way into the kitchen where Sheena was sitting at the table, her head in her hands.

'Good morning,' Nina said distantly.

'Morning,' Sheena's voice sounded hoarse and wretched.

'Were you sick?'

'Mmm,' Sheena nodded.

Nina put the kettle on. She wasn't going to say anything more.

Then suddenly Sheena spoke. 'I'm sorry about last night,' she said in a small voice, 'What I said was totally out of line.'

Nina paused for a second, hesitating about what to say next. She looked at Sheena's young hungover face and softened. The girl looked like she'd been dragged to hell and back. 'Let's forget about it, will we?' Nina said gently.

'Sinéad never said any of those things about you, I swear to God,' Sheena added.

'No,' Nina said, reaching for the coffee jar, 'No, of course she didn't.'

Nina was glad to see the back of her cousin as she got the bus back to Mullingar. The seventeen-year-old had spent the day trying on debs dresses, albeit with a severe hangover. Eventually she'd settled on a gold dress in Clerys. It had cost an arm and a leg and

Nina told Sheena it'd be cheaper to get one made. But Sheena hadn't agreed. She didn't want to be bothered going for fittings and the rest of it. It was only a debs dance after all. It wasn't like she was getting married or anything.

Tired after her day shopping in overheated stores, Nina made her way back to the house alone. Once inside she noticed the light flashing on the answer machine. She picked up the phone. Was Aidan calling already? Her heart gave a little leap. But no. It wasn't Aidan. It was a female voice.

An unfamiliar voice.

'Hi,' the voice said, 'this is Amanda calling on behalf of *The Happiest Couple in Ireland*. Could you give us a call at your earliest convenience?'

Chapter Fifteen

Caroline sat squashed on the sofa between Leila and Suzie. Another mind-numbing night of *Big Brother* was on the cards. Saturday night. Another night in.

This time the contestants were going on about how it was Saturday and how everyone they knew would be out having fun. It was bizarre, Caroline thought. They wished they were out and yet Caroline was sitting in. Watching them wishing they were out.

As were millions of others.

It was funny to watch and it made Caroline think. If she'd continued as a participant in *The Happiest Couple in Ireland* would she have got that kind of media attention? Would she have wanted it? Would she have been able to cope? You'd need to be made of steel to put yourself up for public scrutiny like that. How did you deal with the man on the street calling you a pig? And feeling justified in saying it because he thought he knew you. Because you were in his living room every night.

Leila and Suzie were going out later. They'd got free passes to Chinawhite nightclub. Or was it Sugar

Reef or Emporium? Caroline couldn't remember
now. It was so confusing trying to keep up with
the night-life antics of her two flatmates. Anyway
tonight was something they were looking forward
to. The girls had been promised that Dane Bowers,
Atomic Kitten, one of the guys from Blue, some *Big
Brother* contestants, some *Popstars* contestants and
a couple of kids TV presenters were *definitely* going
to be at the same club.

The drama of it all!

This was about as exciting as things got for Leila
and Suzie.

They never got invitations to A-list events. Not
like some of the top M-City Music execs. No. The
nearest Caroline's flatmates ever got to the real stars
like Madge and Britney was the local record shop.

Tonight the girls spent ages getting dolled up in
the living room. Their tight, leather trousers and
plunging PVC tops made it difficult for Caroline to
know where to look. So she just continued to look
straight ahead at the TV screen.

The girls asked her if she'd wanted to go out with
them but she'd declined. She'd already had one not-
so-funny night on the town with them. They'd both
got lucky within about five minutes. And Caroline
had had to make her way back to Finsbury Park
on her own. With a dodgy cab driver who spoke
no English. And wasn't sure how to get to Finsbury
Park. He was new to the job, he'd explained. And
didn't know north London. Only the tourist areas.

That hadn't been much use to Caroline.

She'd no wish to visit The Tower of London at this time of night.

Eventually he'd radioed in for directions. *Why hadn't he just done that in the first place?*

The night out had cost her almost a week's wages.

She wasn't prepared to suffer another night like that any time soon. No. She just wasn't in the mood for another hair-raising adventure yet. Wrist slashing stuff it might be, but another night watching the *Big Brother* contestants get drunk on TV was a million times better than watching Leila and Suzie get drunk for real.

Leila and Suzie left just before midnight. Caroline yawned. She might as well go to bed now. She didn't like staying awake late at night. Alone. It gave her time to think about Richard. And then the hurting would start again. The despair. The devastation. The hatred. And then the fear. She felt all of it. Deeply. When she was alone. She switched off the telly and cleared away Leila and Suzie's empty wine glasses and crisp bags. Half way up the stairs she heard the phone ringing. Oh God, who was it now? Obviously one of the girls had locked themselves out and wanted her to leave the keys under the mat.

She'd better answer it now really. It would save her being woken up later on. She didn't want anyone hammering on the door at 4:00 am.

She picked up the phone. 'Hello?' she called brightly.

'Caroline, is that you?'

She froze.

That voice was awfully bloody familiar.

Unmistakable.

Richard.

God.

How on earth had he got a hold of this number?

'Ye . . . es?' she felt her voice squeak.

'How are you?'

How was she? How *was* she? Was he insane? How the hell did he think she was? What did he want? She knew Richard. He didn't ring people for trivial chit-chats. Not even people he'd been engaged to.

'I'm fine,' she said stiffly.

'Caroline, there's something I think you should know. I . . . we haven't told anyone yet . . . but Sandra's expecting . . . we thought you should be the first to know . . .'

Chapter Sixteen

'Emily-Ann, that's a beautiful shade of lipstick,' Caroline smiled at the other female contestant through the tinted bathroom mirror. Richard had advised her to become pally with some of the other girls. Said it would put her in a strong position if she came across as popular with her own sex. Caroline wasn't sure. Some of the girls were anything but friendly. Emily-Ann was gazing at herself in the flattering full-length mirror as if admiring an incredibly beautiful piece of art. Caroline discreetly cleared her throat. Perhaps the other girl hadn't heard her. Eventually Emily-Ann turned to look at Caroline. She sported a distinct look of contempt. 'Sorry, do I know you?'

Caroline just stared at her. And said nothing for a while. She could feel her temperature rising. How dare Emily-Ann think she could speak to her like this! Who did she think she was?

'I'm one of the other contestants,' she said eventually, 'We met inside. Er . . . you were saying you work with the homeless. So do I. I was just wondering which charity you work with?'

Emily-Ann looked at her disbelievingly. 'I know

exactly who you are,' she said, *'Are you trying to catch me out or something?'*

Caroline was taken aback. *'Of course not. I work with a group of elderly women. I was just wondering what particular area you work in. I play Bingo on a Thursday night with disadvantaged women.'*

'Bingo'? Emily-Ann sneered. *'You're having me on, aren't you?'*

Caroline felt herself redden. Who did this girl Emily-Ann think she was? Whatever Richard thought, she wasn't going to put up with this kind of rudeness from anyone.

'No, I'm serious. I've been involved in charity work for years. You can tell me what you do. I'm not going to say it to anyone. It's just off the record you know. You can confide in me.'

'I obviously can't confide anything in you,' Emily-Ann said huffily. *'It's obvious that you don't want me to be here. This is not just some little game is it? Everybody is here to win. You just want me to tell you that I'm lying, that I'm making everything up, in case myself and Graham win. Well, all I can say is this,'* she lowered her voice, *'may the best couple win!'*

She flounced out of the bathroom with Caroline staring after her, gobsmacked. What in the name of God, had that been all about?

'Excuse me?' a voice in her ear made her jump. She swung around. Good God it was Lazy Luke's niece from Tele-Fone.

'Oh hello,' she said, a bit flustered.

'I couldn't help overhearing your conversation with Emily-Ann,' Nina lowered her voice. 'She's not very friendly is she?'

'That's a bit of an understatement,' Caroline managed to raise a smile. 'Ah well, maybe she's just having a bad day.'

'You work in Tele-Fone, don't you? With my uncle. He's your supervisor.'

'Um,' Caroline's face flushed an uncomfortable shade of red. What on earth had Luke been saying about her? Did he go around telling people he was her boss? The cheek!

'Well, it's great to see a familiar face,' Nina smiled. 'Maybe we'll meet for a cup of coffee back in work. You, me, and Luke.'

'Yes, em, that would be great,' Caroline muttered uncertainly. God!

'They're serving free wine and cheese outside,' Nina informed her. 'We should go out and get some before it's all gone.'

Caroline searched the other girl's face for traces of irony but found none. So she followed Nina outside.

'Mmm, this wine is lovely,' Nina said.

Caroline took a sip. It was just okay.

'So, this is pretty exciting isn't it?' Nina started off again.

Caroline raised an eyebrow quizzically. 'You mean the wine and cheese?'

'No silly, I mean being on TV and all that. I can't wait to see ourselves.'

Caroline said nothing. She was dreading it.

'I've been on TV three times already.'

'Have you?'

'Yeah, I was on Anything Goes when I was a kid and then I was on the news a few years ago being interviewed about some flooding in the area. They put my name on the screen with "Flood Victim" beside it.'

'Right.'

'And then a cousin of mine was on Spin the Wheel and I went along to lend my support and I was sitting in the front row with a big sign saying "Go on Marty".'

'And did he win anything?'

'Yeah, he won 24 grand but he didn't give me a penny of it the mean fecker.'

'Oh.'

'Well anyway, I'm very positive about this show, you'd never know what it might lead to.'

'That's right.'

'Your fella's very good looking.'

'Thanks.'

'Are you really happy and all?'

Caroline hesitated slightly. 'I think so.'

'I'm happy too. Donal's a nice fella. But I'm not sure if we'll win. I mean, we're not the most glamorous couple here or anything.'

Caroline didn't completely agree. She thought

Nina was very pretty with her sallow skin and slim figure. But it was a pity she didn't make more of an effort. She'd look stunning with the right make-up. Donal was dressed like a workman and was good looking. And he did seem genuinely nice which was more than could be said about many of the contestants.

'Will you have another glass of wine?' Nina offered.

'Ah no,' Caroline said, 'Sure it's not that great, is it?'

'I don't think it's bad,' Nina said, grabbing a glass that looked fuller than all the others. 'Let's put it this way – I wouldn't say no.'

Chapter Seventeen

Caroline was dazed. How could Richard have rung her up and upset her like that? Really though, how could he be so hurtful, so ruthless?

The baby news had been hard to stomach. The biggest smack in the face ever. What did Sandra and Richard expect her to do? Congratulate them? God they were sick. Twisted. Of course Caroline now realised what all of this meant. It meant that he'd been seeing Sandra behind her back. Sleeping with her. They must've lain naked in each other's arms, discussing her. Poor naïve little Caroline. Innocent Caroline who'd had absolutely no idea what was going on. God, it was horrible even thinking about it. She wondered who else had known. Nobody had said anything. But of course, people wouldn't, would they? Nobody liked to deliver uncomfortable news.

Anyway, the incredible thing was, he hadn't phoned just to tell her about the baby. No. As if that hadn't been bad enough . . . there was something else.

According to Richard it was all very simple really. He wanted Caroline to return to Ireland and pretend she was still his fiancée.

Imagine.

And no, unbelievably it wasn't a joke.

Apparently the Happy Television company had got in touch. They'd got new investors and wanted to continue the show, which included the lovey-dovey weekend in Marbella.

Imagine that. A (pretend) romantic weekend in Marbella while he was expecting a child with her ex-best friend. Jesus, he must really be nuts.

She wondered if he'd any idea how much he'd hurt her. Any notion of the nights she'd cried herself to sleep, convinced her heart would physically collapse with the pain. The humiliation. The betrayal. The bitter regrets.

Obviously not. It was all becoming so clear now. Richard thought of only one person. All the time. And that was Richard.

The TV company had been terribly anxious to get in touch. So he'd told her anyway. They were keen to air the show as soon as possible and needed the contestants to finish filming the series. Well, thought Caroline, he could get lost. The cheek of him. How dare he! He must think she was really thick. How could she ever have contemplated marrying someone who'd so little respect for her?

She was staying put. Right here in London. She wasn't coming home. And certainly not for his sake anyway. She'd suffered enough humiliation because of Richard. But it was all over now.

Let him have his child with Sandra. Let them play happy families. And let them stay a million miles from her.

But the real blow came the following Friday. The final straw. The landlord was putting up the rent. His announcement came out of the blue. Caroline was gutted. This was all she needed – good God, as if the rent wasn't high enough!

After a few late night group discussions, the other girls decided they couldn't afford to pay the exorbitant new rates. And applying for other jobs to supplement their glamour work was completely out of the question. There were positions going in the many pubs and restaurants in Finsbury Park but the girls didn't want to take them. In fact they were horrified by the very suggestion of it. Imagine if they were recognised by punters. In the end, they decided to move home to their respective homes in the midlands and commute to London whenever a 'job' came up. Caroline was devastated. As it was she could barely afford to live in London. And now she'd have to go searching for new flatmates.

God how much worse could things get for her? The thought of interviewing strangers to share with was making her feel ill. You heard so many horror stories. But she was in no position to start being fussy. Unfortunately she wasn't even close to being able to afford to live on her own.

The girls moved out the following weekend. On Monday Caroline's ad was in the *Evening Standard*.

The first candidate rang the bell at around 6:30.

Bridget.

That was her name.

She was also Irish.

'Am I first?' she pushed in past Caroline excitedly as if she'd been standing in a queue for once-off tickets to see U2.

Caroline, reluctantly, showed her around the place. Bridget oohed and ahhed at everything. Caroline felt she was a tour guide showing her round Buckingham Palace.

'It's perfect,' she beamed as she stepped inside the shower to have a closer look. 'I was actually thinking it would be wicked to share with someone my own age. I've always kind of lived on my own you know. I used to be quite introverted but I'm not anymore. We could be friends.' Bridget was so excited she could barely breathe.

'Right.'

'It's just I feel I haven't really had a life up to now. I've been working all the time and studying like mad. I'm a real career woman I suppose. Really ambitious. Or if you like I *was*. But then you see I got an ulcer and my GP pointed out that I couldn't keep up with this crazy pace of life. He said . . .' she lowered her voice somewhat and Caroline felt something like a chill running down her spine. 'He said I had all the signs of somebody heading for a nervous breakdown.'

'So what do you do now?' Caroline was curious.

'I've no set plans,' Bridget gave a weird kind of smile. 'I was laid off recently and I was going to get another job but after countless "Dear John . . ." letters I decided to have a rethink. Did I want to head straight back into the rat race? Did I? I don't think so. Now I'm going with the flow. I'm learning to love myself. I feel like I've just got out of prison. You've no idea how that feels.'

'No I . . . don't suppose so.' Caroline admitted. 'Well I've a few more people coming to see the place so I can't make a decision until then,' she added hurriedly.

'Oh,' Bridget looked crestfallen. 'Do you *have* to show it to them? I mean I just love the place. I can definitely see myself here with you. Lots of girly nights in, or nights out – we could head to Kilburn and have a few scoops in one of the Irish pubs – or we could sit in enjoying late night Irish coffees, swapping make-up and having chats, it would be a right giggle. I've never had a sister . . . or a best friend as such.'

'Allo, yis?'

'Hello.'

'Allo yis?'

'Yes?'

'Yis . . . about ze 'ouse.'

'I'm afraid it's gone,' Caroline replied. She felt bad saying that but seriously she couldn't share with someone who couldn't speak a word of English.

If someone rang the house looking for her, they wouldn't even be able to leave a message . . .

The doorbell rang. Oh no, she'd forgotten she'd promised to show the flat to one more person.

But maybe this person would be okay.

Caroline opened the door with a smile.

But the smile soon disappeared as in walked a short, stocky woman sporting an early eighties poodle perm and a brown pom-pommed wool hat, despite it still being summer. Caroline regarded her with surprise. She didn't think people like this existed in the capital city. The woman was probably in her mid-forties. She looked like she'd just swallowed a lemon.

'So do you have some kind of system like where one person does the shopping and the other does the washing up?' the woman sniffed as she ran a finger along the mantelpiece.

'Well no . . . er . . .' Caroline explained. 'I was living with two other girls but we all kind of did our own thing.'

'I see. Okay. I must let you know though that I intend going home every weekend,' she announced while taking a good look behind the cooker. What did she think Caroline hid there? The resident rats? 'So I should really pay a bit less on electricity bills and stuff.'

'Oh okay.'

'And I don't use the phone . . . not ever. I have a company mobile. So the line rental wouldn't really apply to me.' The woman gave a nervous little cough or was it a laugh?

'Right.'

'And I rarely watch TV so maybe we could work out something regarding the cable bill.'

'Mmmm.'

'And I think it's a good idea to put little stickers on things . . . just in case.'

'Uh.'

'In case things get mixed up,' she gave a tight little smile. 'And I don't think it's good to invite people to stay without asking each other's permission first.'

'I . . .'

'And we should keep a spare key or something so that if one of us gets locked out we don't lock the other out.'

'Okay.'

'Not that I really go out much.'

'Right.'

'So do you have any questions you'd like to ask me?'

'No, no,' Caroline answered hurriedly.

'Well, will I call you then?'

'Oh no,' Caroline said, 'I'll call you.'

Caroline slumped down on the little couch. And put her head in her hands. She was exhausted. She just couldn't see a light at the end of this tunnel. Just darkness. A heavy darkness. She even missed Suzie and Leila. The place seemed empty without their random bursts of laughter and heavy midland accents.

They'd both given her signed photos when they were leaving. Topless photos. To put on her wall or whatever. 'They might be worth something when we're famous', Suzie had suggested. Caroline had smiled and said nothing. The world wasn't quite ready for another Jordan.

To top it all, there'd been a second phone call from Richard. He'd told her that *The Happiest Couple in Ireland* were offering extra money for them to return. They only had to appear another five, maybe six more times. And then of course there'd be that quick trip to Marbella to view the actual house.

At first she'd thought he was joking. Surely he was having her on. Imagine! Herself and Richard? The country's most dysfunctional 'couple'. Going on television pretending to be happy. What did he expect her to do? Lie?

Well, yes, apparently. That was the basic idea. It was exactly what he wanted her to do. It was, he kept insisting, worth it. The villa in Marbella was definitely worth lying for. And anyway, they'd already signed a contract, he was keen to remind her.

They'd already signed away their rights.

She rang her solicitor the following morning. Was there anyway she could get out of this?

Not easily, he had informed her. They could bring her to court over it. It could cost her big time.

Caroline's heart had hit the floor.

Chapter Eighteen

Caroline sat in the terraced rented house in London. Alone. Well this was it, wasn't it? She'd have to go home now and face the music. Get a new job back in Ireland – well she sure as hell was not going back to Tele-Fone with everybody asking why things hadn't worked out over in London. But did she really want to stay here anyway? In this city with no friends? Who was she kidding? This wasn't living the high life. This wasn't the life she described to her friends via email. No.

Her emails were full of Hyde Park, art galleries, nights out in the Met Bar, Emporium, Attica and The Groucho Club. Deceptive emails. Describing nights out that took place only in her head. The truth was she never went near those places. She couldn't afford to. She was more familiar with the crowded aisles of Asda than the racks of designer clothes at Harvey Nic's. And an evening queuing at the local Indian take away was closer to the truth than a night dining at The Ivy. A night with friends at Pizza Hut would be a serious treat at this stage.

So here she was living a lie. A fake life. Working for a horribly pretentious crowd who talked the talk but failed to walk the walk.

Anyway it was time to call it a day now. Not that she had much choice in the matter. But she was looking forward to telling Andy where to shove his wandering hands. Anyway at least back in Ireland she knew people. She was somebody. And not just another foreigner on the tube.

The following morning she took the lift up to the trendy M-City offices. Bandy Andy was in foul humour. He had a poster of an Irish girl band whose newly released CD had just flopped, in his hands. As Caroline approached him with her letter of resignation, he tore the poster in two. He was positively fuming. He bundled up the torn poster and fired it at Caroline. 'Get rid of this shit, will you? And get me a coffee while you're at it. Make it strong', he added with a growl. Shocked at his outburst, Caroline slunk from the room. Thank God she was finally going to get out of this rotten place. She made Andy a cup of coffee and brought it into his office where he was roaring into the phone. 'What these girls need is a hit single. They've never had a hit single!'

Caroline tiptoed to his desk with the coffee.

Andy looked up as he slammed down the phone. Caroline thought she could see smoke billowing from his ears.

He was staring at the coffee.

'Is something wrong?' Caroline asked.

'Are you thick or something?' Andy snarled.

'Excuse me?'

'That's not my mug,' he seethed, 'My mug is the green mug. That is the ONLY mug I will drink from do you hear?'

'Right,' Caroline said. 'Bad news, is it?'

Andy frowned, 'What?'

'That girl band. You said they were going to be huge didn't you? You must be really worried. All that money wasted. Oh well, there's no point taking it out on me is there? If you get fired because of your mistakes, you get fired.'

'What the f . . . ? '

'Oh don't mind me . . . I'm just rambling. I'll just get the coffee. The yellow mug isn't it? Oh actually do you know something? I don't think I'll bother. I think I'll just head out for a walk.

Yeah, I don't think I want to stick around here. When the M-City Music bosses in New York find out about all the money that's been squandered on that failed band, the shit is really going to hit the fan and this isn't going to be a very nice place to work now is it?'

She moved towards the door. Andy's face had turned a curious shade of purple.

'Well, I'll be off then,' she added 'so I suggest if you still want a coffee, you should get your own fecking mug.'

Chapter Nineteen

Nina was fretting. Big time. Aidan, the dentist had rung and invited her for dinner, with a group of friends. He'd mentioned an expensive, Italian sounding restaurant. Or foreign anyway. Hmm. Didn't sound much like a date or anything. More like a get together. As in a bunch of good friends meeting up. God, she didn't know if she was happy about this set-up at all. She might stick out like a fish out of water.

They'd probably all be talking about work; rotten teeth and root-canal work and drilling. Nina had a horror of dentists' chairs. She didn't know what she'd be able to contribute to the conversation at all. Should she tell them all about the time her filling fell out on Christmas day last year? When no dentist had been available to see her for two days? Or maybe she'd tell them about the guy she went out with in Irish college. He'd thought he couldn't kiss her because she was wearing train-tracks. Or maybe they'd be more interested in the dentist back in Mullingar who . . .

The sound of keys in the front door broke her train of thought. Dorianne's flight must have arrived in early.

Nina beamed at the sight of her flatmate, who looked stunning although she'd been up all night serving transatlantic passengers.

'Hi Nina,' her flatmate smiled back, 'What are you up to?' she asked plonking herself down on the sofa and setting her coal-black hair loose from her ponytail.

Nina explained her dilemma. Dorianne listened carefully. She failed to see any great problem. She thought Aidan sounded nice, and said Nina was fretting about nothing. 'It'll be a great opportunity for you Nina,' she insisted. 'It's good to get out of the house you know. I'm sure you wouldn't want to be sitting in with myself and Damien for yet another evening.'

Nina wasn't sure if she cared for the way Dorianne had emphasised the word yet. She got on very well with Damien. Extremely well. Sure only last week, she'd given him some useful tips about his tax returns. Nina worked in accounts and was very knowledgeable when it came to things like that.

Anyway nights in with D&D, as Nina jokingly called them, were more fun than most nights out. Damien always brought over decent wine and a few new releases from the video shop. And the atmosphere was always very relaxing. Too relaxing almost. Only last week Nina had fallen asleep on the couch beside the pair during a particularly long film and one-too-many glasses of Damien's superb South African wine. The week before she'd joined them for a scrumptious Indian dinner Damien had spent the whole evening cooking. Fabulous. No, really, she must have taken Dorianne's comment up the wrong way; herself and D&D were the best of pals.

'You should definitely go on this date,' Dorianne said firmly, slipping her feet out of her high heels and tucking them under her, 'You never know what it might lead to.'

'But it might not lead to anything,' Nina frowned. 'And the night might cost a bomb. I don't like going on these dinners with people I don't know. His friends might end up ordering expensive champagne and I might end up having to splash out for it all.'

Dorianne closed her eyes, obviously feeling the effects of jet lag. 'I think you should go,' she repeated before falling asleep.

Chapter Twenty

You had to sit on a little podium with some of the other girls. The men sat in the audience and cheered on the 'birds'. Caroline thought this was by far the naffest part of the competition. The spotlight was on her when she was asked on average how many pints Richard consumed on a Friday night. 'Six,' she said quickly and Richard cheered from the crowd.

Six was the right answer.

Another bonus point.

For Caroline and Richard.

This was worse than a Punch and Judy show, Caroline thought miserably. And to think people all around Ireland were actually going to be watching this at home. With a pizza and beer. Having a right old sneer. Whispering out of the side of their mouths going 'Would ya look at the state of her?' God, it was unbearable even to think about it.

The next question was more complex: If your man was unfaithful to you, would he admit it?

'Not unless he found out he was terminally ill

and thought he had nothing to lose anyway,' was Caroline's answer.

Right answer. The crowd cheered.

Another bonus point.

Phew!

Caroline could feel the sweat beads mounting. Would they ever take the bloody spotlight off her?

Next question: How many sexual partners has your partner enjoyed before you?

'None. Richard's a virgin,' she said with a mischievous grin.

Another laugh.

Another bonus point.

The crowd clapped.

Richard and Caroline were through to the second round.

'Who takes longer in the bathroom? Yourself or Graham?'

'Graham definitely,' Emily-Ann said like lightning.

The crowd laughed.

'That's not a joke,' Emily-Ann added with a deadpan face, 'I've to drag him out kicking and screaming.'

The crowd warmed to her.

Herself and Graham were through to the second round.

'So tell us Donal,' Mikey Mark was getting into the full swing of things. 'What's the worst thing

about Nina? Tell us something that'll shock us to bits.'

Donal paused for a minute as Nina's face fell. What was he going to say about her? This was awful. If he didn't say something to make the crowd laugh, they'd be voted off without mercy.

'To be perfectly honest,' Donal said quietly, 'I'm sure Nina has her faults and plenty of them, but love must be blind, 'cos in my eyes she's nothing less than perfect.'

Nina froze. Oh God, the crowd certainly were not going to like something as mushy as that. But they did. For some reason, they liked Donal's down-to-earth demeanour.

And so Donal and Nina got through to the second round.

Chapter Twenty-One

Caroline boarded Aer Lingus flight EI-179 at London Heathrow. She took her seat just behind the green curtain, which shut people like her off from the first-class passengers. She felt weird. It seemed odd to be coming home already. She hoped that didn't make her a failure.

A lot of people came home having made a fortune in Britain. And let everybody know it. And paid for big expensive houses in Ireland with cash. But then there were the others . . . the ones you didn't hear about. The alcoholics you regularly saw stumbling around the tube in long dirty grey coats, with long dirty vomit-matted beards. They'd also come over to make their fortune, Caroline supposed. But they'd never taken this journey home. And probably never would.

Because sometimes Irish people didn't take kindly to those who hadn't made it in life.

People arriving home without a bob in their pocket.

No.

People were much more interested in the success stories.

Caroline looked out the window at the parked British Airways planes. Tonight some of those planes would be half way across the world. Incredible, wasn't it? She shut her eyes and wondered for the hundredth time whether she was making the right decision. She'd become used to London and its anonymity. It felt kind of safe there. Out of people's sight and minds.

Back in Dundalk people would know her on the street. More to the point they'd be asking her all about her impending wedding. And she'd have to explain. She'd have to tell them there wasn't going to be a wedding after all. She wasn't looking forward to it. Maybe she should just stay in Dublin. After all Fiona from Tele-Fone said she was more than welcome to stay with her until she got sorted. Yeah, maybe she should just stay in Dublin.

After take-off she sipped her glass of white wine and flicked through a copy of the *Irish Independent*. She hadn't read anything Irish recently and it was interesting to see what was happening back home. Her mother had religiously posted her over monthly copies of *U*, *Irish Tatler* and *Galway Now* but apart from reading those magazines, she'd felt very much anglicised. Most of the people in M-City Music had never been to Ireland. Except for Debbie who'd been to Dublin on a hen weekend but couldn't remember anything about it. And Ben who'd kissed the Blarney stone and spent his life telling unfunny Paddy Irish jokes.

She was dreading going back on the actual TV show. How on earth was she going to be able to pull it off? How was she going to act like she was still in love with Richard? Then a thought struck her. God, it was so obvious. Why hadn't she thought of it before?

If she was going to go through with the show she might as well try her best to win it. But to do that she'd have to get herself psyched up for it. Why not sign up for acting classes? That would give her the confidence to go back on the show, wouldn't it? Yes, it all made sense. As soon as the plane landed she was going to enquire about classes. And then she was going to go ahead and emerge the winner of this goddamn show.

All fired up now, she knocked back the rest of her wine.

She felt better already.

Chapter Twenty-Two

'Yes, it was so romantic,' Caroline reddened as she told the interviewer a barefaced lie. 'I mean there I was, at the other end of the world, walking along in the sunshine, lost in my own thoughts when suddenly I spotted Richard.'

'And you'd no idea he was Irish?'

'Not a clue.' Caroline said and worried that she didn't sound convincing enough. 'He was so gorgeous I just presumed he was one of those surfer guys who were always hanging around Eerlie Beach. I couldn't believe he was actually from the same country as me.'

Mikey Mark turned his attentions to Richard. 'What about you?' he said. 'What were your first impressions of Caroline?'

Richard was better at fabrication. In fact he was almost a pro. He closed his eyes as if trying to remember the exact moment he'd clapped eyes on her.

'She was divine,' he answered dreamily, 'She was strolling along the beach with the wind in her hair *and I just thought to myself, "I have to talk to this woman, no matter what it takes".'*

'How romantic,' Mikey Mark said, drearily and unconvinced. He had heard this kind of story once too often. 'So what did you say to her? Did you ask her her name?'

'I wasn't going to be that obvious,' Richard laughed. 'I reckoned Caroline had tons of admirers and I just wasn't prepared to join the queue.'

'So what did you do?' Mikey Mark persisted.

'I asked her to marry me,' Richard said.

'You did?' Mikey Mark's eyes widened. Now this was interesting. Not that he believed it for a second ... 'And she said yes straight away I take it?'

Richard laughed again. 'Oh no', he said. 'She just looked at me like I'd ten heads and kept walking. It made me even more determined than ever to meet her.'

Caroline stood holding Richard's hand. She was intrigued. Richard should be a novelist!!! Where did he get his imagination? She'd never met anyone before with his ability to make things up on the spot. What else did he make up? she wondered uneasily.

What else was Richard capable of?

'I used to spend hours looking at the window at her, as she danced in the garden, or played with her toys,' Graham said dreamily.

'Oh so it was like that then, was it?' Mikey Mark raised an eyebrow.

His questioning look went right over Emily-Ann's head. 'He thought I was unattainable,' she said sweetly.

'So what happened in the end? How did you two love birds finally you know . . . get it on?'

'I was going away to university in France for a year,' said Emily-Ann, 'and my friend pulled up in her car to give me a lift. Graham was looking out the window and saw me and panicked and ran out proclaiming his undying love for me.'

'It seems our Graham spent a lot of time peeping out the window,' said Mikey Mark. 'Part of the neighbourhood watch scheme, were you?'

'So what about you two then? What's your romantic story?'

'Sometimes I bring Nina breakfast in bed,' Donal said. 'I think she looks best in the morning; she's naturally beautiful.'

Mikey Mark secretly bit his tongue. Would this Donal fella ever just get off the stage? Breakfast in bed, me arse. Come on, nobody was that nice. It must all be just an act. It must be.

'So when were you in Australia?' Nina wanted to know.

'Oh about two years ago,' Caroline said breezily though her stomach muscles were tightening.

'*I'd love to go there some day; you must tell me exactly where you went and give me all the details.*'

'*Oh I will,*' Caroline felt nauseous. She wished Nina would go away or at least talk about something other than Australia. Caroline had never even been to the country.

'*Luke's been to Australia loadsa times. My other uncle lives there so he always stays with him. It must have been very handy when you were planning your trip.*'

'*Why?*'

'*Well he must have been able to give you lots of tips about the place.*'

'*Oh I didn't tell him when I was going,*' Caroline said hurriedly.

'*You didn't tell him?*' Nina looked at her oddly.

'*No, I'm er . . . I kind of like to keep my private life private.*'

Chapter Twenty-Three

'The bride looks stunning, doesn't she?' Deirdre's cousin from Roscommon commented.

'Stunning,' Sandra agreed flatly.

'Her own mother made the dress I hear.'

'Really?'

The foyer of The Berkeley Court hotel was crowded with the wedding party.

Richard had disappeared to the bar and hadn't been seen since.

Typical.

'And Stephen seems really nice. I don't know him that well though. What side of the family are you?'

'I'm Deirdre's friend.'

'Are you a nurse?'

'No, no I'm . . . I'm not a nurse,' Sandra told her.

'What are you?'

'I'm on a career break,' Sandra said. Where was Richard? She was going to kill him.

She looked around the foyer to see if she could spot her fiancé.

'I get on very well with Deirdre's friends,' the cousin shook her hand vigorously. 'I'm Bernadette,' she said. 'You're . . .'

'Sandra.'

'That name is familiar. I'm sure I've heard Dee talk about you . . .' she knocked back some wine. Her face was quite flushed. Maybe she wasn't used to drinking. 'Are you married yourself?'

'I'm engaged.' Sandra said.

'Are you? When's the big day? Is Dee going to the wedding? What am I saying?' Bernie started to laugh right in her face and Sandra felt a bit of saliva fly into her eye. 'Of course she's going to the wedding, ha ha. If she's your friend like. Don't mind me now', Bernie continued. She spilled a trickle of wine down her black lace top and nearly knocked her big silly looking hat off when she tried to wipe it off, 'I'm quite merry.'

And quite silly, Sandra thought, wiping her eye.

'Dee goes to loadsa weddings. She's so popular like. She's a really good friend to her friends if you know what I mean. There was this one girl right . . .'

'Oh God, excuse me for a minute but my bladder is about to explode. I'll be right back.'

Sandra ran.

Phew.

That had been close.

Now where was her fiancé?

Holding up the bar.

That's where he was.

With a whole load of lads in tuxes.

It looked like 50 bouncers were holding up the bar.

Or 50 penguins.

'Where have you been?' she whispered in his ear, 'I've been standing out there on my own like a tool.'

'But I thought you were okay. I saw you talking to one of the girls.'

'She was not one of the girls,' Sandra complained. 'She was . . . she was . . . oh I don't know what she was.'

'Hen-pecked already?' one of the lads gave Richard a clap on the back.

Eventually, they were ushered into the magnificent ballroom where dinner was about to be served. Sandra checked the list of table names for seating arrangements.

'We're at table five,' she linked Richard's arm.

'Oh brilliant!' Bernie's face lit up when she saw Richard and Sandra coming towards her.

'Oh no,' Sandra muttered simultaneously, 'I don't believe this.'

'Oh cool,' Richard said when he saw three of his rugby friends sitting at the table. 'Nice one,' he told Sandra, 'How did you manage to pull this off?'

'Here sit down beside me,' Bernie tapped the seat beside her.

Sandra picked up the menu and pretended to read.

Bernie started to butter her roll. 'There's two spare seats here with nobody sitting at them. If the people don't turn up we can take their rolls.'

Sandra gave the girl a watery smile.

The meal itself was absolutely scrumptious even though the company left a lot to be desired. Sandra was almost thankful when the speeches started. At least they'd shut Bernie up for a while.

The lads did their usual betting on the lengths of the speeches.

Alcohol effects had kicked in and Richard seemed to have miraculously reverted back to his rugby days in a very short time frame.

At one stage, she'd seen him trying to balance a pint on his head. 'Would you cop on and put that down?' she whispered, giving his arm an almighty pinch.

'Hen-pecked,' one of the lads said for about the twentieth time.

'God these speeches are very long,' Bernie said as the best man recounted yet another tedious childhood story about the time Stephen fell off his bike.

'Sssh,' Sandra put her finger to her lips.

'Oh I don't think anyone really listens to them speeches.' Bernie continued as if she hadn't noticed. 'I think they're usually so boring. But then again Dee was telling me a very funny story about a girl who got engaged to her best friend's boyfriend . . .' Bernie took a slurp of her wine.

'Sssh,' Richard told her.

Bernie looked up at him.

And shut up straight away.

'I need to go to the bathroom, will you slip out with me?' Sandra whispered to the now highly indignant looking Bernie. 'I don't want to look rude walking out during the speeches.'

'It'll look ruder if I walk out too,' Bernie pointed out.

'Please, I don't feel very well.'

'Oh in that case,' Bernie stood up.

Richard looked up at the two girls in surprise, but before he could object, Sandra had whisked poor Bernie out of the room.

Sandra sat down on the chair in the Ladies, 'I feel much better now.'

'Oh good Jaysus,' Bernie let out a screech.

'What?'

'Me flippin' tights. There's a ladder in them.'

Sandra threw her eyes to the ceiling.

'I paid a fortune for these you know,' Bernie wailed. 'They're not just them cheapy ones you get out of a machine.'

'Here, I've got a spare pair in my bag,' Sandra offered. Would she ever stop talking about her tights?

'Oh thanks a mill, you're an angel. I'll just go into the cubicle here and put them on.'

Sandra waited impatiently for her to come out. She looked at herself in the mirror. She looked tired and drawn and had circles under her eyes.

Pregnancy huh? What was all that stuff about blooming during pregnancy?

She looked blooming terrible.

And felt worse.

Her ankles were beginning to swell. These damn heels were a killer.

Bernie emerged.

'Now that's much better,' Sandra told her.

'But navy tights don't really go with black lace do they?'

'Nobody will notice,' Sandra assured her.

'Will we go back out so?' Bernie made for the door.

'Hang on,' Sandra said, 'What were you saying to me earlier on about that couple?'

'What couple?' Bernie looked at her blankly.

'Remember you were telling me Deirdre knew this couple who . . .'

'Oh yeah,' Bernie leaned drunkenly against the basin, 'Apparently the girl's best friend shagged your man on his stag night. Imagine! The bitch. Someone said the friend was probably up the duff . . . so he proposed to her.'

'Really?' Sandra's voice was icy but Bernie didn't seem to notice.

'I met the girl and all.'

'Caroline?'

'Oh you know her too do you? Lovely girl. She's so pretty as well. Lovely blonde hair. Much prettier than the one he's with now apparently.' Bernie looked doubtfully at her tights, 'I still think they look a bit blue,' she said.

'What else did you hear about Caroline and the . . . the other pair?' Sandra felt like throwing up but was determined not to let Bernie get side-tracked. Not until she'd got the last bit of information out of her.

'Oh, apparently everyone was talking about it and saying what a bitch the friend was.'

'Did everybody else think that . . . Caroline's friend was pregnant?'

'Ah, no, I don't think so' Bernie explained, 'They all know that, Richard . . . I think that's your man's name . . . that Richard proposed 'cos she's from a wealthy family. He's a right old money grabber apparently.'

Sandra was gobsmacked. 'But Caroline's family don't have any money,' she countered, nearly choking to get the words out. 'And he was going to marry her, wasn't he?'

'Ah, but he thought she did,' Bernie laughed, 'You see he thought she was one of the Kreevans from Dundalk. He thought she lived in a penthouse and was rolling in it.'

'She *is* one of the Kreevans.'

Bernie chuckled. 'Well technically yes. But her father was bought out of the family business a few years back. Richard obviously found out. It's her uncle that owns the clothing empire. Not her da. But rumour has it he's getting back with Caroline now. Funny that isn't it?'

Sandra steadied herself against the basin. Was she imagining it or had the bathroom actually begun to spin?

'It's a small world isn't it?' Bernie gave a loud guffaw.

'No, it's actually . . .' Sandra said faintly, '. . . it's actually quite a big world. It's just the circles . . . the circles that we move in . . . are quite small.'

Chapter Twenty-Four

It was Richard who got the long awaited call. They'd
made it to the final 14. Himself and Caroline. Thank
God. They'd finally made it. Seven couples had
in total. Just seven. But they'd a long way to go
yet.

The bad news was that Emily-Ann and Graham had also reached the finals. As had Nina and
Donal. And they were all going to have to go down
to Marbella together to stay in the house for the
weekend.

Caroline was nervous about all the media attention. The ball had started rolling. At tremendous
speed. The Sunday World had expressed interest
in interviewing herself and Richard. A late night
talk show wanted them to join a panel. Could they
perhaps explain to viewers what made a great relationship? And a giant DIY store was keen to spon-
sor them. Were they interested? Were they what?
Richard had signed the dotted line before Caroline
could get her head around the whole thing.

God, where was it all going to end? Who would

approach them next? Playboy? Perhaps approaching them to do a special 'naked couple' spread? Would they get married on TV? The Oprah Winfrey show? Maybe. The whole thing was ridiculous. So comical you just had to laugh at it. It was frightening too. Would they be able to pull it off? Would they be able to convince the nation that they were in fact the happiest couple in Ireland?

Would the media start looking for skeletons in closets? Would their families and friends be hounded for childhood stories and quotes?

A source said . . . an insider confirmed . . . a relative hinted . . . a close friend suggested, that kind of thing. It was a bit worrying when you started thinking about it. It was best not to think about it too much. At the end of the day you couldn't be going around assuming the worst.

Then there was a press conference. For the 14 finalists. All the media had been invited. Interest in the seven happy couples was spiralling. People in the know, reckoned this show was going to be bigger than Pop Idol and Big Brother put together. It was to be screened during the month of November. Richard knew he had to do something drastic. Something that would win the hearts of the Irish public. Something to make them pick up the phone and vote for himself and Caroline. They'd already seen the photos of the dream house. It was luxurious with breathtaking views of the Mediterranean. And best of all, it was ready to walk into and call home. It even had a jacuzzi in the ensuite bathroom. Richard wanted it badly. He had to have it. So at the press conference. In front of 30 hacks he got down on one knee.

And proposed.

Chapter Twenty-Five

Nina decided on her good wine-velvet dress. She'd bought it on the very last day of the sales last year when everything had been slashed to practically nothing. She took it out of her wardrobe, held it up to her and frowned at her reflection in the mirror. It looked very big didn't it? After all, it was a size 14 and Nina was only a size 10 but it had been such good value. It would have been madness not to buy it.

Aidan arrived at 8:00 on the dot. Nina tugged at her pearls nervously. She hadn't worn them since her grandmother had died. Her grandmother had told her to save them for a special occasion. Well this was a special occasion, wasn't it? After all, it wasn't every day of the year you were asked out by a dentist. Aidan didn't tell her she was looking well. In fact he looked almost uncomfortable as he led her to his car. Maybe he was nervous, Nina told herself. Maybe he was embarrassed that he hadn't made a huge effort to dress up. He was only wearing jeans and a shirt.

*   *   *

The restaurant wasn't an expensive one. It was a pizza place and everybody seemed to be wearing jeans. Nina felt awkward as she tottered unsteadily in her new high heels. Suddenly she began to feel ridiculous. She sat down at the table of about ten people with Aidan. Aidan introduced her and hands were shaken. The waiter came round and everybody ordered starters. Nina noticed that some people were ordering very expensive starters and somebody else had ordered cigars to the table. She ordered a Caeser salad.

'Lovely dress,' one girl said. Her name was Lillian and she was very pretty with long-blonde hair, although her eyes were a bit red. As if she'd been drinking.

'Thank you,' Nina said.

'I have a dress just like it.'

'Really? Well I'm glad you didn't wear it out tonight or we both would have looked stupid.'

Everyone laughed and Nina was delighted with herself. This was a great start. It was important to fit in with Aidan's friends.

'Well,' Lillian continued in quite a slow voice. 'I don't think it would have fitted me even if I'd tried to put it on. See, I wore it to my tenth birthday party.'

Lillian laughed but nobody else did. Nina stared at her napkin. And felt the blood rush to her face.

The waiter came round again and Lillian ordered another bottle of wine.

'I think you should have a coke or something,' Aidan said.

'I think you should mind your own business,' Lillian snapped back.

Fintan, the man sitting to Nina's left, tried to start a conversation.

'What do you do with yourself Nina?'

'I work in Tele-Fone.'

'What do you do there?'

'I work in accounts,' she told him, aware that everybody else was listening.

Lillian snorted.

'Right that's it,' Aidan threw down his napkin. 'I want a word with you.' He pulled Lillian to her feet and escorted her outside.

'What's that all about?' Nina asked Fintan, startled.

'That's his ex,' Fintan explained sheepishly. 'Aidan went out with her for six years.'

'Six years?' Nina's heart fell to the bottom of her shoes. 'How long is it off?' she asked in a small voice.

'Not long,' Fintan told her. 'About three weeks.'

Nina's Caeser salad arrived but she didn't touch it. Talk about disaster.

'Who broke it off?'

'She cheated on him,' Fintan explained. 'So he ended it.'

'But he still has feelings for her?'

'I don't know.'

But Nina knew. It didn't take a genius to figure out that she was just being used. Oh what a nightmare this was. Her head was spinning and she began to feel faint. The rest of the group were looking at her uncomfortably. She was obviously a prop in this little drama. Nina got to her feet unsteadily and opened her little wine-coloured velvet purse. She took out €20 and left it on the table.

'I hope this is enough,' she said in a small voice.

'Don't be ridiculous,' one girl said sympathetically, 'You haven't eaten a thing. Go on, put your money back in your purse, would you?'

Nina hesitated slightly. But then said firmly, 'It was nice meeting you all and I hope this hasn't ruined the rest of your evening.' She left the note on the table, walked towards the door and went out.

She could almost hear the whispers rising excitedly behind her back.

She stood outside the restaurant and hoped a taxi would come by shortly.

Out of the corner of her eye she could see Aidan and Lillian wrapped around each other under a lamppost and Lillian was sobbing like someone had died. And Aidan was stroking her hair and saying, 'It's all right.'

Nina hoped they wouldn't see her standing there. But thankfully a taxi pulled up within minutes and Nina was safe. Heartbroken, humiliated but somehow safe.

The house was empty. Donal's flat was in darkness. Nina walked upstairs and let herself into the flat. An empty can of beer had been left on the kitchen table. Damien and Dorianne had obviously shared it before going out. She wondered where they were. Where was Donal? Where was anyone when she needed someone to talk to?

She should have known. Should have known that a great catch like Aidan would only be interested in a drama queen like Lillian with her posh voice and helpless tears. Even though she'd cheated on him, he still wanted her. Not Nina.

She was just a fill-in.

Nina's heart felt as heavy as it had the day her dad had told her there wasn't enough money for her to go to university. Even though she'd got enough points to get into UCD. That was the day she'd thought that she'd never be anything ever in life and that there would be no escaping the small town she'd grown up in. Thankfully her job in Tele-Fone had enabled her to live in the city. But still, Aidan's friends didn't think she was much. She'd love a little drink now but there were no beers in the fridge. There was a bottle of wine in her bedroom that she'd won in a raffle in work. Nina had been keeping it for a special occasion. But now seemed a good time to open it. Yes, she'd open it and have a glass or two and then when Damien and Dorianne came home she'd offer them a glass too. After all they were always sharing things with her and it was important to share stuff with friends.

*　　*　　*

'Dorianne, Damien,' Nina walked slowly into the kitchen, hungover as hell. Her head was throbbing and she felt ashamed at the sight of the empty bottle of wine. They'd think she was sad drinking it all by herself. 'What did you get up to last night?' she asked them, 'I waited up for you but you never came home so I must have drifted off finally at about 2:00 am.'

'We decided to stay in Damien's brother's house for er . . . for a change,' Dorianne explained, '. . . didn't you stay out yourself though?'

Nina shook her head, too mortified to tell them the truth. 'I came back early. It was too boring, they were just all talking about work. People always do that don't they? Have you finished with those Sunday papers?'

Dorianne buttered herself a croissant. 'I have to say I don't agree with you,' she said, 'I mean not everybody talks about work while they're out. I rarely talk all about my passengers and Damien doesn't always talk about the garage where he works.'

'Well he should,' Nina said, eyeing the freshly baked croissants, 'I mean I found it so interesting when he gave me all that advice about buying a second-hand car.'

'But it obviously wasn't much use to you when you didn't buy the car in the end Nina,' Dorianne countered.

'Oh I know, but it's good to know the prices of things. You don't want to be going around not knowing the price of anything. No, I have to say I always find conversations with Damien very interesting,' she insisted. 'But talking about teeth is different . . . completely different.'

'So you're not going to see him again?' Damien enquired.

'Er . . . probably not.' She sat down at the kitchen table with a cup of black coffee, hoping they wouldn't probe for more information. The last thing she wanted to do was talk about Aidan. She wanted to forget she ever met the man. 'Those croissants smell delicious,' she said, 'If you've any left over will you let me know?'

After Damien left, Dorianne told Nina there was something she wanted to tell her.

Mildly surprised, Nina looked up from the TV. It wasn't often Dorianne suggested a little one to one. Her head felt like someone was hitting it with a piece of concrete. The last thing she wanted was a serious conversation.

'I didn't like to tell you when Damien was here,' Dorianne said somewhat awkwardly, 'but we've decided to move in together.'

Nina looked at her in astonishment. Gosh. This was a surprise. 'Right,' she said slowly, after a pause. 'I see, er . . . when do you think you'll be moving out?'

'Well the thing is,' Dorianne continued, 'Damien would like to move in here.'

'Move in here?' Nina raised her eyebrows. 'Well . . . God he's very welcome to. I mean I get on very well with Damien and I must admit it often gets a bit lonely when you're off on your trips.' Privately, she thought it wasn't a bad idea at all. Damien was very handy at fixing things that got broken and anyway a third tenant would mean less rent and less to pay on bills and that.

Dorianne sighed. This was more difficult than she'd expected. Obviously the message wasn't getting through to Nina.

'The thing is Nina,' she tried again, 'The thing is . . . we want to make a go of this . . . you know live as a couple.'

'Right,' Nina said quietly as if all this was beginning to sink in. 'Right . . . I er see what you mean. You don't want me here, do you? I mean is that what you're trying to tell me?'

She looked so hurt and hungover that Dorianne automatically felt guilty.

'Of course Nina, we'd keep in touch and everything. I mean it wouldn't change our friendship and I'm sure you'll have no problem finding someone else to live with. Try putting an ad up in the local supermarket – after all that's how we found each other. It's just that Damien and I want to make a go of this you know . . . just ourselves.'

'Right,' Nina sounded utterly deflated. 'I see.'

Chapter Twenty-Six

Emily-Ann walked briskly along Baggot Street. The sky gleamed, turquoise and blue but there was a definite chill in the air.

Autumn had arrived unannounced.

She spotted plenty of talent walking along the footpath at 11:15. A horde of handsome men in suits flitting from one office to another. What did they all do in their spare time?

Where did they go?

After all they didn't stay at the office all weekend. Of course they didn't. But it was mystifying all the same. It was as if they all mysteriously disappeared come nightfall only to be replaced by muckers and savages falling over themselves, scoffing kebabs and yelling 'Are yis all right, gerils?'

She stood at the lights at the corner of Baggot Street and Pembroke Road. Stood for ages in her own little world until a woman came along and pressed the STOP pedestrian button.

Emily-Ann pretended not to notice.

When the lights eventually changed she continued

to walk. There had to be life outside O'Donovan PR, hadn't there? Wouldn't it be so nice to be a model and be driven around to exotic shoots all day and to get your hair and make-up done into the bargain? That would be more like it. After all, she'd been in this PR business for nearly two years now. And they still weren't giving her any responsibility. So what did the future hold for her? Where was she going in life?

You had to have some kind of master plan to succeed. You couldn't just drift. Nothing ever happened to people who said 'I'll wait and see what happens'.

How come other people seemed to know exactly where they were going?

People in banks and things.

Not that she wanted to work in a bank.

No.

She'd been crap at maths at school so they probably wouldn't want her anyway.

And she didn't want to wear a uniform and look the same as everybody else.

But PR definitely wasn't her thing. Stuck in a stuffy office with a boring crowd of women.

Very few men opted to work in PR.

And who could blame them?

This wasn't her life's calling by any means. At first she'd thought the job would be really exciting. Working as a 'Public Relations Executive'. At least that was the title she put on her business card. Well everyone put the word 'Executive' on their card, didn't they? Sure even if you were a cleaner in Dublin these days you'd probably put 'Cleaning Executive' on your card.

Dublin people had become very pretentious.

The PR world eh? It sounded so glamorous. Long boozy lunches with clients. Schmoozing in places like the Shelbourne and Doheny and Nesbitt's after work with the 'suits'.

The reality was bleaker however. Lunchtime was usually a sandwich from O'Brien's. And Friday evening frolics involved nothing more exciting than getting the number 10 bus home to watch a video. It was crap. This mundane existence was not what she'd expected from life. She was going to have to do something about it. And fast.

Emily-Ann, before she'd decided to become famous, had contemplated many careers.

She'd wanted to be nurse at one stage. When she was very small. And then a doctor when she realised they earned more money. She'd played with the idea of being a dentist or a lawyer. Then she decided she was going to be just like Madonna.

When she started secondary school, she thought a dietician would be a nice job. Until she realised you had to study chemistry. At twelve she thought she'd forget the whole studying thing and be a singer or a dancer.

She went through school cutting out pictures of famous people and gluing them onto her copy books.

So that she could look at the pictures while pretending to listen to the teachers.

At seventeen she'd left school and enrolled in a secretarial course.

At eighteen she decided to be an air hostess with a middle-eastern airline and see the world. But didn't get the interview when she told them she wouldn't wear a veil. She'd also quite fancied being a photographer, or a journalist, a vet, a schoolteacher and a driving instructor.

But now she had her heart set on being a model. If she was just a little bit slimmer she could be a top model. A real model. Not just one of those girls who hung about nightclubs saying they were models. Out-of-shape girls that you never actually saw in anything. No, if she was going to do it, she'd do it properly. And then she'd have every man in Ireland after her. And could get free into all the nightclubs with the gossip columnists chasing after her. Trying to find out which eligible bachelor was courting her. What fun!

She headed up the steps to her office, still thinking about her future. Yes, she'd better get a move on and strike while the iron was hot. She wasn't going to be this beautiful all her life. In a few years time it would be too late.

Back in the office, Emily-Ann switched on her PC to make it look like she was doing a bit of work. She started looking up model agencies on the Internet. She carefully wrote down the names into her diary. She felt very business-like and organised. She rang the first agency and made an appointment. The woman told her to come in during the week. Emily-Ann arranged a time, gave a satisfied smile and put down the phone. She was on her way now . . .

Well on her way.

Chapter Twenty-Seven

Caroline rang the doorbell of the chic-looking Sandymount townhouse. She'd seen an ad in the *Irish Times* about it. A big girl with a friendly warm face and dark-wavy hair answered the door. 'Hi I'm Josie,' she introduced herself, 'you must be Caroline. You were talking to Verda on the phone.'

'Oh right,' Caroline smiled back.

'Come in out of the cold – it's chilly outside.'

Caroline stepped into the hall. The whole place was cool, chic and compact. The type of place where you'd be proud to have visitors dropping in to say hello. A million miles from the damp red brick she'd left behind in north London. This was more like *Melrose Place* on TV. Only there wasn't a pool in the courtyard. Pity really. But with the Irish weather, there probably wasn't much point.

Still there was a fountain . . . that was something.

It was a nice touch. Perhaps the residents all got together in the summer and sat around the fountain.

And had communal barbecues.

Maybe not though.

This was Ireland, not Florida.

Caroline noticed that there were lots of fabulous cars parked in the car park.

Inside, the townhouse was decked out in plush luxury carpets and cream upholstered sofas. The pale walls displayed tasteful prints. None of that psychedelic nonsense that gave you a headache to look at. Caroline couldn't believe this place. It really looked like someone's home, not the type of place you'd rent out to strangers. She said as much to Josie.

'Oh but it is someone's home,' she pointed out. 'It's just that Ronan, the owner, doesn't live here. He works mostly in the States. I think he must have a girlfriend over there.'

'So it doesn't get too crowded here then,' Caroline said, relieved.

'Well I usually go home every weekend,' Josie explained. 'To my fella' she added, blushing furiously.

'I see,' Caroline pretended not to notice. 'And the other girl is Verda.'

'That's right.'

'Does she go home?'

Josie frowned and pushed back her glasses. 'I don't think so. She doesn't go home every weekend anyway.' she said. 'That isn't to say she stays here in the house though,' she added quietly. 'If Verda gets lucky we don't see her for days. She's a bit of a wild thing our Verda, so she is.'

God, this whole set up was intriguing, Caroline thought popping into the main bathroom for a look. Inside were his 'n' hers cream porcelain sinks and a huge walk-in power shower.

Josie was obviously the mother figure in this household, Verda, the resident freak, and the owner sounded like some kind of Mr Darcy figure, always away on business. The wealthy owner whom nobody really knew anything about.

God, what an exciting place to live in. Like a TV drama.

She wondered if anyone else had been to see the house.

'Well, a couple came to see it,' Josie told her. 'But Verda said she didn't want a couple staying here. The room is just beside hers see, and she said you'd be able to hear everything. She doesn't really approve of that kind of thing.'

'Right,' said Caroline. 'But didn't you say she was a bit of a wild thing herself?'

'Well, she does disappear, but we never actually meet the gentlemen in question,' Josie said without a trace of sarcasm. 'Verda's quite moralistic in her own way.'

God, the plot was thickening at a great rate.

And people thought The Addams family were strange!

'And a few other people rang about it but . . .' she trailed off.

'Now, let me show you where your room would be,' Josie said, leading the way down the corridor like Mother Hen. 'Let me warn you, it's extremely small, but that's why you pay less rent,' she explained. 'And if either myself or Verda move on you'll be able to move in to one of our rooms.'

The lady doth protest too much, thought Caroline *Just how small was this place?*

Her room was the boxroom.

No surprises there.

A bare room with off-white walls, and a small mirror.

One slim wardrobe, its door half opened.

A single chair.

A single bed.

For one person.

It would do.

For the moment.

She could save her money.

How nice to live by the sea. She looked out the tiny window. It looked onto the garden of another townhouse.

Someone had hung washing on the line.

Baby clothes.

Well so much for living next door to a bunch of hunks.

Melrose Place?

Eh . . . probably not.

'So when will you let me know?' Caroline asked.

'It's yours if you want to move in,' Josie offered. 'You look like you'd fit in here.' *God was that a compliment?* 'It's a really easy-going house. And Ronan, the landlord is dead on. It's funny calling him the landlord really. He's only about our age and drives one of them sports cars, so he does. And he's good looking too. But as I said, he's never here anyway and he lets us do our own thing.'

'Great,' Caroline eyes lit up. 'I'll start moving my things in right away if you just give me the details, the deposit and that kind of stuff.'

So what if Verda was a bit on the strange side. People weren't perfect. And when you added up the pros and the cons of this place . . . well it was a bit of luck that she'd found it, wasn't it?

Chapter Twenty-Eight

Everyone said it was bad luck to buy things for an unborn baby. Personally Sandra thought it was a load of nonsense. Buying things for the baby gave her something to do. Kept her sane. Gave her some sort of ludicrous perspective on an otherwise duller than dull life. And when she was busy she'd forget about things. Like how unhappy she was. Yellow was the best colour really. Yes. You could put yellow on boys or girls. It didn't matter. She didn't know what sex the baby was. Didn't want to know. Yet.

It was bad luck, they said.

Bad luck, eh?

Everything seemed to be unlucky these days, didn't it?

Sandra wondered what she'd done to deserve her run of it.

She wandered round the baby shops lost in a world of her own. She'd no interest in shopping for herself any more. Nothing looked nice on. She felt like a big old blob. A bloated blobby balloon. And the media wasn't helping by portraying pregnancy bumps as something sexy, on the cover of magazines.

The expectant celebrity mummies lapped up the attention. Played to the cameras. By wearing a small jumper. Or an unbuttoned shirt. But it did nothing for the confidence of real mummies every-where.

Why did every female celeb in the world seem to be pregnant at the moment? Making Sandra feel even worse. God, you couldn't open a magazine without being assaulted by the sight of someone's perfectly-formed bump. And then there was all the fuss about celebs getting their figures back after the pregnancy. Sandra didn't like it one bit. It put too much pressure on other mothers to get their figures down to a size 8 afterwards. Ordinary mothers. Mothers who couldn't justify paying for personal trainers, dieticians and 24-hour nannies.

She almost wished maternity frocks and denim dungarees would become fashionable again.

Since Deirdre and Stephen's wedding, Sandra had barely ventured out socially. Apart from not wanting to wear a hideous maternity dress in public, she was now also aware of what her so-called friends thought of her.

They obviously despised her.

Babble-mouth Bernie had more or less made that clear at the wedding.

And it had hurt.

Big time.

According to that girl Bernie, Deirdre's friends thought she was nothing.

Just some slut.

And a sly little schemer for having snatched Richard away.

But they didn't know the truth.

The truth was so *so* different.

She hadn't snatched him away.

She'd been so hammered the night of his stag.

In fact she barely remembered anything that had happened after the nightclub.

She certainly had very little recollection of being in bed with Richard.

Often she wondered if her drink had been spiked or something.

Mind you, she had had an awful lot to drink that night.

Never again would she drink to the point of no return.

If only she could turn back the clock.

Sandra had never wanted Richard in the first place.

Grant it, he wasn't the worst looking. And handsome men in Dublin were a bit thin on the ground. He had an all right job, a respectable background, was popular with the lads and knew a lot of people around town.

Technically there was nothing wrong with him.

But there was something wrong with him being her fiancé.

It had never felt right.

And it didn't feel right now.

He was supposed to have got married to Caroline.

Caroline.

Her best friend for God's sake.

And now Bernie was saying that apparently Richard and Caroline were getting back together.

What on earth was that about?

Surely, in a million years, Caroline wouldn't consider taking him back.

Would she?

The whole thing was a fiasco.

Richard had never ever told Sandra he loved her.

Not that she expected him to lie.

Even on their recent holiday to Corfu, he'd hired a jeep and had driven around the island by himself.

Of course her father still didn't know about the baby. But she was going to have to tell him. And soon. God, she was dreading it. Not that her parents would go all moralistic on her or anything. No, it wouldn't be like that at all. But she hated the fact that her dad would be disappointed when she eventually told him. Sandra's father had always had high hopes for her. He had no time for Champagne Charlies. People like Richard. He'd barely accepted his only daughter's engagement to Richard but he hadn't passed judgement. That was just the kind of man he was. And he'd given them one of his many properties to live in. A place on the grounds of the family mansion.

The place was a bit run-down, he'd told them as he'd handed over the keys. But Richard hadn't minded. He'd assured Mr Krayne he'd take pride in doing it up. And he had. Hence the countless Sunday afternoons in garden centres and DIY stores.

The house was spacious but lacked warmth. Or maybe that was just the way Sandra felt about it. After all, it was totally respectable with every mod con known to man. But sometimes it took quite a long time to heat up because of the high ceilings.

Of course the house wasn't theirs. It still belonged to her family. Very much so.

That was a sore point with Richard.

An open wound.

To know that the house wasn't theirs.

Legally.

But Sandra's father had refused to sign the property over to them.

He said they'd have to wait.

Richard seemed really pissed off about that.

She hadn't really noticed at first.

But since her conversation with Bernie the night of the wedding, a lot of things made more sense. Would he have married her if she hadn't been TK Krayne's daughter? If she'd just been some slapper in the nightclub the night of his stag? Instead of a millionaire's daughter? After all everybody knew TK Krayne was a major player in the Irish music industry, and was now managing a couple of big name British bands that never left the top ten. And as everybody in the music industry knew, it was the managers who made the big bucks.

Not the thrown together starlets singing their little hearts out, and collapsing with exhaustion after six months.

Mr Krayne had always been adamant that his daughter steered well clear of the murky music industry. Not that he'd too much difficulty keeping her away from it ... Sandra hadn't a note in her head. God, even her music teacher at school had begged her to mime at the annual Christmas concert.

Later, when she got home, laden with baby clothes and toys, Sandra decided to put her feet up on the little footstool in front of the telly.

Judge Judy was on.

Richard was out.

At work.

Everybody else was out.

At work.

She was in.

With *Judge Judy*.

And everybody else who wasn't working.

It was funny wasn't it? Every dark cold wet winter's morning over the last few years, Sandra had dreamed of this. Every time her alarm clock had gone off and she'd had to fly to London for a meeting, she'd cursed the damn thing, thinking if only she could just lie on a bit ... just another half hour ...

Now she couldn't stand sitting at home all day.

She was well able to work.

She'd always loved being out and about with people. The buzz of sales and marketing, even the pressure, and the satisfaction of completing a successful campaign.

This moping about the house business didn't suit her at all.

She was losing her mind.

Things weren't working, Sandra thought, as a lone hot self-pitying tear slid down her cheek.

She wanted out of this relationship. To hell with what other people thought. Other people didn't have to live her life.

The phone rang. Absently Sandra made her way towards it.

'Hello?' she answered.

'Good afternoon. This is the Happy Television company calling. Is this the right number for Caroline and Richard?'

'This is Richard's number,' Sandra said, suddenly feeling her blood run cold. What the hell was this all about?

'I wonder if I could leave a message for him then?' the voice at the other end continued cheerfully. 'My name is Amanda from the Happy Television company. I'm a researcher for *The Happiest Couple in Ireland* television series. We just wanted to confirm that Richard and Caroline are definitely coming back to the show.'

Chapter Twenty-Nine

Nina let herself into the empty flat. Dorianne was in New York and it was kind of nice to have the place to herself. She needed time alone. To think. Her whole world had been turned upside down. In a matter of days. She couldn't believe she was going to have to move out of here. Moving was so stressful. As bad as death or divorce, they said. Where was she going to live? She was so happy here.

But now she had to vacate the place. Where was she going to start looking? She couldn't rent a place on her own. Rents on one-bed apartments in Dublin were astronomical and she had no particular desire to live in a dump.

She heard somebody downstairs. Donal. He must have arrived home early from work. She needed to talk to him urgently. She hoped it wouldn't be too difficult to persuade him to go back on to *The Happiest Couple in Ireland*. If he refused, her dream of winning the coveted prize would be out the window. And God, wouldn't it be nice for her to win a luxury villa in Spain? Especially now that she was on the verge of being evicted. And winter would soon be upon them. She'd better go down and ask him now. She hadn't spoken to him since that time Sheena had gone into his flat and made a fool out of herself. She stood up and patted her hair in the mirror. Now was as good a time as any.

She crept downstairs, her heart beating rapidly. Was she doing the right thing? Suppose he saw right through her? Suppose he thought she was only trying to use him to win the house? *Ah no*, she told herself. *Sure anybody else would do the exact same thing.* And anyway, she thought as she tapped on his door, wasn't she doing him a favour in a way? After all, if they won, he was going to get half a house!

Donal looked suspicious as he opened the door to Nina. She was annoyed. Did he think she'd only come down looking for some milk or a free look at his copy of the *RTÉ Guide*? 'Can I come in?' she asked him as sweetly as she could. He was only wearing a towelling robe, as if he'd been about to take a shower or something. She hoped he'd excuse himself to go and get changed, but he didn't. She wondered if she should offer to come back later.

She accepted his offer of a cup of tea. Not because she particularly felt like one, but because she couldn't just say straight out what she had to say. You had to be subtle when you were looking for something. Make people think you were doing them a favour. Give the impression you'd just come down for a bit of an oul chat and then just . . . you know . . . make your announcement.

The atmosphere was pretty awkward; after all, the last time she'd sat here, it had been to explain that their relationship couldn't continue. That she was too young to be getting involved, far too young to be thinking about moving in . . . MOVING IN! Good God, a thought just struck her. But no, that was out of the question. She banished it immediately. It wasn't worth even contemplating. And anyway, it would only be giving Donal ideas. She couldn't possibly just change her mind now and start carrying her things down from the upstairs flat. What would he think of her? Putting him on the spot like that? Asking him to clear out his spare bedroom so she wouldn't have to go through the hassle of finding a new place to stay?

No, it was unfathomable. She remembered the last time she'd sat here all right. It had been so uncomfortable watching tears form in a grown man's eyes. The eyes of a man she liked but didn't love. How could she forget? Trying to leave as he'd implored her to change her mind. Telling her he couldn't live without her. But she'd stood her ground, insisting it was over, there was no turning back. He'd gazed into her eyes longingly, like a wounded puppy. And asked her for one last shag.

One for the road.

'So, it's nice to see you again Nina,' he interrupted her train of thought. 'Just like old times.'

'Yes,' she said.

'How have you been keeping?'

'Busy, you know, work and all that.'

'Was your cousin all right after the other night?'

'Yes,' Nina said abruptly, 'she was fine.'

She didn't want him to think she'd come down to discuss her drunken cousin. Sheena was the last person she wanted to talk about.

'What about the man in the car? Are you seeing him?'

'No,' Nina said truthfully.

Did she imagine it or did Donal look ever so slightly pleased about this?

'I'm glad you called in,' Donal said looking her straight in the eye. He'd nice eyes; chocolate brown, and nice hair, clean and short. Respectable. No sideburns or goatees. Nina's two pet hates.

'Yes, well I think it's important to remain friends,' Nina said matter-of-factly. 'We've always got on well so it would be a pity to . . .'

'Yes we have always got on well, haven't we?' Donal interrupted meaningfully.

'*The Happiest Couple in Ireland* were on to me,' she said searching his face carefully for a reaction. She got none. He didn't flinch.

'Anyway,' she continued trying to sound like she was just making ordinary conversation, 'they wanted to know if we'd be interested in coming back onto the show.'

'Really?'

Still no emotion. God, this was like trying to manually remove teeth.

'I thought it was funny,' Nina said.

'Very funny,' Donal agreed.

Nina could feel herself getting flustered. He was doing this on purpose. She was sure of it.

'Anyway I was thinking of going back on, you know. After all, you'd be a long time saving before you'd be able to buy a villa in Marbella, wouldn't you?'

'That's true.'

'So I thought I might as well, you know, I've nothing to lose.'

'I see.'

'I was wondering,' Nina felt herself getting hot under her shirt collar, 'I was wondering, er if you would be interested in going back on to the show?'

'Me?' Donal looked flabbergasted, as if it genuinely hadn't crossed his mind. 'With you?'

'Of course,' Nina smiled rigidly.

'You mean you want us to get back together?'

Nina paused. Her head was reeling and she didn't quite know what to think.

'Well, okay, then,' he said before she had a chance to say anything else. 'But I really expect you to treat me with a little more respect this time round.'

'Uh . . .'

'And I'm really pleased about this Nina. I can't tell you how hurt I was when you ended it.'

'I . . .'

'Say nothing. Okay? This is a wonderful moment for both of us. You know, I always had a feeling that you'd come back . . .'

Chapter Thirty

Sandra sat upstairs in the big double bed flicking through *Image* magazine. But the words just blurred in front of her. Richard had wanted to replace this bed. He'd said they needed a bigger one, one with built-in drawers. Only Sandra had put her foot down. They didn't need a bigger bed. And besides, she wasn't going to spend any more afternoons in furniture shops. She wondered where Richard was now. There weren't many furniture shops open at this time of the evening.

The pubs were open though.

Of course.

Not that Sandra was ever invited along.

After all, it was embarrassing bringing the pregnant bird to the pub, wasn't it?

She was beginning to expand now. They couldn't pretend for much longer.

He didn't want to be seen with Sandra. She knew he didn't. It was obvious. It was uncool having the pregnant bird with him.

And it probably put other women off.

She placed her hands on her stomach. The foetus was definitely moving. She hoped the little one wasn't stressed. Was Richard out with Caroline? Had they decided to get back together behind her back? Were they discussing *The Happiest Couple in Ireland*? When did they plan on telling her that they were going back on the show?

She felt a little kick in her stomach.

'We're going to be all right you and me,' she rubbed her tummy. 'Your mother is very strong. Yeah,' she added, 'stronger than most people would ever believe.'

She'd spoken to her parents earlier in the week. And told them about her pregnancy. Her mother had been angry, then upset. Her father hadn't said much. Her mother said that she'd have to get married straight away. Her father hadn't agreed. He'd said Sandra would have to think long and hard about what she was going to do with the rest of her life.

But now that phone call had changed everything. All Sandra's suspicions had been confirmed. Ah yes. It hadn't taken Richard long, had it? A woman's instincts were usually right. She lay on the bed thinking. Just thinking. She hadn't been able to think this straight in a long time.

Everything was different now.

Very different.

Richard was obviously planning on getting back with Caroline, and they were going to pretend to be the happiest couple in Ireland while Sandra stayed at home with his child.

Was that the plan? But did they honestly think she was going to stay 'mum'? Did they think she was that stupid?

It would be a lot easier to move on now.

She wouldn't feel guilty for leaving him.

At all.

In fact Richard had left her with no choice. Sandra rolled over on the bed, fingering the soft pillows. She liked this bed. She was going to keep it for herself. There wouldn't be a new bed.

No.

There wouldn't be a new anything.

Just a new life.

A life without Richard.

Of course he'd always be welcome to have access to the child. In fact she'd positively encourage it. Sandra's own father had been a major influence in her life. But he hadn't worked his ass off for nothing. He wasn't a bum like Richard. A spoilt bum who was all talk. But very little else. It was obvious now why her dad hadn't signed over the house to herself and Richard. He hadn't trusted him. No wonder.

He'd never exactly welcomed Richard into the family anyway. But hadn't said too much; Mr Krayne was a man of few words. When he spoke however, his words made sense.

And now the unwanted fiancé-in-law would get nothing.

Mr Krayne would make sure of that.

Sandra knew him so well.

She closed her eyes and began to think about Chris Fennell. Now living in Boston. Marital status unknown. Gorgeous kind Chris, who'd written to her over and over again.

But she hadn't answered the letters. Because she hadn't wanted to emigrate to be with him. And he hadn't wanted to move back to Ireland to be with her.

She'd always fancied him. But had been terrified of settling down. She thought about him now and thought about Richard. And she smiled. A sad smile. And then she laughed. She laughed and laughed and laughed. Hysterically. She laughed until she howled. And then she just howled.

Because she knew she'd made the mistake of a lifetime.

Chapter Thirty-One

Caroline arrived at her new Sandymount address in a taxi. She made her way into the complex of townhouses, pressed the buzzer and waited for somebody to answer. It was a gorgeous Saturday afternoon with wisps of cloud streaking the faint blue sky.

'Pleased to meet you,' Verda said, answering the door. She was a slight sallow-skinned girl, attractive in an obvious kind of way. She held out what looked like a dark-brown claw, five spindly fingers topped with nails so long they were beginning to curl. 'I'm on my way out now; Josie will sort you out.'

Josie appeared and gave Caroline a welcoming hug. She was literally twice Verda's size.

The two girls watched Verda totter down the steps. She was wearing a black skin-tight beaded mini, fake-fur shawl, gold hoop earrings and a mountain of make-up. Her stringy jet-black hair looked like it had died along time ago.

Through over-dyeing.

'Is she foreign?' Caroline asked as they watched

Verda hitch her skin-tight mini so far up you could clearly see her black and red knickers. She opened the door of a nifty little red two-seater sports car and turned on the engine.

'Yes, she's half Russian, half Portuguese and half English,' Josie said without a trace of irony.

'I see,' Caroline said, trying to maintain an air of seriousness. 'What does she do? I mean that's a cool car.'

'Oh she doesn't own that,' Josie explained, 'She has a lot of friends who lend her their cars.'

'But what does she do?'

'Sales,' Josie said.

Chapter Thirty-Two

Richard was late home from work. He threw his coat across the kitchen table. Then planted a big slobbery kiss on Sandra's lips. She tasted and smelt the alcohol simultaneously.

She wondered how long he'd been drinking.

She also wondered what went on in other people's homes. Did other couples throw their arms around each other in the evening? Thrilled to see each other after a long day at the office? It was hard to know, wasn't it? Sandra had never lived with anyone before, so she didn't know. She only knew stuff that happened in films, where couples fed each other ice cream on leather sofas, with the music turned down low, and the place full of candles.

But maybe that only happened in films.

Who knew what other couples did?

Wouldn't it be great to be a fly on the wall?

Imagine being a fly on the wall of the Beckingham home?

Or the Ritchies?

What *did* those couples say to each other?

'How was your day?' Richard slumped on the couch beside her.

But Sandra wasn't paying attention. She was wondering if Tony Blair slumped on his couch after a day in Downing Street and asked Cherie how her day was.

Did Jennifer Aniston yell at Brad Pitt 'Hey it's garbage day today. Your turn buddy, I did it last week.'

She thought about it; was Jennifer funny all the time like she was in *Friends* or did she sit around in her pyjamas scratching a head of greasy hair? Like normal people did on a day off. The head of hair that launched a million 'Rachel' haircuts. Was it ever greasy?

Richard cleared his throat. Sandra mentally banished Jennifer's image.

'I got a phone call,' she told her fiancé in a monotonous tone of voice, 'from the television company. They wanted me to confirm that you were going back on the *The Happiest Couple in Ireland* show with Caroline.'

She paused for a moment before continuing. 'I couldn't confirm of course,' she said with a deadpan face, 'You see I wasn't sure what I was supposed to say. I didn't know . . . because . . . because I don't know anything. I'm just the person carrying your child.'

'Did you tell them that?' Richard paled.

'Why? Was that not the right answer?' Sandra

enquired ironically. 'It's just I wasn't quite sure . . .'

'Listen, I can explain . . .' Richard began.

'Good. Because I've a feeling this could be interesting.'

'It's like this . . .' Richard began.

Sandra waited patiently.

This'd better be good.

'It's like this,' he repeated himself. 'We don't have a house right?'

'We live in a perfectly adequate house,' Sandra replied numbly.

'But it's not ours,' Richard stressed. 'It belongs to your father.'

'Go on,' Sandra said.

'Eventually it might be ours maybe,' Richard sighed. 'But think about it realistically, I mean, your dad could leave it to us when he dies, yes. But he could live into his nineties, which means we could be waiting until we're seventy. Or else your mum could die and he could remarry and then where would we be? Not exactly an ideal situation, is it?'

'Just what are you getting at here Richard?'

'Just think about it Sandra . . . if we won this dream house in the sun, think of what we could do with it? It's worth a million euro. A million euro Sandra!!! We wouldn't have to live in it if you didn't want to. We could sell it and buy something else. Without having to take out a mortgage.'

Sandra just stared at him. God everything was beginning to make sense now. It was all about money with Richard wasn't it? He badly wanted a house. He knew now he wasn't going to get one from Sandra's father but . . . if he got back with Caroline, he could still win one.

'Sandra, the first part of the show is going to be aired regardless. We signed away our rights at the onset. They have the right to air it. There isn't a damn thing we can do about it. Now, if myself and Caroline refuse to continue the show, then people will start asking questions. The press could get wind of you and me and then we'd be in a right mess. It'd only be for a few short weeks.'

'And Caroline doesn't mind?' Sandra said without expression. 'You mean she's just going to pretend to be with you?'

'Yes,' Richard said, refusing to look her in the eye, 'That's exactly what she's going to do.'

Chapter Thirty-Three

'Now pretend you're a chicken,' the acting coach yelled.

Caroline ran around the freezing-cold room flapping her arms underneath her, making a squawking noise. Tonight was her first evening at drama school.

To say that it was not a fun experience was an understatement. There were 15 people in the class. They all seemed mad. Actually that wasn't completely true. Two of the girls were primary school teachers and were a total hoot. But as for the rest of the head-bangers . . . they just reminded Caroline how so many people in the world just wanted to be famous.

But handing over hard-earned cash to a drama school was not the way to go about it obviously, Caroline thought as she got down on her honkers and pretended to lay an egg.

The other students were mostly 'alternative' types wearing little woolly hats and colourful smocks.

Four of the group were foreigners and half of them worked in restaurants and clothes shops.

'Now pretend you're a signpost. Stand very still. Don't move,' the acting coach roared. She was a weird looking thing with wild bushy mousy-coloured hair, wearing a pair of black and white check dungarees that most normal people wouldn't be seen dead in. Caroline thought she looked like a clown.

She stood pretending to be a signpost for what must have been at least five minutes – it felt like five hours. The students had been told to keep their eyes shut. The room was very quiet. Caroline kept wondering had the teacher slipped out for a fag or something. She was too afraid to open her eyes though. The teacher might yell at her in front of everyone. And that would just be too embarrassing.

Everyone was going to the pub afterwards for a drink. Caroline decided not to. Not that she didn't need a strong measure of alcohol right now, but the wind outside was turning to driving rain and she didn't want to miss the last DART home. It was 10:00 pm before she got back to Sandymount.

Josie was sitting cosily by the fire watching MTV.

Verda was out.

But then again, she was always out.

'How was the acting?' Josie gave her a big encouraging smile.

'Oh I dunno,' Caroline slumped on the sofa. 'It was a bit of a let down, but I'd say I'll probably get used to it.'

'Wouldn't it be great if you became like a really famous person on the telly and then I could say that I knew you?'

'Yes,' Caroline smiled warmly, 'but somehow I don't exactly see myself at the Oscars.'

'Don't you want to be a big film star so?'

Caroline laughed. 'Not really. I'm only doing this for a laugh you know. I think acting must be a desperately hard way to make a living.'

'You're probably right,' Josie agreed.

'Anyway, I'm just happy to do the course and we'll see what happens.'

'I was in the school nativity play once,' Josie said. 'I was a sheep.'

'Well somebody has to be the sheep,' Caroline said good-naturedly, 'I'm sure I've played worse than that.'

'My parents wouldn't come to the play,' Josie continued gloomily, 'because Jackie, the girl next door, was the Virgin Mary and I was just the sheep.'

'Well that was wrong,' Caroline frowned, 'I mean everybody has to start somewhere, don't they?'

'I suppose,' Josie said quietly, 'It kind of put me off acting for life though.'

'It's not for everyone,' Caroline agreed, 'It might not even be for me. Who knows?'

'Ronan's really into all that.'

Caroline raised her eyebrows in surprise, 'Ronan the landlord? He's an actor?'

'Um no,' Josie shook his head. 'He's involved more

in the production side of things. He was doing all that stuff in America. He's come back to take over an Irish production company.'

'Gosh, I didn't know he produced films!' Caroline said excitedly. 'This is great news. Maybe he'll be able to give me some tips about how to break into the business.'

'Oh I don't think it's films he produces,' Josie was keen to get her story right. 'Because Verda was asking him all about it. I think she also got her hopes up. Thinking it'd be a foot in the door and all that. He's producing one of those series – kind of reality/quiz things. I'm not sure what it is really. Verda said it sounded silly.'

Caroline just stared at her. She could feel the colour drain from her face. 'What's the name of the show, can you remember?'

Josie chuckled. 'Oh you'll laugh when you hear the name.'

'Tell me,' Caroline urged.

'It's . . . ha, ha . . . it's called *The Happiest Couple in Ireland.*'

Chapter Thirty-Four

Thank God Richard had gone to the south of Spain, Sandra thought as she nestled into the sofa with a glass of rich red wine and a huge bag of tortilla chips. Yummy. He'd gone away with the lads. She was glad he'd gone. So glad.

He'd be away for a full week. In Marbella. Playing golf. And whatever else people did on those 'golf' trips. He'd said he was going down to see if he could find out where the villa was and get a sneak preview. But Sandra hadn't fallen for that excuse. Sure, hadn't Richard already been sent a poster of the villa? She bet he was down there posing in Sinatra's in Puerto Banus every night, and dancing in Olivia Valere's.

She could just imagine him now. This minute. Dining in one of those chic little restaurants on the marina with all the other 'golfers'. Drinking champagne and drooling at the yachts and the sports cars and . . . other things.

Drooling over the grown-up toys they'd probably never have, but could aspire to have . . . maybe . . . in another life. Maybe.

Sandra didn't care one way or another. She wouldn't have minded if he'd gone fishing in Iceland. As long as he was far far away from her. She picked up the remote control for the CD player. Strauss. Perfect. That should relax her. God knows she was stressed enough.

After Richard's extraordinary bombshell.

What was he thinking anyway?

Trying to bully her into agreeing to let him go on the TV show.

And expecting her to go along with it as if everything was fine.

Anyway this week would give her the perfect opportunity to sort everything out. There was lots to be done and she'd have to move fast. She was signing a load of legal documents tomorrow and then she'd have to pack all Richard's belongings and change the locks. When he came back from Marbella he could move straight in with Caroline wherever she was living now.

And that would be nice for him.

After all, Caroline and Richard wanted to be the happiest couple in Ireland now, didn't they?

And everybody knew that three was a crowd.

Chapter Thirty-Five

Setting up your own business was terrifying. Everybody knew that. One minute you'd be thinking 'This is great, sure doesn't it make sense to be working for myself?' The next minute you'd be panicking, going 'Oh my God, what am I doing?'

It was far easier just to work for other people and just let them take care of your pay slip. Once you were on your own you had only yourself to fall back on. Sandra was aware of the risks. And yes it was simpler to work for the other fellow, but then the other fellow made all the money didn't he?

Her dad had warned her. He said you needed a hard neck. But maintained it was still the only way to go. And he was the expert after all. He'd spent enough years banging on doors, only to get them slammed in his face.

But that was a long time ago now.

Before he'd hit the big time.

Now everybody was nice to him. He was invited everywhere. To venues he'd never heard of. By people he'd never heard of. By those who'd trampled all over him when he'd been looking for his first break.

Of course he never turned up to their parties.

He was a busy man.

And who was laughing now?

Certainly not the kids from his hometown. The ones who'd thrown stones at him when he'd delivered newspapers, the rain seeping through the holes at the bottom of his shoes.

'Where are they now?' Sandra had asked him once. A long time ago.

'God knows,' he'd shrugged, 'And who cares?'

'But what kept you going Dad? All those years? All the knock backs?'

'Revenge kid,' he smiled and ruffled her curly head. 'I hate to say it but revenge got me where I am today.'

'Revenge?' Sandra had looked up at him with big baby-blue eyes. Revenge? It was a big word. She wasn't sure what it meant.

'Sweetie, not many admit it but it's what gets you to the top. If someone treats you badly, picture their face every time you're feeling down, it'll give you just that little bit of encouragement to keep going. Because one day the look on their face will give you the last laugh. And their face won't look pretty then. But yours will.'

Sandra thought about it.

There was a girl in school with her who hadn't been very nice to her. Who used to make up things about her and had often pulled her hair. When Sandra had got her job in fashion buying, her manager had taken her out for a fancy lunch in a top restaurant. Guess who'd been the waitress?

Sandra smiled. She shouldn't really be thinking those kind of thoughts. Her mother had always told her to forgive and forget. And to follow her heart.

'Don't listen to your mother!' her father had warned her. 'She's a good woman – the best. And she means well. But if you follow your heart, you'll end up with heart disease.'

Sandra parked her car in the Jervis Street Shopping Centre. Her father was right. She should have listened to him more carefully. But she was listening now. By God, she was. She wasn't going to end up with heart disease. Ever.

She locked the car door and headed for the exit door. She was excited about her little venture. Her father would admit that it was worth it. Working for yourself. Mr Krayne had always been determined to work for himself. 'What was the point in working for another fellow?' he'd always argued. 'You get no thanks for it whatsoever. You work 35 years and get a pitiful pension at the end of it. If you're lucky, you get a plaque and a handshake.'

Sandra stepped into the little clothes shop in the city-centre store. It was hard to miss the huge For Sale sign above the shop outside. It was the prettiest little shop she'd ever seen, with wooden shelves displaying tiny yellow, pink and baby blue garments.

On the wall were painted cartoons; bunnies, smiling zebras and laughing giraffes. It was like a magic little kingdom. In the corner was a ball crawl where kids could mess around in while their parents did some serious shopping.

The owner, a middle-aged woman came over to help her.

'Do you know if it's a boy or a girl?' she smiled at Sandra in her black-velvet maternity dress.

She was beginning to show now.

Sandra shook her head. 'They say it's bad luck.'

She ambled through the aisles. The clothes were so beautiful, so dainty. She picked up a pair of tiny lemon felt shoes. Were there really feet so small that could fit into these?

'You've such wonderful taste,' Sandra told the woman. 'The shop is such a dream. Why are you selling up, do you mind me asking?'

'Well it was a difficult decision. And it'll kill me to say goodbye to this place. I started in childrens clothing when I was nineteen. By the age of twenty-one, I had my first place. It was a little corner shop in Drumcondra. All my friends and neighbours used to buy from me. If they hadn't I wouldn't be here today.'

'Why wouldn't they have bought the clothes?' Sandra picked up a miniature pair of pink and white socks and put them in her basket. 'You have such impeccable taste.'

'I'll tell you a secret,' the woman leaned towards

her and spoke in hushed tones. 'Of course I never told anyone before now, but,' she smiled almost resignedly, 'now I'm packing up and leaving the country I might as well tell you.'

Sandra was all ears. 'Years ago I stumbled upon a dressmaker in Paris. A wonderful dressmaker. She had a gift from God I think. She used to make the most exquisite children's clothes.'

'Really?' Sandra perked up.

'She used to sell them to me for half nothing. She wasn't in the business to make money you see, she was just exceptionally creative.'

Sandra waited for her to continue.

'She died a few years ago. I thought that was me finished. I never thought I'd ever get anyone as good ever again.'

'And then you did?' Sandra offered.

'Her daughter took over and now employs 16 women.'

'Sixteen? Well she's obviously not in it for love alone.'

'Unfortunately not,' the woman laughed, 'the day of doing anything for love is dead and gone.'

'But she's still good, excellent, judging by these clothes.'

'She has the gift,' the woman explained dreamily. 'And she trains her staff under a watchful eye.'

'So where are you off to?'

'North Florida. My husband's got arthritis. He's had enough of the Irish weather. He's been at me to leave for years now. To be honest I'm getting a bit old for it now. It's quite hard to get reliable staff these days. Staff that'll treat the customer the way she should be treated.'

'I know what you mean, there's nothing worse than handing money over to a surly brat. Anyway you'll love the sun. My parents have a place in the north of Florida, not too far from the border of Georgia. It's wonderful up there and not as touristy as the South.' Sandra assured her. 'Have you had many offers for this place?' she was almost too afraid to ask.

The woman sighed. 'A few. Our highest offer is from a foreign gentleman. He wants to turn this place into an Internet café. I think it would be a shame.'

'Oh so do I,' Sandra nodded, 'really. So do I.'

Chapter Thirty-Six

The women in St Bridget's nursing home loved to hear Caroline sing *The Fields of Athenry*. Caroline gave a little bow, ignoring their pleas for another song. 'Another night,' she promised, 'Sr Breege will kill me if I don't get the tea ready, it's nearly 8:00.'

Bedtime was 8:30 at St Bridget's home. Caroline reckoned it was because the nuns were so mean. If you put the old folks to bed early then you didn't have to pay as many night staff to look after them.

Caroline was settling into her new job with ease though. It was only temporary. To keep her going until the show started again. Caroline had been visiting this home for years anyway as part of a charity group. Herself and a few others had always organised the annual Christmas party (the most talked about non-alcoholic Christmas party in Ireland!).

She was fonder of some inhabitants than others. But she was especially taken with Maggie. Maggie was her favourite lady; a sweet old soul in her mid-seventies, her face resembled an American Airlines destination map. Caroline had never seen so many lines on one face. But it was a kind face. Not like some of the others.

Some of them never smiled.

Not that Caroline blamed them really.

It wasn't a barrel of laughs in this place.

The inhabitants weren't here by choice.

It was like summer camp.

Without the summer.

Without the entertainment.

Without a departure date.

Maggie was different though. She was like a rose among a clutter of thorns. She always greeted Caroline with a radiant smile, when some of the other old folks simply ignored her.

Marion, who worked in the kitchens had told her Maggie's story.

Maggie had been in the home since she was fifteen. An unmarried mother, her God fearing Catholic family had been anxious to bundle her out of sight.

The sooner the better.

Maggie had come to the home to work.

For the nuns.

The kind nuns.

The good kind nuns.

Who'd forced her to kneel in the courtyard every morning at 6:00 am.

To beg God for forgiveness.

Caroline thought the story was shocking. Such a

waste of a life. Of course Maggie's child had been
taken away from her the minute 'it' was born. The
nuns hadn't told her the sex of the child.

It was none of Maggie's business.

Caroline shook her head. 'Do any of them ever
visit? I mean, the families?'

'Some do, most don't,' Marion shrugged, 'Most
of their parents are long dead I'd say now.'

'What about Maggie?'

'I've been here 30 odd years now and I've never
seen nobody call for her,' Marion folded her arms
over her huge bosom and muttered out of the side of
her mouth. 'Sometimes she does be all dressed up and
waiting by the door pretending she's got someone to
take her out. Says her brother is coming. She carries
a photo of him. It's so faded now though . . .'

Caroline put away the teacups and disposed of the
digestive biscuits' wrapper.

Poor Maggie.

A woman with a past.

But no future.

And a present hardly worth living for.

She made Caroline feel guilty for complaining
about her lot.

'Sure haven't I my health?' Maggie would say.
'There's ones in here can't walk. They need a wheel-
chair to get around and someone to bring them to the
toilet. I have my health, thank God, and my dignity.
For the moment anyway.'

Caroline was sleepy now. She was kind of glad

that the day was nearly over. She was going to be taking a break from this place now. Sister Breege had told her there was no problem getting time off to do the show and her job would be waiting for her at the end. Caroline knew she'd miss Maggie and the others when the TV show resumed because God, it might not sound trendy saying you worked in a nursing home but it beat M-City Music and Tele-Fone any day.

Chapter Thirty-Seven

Sandra parked her car outside the solicitor's office. Her heart was pounding but she allowed herself a slight smile. The documents were ready to sign.

Her dad was waiting inside the office, along with the shop owner and her solicitor. Sandra shook hands and then got straight down to the legal stuff. It didn't take too long. All the documents were clear. Her dad had done a bit of research, concluding that buying this shop was in fact an excellent investment. 'But of course, there's always some risk involved in working for yourself,' he said.

'I know,' she said, 'But that's why I won't mind putting in all the hours in the world. When you work for yourself, you never have to work another day again. So they say anyway. And it'll be worth it.' Sandra was so excited she could barely breathe. She was going to travel the world now, looking for baby clothes for her shop. She'd bring the baby with her naturally. She wasn't going to leave the child at home with a nanny. Not yet anyway. If the shop did as well as she thought it would do, maybe she could get an au pair who could travel with her?

The possibilities were endless anyway.

The first thing she was going to do was paint the front of the shop a bright yellow. Yellow was eye catching and sunny. At the moment the exterior was a faded green. Not exactly the kind of place that would draw in the punters.

She was going to put kiddies books and games in the corner so older children could read instead of pulling at their mother's skirt. That way, parents could browse in peace instead of being literally dragged out of the shop by the coat tails.

Mr Krayne suggested she should have some kind of opening. Under its new name, *Kids around the Korner*. A cheese and wine evening event where mums could meet other mums. And then perhaps an afternoon party. On a Sunday (to show customers the shop would be open for business every day of the week). She'd invite every young parent she knew and get them to bring others.

In the future she might organise a fashion show, maybe around Christmas time. And give some of the kids a chance to be models for the evening. The parents would love that.

There was just one thing she had to do now.

She had to tell Richard.

That their relationship was over.

Completely.

Chapter Thirty-Eight

'A new start, a new life,' Sandra repeated as she stood, arms folded in front of her disbelieving fiancé.

Richard just stared at her.

Where had this come from?

The announcement.

Out of the blue.

'What on earth are you talking about?' Richard zapped the remote control, turning up the volume on the soccer.

Sandra sat down on the end of the sofa and stared at him. 'This is not me being dramatic Richard. I've thought about this very *very* carefully. Now, you heard what I said and I've no intention of repeating myself.'

Her fiancé continued to stare at the screen. But his eyes weren't following the ball.

And Sandra couldn't help noticing how terribly pale he'd gone. It was like a scene from a movie. A scene where the music would be playing peacefully, but you just knew something terrible was about to happen.

'You need to get out more,' he said suddenly, brushing her off. 'When you spend too much time thinking Sandra you go all weird. It's not nice.'

'If you didn't want me to *think* so much, maybe you might not have left me at home all the time Richard. But you did, and in a way I'm glad you did now.' Sandra turned away from him and started to empty the dishwasher.

'Of course I could cause a scene,' she pointed out slowly, 'and maybe sell *my* side of the story to the press once your silly TV show is aired but I don't think there's any need for that. We're still going to be the parents of a much loved child so it's best if we can, you know, remain civil to each other.'

Richard still said nothing. He continued to watch the screen.

'Of course, if you *prefer*, we *could* get lawyers in,' Sandra continued, 'if you felt there was no way we could sort everything out as two adults,' she took a pile of plates and put them carefully in one of the kitchen presses, 'or we could . . .'

'Shut up, would you Sandra,' Richard said irritably, 'you're beginning to annoy me.'

'I annoy you most of the time, don't I Richard?'

He stood up. 'We can talk about this Sandra. I know this is really rough for you, with me and Caroline on the show and everything. but please don't blow it for us all now.'

'I'm sorry,' Sandra spoke like a robot, 'But it's too late.'

'Come on Sandra.'

'As I *said* Richard, it's just too late now.'

'You won't be able to make it on your own you know Sandra, you'll end up coming running back to me,' he said peevishly. 'If you leave me, you'll end up a lonely old woman.'

Sandra looked at him incredulously, 'There's more men out there besides you Richard, a lot more men,' she added reaching for her coat.

'Do you honestly think anybody's going to go near you while you're carrying my child?' Richard moved towards her threateningly.

'If you touch me Richard, I'll ring the police. And then I'll ring *The News on Sunday*. I think they'd be *very* interested in my side of the story, don't you? And as for me carrying your child? I'm carrying *our* child Richard. A *child*. Not a disease. And I'm sure I will get someone else. If that is what I decide I want. It shouldn't be too difficult. After all, I got *you* didn't I?'

Chapter Thirty-Nine

'Caroline, welcome, welcome, come on in.' Tony made sure he gave his friend's fanciable cousin a great big slobbering kiss. She could smell whiskey off his breath.

'Now what can we offer you to drink? You look absolutely amazing.'

He disappeared with her coat.

Caroline glanced around the crowded front room. It was half full. Thank *God* she hadn't been the first to arrive.

All the usual faces were here.

Tired faces.

Like old reliable pieces of furniture.

Pieces of furniture usually confined to attics.

God, some things never changed.

Tony was back with a glass of champagne for her. 'Your tipple as far as I can remember,' he said good-naturedly.

She took it from him smiling. She was going to enjoy herself tonight.

'You look so beautiful,' he whispered. 'If Richard could see you now he'd be kicking himself.'

Caroline's face fell. Why did Tony suddenly have to remind her of Richard? Why did people always do that? Couldn't they just leave it? Where did she have to go to escape the countless little reminders and painful memories? The moon?

She made her way into the kitchen to see what food was on offer. The kitchen was jammed. You could hardly move in there. Wasn't it funny the way people at parties always congregated in the kitchen?

Caroline helped herself from the buffet. It was absolutely scrumptious. Tony must have paid someone a great deal to prepare this. Obviously he didn't do it himself.

'Hey cous,' Colin appeared out of nowhere and gave her a great big bear hug. He was totally pissed.

'Hi Colin,' Caroline threw her eyes to heaven. 'Nice to see you're already in the party mood. What time did you and Tony start drinking at?'

'I've only had a few,' Colin assumed an air of seriousness. 'I'm not wasted, I shwear I'm not,' he said very deliberately, which only really confirmed that he was even more locked than Caroline had initially thought. 'Here let me introduce you to Lucindra.'

Oh God, Caroline groaned inwardly, this was the part where she was about to meet Colin's Miss Right-for-tonight. She'd been through this a thousand times.

Lucindra was pulled out from among the crowd. Her curly-blonde hair cascaded down her back. She wore so much make-up it was hard to imagine what she looked like without it. 'Oh hi Caroline, I've heard so much about you,' Lucindra said, obviously eager to chat.

Oh no, Caroline thought, the poor girl had obviously read somewhere that it was a great idea to get in the relatives' good books.

She had to get away. Had to escape. She hated meeting Colin's conquests. It was so embarrassing when they shot dagger looks at you for months afterwards. When it didn't work out. As if you were the reason he hadn't phoned. Caroline wanted nothing to do with it all. If Colin wanted to make half of Dublin his enemy, let him do it all by himself. Caroline didn't mess with people's feelings. One day Colin would hopefully meet a strong woman that would give him a good run for his money. The problem was, that the strong women of Dublin never seemed to give Colin and his rugby-obsessed friends the time of day. 'Do you know where the bathroom is?' Caroline asked Lucindra who gave directions.

She bumped into Tony on the way to the bathroom. 'Where are you running off to sweetheart? Are you all right for champagne?'

'Yes thanks,' Caroline said, promising herself to drink three glasses all at once so she'd feel on the same wavelength as all these drunks. Mind you, she didn't want to get too drunk. She had to meet Richard tomorrow to discuss *The Happiest Couple in Ireland*. He was flying in from Marbella tonight and she'd arranged to meet him in the afternoon. She was dreading it.

'Did I ever tell you that I have always fancied you Caro?' Tony slipped an arm around her waist and urged her to drink up.

'Many times,' Caroline answered truthfully.

'I fancied you since you were ten and I was eleven.'

'I know,' Caroline said patiently. In fact it was a pity she didn't fancy Tony really. He was very handsome. And nice enough when he wasn't pissed. But she could never realistically consider Tony. She'd known him since she was like two. Going out with him would feel . . . would feel . . . well almost incestuous!

'Colin would kill me if he knew.'

'He knows,' Caroline told him.

'He does?'

'He's known for years. Do you not remember him beating you up in boarding school when he found my photo in your locker?'

'You know about that?'

'I know everything,' Caroline smiled.

'Caroline, there you are!' Oh no, it was Colin's Lucindra. Looking a bit frantic. She grabbed Caroline's arm. 'Have you seen Colin? I've been looking for him everywhere.'

'Actually . . .' *I have seen him, heading outside, with a tall scantily-dressed red head actually.* '. . . I think I saw him in the kitchen. Let's go and look for him.'

'Are you sure he's in the kitchen?' Lucindra didn't sound too convinced. Caroline's heart went out to her. Why was her cousin being a prick? And why on earth did any woman put up with his behaviour? It was baffling.

'It's just I was in there only a second ago and he wasn't there. I checked upstairs too . . . in all the bedrooms,' Lucindra said a little shakily as if she thought there might be a very good chance that he'd be there.

'Well you might have missed him,' Caroline said absent-mindedly. She wasn't really listening to Lucindra. Her head was beginning to spin.

'Somebody said they saw him leaving with another girl,' Colin's Miss-Right-for-the-first-part-of-the-night's face crumbled. Caroline put an awkward arm around her shaking shoulder and tried to convince her that even though her cousin was a really nice guy, he wasn't really that good with women.

'Not really that good? That's the bloody under-statement of the year,' Lucindra sobbed before blowing her nose into a man-size tissue.

She was going to kill Colin for doing this yet again, Caroline told herself. When he was younger he'd been almost admired for playing Jack the lad.

But really it was time he grew up. And if he couldn't be good, he could at least try and be discreet.

Why did he have to go off with that other woman? If he'd found her that irresistible, could he not have quietly got her number or something? But no, Colin always had to be creating a scene.

'Have you his mobile number?' a red-eyed Lucindra wondered.

'I don't think ringing him would improve the situation,' Caroline said wisely.

Caroline wondered what she should do with her. The girl was tired and emotional and shouldn't, under any circumstances, ring Colin and make a fool of herself.

'You'll thank me in the morning if I don't give it to you,' Caroline handed her another tissue. Christ this was awful. She should be outside dancing and enjoying herself. This party had the potential of being a lot of fun.

Eventually she got Lucindra to calm down.

Then, later on, she noticed Tony and Lucindra chatting on a seat in the hall, their heads very close together. Tony was hanging on Lucindra's every word. And he was holding her hand too. Out of the frying pan and into the fire, Caroline thought.

Caroline decided it was time to hit the road.

The party was well and truly dwindling. A couple were slow dancing among the empty beer cans and half-empty bowls of nachos. A few bodies were strewn across floors and sofas. Somebody in the kitchen was making toast and someone else had optimistically opened a bottle of Bailey's.

In a vain attempt to relight a party.

A party that was probably best left to fizzle out.

As she was ringing for a taxi, a female guest offered her a lift.

Caroline gratefully accepted.

The girl dropped Caroline off at her house.

Pretty merry at this stage, Caroline tried walking in a straight line towards the house, but couldn't. She felt dizzy. All that champagne. It was lethal.

As she reached the door, she started fumbling in her bag for her keys. And couldn't find them. She sat down on the cool concrete. And let her head collapse in her hands. God.

Suddenly the front door opened.

'Are you okay?' enquired a deep well-spoken voice.

'Oh thank God somebody's in,' Caroline muttered, looking up, into the darkest-blue eyes she'd ever seen. Their owner smiled. He brushed away his ash-blond hair with his fingers. 'Hi,' he smiled, 'you must be Caroline.'

She opened her mouth to say something, then shut it again.

'I'm Ronan,' he said, 'Ronan Dexter.'

'I'm Caroline,' she whispered. *And I must be dreaming.*

Chapter Forty

'I just popped in to get my spare pair of keys,' Ronan explained. 'I always keep a spare pair here 'cos I'm forever losing them. I hope I didn't give you a fright or anything.'

Caroline paused. She'd had a bit too much to drink already but could still see he was one of the most attractive men she'd ever seen. Ronan Dexter, wearing a tux with his collar open and his necktie loose around his neck, was leaning against the frame of the door, smiling at her. She hoped he wasn't going to just run off or anything. Now that she'd finally met him. Wasn't he even going to stay for a drink?

She looked into his startlingly deep-blue eyes and offered him a beer. He looked American, very Californian, tanned with fair highlights but his accent was D4 and the half-lit cigarette dangling between his fingers was a dead give away. He might have lived in the US but he was an Irishman at heart. Caroline cracked open two beers. She wondered what age he was and why he was dressed like this.

'I was at a film festival,' he explained, as she handed him his beer.

'Any good?'

'Nah,' he laughed, 'too many couples and single blokes but sure who's complaining when I arrive in here and find a cracking bird like you waiting for me? In fact if I'd known you were here I'd have popped in earlier.'

Caroline laughed. He really was very cheeky. But he looked perfect. His face looked like it had been painstakingly crafted by a world-class sculptor. His only imperfection was a slightly crooked tooth. It looked odd, as if the sculptor, in a moment of madness had gone, 'What the hell, let's not make him perfect after all.' He seemed to be having severe difficulty pouring the beer into the glass. Caroline wondered how much he'd had to drink.

'Hey I'll do that', Caroline giggled, 'go on, you sit down.'

'Ah you're a star. So tell me, what do you do with yourself when you're in Dublin? Have you a boyfriend?'

Caroline wasn't sure what to say. As far as Josie was concerned, Ronan was one of the new producers of *The Happiest Couple in Ireland*. She'd better tell him she was one of the contestants, in case he thought she was leading him on. And that she was happily engaged to Richard. God why did she have to tell him that? Dammit, why was life so unfair?

Ronan noticed she wasn't saying anything. 'Right,

sorry, give me a slap. I'm a cheeky bastard. I shouldn't be asking you personal questions. Let's talk about something else. Are you single? Oh God, I've done it again! Sorry I'm so nosy, it's a disease, I'm getting help for it I swear. In fact there's a group in LA called: Interfering Blokes Anonymous. I've signed up for it. It's great, very therapeutic. Although I was almost kicked out . . .'

'Why was that?'

'Um, I kept asking the other people why they were there.'

'God, you really do have a problem, don't you?'

'Sit down here on the couch and tell me all about yourself. You can tell me anything, I've had a few drinks so I'll remember nothing in the morning.'

'I think I'll pass,' Caroline giggled. 'Listen I've something to tell you . . . it's about a TV show I'm doing . . . em, it's really exciting.'

'You're doing a TV show and think it's exciting?' Ronan looked at her and smiled.

'Don't you think working in TV is exciting?'

'Exciting? I dunno, I do it for a living so I'm kind of used to it. But people always think other people's lives are exciting, don't they? I suppose it depends on how you define excitement. Sitting around all day. Decision making. Working round the clock on stuff, only for it to be scrapped days later for one reason or another . . . that more or less sums up my life.'

'I'm sure it's not that bad,' said Caroline.

'Yeah, there's good stuff as well. It's just not as

exciting as people make out. You know, I always thought being an airline pilot would be a fascinating job until I got talking to a pilot in a bar in New York. He says most of the time you're cooped up for hours with just one other bloke looking at nothing but clouds. It really made me think. You always want to be something you're not, don't you?'

Caroline shrugged, 'Maybe you're right. Well the thing is . . . about the show . . .'

The bell rang suddenly. Caroline stood up. She was surprised. She was sure Verda and Josie had told her they wouldn't be around this weekend. She opened the door and the blood drained from her face. Richard was at the door, two big suitcases at his feet.

Caroline was stunned. What the hell was he doing here?

'I've come to stay my darling,' Richard grinned manically. Then he spotted Ronan and his jaw fell open.

'Ronan Dexter,' he sounded startled. 'What are you doing here?'

'Hiya Richard,' Ronan also looked baffled. 'Why am I here? Well, this is actually my house.'

Caroline looked from one man to another. It wasn't too difficult to figure out how the two men knew each other. Richard had worked in TV for years and Ireland was very small.

'When did you get back from America?' Richard asked him suddenly.

'I was headhunted to come home and produce a TV show here. To be honest I haven't even started work on it yet. We resume filming shortly though,' Ronan explained. 'The new investors think it's got the potential to be huge.'

'Oh you don't have to explain. We know all about the show,' Richard's face broke into a cheesy grin. 'And you're in luck my friend,' he put an arm around Caroline. 'Ronan Dexter, meet "The Happiest Couple in Ireland".'

For a few seconds Caroline tried to remember how she'd ended up with a hangover. Oh yeah, Jesus, the party . . . and then that scenario with Richard and Ronan. God it was like a truly awful dream.

After Ronan had left, Richard explained everything. Sandra had thrown him out, he'd said. And naturally he'd turned to Caroline for comfort.

Naturally?

Well he couldn't stay here that was for sure, she'd told him.

She'd ordered a taxi and sent him to his parents. Let them take care of him! He wasn't her problem anymore.

She was furious with him. How dare he just turn up on her doorstep as if nothing had ever happened.

Most of all, she was annoyed that she hadn't been able to talk to Ronan for a bit longer.

God, he was different from the average run of

the mill, wasn't he? You certainly didn't meet men as sexy as Ronan every night of the week. And he was funny. God knows what might have happened if Richard hadn't turned up to ruin everything. She dragged herself out of bed and wandered into the kitchen. Josie was making tea.

'I like the flowers,' she grinned.

'What flowers?' Caroline asked, confused. She was parched with thirst and made her way towards the sink.

'The ones Ronan sent; you must have made a good impression. Myself and Verda have never got flowers from him.'

Caroline made her way towards the magnificent display of white lilies and picked up the card.

Sorry, sorry, sorry about last night. Hope you don't think I'm some obnoxious drunk. Sorry again, Ronan.

'That's funny,' Caroline said with a smile. 'He wasn't that drunk.'

'I've never seen him drunk in my life,' said Josie almost mournfully. 'I wish I hadn't missed that. Ronan's normally so conservative. Why is he apologising though? Did he make a pass at you?'

'Not as far as I'm aware of,' Caroline said with a laugh, 'but if he had, I wouldn't have beaten him off with a stick.'

Josie grinned. 'I know exactly what you mean.'

They sat down. When the phone rang, Josie answered it, then handed it to Caroline.

'Caroline, is that you?' Richard's deep voice was unmistakeable. Caroline felt a rush of panic at the sound of his voice, but any fear soon turned to annoyance. 'What do you want?' she said coldly.

'It's about *The Happiest Couple in Ireland* Caroline. We need to talk about this.'

She took a deep breath. 'Yeah?' She wasn't going to make this easy for him. *The Happiest Couple in Ireland*? Well, that's hardly us now Richard, is it?'

'The house in Spain would be sold and the proceeds split,' Richard said crisply. God, he was so calculating about the whole thing, wasn't he? He was just unbelievable. He'd probably consulted a lawyer before consulting her.

'And it's not just about the house,' he continued. 'There's sponsorship deals involved and just think of the exposure.'

'I'll call to your parents' house later Richard,' Caroline said sourly.

'I think they'd be pleased to see you.'

'Listen, don't read into anything, the only reason I'm calling is because I don't want to be seen with you in public,' Caroline insisted. 'By the way, why exactly did you move out of Sandra's house?'

'I had to leave her Caroline. I finally realised I'd never be able to love her the way I used to love you.'

Caroline stared at the phone in stunned silence. What on earth was he talking about?

Chapter Forty-One

Emily-Ann reckoned the TV show would propel her straight to stardom. After all, just look at what TV exposure had done for other unknowns?

There was Anna, the Irish lesbian who'd got herself a job on RTÉ and then Brian Dowling, the Irish gay, former air steward, who'd gone on to do all kinds of amazing things in Britain. Emily-Ann wasn't sure what all the other contestants were doing but no doubt they were all living it up somewhere. And their 15 minutes of fame would guarantee invitations to all sorts of things for the rest of their lives.

Anyway, wouldn't it be really cool to say you were a model on TV? Not many TV contestants were models. Emily-Ann reckoned it would give her that special edge. Over people like Caroline who was as dull as ditchwater. Or Nina who was as attractive as a fly in a bottle of sun tan oil. Not that the girl was bad looking or anything. She'd a slim figure and nice dark eyes but she was just so boring it was untrue.

Graham also modelled part time. Like herself. But not that much though. There wasn't enough work for male models in this country. Not that Graham seemed to mind particularly. He was a fly-by-the-seat-of-his-Calvin's kind of guy who turned up to countless openings of bars, clubs and leisure centres.

Being a part-time Irish male model didn't sound sexy enough though. That was Emily-Ann's opinion. It wouldn't win the public over. Graham would need to start convincing people that he was 'international' darling.

Hopefully this recall to *The Happiest Couple in Ireland* would guarantee even more exposure. And model agencies would come banging on the door. Emily-Ann took out her nail file and started sawing away at her talons. Many existing Irish models were old boots, she thought. Hanging around nightclubs just because they got in free. Emily-Ann thought none of them were any great shakes. Why shouldn't she join an agency and grab all the work? After all it was an easy way to earn dosh. A photo shoot here, a bit of catwalking there. Why not indeed? Anyway it'd be better than this gloomy place. And people might look up to her if she was a famous model.

'Emily-Ann?' Her boss, Samantha's annoying voice shot across the room.

Oh what now? Emily-Ann stretched in her seat. She thought for a moment about disobeying but Samantha's voice was unbearably sharp so . . . maybe not. 'Yes?' she muttered sulkily.

'Emily-Ann could you come here for a moment?'

Emily-Ann sighed and dragged herself to Samantha's desk. The woman wanted her to type a whole pile of letters. Emily-Ann looked at the long list in dismay. Women were so bitchy weren't they? If she decided not to pursue her modelling career, Emily-Ann was going to work in a male-dominated office. Yes definitely. The atmosphere would be much more laid back, she reckoned.

Men wouldn't be 'out to get her'.

Not like the staff in here.

Chapter Forty-Two

Nina had been reading up on Spain on the office Internet. Lots of Irish and English people lived there apparently so it wasn't like everyone would be speaking Spanish with nobody being able to understand you. And there were advantages too. Like, if you lived in Spain, your heating bills would be practically non-existent. And you could teach English to earn cash. It'd be exciting. More exciting than Tele-Fone anyway.

She'd also borrowed a book from a girl in work. An interesting book about working and living abroad. Spain was apparently much cheaper than Ireland, which was always a bonus. And because it was hot over there she'd be able to walk everywhere. No more wind, rain and icy winters or hours shivering at horrible bus stops. Hurrah!

'What's on your mind?' Donal asked, putting an arm around her. They were strolling around Stephen's Green admiring the ducks.

'Ah nothing,' she said, brushing him off.

It was a silly question, she thought. Asking people

what was on their mind. As if they'd ever tell you the truth. Anyway, it was often better not knowing what was on people's minds.

'Do you fancy going to the cinema?'

'Ah no, it's too crowded on Saturdays.'

Nina didn't tend to go to the cinema much. You always ended up sitting behind a really tall man or a courting couple. And anyway if you were prepared to wait, you could see everything on video eventually and then you could watch the same film a couple of times. Better still, if you waited a couple of years you could see it on TV and tape it. Then you'd have it forever.

Endless hours of enjoyment.

In your own home.

Much better than sitting in the cinema.

With a bunch of people you didn't know.

'Would you like to go for a drink so?'

Nina looked at her watch. 'In the middle of the afternoon?'

Donal shrugged. 'I wouldn't mind doing something,' he said.

'How about we head down to the National Gallery?'

'That's a great idea,' Donal agreed 'and then we can go to the café in the gallery for coffee and a piece of cake.'

'Well, we'll see,' Nina stood up straightening her skirt with the palms of her hands. *A slice of cake in the gallery shop? Sure you'd probably get a whole cake in Supervalue for less!*

After traipsing around the gallery, Nina yawned. She was exhausted and wanted to go home. Donal didn't. He said life was too short to be staying in all the time. He wanted to go out. Do something exciting. Go to the pub.

'Why not get a bottle of wine?'

Donal thought it was a great idea.

They stopped at an off-licence on the way home. He wouldn't hear of Nina putting her hand in her own pocket. What a sweetie, Nina thought.

They sat on the sofa back in Donal's tidy flat drinking wine and nibbling the packet of peanuts Nina had bought (well you couldn't just turn up empty-handed now, could you?).

It was so comfortable, so familiar. That's what Nina loved about this place. The familiarity of it all. Donal's slippers sticking out from under the sofa, the smell of his favourite woolly jumper, the way he knew that she took milk and no sugar in her tea. The way he knew not to be annoying her when she was 'on'.

She didn't want to go through all of this again. With someone else. She didn't want to be undressing in front of another stranger again. Or explaining her life story to another guy who might, or might not, stick around. And most of all, she didn't want to be meeting a new set of relatives and being on her best behaviour, only for them to size her up and then decide she wasn't good enough.

Of course she didn't particularly want to be in

a heavy relationship. Especially not one which was going absolutely nowhere. But she didn't want to be in clubs all the time either. Searching for Mr Right when she already had Donal. Looking for the perfect partner was like playing the stock market. You just had to hedge your bets – and hope for a decent return.

Then again, playing the market, you took the risk of your investment going very wrong, didn't you? Imagine if your returns resembled a bunch of Eircom shares? Nina knew a girl back home called Fidelma who'd invested seven years in a relationship.

Nigel was studying medicine and she'd had a steady job in the bank. He didn't have any money so she was happy enough to foot most of the bills. After all it was only fair, she told Nina. One day he'd be making a lot of money and then she wouldn't have to pay for anything. Nina thought she was mad in the head but said nothing. Country women were funny if you went around criticising their fellas.

Anyway, last New Year's Eve, Fidelma had gone to see a fireworks display with Nigel, now a trainee doctor. Fidelma said it had been so romantic. Just the two of them sitting on a bench watching this magical display.

It should have been the perfect opportunity to propose. After all Nigel had completed his training now so there was no excuse. He'd put his hand in his breast pocket and Fidelma's heart had given a little leap. Maybe . . . just maybe . . .

But alas, Nigel hadn't reached for a little black velvet box.

No.

He'd pulled out a massive big hanky and blown his nose loudly.

Fidelma had burst into tears.

Nigel had been baffled apparently.

'In the name of God woman, what is the matter with you?' he'd asked her.

To make matters much worse he'd suggested a break. Imagine! A break after seven years! Nina would have strung him up by the balls for that. But Fidelma had agreed. And then he'd met someone else. A radiographer. In the hospital.

They'd got engaged almost immediately.

The story had been a lesson to Nina. At least if you'd an education, nobody could take that from you. But a man? Now that was a different matter entirely. A man could walk any time. Leaving you with nothing to show for your time and effort. Even if you were married, he could still walk out the door, calling 'So long' over his shoulder. Nina was in no doubt. A man was a pretty useless investment.

The house in Spain, however . . .

'So have you decided where you're going to live?' Donal asked as he topped up Nina's glass of wine.

'Not yet,' she shook her head sadly.

'Of course, you're more than welcome to move in

here you know . . . until you . . . er find somewhere else. You could have the spare room.'

Nina smiled at him over the rim of her wineglass. 'Really?'

'Sure, I'm not using it at the moment anyway so why not?'

'No strings attached then?'

'Absolutely not,' Donal promised, happily slipping an arm around her shoulders.

Chapter Forty-Three

Verda had rung Ronan about a bulb that had blown. Caroline didn't know anything about a bulb and was surprised to see Ronan standing in the hall on a stool. He was wearing grey combats and a white T-shirt. His arms were toned and tanned.

'There was no need to call,' she said shyly, 'Sure I can change the bulbs myself.'

'Ah well, I wanted to call over anyway,' Ronan winked at her and jumped down off the stool. 'The truth is, I feel like a tool after our meeting the other night. I hope I didn't completely scare you.'

'Of course you didn't,' Caroline assured him, 'and thanks a million for the flowers Ronan. I was flattered. But seriously, don't be apologising. I just thought you were funny, that's all,' she added.

Suddenly not being able to think of anything to say, she walked into the kitchen to put on the kettle.

'Anyway,' she called from the kitchen, 'it's not like I was dead sober myself. Do you take milk in your coffee by the way?'

'Am I invited to stay for coffee? Well, yeah then, I take milk thanks,' Ronan appeared at her side and dazzled her with a smile. When he smiled, laughter lines appeared, making him even more desirable.

'What have they been saying about me?'

'Who? Josie and Verda? They haven't said that much. Especially Verda, she hardly ever says a word.'

'She's unique,' Ronan said cryptically.

Caroline laughed as she fetched two matching blue and yellow mugs, 'you said it.'

'I still can't believe you're the same Caroline who's in *The Happiest Couple in Ireland* show,' Ronan sat down on the sofa. 'You're very popular you know. All the crew think yourself and Richard will run away with the prize.'

'Really?' she looked astonished as she handed him his mug.

'Absolutely. Thanks, you're a star. You're lucky you know . . . to have found your soulmate.'

Caroline swallowed. 'Yes, well, sometimes you meet your soulmate when you least expect it,' she said cautiously, refusing to look at Ronan directly. Determined not to be captivated by his magnetic blue eyes.

'That's what he said too,' Ronan said casually.

'Richard? Did he?'

'He said yours is a very passionate relationship.'

'Really?' *The bloody nerve!*

'Is it like a love/hate relationship?' Ronan questioned.

'Er . . . kinda.' *Just a hate relationship actually.*

'He's a lucky bloke though,' Ronan said.

Caroline felt herself go scarlet. She looked up at him slowly, swallowing a lump in her throat.

'Why?'

'He just is,' Ronan teased, but avoided catching her eye.

Caroline paused. Was he playing games with her? Maybe she shouldn't say anything else just yet.

'That's my dream you know,' Ronan continued vaguely.

'What is?'

'You know, meeting the perfect woman . . . sharing stuff. Somebody to love you no matter what.'

'Mmm,' Caroline stared at her feet. 'Have . . . have you ever been in love?'

Ronan rubbed the handle of his mug thoughtfully. 'I think so,' he said. 'Well I thought I'd found my soulmate but . . .' he broke off.

'Don't tell me if you don't want to,' Caroline said gently.

'No, I want to, it's nice to be able to talk to someone. I've kept all this stuff bottled up for so long. It's not something you can talk to blokes about.'

Caroline waited patiently for him to continue.

'I went off on business . . . for three days. When I

got back she told me she'd met someone else and that was that. Nothing I could say to her would make her change her mind. She married the other guy shortly afterwards. I think I've got over her now but I don't know if I'll ever allow myself fall for anyone like that again.'

'I understand,' Caroline said softly.

'I've bought the shirt, worn it and it stank. It was the ultimate betrayal, but . . .' he paused and looked up and she could see the pain in his eyes. She recognised it – it was the same pain she'd seen in the mirror for weeks after Richard left her.

'Time's a healer,' she said patting his arm and hoping she didn't sound insincere.

'You probably can't even begin to imagine what it was like.'

Oh I can, thought Caroline wryly. *Believe me, I can.*

'You know the prize is fantastic,' Ronan suddenly changed the subject.

'Hey, just because you're the producer,' she shrugged. 'Of course you're going to say that.'

'The girls tell me you're trying to break into acting? Maybe this is just the show to get you noticed?'

'God, what else did the girls tell you?'

'A bit,' Ronan said with a smile. 'But not enough unfortunately. I guess I'll just have to figure the rest out for myself . . .'

Chapter Forty-Four

'But I do kind of feel sorry for her,' Caroline fiddled with her beer mat as they sat in the Ice bar in The Four Seasons Hotel. 'Despite everything, she must be going through hell.'

'She is,' Richard nodded. 'But I just can't help the way I feel. I can't make myself love her. Anyway, I must say I'm very happy to be back living with the folks again for a while so I can get my head straight.'

'I still feel sorry for her though, even after everything that happened,' Caroline sympathised. 'I mean I know she betrayed me and everything . . . but still, she can't have been looking forward to seeing us on the TV acting all lovey dovey.'

She looked up at Richard. She wondered what was going through that head of his. He still looked handsome despite looking like he hadn't slept for about a week. But the funny thing was, she wasn't attracted to him anymore. Not even in the slightest.

Richard reached for Caroline's hand and squeezed it.

'It's for the best. She'll just have to come to terms with it.'

'Will she cope?'

'She'll be fine. I've promised to provide for the baby. And I'll always be there for her. As a friend. But there's no longer a spark between us. I realised that when I met up with you again. I can't help the way I feel. That doesn't make me a bad person now, does it? It just proves I'm human like everybody else.'

Caroline stared at him too shocked to speak.

He had got to be joking.

Inexplicably a vision of Ronan appeared in her mind. She banished it immediately.

'Did you ever actually stop loving me?' Richard asked her. 'I know I never stopped loving you. I really do feel part of the happiest couple in Ireland sitting here with you.'

Caroline stared into the fire, too stunned to speak. He thought she was nothing, didn't he? Imagine. He thought she didn't even have the brains to figure out what he was playing at. Incredible.

'I know I probably don't deserve a second chance,' Richard added, his eyes fixed on the floor, 'but I knew for definite, when you were living in London, just how much I really loved you. You've got to try and understand what happened. I was trapped. What happened was . . .'

'I don't want to hear,' Caroline winced. 'I don't want to know how it happened.'

'She was pregnant . . .'

'I told you Richard, I don't want to know.'

'I had to stick with her Caroline. I thought an illegitimate grandchild would just be too much for the folks to bear. But I know now that I can't stay with Sandra just for the sake of the child. That wouldn't be fair on anyone. To be honest, Sandra was putting a lot of pressure on me. I think her main aim in life was to be married to me. I'm just beginning to see it all so clearly now.'

Caroline frowned. She'd known Sandra for most of her life. She couldn't remember her being keen to trap anyone into marriage.

Funny that wasn't it?

'Do you think you could ever forgive me?' Richard looked sheepishly into Caroline's eyes.

'There isn't . . . there isn't anybody else on the scene?'

She paused, thinking about it.

She thought about Ronan.

Kind, handsome, clever, gorgeous Ronan.

A charmer.

But that was her secret. Nobody else's business. And certainly not Richard's.

'No,' she said quietly, 'no, there isn't.'

He leaned forward. 'Can I kiss you Caroline? It's something I've wanted to do ever since we met up again.'

'Certainly not,' she retreated, appalled. 'In fact I think you should be ashamed of yourself. Either that, or you are truly mixed up. I'm going to go home now. I've had enough. I'll talk to you tomorrow. And only so we can discuss the show.'

Chapter Forty-Five

Josie was plonked in front of the TV as usual. Verda was out as usual. 'Hi,' Caroline said wearily, slumping down beside Josie. She was drained. Her little heart to heart with Richard had knocked the hell out of her. 'I'm so tired now I don't know whether I have the energy to take off my make-up, undress and get into bed,' she muttered.

'How was the acting class this evening?'

'Oh same as ever . . . all these fruitcakes talking about the day they're going to win an Oscar, and then I met Richard for a drink. A very quick drink.'

'Don't take off your make-up yet,' Josie advised. 'Ronan rang to say he'd be popping over with a pal.'

Caroline felt her heart somersault. 'With a pal? Calling over at this time of night? Why?'

'Beats me,' Josie shrugged. 'I didn't invite him over anyway. And I don't think Verda did unless she's planning on staying here tonight for once.'

'I wonder why he's bringing a friend?'

Josie frowned at the TV. 'Yeah it's strange. I think

he said something about his friend maybe wanting to move in – but I must have heard wrong. I mean where would he sleep? Verda never told me she was planning on moving out. Did she say anything to you?'

'Not a word,' Caroline fished a little mirror out of her handbag and gave her reflection a quick check.

'Don't worry, you're gorgeous,' Josie teased. 'You vain thing.'

'Stop slagging me,' Caroline pulled a face. 'I hope he's nice anyway.'

'The friend?'

'Yeah. Well, what I mean is, I hope he's nice if he's going to be living here with us.'

'Could be a she?'

'Yeah, I suppose it could,' Caroline said slowly. She hadn't thought of that.

'It's a pity Ronan wouldn't move in himself,' Josie said wistfully. 'This place could do with a good-looking man. Mind you, he's calling round here an awful lot recently. Before you moved in he was never here.'

'Mmm.'

'I wonder why that is now?' Josie said suggestively.

'No idea.'

'Really? Have you really no idea?'

Caroline shook her head uncomfortably. What was Josie hinting at? The bell rang. Ronan entered alone. His hair was damp but he still could have passed off as Brad Pitt's younger brother.

'Where's your friend?' Josie asked. 'Would they like a cup of tea?'

'She's out in the car. I doubt if she'd like a cup of tea though. Can I bring her in?'

'Sure,' Caroline said cheerfully trying to assume an air of nonchalance. So it was a girl. What on earth was she like? Why hadn't she just come in with Ronan instead of sitting in the car, waiting to be invited in? Herself and Josie exchanged puzzled glances as he went back out into the rain.

He arrived in again. Alone. Caroline and Josie just stared at him. What was going on? If this was a joke, it wasn't exactly funny.

'She's shy,' Ronan sighed.

Still Caroline and Josie said nothing.

From the top of the zip of Ronan's leather jacket appeared a jet-black furry head. The curious green eyes scanned the room. Her whiskers twitched and she let out the tiniest sneeze.

'Oh my God,' Caroline shrieked as she ran towards Ronan and slipped her hand into his leather jacket. The kitten seemed quite at home close to Ronan's chest. She was warm in there and Caroline wasn't sure whether to pick it up. 'Go on,' he urged her. He took Caroline's hand and stroked the kitten's head with it. The feeling of her hand inside his warm jacket sent waves of electricity through her body. She hoped he couldn't hear her heart pounding.

The kitten, unaware of all the chemistry going on above her head, let out a mournful meow. Josie was already pouring milk into a bowl and the kitten was watching her out of the corner of its eye.

'Where did you get her?' Caroline asked Ronan.

'I had my car parked in town. The rain was pelting down and I spotted this little thing crouched behind the wheel. I couldn't leave her there.'

'Of course not!' Josie and Caroline exclaimed in unison.

'The thing is . . .' he looked from one girl to another, almost beseechingly '. . . the thing is, the bloke I'm staying with has a dog, so I can't bring this little thing home. So I was wondering if . . .'

'Of course we'll take her,' Caroline was definite.

'I'll build a shed out the back with a little bed and install a heater for her,' Ronan continued enthusiastically.

'She can sleep in my room,' Josie offered.

'Or mine,' Caroline offered immediately.

Ronan laughed. 'Are you sure you don't mind girls? I'll give you money for all her food and everything.'

'We'll all look after her,' Caroline squeezed his arm, feeling his muscles through all the layers of clothes. God! 'Between the three of us, she'll be the best looked after cat in Dublin.' *And it'll give you a legitimate excuse to call more often*, she thought happily.

Josie took the kitten off Ronan and put her down beside the bowl of milk, which the kitten sniffed cautiously. 'What'll we call her?'

'Blackie?' Ronan suggested.

'Get away out of that, where's your imagination?' Caroline laughed.

'How about Fluffy?' Josie offered.

'Ugh,' Caroline and Ronan said together.

'I think she looks like a mon chi chi,' Caroline said.

'Chi-Chi for short.'

'Hey, I like that.'

'I like it too,' Josie agreed with Ronan. 'Well Chi-Chi,' she bent down to pet the kitten. 'Welcome to the family.'

Chapter Forty-Six

Monday morning. And Emily-Ann was lying in bed listening to Gerry Ryan. It was great just being in bed. When everybody else was at work. It beat not having to get up in the cold and face the bumper-to-bumper traffic.

Emily-Ann pulled the warm duvet cover over her head and wondered smugly how they were all getting on in O'Donovan PR. She was well shot of that place. Where she'd been completely taken for granted. They hadn't even organised a going away party for her.

Imagine!

Emily-Ann had decided to give herself a few days holiday before the filming for the show started. She wanted to be in top shape. Her diary was jammed for the next few days. She was going to treat herself to a luxury makeover at Bliss salon in Sandycove. And then a haircut in a fancy salon. A new wardrobe of clothes was also called for. Unfortunately you had to go abroad for decent clothes these days, to Milan, Paris or New York. London was out now 'cos of the sterling difference. If only she could jet off to the Big Apple on a shopping spree! She wanted to knock them dead on the show. She, Emily-Ann, was going to have the entire country (including Ronan, the dishy new producer) eating out of her manicured hand.

He really was divine wasn't he? Ronan looked like an American film star. All chiselled cheekbones and a smile any orthodontist would be proud of. It was so exciting having a guy like that produce *The Happiest Couple in Ireland*. She'd honestly expected some fat old cigar-smoking git, and had been pleasantly surprised when she'd gone to the meeting to discuss her contract.

With Graham.

Of course, she'd warned Graham beforehand to be on his best behaviour. He was a volatile creature. And it was pretty hard to know what was going on in his head most of the time. Emily-Ann had to drill it into him that he wasn't to say anything that might hurt either of their careers. He'd agreed of course. But Graham was as bad as his word. On seeing Ronan, he'd lowered his eyes and whispered 'What a ride' into Emily-Ann's ear. She had almost clocked him over the head.

When she finally hauled herself out of bed, she went into town and found Sandy's model agency. In she strode, armed with a few photos in a black-leather folder. She knew it wasn't much of a portfolio but it wouldn't take long to get a first-class book filled. She wore a camel-coloured skirt, showing off her long legs in knee-high boots and, a tight figure-hugging black top, emphasising her newly slim waist. She looked sensational, she told herself, as she mounted the steps to Sandy's offices on the second floor of the four-storey Georgian building.

Sandy herself was out of the office.

'You can talk to Joe,' the bored looking receptionist looked her up and down. 'Take a seat, I'll check if he'll see you.'

Emily-Ann took a seat and had a good look around the foyer of the offices. The walls were plastered with cards of some well-known Irish models. Some of the cards looked pretty outdated. Emily-Ann wondered if some of the girls even still worked as models. *Well, they'll be working less once I'm on the scene,* she thought smugly. Glancing at her watch, she hoped this Joe fella wouldn't keep her long.

Eventually, a short ropey-looking guy of about forty appeared, a cigarette hanging from the side of his mouth. His face was disagreeably red.

There was something odd about him but Emily-Ann couldn't put a finger on it.

'Come in,' he said brusquely.

Well, he didn't seem to be too bowled over by her beauty, Emily-Ann noticed. Huh, maybe he was gay. She followed him into his office. He nodded at a seat. She sat down.

'What can I do for you Emily?' he stubbed his
cigarette out.

What could he do for her? This was a model
agency wasn't it? What did he think she was after?
A cleaning job?

'I want to join your books as a model,' she
informed him, not sounding as confident as she
would have liked.

'What experience do you have?' his eyes skimmed
her cleavage.

'I've done quite a bit of publicity for a company
called *Great Gardeners of Ireland*,' she told him,
producing the folder. 'And I'm going to be on TV
soon. On a new show. It's going to be huge.'

He skimmed through her folder and sniffed. 'It's
hard to tell from these shots,' he said. 'You'd have to
get some more professional ones done, if you know
what I mean. Maybe a full length business shot, you
know wearing a business suit or something, and a
bikini shot.'

A bikini shot? What on earth was he talking
about? Emily-Ann only intended doing covers. Or
classy editorials. Or catwalk shows. On the runways
of top designers. She certainly had no intention of
appearing in tacky rags. Imagine donning red lace
for builders to be leering at her! Good God, if she
did that, her father would disinherit her and no
decent man in Ireland would look at her in the
same way again.

'Sure,' she said, deciding to humour him. She

didn't want to come across as being too difficult at this early stage. After all Naomi Campbell had got herself into a bit of trouble throwing her weight about. She'd read that somewhere.

'Leave this with me,' he said, referring to her folder. 'Sandy will want to run her eye over the pictures. I reckon we'll be able to get you a bit of work. Are you sure you're going to be on TV? You're not messing are you? The clients usually like to book a familiar face you know?' He gave her what Emily-Ann felt was a most unpleasant smile.

'Yes I'm definitely going to be on the show,' Emily-Ann said haughtily. 'And what's more, I'm going to win it.'

Chapter Forty-Seven

Caroline wasn't really enjoying the acting classes anymore. Pretending to be a tree or a fish. And all that breathing. BREATHE IN . . . AND BREATHE OUT AGAINNNNNNN AHHHHHH. It was so annoying.

She hadn't really wanted to come tonight. She wanted to be at home. In case Ronan called again. She wanted to be in the same room as him. Near him. God, she was like a woman obsessed. But why wouldn't she be? Ronan was the type of man who looked at you as if you were the only person in the world. What woman wouldn't be attracted to a man like that?

Tonight all the acting students were going out together for a few drinks. Caroline hadn't made any friends in the class yet. But hopefully that would change. Then again, maybe all evening classes were the same.

The last time Caroline had joined a night class, it hadn't been a huge success.

It had been a creative writing class. There'd been

nine women in the class. And four men. One man was about ninety. One was married. One was as gay as the fairy on a twinkling Christmas tree and the fourth was just out of school. And convinced he was the next James Joyce.

The teacher, a small grey-haired woman who always wore a maternity smock although she wasn't pregnant, actively encouraged her pupils to read their work aloud in class.

Caroline's memories of the class weren't exactly fun. She remembered spending all night one night composing a beautiful poem about love. She could hardly wait to come in to class the following Thursday to share her beautiful piece of work with the others.

The classroom was consistently cold and draughty. And the machine outside the room only dispensed half-full polythene cups of watery tea. But it had all seemed worth it. At the time. Putting up with the less than comfortable conditions in the name of art. That night, Caroline had barely listened to the other pupils' poems because she was so anxious to read out her own piece of tear-inducing, heart-rending writing.

Finally it was her turn.

She stood up and took a good breath.

'I wandered lonely through the fields . . .' she began.

'Is that not that Wordsworth poem?' the pseudo James Joyce peered at her through little roundy glasses. 'You can't just steal other people's lines like that.'

Caroline was puzzled. Had Wordsworth really used the same line? No *wonder* it had seemed kind of familiar. Oh God how embarrassing. Then again, great minds thought alike, didn't they? Maybe this was just a sign. A sign that proved she was destined to compose masterpieces.

'Wordsworth's line is actually different,' one of the women said sympathetically, 'it's "I wandered lonely as a cloud".'

'Continue Caroline,' the tutor continued in an 'I can't believe one of my pupils is actually so thick' kind of way.

'I wandered lonely through the fields,' Caroline began again; her face slightly flushed this time. 'Drifting through all the fallen leaves. When suddenly I heard an angel weep . . .'

And then her mind had gone completely blank. How could this have happened? She'd learnt it off by heart.

'Sorry . . .' she said quietly, 'I've just completely forgotten the rest.'

'Was it something to do with daffodils?' the pseudo James Joyce had asked.

Caroline had never gone back.

Chapter Forty-Eight

'So what should I wear? How should I do my make-up?'

'Oh you don't have to worry about any of that,' Clive told Emily-Ann over the phone.

Sandy's agency had passed on Clive's number.

She didn't know anything about him. But he was probably reputable enough. After all, the agency had recommended him.

'Oh right, I see.' Of course, Emily-Ann nearly kicked herself. God, she'd really gone and put her foot in that one. Models didn't do their own hair and make-up. They'd professionals to do all that kind of stuff. Right, well no harm done really. She was learning all the time. After all she was still only new to this game. Give her a few weeks and she'd be a pro.

'So what time should I be there at?' Emily-Ann was determined to come across as professional. It was important to make a good impression. She'd read somewhere that Cindy Crawford always turned up to her appointments at least 15 minutes early.

Clive gave directions to the venue and Emily-Ann took the details down meticulously. She was leaving nothing to chance.

She woke up the next morning, earlier than usual and hopped straight in to the shower.

Normally she shampooed, conditioned and blow-dried her hair every morning, but there was no point in doing that today. The professionals would only be washing it again later on. She wondered which one of Dublin's celebrity hairdressers was going to work on her hair. She might get some juicy gossip off them about the 'stars'. Ireland didn't have too many 'stars' but you might be fooled. Some people carried on as if they were. For absolutely no reason at all. Just 'cos they'd played a bit of rugby in college or were a runner up on some quiz show. God help me if I ever end up having illusions about how great I am, Emily-Ann thought before sticking on her shower cap and turning on the hot water.

Arriving at the venue, make-up free and shampoo free, Emily-Ann felt almost naked. She took the lift to the second floor, full of nervous anticipation. What would the other girls be like? Would they automatically hate her just because she was tall and toned? Would they be jealous of the new girl? Would they see her as competition? After all some models in Ireland became 'tired' very quickly, turning up to opening after opening and grinning into the camera of any photographer who bothered to show up. The photos might show up months after the particular event as 'fillers' when the magazines were celebrity-starved for a particular issue. But more often than not the photos weren't used. Emily-Ann knew this much from her PR. Enter the backstage world of bitching, she told herself as she pressed her finger on the buzzer that read Apple G. Promotions.

She pushed open the door. And was greeted by the back of a man wearing a purple blazer. He'd a mobile phone stuck to his ear and didn't even turn around, just continued talking. She took a seat. And waited.

He'd a strange kind of Dublin accent, she noticed, mixed up with other accents. As if he'd travelled a bit, or was trying to cover up his own accent or something. It was funny the way some people were like that, wasn't it? Emily-Ann knew some guys who'd gone to the States for the summer and were still speaking with an American accent. Two years on.

The guy was still talking. It sounded like he was making some kind of deal. Hmm. Dodgy. Emily-Ann noticed his black hair was greasy.

Just like her own.

She noticed the hairdresser hadn't arrived yet either.

Suddenly she began to feel slightly uncomfortable. Maybe it hadn't been such a good idea to turn up so early. It certainly didn't look like her efforts were being appreciated too much.

Finally, much to her relief, the door was pushed

open and two girls walked in. Two very ordinary girls. Certainly not models. The make-up artist and the hairdresser obviously. Mind you, they'd seemed to have forgotten their bags of tricks today.

'Hello,' Emily-Ann gave them a smile.

'Hello,' they smiled back and sat down beside her.

'I wonder is it just the three of us?' one of the girls said.

What was she talking about? Emily-Ann wondered. *Just the three of us.* Surely those girls weren't models. They were neither tall nor slim, and both were wearing a load of gunk on their faces.

The greasy black-haired guy had finished his conversation. He stuck his mobile in the back pocket of his jeans. 'Right then,' he looked from one girl to another, 'We're all here then, are we?'

Emily-Ann looked at him blankly.

'I know Debbie and Sadie, all right girls?'

'Fine,' they answered.

'And you must be Emily-Jane. Right then, okay Debs and Sadie, you lot know the score. The outfits are in the backroom, you've 15 minutes to get sorted. You can show Emily here the ropes.'

The girls stood up. 'Are you right then?' the girl called Debbie looked at Emily-Ann.

She followed them in to the back room. What on earth was going on? Where was the hairdresser and the . . . 'What's the story with our make-up?' Emily-Ann blurted out.

Sadie looked at her like she'd ten heads and a

tail. She was wearing enough make-up to last her for a year.

'Oh you won't need any make-up,' Debbie announced. 'We usually wear masks you know.'

'Wh . . . at?'

Sadie started to snigger. 'Would you prefer people to recognise you? I'm much happier wearing the mask thank you very much. In fact they'd have to pay me more to take it off.'

'I don't understand,' Emily-Ann said slowly. What was this? Some kind of set-up? Some kind of sick joke? Debbie pulled three pink-leather catsuits out of the wardrobe. 'Christ,' she shouted, holding one of them in the air, 'these things seem to get smaller by the week. How the fuck am I supposed to squeeze me arse into this thing? By the way,' she looked at Emily-Ann curiously, 'what's the story with the long face? Didn't Clive tell you what you'd be doing?'

Emily-Ann shook her head. 'Nope.'

'He's a bit of a prick like that,' Sadie said. 'I suppose we're used to him by now. Come on girl, get changed,' she nodded at Emily-Ann. 'When these guys say 15 minutes, they usually mean ten.'

'But I'm here for the modelling,' Emily-Ann protested.

Sadie laughed. 'Oh you've a lot to learn. Modelling', she made a funny face, 'covers a wide range of stuff. Champagne and catwalks it usually isn't. You have to take the good with the bad. If you turn stuff down, you don't get booked for the good gigs. It's pretty shit at the beginning but it gets better. Or maybe you just get used to it. Yeah, that's probably it. You get used to it.'

'B . . . but how long have you been a . . . m . . . model.'

''Bout two years. Debbie's been at it nearly three. It takes a while to get your name known.'

'Right,' said Emily-Ann. She looked at the catsuit dubiously and hoped to God it wouldn't split on her. 'By the way what are we supposed to be doing anyway?'

'This is the launch of some new radio station,' said Debbie knowingly. 'I couldn't tell you how many radio stations I've launched in my career. Basically a new one pops up every few weeks. This one's called Love FM I think. Tacky or what? Basically they just want us to hang around traffic lights and hand out car stickers, caps and lollipops.'

'Is that it?'

'Yeah, it's a good gig this. €85 into your hand for two hours work. Beats working in an office eh?'

Emily-Ann wasn't so sure. Suddenly, the thought of working in an office for the rest of her life didn't seem too horrendous any more.

'Sometimes it's pretty embarrassing though,' Sadie said as she fought to pull up the zip of her catsuit. Remember Liverpool Debs?'

'Jesus, will I ever forget?'

'What happened in Liverpool?' Emily-Ann shook

some of Debbie's talc onto her legs to make it easier for her to squeeze into the rubber.

'We were promoting safe sex and basically had to give out free condoms.'

'Well I would have absolutely refused to do that,' Emily-Ann insisted.

'It was well paid,' said Sadie.

'I don't care if they offered me a million euro,' Emily-Ann insisted.

'Ah you can't be having that kind of attitude. Nobody knew us over there, and besides the rent has to be paid somehow. I've a two-year-old kid at home. You can't just go home and tell a little kid there's no food 'cos Mammy didn't want to do this and Mammy didn't want to that. Christ my arse looks fecking enormous in this thing, doesn't it? Sadie scrutinised her bum in the rusty mirror.

'No, it doesn't,' Emily-Ann lied. She suddenly felt really uncomfortable with these two girls. They were from a very different world from the one she inhabited. These girls were actually trying to make a living here. They weren't doing this to get invited to parties or automatic entry into the VIP bars. They were doing it because there was money to be made. And they weren't really qualified to do anything else. It was a real eye opener.

Soon the girls were ready. Emily-Ann was so thankful for her mask. She'd just die if anyone spotted her. It really didn't matter doing this kind of stuff as a once off as long as she wasn't recognised. She'd better not be recognised.

The girls waited on the street for the taxi that had been ordered for them. They'd been presented with their huge sacks of goodies. It was just as well they were giving out freebies and not just fliers. Joe Public tended to be a lot friendlier when you were giving him something for nothing. Anyone in PR knew this.

At least there were three of them, Emily-Ann thought gratefully as fellas sped past in vans shouting obscenities and cat calling at the girls. Debbie and Sadie simply ignored them.

'You get used to it,' Sadie advised. But Emily-Ann wasn't fooled. You never got used to this kind of work. You endured it.

Maybe.

At O'Connell Street, Debbie asked the taxi to stop. 'You don't mind if I take this one, do you girls? It's nearest to where I live.'

'You take it Debs, O'Connell Street usually does my head in anyway.'

'Cheers girls,' she hopped out, pulling the mask down over her eyes. 'Nice meeting you Emily-Ann.' She slammed the door shut. She was gone.

'Baggot Street and then Donnybrook, right?' the taxi driver enquired.

Emily-Ann thought she was hearing things. 'I didn't realise we'd all be separated,' she said to Sadie.

'Yeah, a lot of the time you have to work on your

own. These guys really know how to get their pound of flesh. So which would you prefer? Donnybrook or Baggot Street – I'll let you choose as it's your first day.'

Emily-Ann just looked at her. What a choice! It filled her with total panic. Sadie might as well have offered drowning or strangulation as a form of suicide. Her old workplace was in Baggot Street and she lived in Donnybrook. How on earth was she supposed to stand in either of those places and hand out lollipops? Stop the world; she thought desperately, I just want to get off now.

'The choice is yours,' Sadie re-iterated. She sounded almost impatient.

'I'll take Baggot Street,' Emily-Ann said faintly. She might look back and laugh at this some day, she thought. But more than likely she wouldn't.

She got out at Baggot Street.

'Just stand at the lights,' Sadie advised, 'and don't work a minute over your two hours.'

'Right.'

'And don't worry, it's not always this bad. I have a photo shoot with Westlife next week. So you know it gets pretty glamorous sometimes.'

'Right,' Emily-Ann smiled weakly and closed the door of the taxi. Westlife? Huh!

She stood at the lights in Baggot Street just near Tescos with her santa sack. If my friends could see me now, she thought painfully. Nobody, least of all Emily-Ann, knew exactly why she was there.

When the lollipops were produced, people in cars suddenly expressed a huge interest. Like she'd often been told in the PR world, Joe Public was very keen to get his free cap and candy. He wasn't as interested in the car bumper sticker. But of course from a promotional point of view this was the most important item to flog. It was all about free advertising at the end of the day. Women were the worst. Some of them asked for five caps for their five little brats. Men just smiled and some of them just openly tried to get a good look at her arse.

'Do you come here often?' one man asked her as he lowered his window, his eyes glued to her chest, straining against the pink rubber.

'Ha ha very funny', she shoved a load of lollipops into his face. *Dickhead.*

It wasn't as bad as she'd thought it was going to be. Emily-Ann's sack began to empty and it was nearly time to go home. She'd just a few goodies to dispose of now. But the traffic had thinned and it wasn't as easy to get people to stop when they weren't going bumper to bumper anyway. The traffic lights turned red again and Emily-Ann rushed over to the first car. It was a brand new red BMW and to her surprise, she saw her friend Celine in the driving seat. Gosh, this must be the car her mum had just bought. Celine had been dying to get behind the wheel of it.

She rapped on the window. Celine just looked at her and looked away. She was wearing her designer sunglasses and black leather jacket and obviously thought she was too cool for words. Oh God, she doesn't recognise me, it suddenly dawned on Emily-Ann. She was half tempted to take off her mask but then thought better of it. Imagine if someone recognised her now when she was just about to go home. She banged on the window and to her horror Celine seemed to be shooing her away. As if she was one of those tinker kids who splashed dirty water on your windscreen and then harassed you for money. God this was mortifying. She stood rooted to the spot aware that people on the street were staring. 'Hiya,' Emily-Ann said.

'Do you people not understand English?' Celine said cuttingly.

The lights turned green and Celine revved up the engine and sped away, nearly taking Emily-Ann's toes off as she did so.

Emily-Ann was stunned. Had she just imagined that horribly unpleasant encounter with one of her best friends? Emily-Ann had known Celine since they were in playschool together. Had she always been that nasty to strangers? Emily-Ann was suddenly grateful that Celine had insulted her and not Sadie say. People like Sadie were decent. Just out to make themselves a living. After all it wasn't like Sadie was out begging with her baby. In fact the more Emily-Ann thought about it, the more outraged she felt.

She could hardly believe that the only member of the public who'd outwardly insulted her was one of her own best friends! She looked at her watch. It was time to go home.

Suddenly she had an idea. It wasn't the best one in the world but it was the best she could think of right now. She'd hop into Burger King and get changed in the loo before going home. She wasn't standing at the 10 bus stop wearing this thing.

She walked into the fast food restaurant, aware of the intrigued looks she was receiving from the customers and staff alike. She headed straight for the Ladies and peeled off her catsuit. Never in her whole life had Emily-Ann been so glad to take a particular garment off. Ugh. She hoped she'd never have to don a catsuit again.

As she walked out of Burger King, nobody batted an eye-lid. They obviously didn't recognise her as the ridiculous looking 'pink freak' that had walked in minutes earlier. Thank God. She'd her make-up on now and the catsuit safely bundled away in the bottom of her tartan shoulder bag. Her hair was still as greasy as hell but there was nothing she could do about that now.

Chapter Forty-Nine

The sun was seeping through Caroline's bedroom blinds. She opened one eye sleepily and then another. She was hungover and exhausted from the night before and was to start her 12-hour shift at St Bridget's in an hour's time. Still, she enjoyed working with elderly people. It was very rewarding. She'd worked with these particular women before. As part of the charity group. Playing bingo and organising sing songs and that kind of thing. Sounded stupid maybe, but it was actually a lot of fun. More fun sometimes than nights out with her peers.

God what a weekend though, she thought as she dragged herself out of the bed and into the shower. Friday had been a major pub crawl with Fiona – starting at The Merrion Inn, then The School House, SamSara, The Duke, The Bailey, Kehoe's, and then back up to the Shelbourne Hotel before heading off to Renards. She'd got home at about 6:00, falling into bed with her make-up still on, her contact lenses still glued to her eyes. Then on Saturday, one of her old school acquaintances rang to remind her about a buffet party.

'I hope you haven't forgotten,' Audrey said breezily down the phone.

'Of course not, 'I'll definitely be there.'

'Yourself and Colin?'

'Huh?'

'The invitation is for you both. Remind him, won't you hon?'

'Yeah, yeah, sure,' Caroline said. She'd forgotten that Audrey had had a crush on Colin since she was about five.'

Most people were invited to a party alone or with a partner. But Caroline always seemed to be invited with her cousin.

The last time she'd seen her cousin was in the most recent edition of *Social & Personal* magazine. Flanked between society girls and champagne flutes. She rang him to see if he was interested in coming along to the party.

'Who else is going?' he'd wanted to know.

'Dunno,' Caroline said.

'I haven't heard of anyone else going. But I might pop along if nothing else comes up. It depends on how I feel later.'

'God, you're charming Colin. By the way are you still seeing your woman?'

'What woman?'

'The one you brought along to the last party up the mountains.'

'God no, she was mad, absolutely hysterical. She kept on asking me what the story was. I was like, what story? She was a nutter, a head wrecker.'

'You're impossible.'

'So you keep telling me. Will there be any decent birds going to this party anyway?'

'I doubt it. Audrey usually just invites humans to her bashes.'

'You're a panic Caro.'

'Yeah, well listen I'll let you go. I might see you later.'

'Sure, maybe.'

She'd put the phone down and sat by it for a while. She wondered where Ronan was this weekend. He had called by to leave in a furry mouse and some smoked cod for Chi-Chi but she'd missed him.

At the party, Caroline was one of the first to arrive. Did she imagine it or did Haughty Audrey look ever so slightly pissed off to see her arriving on her own?

She'd brought an extremely expensive bottle of champagne. Now she was thinking she needn't have bothered.

'Thank you,' her hostess almost snatched the bottle from her, glancing at the label to make sure it was really champagne and not sparkling white wine. 'Is Colin not here?'

Blunt and straight to the point, that was Haughty

Audrey for you. She was probably having the party in Colin's honour, knowing her. She'd especially had her eye on him ever since Meek Mike (her boyfriend of 11 years) had turned out to be not as meek as everyone imagined and was now the proud father of twins.

In America.

Mike had always had a thing for Americans.

'He's probably coming later. You know Colin.' Caroline removed her coat and looked around for a suitable place to hang it up. 'Who else is here?'

'Shane and Geraldine, Larry and Lucy, Peter and Sheila and . . . Rory.'

'Rory?' Caroline was amazed. 'As in Gory Rory, as in . . . as in the one I used to go out with? Oh God, Audrey thanks a lot.'

'Well I didn't want you feeling left out . . . with all the couples you know.'

Caroline groaned, suddenly remembering why she hated Saturday night parties so much.

'But what about you? Won't you be feeling left out?'

'I'm not looking for a relationship at the moment,' Audrey said thoughtlessly. 'Go on into the sitting room, I'll look after your coat.'

Caroline entered the sitting room nervously. She hadn't met Rory since the night she'd caught him snogging another woman in The Sugar Club. She was supposed to have been in Newcastle on a hen night but the flight had been cancelled due to fog. So they'd hit Dublin instead.

Unexpectedly.

The couples perked up when Caroline appeared. Nobody had dared leave the room for the last 15 minutes, not even to go to the bathroom. Just in case they missed the show down; of two ex-lovers meeting face to face after all these years.

But severe disappointment was felt all round when Caroline gave everybody a cheerful hello and gave Rory a friendly hug.

'Punch?' he gave her a huge grin.

I'd love to, she thought. 'That'd be great,' she said.

'You look absolutely fantastic,' he complimented her.

'Do I?' Caroline was pleased. She had been making a huge effort of late so it was nice that someone had noticed at last. Although, maybe Rory was just being polite to make up for the caddish way he'd treated her.

'Are you here on your own?' he handed her the glass of punch.

No, I've actually a man hiding outside in the boot of the car.

'I am tonight,' she said, hoping to sound mysterious yet aloof. If Rory thought there was any chance of a snog for old time's sake he could absolutely forget it.

Some men had an awful cheek. Did he really think she'd spent the last few years pining for him or something? Suddenly she hoped Colin would show up. With a single friend or two. There was something pretty depressing about being outnumbered by couples on a Saturday night.

'What are you up to these days?' Peter asked her. 'We haven't seen much of you since our wedding.'

Oh no, Caroline thought. Please don't start the 'wedding' talk until I'm too pissed to notice.

'This and that,' she said lightly.

'How's the love life?' Sheila asked.

Everybody looked at Rory who had the savvy not to look remotely bothered.

'It's great,' Caroline said flatly. *I'm here on my own. Does that not speak for itself?*

'Are you still out on the town every night?' Lucy asked.

'More or less,' Caroline answered, swigging back the punch.

'Where do single people go these days?' Geraldine piped up. 'It seems so long ago since I was out in a nightclub. It's so hard to organise to stay out late, what with the kids and . . .' she drifted off.

'Oh the same old haunts,' Caroline explained. 'Nothing changes. I really believe that if you emigrated for ten years you could still go back to Leeson Street and find the exact same pictures on the walls, the same people sitting on the exact same stools, having the same conversations.'

'I'm so glad I'm not back there,' Geraldine shuddered, giving Shane's thigh a reassuring squeeze. 'More nuts anyone?'

'Is anyone else coming tonight?' Caroline asked as Audrey came into the room armed with a fresh tray of canapés.

'David and Eimear are supposed to be coming,' she announced. 'Eimear went for her second scan this afternoon. They're both so excited. She's saying she doesn't know whether it's a boy or a girl. I think she probably knows and just isn't telling anyone.'

'I'd say it's a girl,' Sheila said. 'She's very big. Remember when I was expecting Shannon?' she asked the group proudly.

Never again, thought Caroline as she gratefully accepted a fresh glass of punch from Gory Rory. This night was wrist-slitting stuff. Any minute now the 'couples' would start comparing Woodie's DIY to Atlantic Homecare. On second thoughts maybe it'd be better if Colin didn't show up. She reckoned this little get together wouldn't really be his scene.

She looked around the room vacantly. If she had married Richard, would she be sitting here holding his hand and boring everybody stupid about matching sets of Tipperary Crystal tumblers?

God, she hoped not.

The doorbell rang. Caroline felt her heart give a little leap. Hopefully Colin had showed up with a bit of single talent. Was her hair all right?

But she needn't have panicked.

It was only David and Eimear.

They'd brought along the most recent photo scans of their foetus.

Caroline looked at the photos politely. It was hard to make out anything. 'Wow,' she said flatly, hoping that sounded appropriate.

'That's the head there. I think he or she was asleep.'

'It's incredible. An absolute miracle.' God that punch was going straight to her head. Would Rory have spiked it? Out of spite or sheer desperation?

'Don't tell me you're getting broody,' Eimear joked.

'Oh no, not at all, not at all.' Caroline handed back the photos. 'In fact I couldn't bear to have kids', she added thoughtlessly and then noticed the look of absolute shock on Eimear's face. 'God I'm sorry, I really am. That was a terrible thing to say, I don't honestly know what came over me. I . . . God . . .'

'Don't worry about it,' Eimear said eventually, once the sheer disbelief had faded from her face. She patted Caroline's arm. 'I know you didn't mean it. It's me who should be feeling guilty,' she said kindly. 'After all, here we are all talking about weddings and babies and you're . . . you know . . . I don't know what to say really.'

'I'm not terminally ill or anything,' Caroline reached for her glass of punch although she was wondering should she just quit while she was ahead and order a taxi home. At this stage it looked like Colin was going to be a no-show.

'I felt really bad when Richard got engaged to Sandra. We all did,' Eimear sat down beside Caroline. 'I just kept sitting there thinking he shouldn't have left you.'

'Well don't worry about it,' Caroline said flatly. 'I'm fine about it anyway.' She wondered if she should tell them that Richard had left Sandra and tell them about *The Happiest Couple in Ireland*. After all they were going to find out sooner or later anyway.

'Are you?' Eimear didn't seem to believe her. 'So er . . . how have you been? Have you taken any holidays this year?'

'I went to Santa Monica in Los Angeles,' Caroline told her. 'It was great. We went to Beverly Hills and I got a suit in Rodeo Drive. It was half price in the summer sale. It was really cool shopping there. The shop assistants even offer you champagne and canapés.'

'Really?' Eimear said encouragingly. 'And did you do the tour of the stars' homes?'

'No,' said Caroline. 'I don't really care where people like Sylvester Stallone live. I couldn't justify paying money to someone to drive me around like a Peeping Tom.'

'We went there last year on our honeymoon and did the tour. We bought a map of the homes so we could see exactly which house belonged to whom.

God it does seem really naff, now that I think about it.'

'Don't mind me, I'm just being disagreeable,' Caroline laughed apologetically.

'Well you're definitely not yourself,' Eimear looked concerned. She'd known Caroline since they were toddlers. Caroline was far from her usual bubbly self. 'It must be a real pain in the arse sitting in with a bunch of couples.'

'I dunno. I did my girls' night out thing last night. I can't seem to manage two nights out on the tear any more. Anyway,' she sighed, 'It's not my social life that's getting me down, it's everything. I mean I'm working in a nursing home at the moment and I love it but that's not what I want to do for the rest of my life. I don't seem to have any direction anymore. Don't know where I'm heading. It's scary. At least you know you're going to be a mum.'

'Yeah, yeah, yeah, I'd kill for a really wild night out though,' Eimear admitted. 'Or at the very least, a drink,' she patted her stomach mournfully. 'Don't get me wrong I'm thrilled to be pregnant. But sometimes I wonder is the fun all over.'

'Do you still meet up with Richard? And all our old friends?'

'Ye . . . es, it's very awkward. Because Sandra . . . Sandra isn't as good a friend as you were . . . *are*. Er . . . more punch?'

'Why not?'

Caroline didn't even notice Colin and his friend come in. At that stage she'd probably consumed more punch than the average person consumes in a lifetime. So Sandra obviously hadn't told anyone she was pregnant. Mmm. Well that was something at least. But could Caroline realistically go on a TV show with her ex and pretend everything was rosy? And did Richard honestly think they could pull this off in a country as small as Ireland?

Some people had already left the party. Couples often tended to leave places early. God you wouldn't wish coupledom on your worst enemy would you?

Of course Gory Rory was showing no signs of leaving and looked a bit put out by the arrival of the extra lads.

Word had it that he later ended up with Audrey.

After everyone else had gone home.

Caroline was sitting on the sofa with her feet tucked under her, reminiscing about her school days with Lucy when she saw Colin's friend. 'Is that Declan?' she squinted over her umpteenth glass of punch.

'So it is,' said Lucy perking up. Although in a long-term relationship, Lucy never had any qualms about openly showing her approval of other men. 'God, he's not bad is he? Is he seeing anyone?'

'I'm not sure,' Caroline said, her eyes closing. 'Jesus Lucy you know I'm afraid to get up. This stuff,' she stared at the punch with a glazed look in her eye, 'has gone right to my head.'

Luckily she didn't have to move. Colin and Declan joined them on the sofa.

'You look locked,' her cousin told her before launching into a major flirting session with Lucy. Larry, her partner, had left earlier as he had an early flight to catch on Sunday morning.

Declan kissed Caroline's cheek. 'Hi ya gorgeous,' he said and she noticed his eyes were quite blood-shot. 'It's great to have you all to myself for once.'

'Well Lucy and Colin also happen to be sharing this couch.' Caroline laughed.

'How are you anyway? Have you resigned from Tele-Fone yet?'

'I'm on unpaid leave,' Caroline explained. 'I didn't have the nerve to give up my security just yet. But I'm doing a bit of casual work and trying to decide what to do with the rest of my life.'

'Hang on here 'til I get another beer?' Declan went to stand up but keeled over instead. Caroline rolled her eyes to heaven. Typical. The only single man at the party (apart from Colin) was completely out of his mind.

Caroline was left on the couch with Colin and Lucy.

She could hear her cousin telling Lucy that he'd always fancied her and that if she ever split up with Larry he'd give her a call.

Caroline half expected Lucy to throw her drink

over him for being so presumptuous. But to her
absolute astonishment, Lucy simply took a business
card from her bag and gave it to him.

'What did you do that for?' Caroline accused her
the minute she got her on her own. 'You know what
Colin's like. He'll plague you until you go on a date
with him. Believe me I know what he's like. I lived
with him for long enough.'

'Do you see a ring on my finger Caroline?' Lucy
held up her left hand belligerently.

'That's not the . . .'

'. . . point is I'm keeping my options open. Who's
to know what Larry gets up to on his trips away?'

'But you don't think . . .'

'I don't know Caroline. I used to spend my time
worrying about Larry and being suspicious, you
know, checking his coat pockets for strange little
notes and trying to find out from his friends if he
behaved when he was away, and trying to get bits
and pieces out of his PA when she was sozzled at
the annual Christmas party. But then I got tired of
it. It wasn't doing me any good.'

'And who's messing around now?' Caroline was
blunt.

'Larry isn't prepared to discuss the future. He's
thirty-four Caroline. The "too young to settle down"
thing doesn't wash anymore. God you know,' she
sighed, 'sometimes I wish I was single again. When
your cousin asked for my number it actually reminded
me that men used to find me attractive.'

Caroline lit a cigarette and took a long drag. God this party had produced a few thought-provoking issues. She'd felt so self-conscious at the beginning of the night, trapped like a prisoner in Couple-Happy-Land. Now it seemed that some of those couples weren't so blissfully, deliriously, ecstatically, thrilled to be with one another the whole time.

The revelation cheered her up.

'Caroline?'

Declan seemed to have miraculously woken from his coma.

'Mmmm?'

'I was wondering . . .'

'Mmmm?' Gosh he was struggling. This was unbelievable. Maybe he was trying to pluck up the courage to ask her on a date.

'Yes,' she decided to put him out of his misery. She ruffled the top of his head playfully.

'How did you know what I was going to ask you?'

'Er . . .' Oh God this was embarrassing. Had she gone and completely taken him up the wrong way?

'I was just wondering . . . if you're going in to the kitchen could you get me another beer?'

'Oh sure,' Caroline felt her face redden beyond belief.

She bolted towards the kitchen where Audrey and Rory seemed to be participating in a deep meaningful conversation next to the salad spread.

'Excuse me,' Caroline muttered as they slinked

away. She opened the fridge. It was still full of beer. That was the best thing about going to a 'couply' party. Most people drove, departed early and left a load of booze behind.

Maybe she should start coming to more of these things.

She should really stop drinking now though. Just to be on the safe side. She bent down to retrieve a cold Carlsberg. A pair of hands on her hips made her jump. She swung around.

'What I meant was,' Declan had his hands on her shoulders and his eyes locked hers. 'What I meant was . . .'

'Carlsberg? Or did you mean Heineken? There's also cans of Guinness in there although they say it's not as good as the real . . .'

Suddenly he lunged forward and tried to stick his tongue in her ear.

'Get away from me,' Caroline pushed him away indignantly. What did he think he was playing at? How dare he presume anything!

'I thought . . . I thought . . .' he slurred as he keeled over again, this time grabbing the tablecloth. The sound of smashing glasses encouraged all the partygoers to rush into the kitchen.

Audrey looked absolutely horrified.

Lucy asked what was going on.

Even Colin looked concerned.

Everybody was looking at Caroline like it was her fault.

'I didn't push him,' she announced.

'He made a pass at you didn't he?' Gory Rory asked excitedly.

'I'll kill him,' Colin said. 'I warned him you were on the rebound.'

Caroline grabbed another glass of punch that somebody had left on top of the fridge. She'd had enough. Enough of people feeling sorry for her and thinking they could pity her like she was some freak.

'I've an announcement to make everybody,' she said raising her glass and spilling half of it. 'I am no longer single. I am back with Richard,' she said, 'and we,' she added drunkenly, 'we are *The Happiest Couple in Ireland*.'

Chapter Fifty

'Hello!'

Ronan was standing at the door, looking his usual devastatingly good-looking self. Caroline was surprised and delighted to see him.

'Did one of the girls ring you?' she wondered.

'No,' Ronan looked sombre. 'Nobody called me. I just wanted to talk to you, alone,' he stared at her intently and she thought, for the thousandth time, he was the sexiest man she'd ever seen. In fact, he looked even more desirable when he was trying to be serious.

She wondered who he reminded her of. Probably a cross between Jude Law, Ed Burns and a Calvin Klein model. You couldn't get better than that could you?

'There's a television company in the States mad keen on getting the US rights to *The Happiest Couple in Ireland*,' he told her. 'If we can sell them, we're talking major exposure, you'll make a fortune.'

'And so will you,' Caroline couldn't help herself saying. 'Only you won't be recognised on the street as being the eejit on TV. Come in.'

Ronan looked genuinely put out. He stepped
inside. 'Caroline, yourself and Richard have an excellent chance of winning. Those first few scenes are
riveting. The viewers are going to love you two.'

'Well the first few scenes were different,' she
said testily.

Ronan was suddenly standing very close to her.
So close she could feel his breath on her face.

'Listen,' he said gently, picking a piece of fluff off
her shoulder. 'That wasn't the only reason I called.
In fact, I dunno, maybe I shouldn't be here, after all
it's not really any of my business.'

'What's none of your business?'

Ronan looked highly uncomfortable.

'Go on,' Caroline began to worry. It wasn't like
Ronan not to be smiling.

He took a deep breath. 'Well,' he began, 'I was
out with some of the lads I used to go to school with
last night.'

Caroline waited for him to continue. He was
struggling. She was intrigued.

'We ended up in Leeson Street.'

'Oh God,' Caroline smiled sympathetically. 'No
wonder you're not feeling your best.'

'Ah you know, I didn't have too much to drink,'
Ronan smiled but his usual sparkle was absent. What
was going on?

'Caroline, you're the most attractive women I've
ever laid eyes on.'

Caroline felt her face flush. Where had that come

from? She didn't know where to look. Didn't know what to say. To say she was completely stunned was an understatement.

'And that's why,' he added, placing a hand on her arm, 'That's why I'm telling you what I saw.'

'God Ronan you're frightening me now. What did you see?' Her eyes searched his.

'It's not what I saw. It's who I saw. Well . . . ,' he hesitated, 'I'm almost 99 per cent sure.'

And then it dawned on her. Of course. Who else could it be? No wonder Ronan was shocked.

'I know who it was,' she grimaced. 'It was Richard, wasn't it? With some old tart?'

Ronan looked baffled. 'You knew?'

She shrugged. 'I can guess.'

'I'm not 100 per cent sure.'

'Oh don't worry. *I* am. He's a lying cheating scumbag. And he loves Leeson Street.' She laughed again at Ronan's worried expression. But her laughter was verging on hysteria. 'Anyway why would I care? It doesn't bother me in the slightest. Our relationship has been over for a long time. We can't stand each other.'

Ronan's eyes bore into her. 'Do you want to talk about it?'

Caroline bit her lip. God, maybe she was mad. After all, the last thing she wanted was to be kicked out of the show at this stage. But the relief of being able to tell someone was overwhelming. 'I'm sorry,' she said. 'You must think I'm nuts.'

Ronan put his hands on her shoulders and forced her to look at him. His face was very close to hers. 'I don't think you're nuts,' he said softly. 'But I do think you're beautiful.'

Her heart was pounding so loudly she wondered if he could hear it. She closed her eyes and he brushed her cheek with his lips.

She opened her eyes again. And he withdrew from her. The moment had passed. But her heart was still accelerating.

'You don't know how much I wanted to do that.'

'Mmmm.' She was finding it hard to speak. Her emotions were all over the place. Finally she found her voice. 'So now you know. Maybe all the happy couples in your TV show are actually dysfunctional?'

'If I'd known you were on the market, I'd have put in a bid ages ago,' Ronan said quietly.

'Well now you know,' she grimaced. 'Richard and I are probably the unhappiest couple on the show. So are you going to fire us?'

'No, the show must go on at all cost. There's too much at stake now and advertisers have poured enormous amounts of money into the programme. So I'm not going to fire you. I'm going to do one step better. And ask you out.'

'Really?' Caroline's heart did a back flip.

'Richard didn't deserve you anyway. The first time I saw you with him I just thought 'What a waste!''

'Really?'

'Absolutely. But this has to be our secret, understood?'

Caroline was on the verge of bursting into tears. 'Actually Ronan, I . . .'

He put his hand gently under her chin. 'Be quiet you,' he whispered as he bent down again and kissed her fully on the lips.

Part Two

Chapter Fifty-One

Showtime! D-Day. The cameras would soon be rolling and Caroline had butterflies in her stomach. Would she be able to pull it off? Would the acting classes help? Would she able to pretend it was Richard she was in love with? Instead of Ronan. God, she was in bits.

Richard collected her and she sat in his car for the first time since they'd split up. He was wearing the same brand of aftershave he'd been wearing when he'd broken off the engagement. She remembered it. How could she forget it? It was her favourite. She'd given it to him for Christmas. She'd made love to him, smelling that aftershave. And now she was sitting in his car. In silence. Smelling the aftershave. And thinking of Ronan.

'You're not saying much,' Richard said eventually.

'What's the point?' she stared out the window. 'What's left to say?'

Richard turned to look at her when they stopped at a set of traffic lights. 'You know,' he said quietly, 'this isn't the way I believed things would work out.'

'Oh believe you me Richard,' she answered, 'this isn't the way I thought things would turn out either.'

'Listen,' he said, his voice softening. 'Now, let's try and get on with each other anyway, now that we've agreed to go through with this. What are you up to these days anyway? You'd better fill me in, in case they go fishing for info and catch me out.'

'Well I'm still doing the acting and still working in the nursing home. Just a bit of reception and administration work. Part-time. I'm not looking for a major career just at the moment.'

'I dunno about this acting stuff,' Richard shook his head negatively, 'Aren't you a bit long in the tooth to be starting off in that now? There's kids who've been in acting school since they were like, three.'

'Well look at Robert Redford – I don't think he started until he was in his thirties.'

'Hmm,' Richard shrugged, turning to drive into the studio car park.

At the television studios they bumped into Emily-Ann and Graham. Emily-Ann was draped all over Graham like a new fashion accessory. Her face clouded when she saw Caroline and Richard.

'Nice shoes,' she said stonily to Caroline before deliberately turning her back.

Caroline looked down at her black shiny high heels, suddenly feeling very self-conscious. They did look a bit OTT, didn't they?

Mikey Mark appeared. 'Hello everybody,' he greeted them like a puppet on a Punch and Judy show. 'How is everybody today? I can't tell you how nice it is to see everybody back on the show looking so happy.'

Caroline felt like grabbing his microphone and hitting him over the head with it. But restrained herself. This, she had to remind herself, was not The *Jerry Springer* show.

Ronan arrived shortly afterwards. And was doing a very good job of ignoring her completely. She knew why he was doing it though. He'd already explained that it wouldn't do any good letting people know that he was her landlord and that they'd met outside the show already. People wouldn't believe it was just a coincidence. They might say it was a fix.

He wasn't ignoring Emily-Ann though. No. She was all over him, flirting shamelessly, and he seemed to be lapping it up, while Graham was checking out one of the hunky assistant cameramen.

Caroline wondered how long was he going to stay in the country? When would he be returning to the States? She'd love to know his plans, spend a lot more time with him. Alone. Without Josie sitting in between them, munching on hobnobs, updating them on the latest *Eastenders* developments. But of course, there was little she could do. At the moment.

*   *   *

Nina was dying for the weekend away and hoped
that all the contestants would get on well during
the weekend in Marbella. It was going to be a
challenge though. The camera was going to be on
the 14 finalists for most of the time so the public
at home would be able to see how they interacted
with each other. Nina hoped they would like what
they saw of her and Donal. She really did. She
desperately wanted to be liked. When they got back
the public would vote one couple off. She hoped it
wouldn't be herself and Donal.

When she was little, she'd gone away to Wales
with the Girl Guides. And they'd all slept in tents
and had a midnight feast. It had been madly exciting.
She hadn't really gone abroad since. Except to an
uncle's funeral in Birmingham. She wondered what
the south of Spain would be like.

When the TV company announced that the show,
including the trip abroad, was back on again, she'd
nearly fainted with joy. Imagine. Marbella. Haunt
of the rich and famous and all that. She hoped
she'd spot a few celebs down there and then she
could ask them for their autograph. She'd once
got an autograph from Daniel O'Donnell and it
was her prize possession. Another time she'd met a
newsreader from TV3 and had got her photograph
taken with her.

Most of all, Nina hoped she was making the
right decision in seeing this TV show through to
the final stages. It had been quite a struggle to get

the time off work. But it was a challenge after all. Of course it was.

A chance in a lifetime.

The seven couples were rounded up like sheep. They were outside the studios in Wicklow and it was absolutely freezing. The cameras were ready to roll. Ronan came out and had a few words with the contestants as the stylists and make-up people rushed around frantically trying to sort out hair and make-up. The chief stylist told Emily-Ann that she had to wear wellingtons in the garden and an apron in the kitchen scene.

'You have GOT to be joking,' Emily-Ann scowled.

Caroline saw her storm up to confront Ronan.

'Listen Emily-Ann,' he told her firmly, 'I want you to put on your overall immediately and start gazing lovingly at Graham.'

Caroline tried not to laugh as Emily-Ann flounced off.

That had certainly put 'the model' in her place.

The other six couples were 'strange' to put it mildly. One couple (both divorced and very OTT) had turned up in matching polka dot shorts and white T-shirts. They were given a pair of fleeces to don before they perished of the cold. What were they thinking? Caroline wondered. It was the middle of the winter in Ireland, for God's sake, not summertime in the south of France. The two lesbians had also made the final cut (the shock factor of the show presumably). As had Nina and Donal. The remaining two couples (an Australian couple and a couple from Cork) had also made it to the finals.

'Not too much competition here,' Richard had whispered to Caroline when the cameramen had temporarily stopped filming for a quick cup of tea.

'But you never know who the public will vote for,' Caroline argued. 'It's impossible to guess. We certainly haven't won yet.'

Caroline and Richard were given a Mediterranean dish to prepare, with lots of garlic and vegetables and olive oil. Actually, they didn't have to do anything at all really. One of Ireland's up-and-coming celebrity chefs was on hand to do everything. He had offered his services for free in order to promote his new south Dublin restaurant. He told Caroline and Richard (off camera) that his new place was going to be the place to see and be seen in. He offered them dinner for 12 as long as they were prepared to be photographed for a local newspaper.

'Nice one,' said Richard.

'Could we possibly have two tables for six?' Caroline asked sweetly. 'Preferably not on the same night?'

'Sure,' the wannabe celeb chef said, slightly baffled.

Then Nina appeared and managed to wangle a

table for two from the poor guy and Emily-Ann scooped a table for 16 after she told him her father was a big-shot business man.

'I'll bet he'll be sorry he ever agreed to appear on this show,' Ronan muttered to Caroline under his breath as they made their way to the gardens to start digging. 'By the way,' he whispered, 'You look beautiful this morning, you really do.'

'Thanks,' Caroline blushed. She wanted to tell him that he looked gorgeous too, but then didn't.

'How was your weekend in Dundalk anyway?'

'Oh you know, fine, I was out at the rugby club catching up with old pals and mum and dad are so proud that I'm going to be on TV and all that. Dad used to have a bit part in a soap before he got into the clothing business and he thinks all that stuff is great. I just hope he's not too disappointed when the first episode is aired tonight!'

Richard suddenly appeared and wrapped his arm possessively around Caroline's waist. 'Are you chatting up one half of Ireland's Happiest Couple?' he winked at Ronan.

'Do you know something?' Ronan gave him an odd look. 'I'd never, not in a million years, come between two people that were truly happy together.'

He strolled off with Richard staring after him, bewildered. 'What's his problem?'

The gardening scene was next to be shot. The frost on the ground was so hard that the scene had to be shot indoors on a little man-made patch. Emily-Ann looked hilarious as she tried to get the dirt out of her nails and Graham absolutely refused to get his fingernails soiled.

Emily-Ann threw him dagger looks as he sat to the side and observed, his hands firmly in the pockets of his white Versace jeans.

The Australian couple scored higher than anyone in the gardening category. They were what you'd call extremely outdoorsy. In fact, both admitted happily that they could spend all their time outside.

'We even make love outdoors,' they said grinning at each other.

'You can get arrested for that you know,' Emily-Ann sniffed in disgust.

The day dragged on and on. There was a fake little party at the end where contestants had to either sing a Christmas carol, even though it was only October or pull a Christmas cracker and tell the joke inside. Caroline caught Ronan's eye and gave him a wink as she pulled her cracker with Richard and a plastic ring popped out and hit him in the eye.

The girl from Cork was some kind of opera singer and sang the most beautiful rendition of 'Silent Night'.

After her piece nobody dared sing. Not even Graham who had been all set to perform '*Rocking around the Christmas tree*'.

Considering, there hadn't been a squeak from the Cork people all day, they certainly left the show as the current 'stars'.

Everybody else seemed to be extremely put out.

Who did those Cork people think they were anyway?
Stealing the show like that!

Mikey Mark and Ronan exchanged knowing
glances as the limos rolled up to take the 'happy
couples' home.

This show was about to get very interesting indeed.

At 7:00 that evening, the first episode of *The Happiest Couple in Ireland* was screened on prime time
Irish television. Every paper from *The Irish Times* to
The News of the World covered the show. Audiences
were hooked.

Josie, Ronan and Caroline watched it in the house.

Ronan had seen it all before in the studios.

But was keen to see it again with Caroline.

The credits rolled.

The intro was from a big Irish rock band.

Impressive.

The first scenes showed the hundreds of couples,
queuing outside the Dublin hotel.

It was very funny to see the hopeful sea of
wannabes all searching out the cameras. Couples
making an absolute show of themselves, clamouring
for the spot light.

Ronan and Caroline couldn't stop laughing as the
camera honed in on Emily-Ann and Graham fighting
to get a look at themselves in one of the hotel lobby's
full-length mirror.

'Ooh, they won't like that,' Caroline chuckled.

'No, but the viewers will love it,' Ronan laughed.

'And that's what this is all about at the end of the day. If the ratings soar, we get more advertisers and that's basically when the TV stations start to sit up and take notice.'

Richard came across as playing the 'protective boyfriend' extremely well.

'God, he really does look happy, doesn't he?' Josie observed as Richard beamed into the cameras.

'Well it wouldn't be too hard to act like the happiest man in Ireland if Caroline was on your arm,' Ronan said, giving Caroline's thigh a squeeze.

Caroline turned scarlet and stared straight at the television.

Josie said nothing.

Just smiled.

Caroline hadn't told her about the kiss.

But she didn't have to.

Josie hadn't come down in yesterday's shower.

Caroline didn't know whether to laugh or cry upon seeing herself on camera. This was head-wrecking TV. She cringed every time the camera picked her out and thought she looked quite fat. She wondered what people were saying about her. Now. At this very moment. She wondered what Sandra was thinking.

And all her old friends.

Mind you, you were better off not knowing what they were saying, weren't you? Irish people had a habit of not praising people they saw on telly. 'Would ya look at the state of her?'. Or 'I know your woman. She works in Tele-Fone, so she does. Who does she think she is?'

Caroline was glad she didn't have to go back to the Tele-Fone office any time soon.

At this stage she'd probably never go back. But at least these last few months had given her a good break from the dreary Tele-Fone existence. And that was a good thing.

Her father rang during the ads. 'We're taping it here,' he said excitedly. 'You look gorgeous. The neighbours are saying you look the image of your mum when she was your age.'

'The neighbours?'

'Yeah, half the town's here watching the telly in our house.'

Oh Jesus.

Her mother got on the phone. 'The pink doesn't really suit you love,' she said. 'It clashes with your green bag.'

'Well there's nothing I can do about it now, is there?' Caroline groaned.

'Richard looks grand too. Is it all back on again? I think you should think carefully before opening your heart to that man again. What about Sandra? Is that all off now? We're all very confused here.'

'It's a long story Mam.'

'Anyway I bet you're going to win. Everyone round here is saying it. People are placing bets in Paddy Powers.'

Oh God.

'Oh, I better go now,' her mother squealed, 'It's back on again.'

Caroline sat back down at the telly. This was terrible. Her parents actually thought she was back with Richard for real. They didn't even know Sandra was pregnant. Nobody knew. Should she tell them the truth? That she was actually on TV lying through her teeth? Maybe not. They were both in their sixties now. There was no point in upsetting them unnecessarily. She'd let them know when she went home for Christmas. Yes, the show would be over and she'd tell them then.

Richard watched the TV with his mother who looked as proud as punch. He turned up the volume on the TV. It was great the way the first episode had turned out. He looked smooth. That shirt that he'd bought in London really stood out. What a pity he hadn't invested in a few more. He wondered how many people would recognise him from the show. He hoped all his exes would see the show. Then they'd be sorry they hadn't appreciated him when they had the chance. Most of all he hoped he'd be spotted by a talent scout and be catapulted into stardom.

The stardom he deserved.

Chapter Fifty-Two

Richard was waiting on the steps of the Radisson Hotel. He'd wanted to meet Caroline in private to discuss their next move. Whatever he meant by that.

It was his idea of course. Caroline wasn't sure what he was playing at. And she wasn't comfortable meeting him alone. It didn't feel right. Not now, when he was about to have someone else's child and there was no chance of them ever getting back together.

She wore a black off-the-shoulder cashmere top and her figure-hugging leather trousers. Thankfully they still fitted her.

Inside the bar area, Caroline and her ex-fiancé took a seat beside a roaring log fire. A year ago, Caroline would have loved this. Herself and Richard, snug by the warmth of the fire, browsing through the newspapers, drinking Irish coffees. Now it was different.

So different.

She ordered a Coors light and Richard opted for

a glass of Guinness. As they waited for the order, Richard turned to Caroline, his face assuming an air of seriousness.

'I'm worried about the show,' he said.

'Worried?' Caroline looked at him quizzically, 'But why? There's nothing to be worried about, is there?'

'It's going to get really competitive down in Marbella. You do realise that don't you? The Corkonians will be singing like mad once we get there and all the oul' ones will be voting for them. And Graham will get all the kiddie votes 'cos of his sweet boy look. Having said that, I don't think the Australians will give us cause to worry – they're too loud and brassy.'

'But you never know,' Caroline countered, 'They do seem popular with their happy-go-lucky attitude. Aussies are loved by Irish people. We love the kangaroo connection.'

'Mmm, maybe you're right. Every Irish person has a relative of some sorts living over there – and just look at all our Aussie soaps.'

'Exactly.'

'Well that makes it even more vital that we come up with a story.'

'A story?'

'Yeah, something that'll propel us into the limelight. You know. Get us noticed over the others?'

'You mean just make something up?' Caroline asked incredulously.

'Not make up exactly, but we have to give the papers a hook you know. Celebs do it all the time. Wasn't there a boy band a couple of years ago who faked a helicopter crash to get front page coverage?'

'You want us to fake a helicopter crash?' Caroline laughed.

'What I'm trying to say is,' Richard wasn't laughing, 'that we have to give the media an angle that's all. Emily-Ann worked in PR you see. She has it all worked out, going on about her modelling all the time. She's using her looks to win votes.'

'Well what do you think we should do?' Caroline asked.

'Is there anything you can dig up? Any kind of family tragedy or anything?'

Caroline frowned at him. 'I've never had a family tragedy,' she said. 'And anyway I don't think it's appropriate to use the death of a family member to promote yourself. I think it's a bit sick actually.'

The lounge girl arrived with their drinks.

'What about your dad? Doesn't he have a bit of a drink problem? Couldn't you make out that that affected your childhood or something?'

Caroline looked at him incredulously. 'You're skating on thin ice there Richard. 'Dad always liked a few drinks, he still does, but he most certainly does not have a drink problem.'

'Okay, okay I suppose it's not fair to drag your family into this. How about you personally? You could say how you survived as a down-and-out in London?'

'You're taking the piss aren't you Richard?'

'Well what about that mole you had removed? You could do an interview like 'HOW CANCER NEARLY KILLED ME.'

Caroline stood up. 'I'm not having this conversation Richard.'

'I'm joking Caroline. When did you lose your sense of humour?'

'I guess the day you told me yourself and Sandra were getting married Richard,' Caroline sat down again. 'Yes, I think was the day I began to think we no longer shared the same sense of humour.'

'Sorry, I didn't mean to upset you, I was just trying to get you to see my point of view.'

'But why should I be digging deep into my past to dig up the dirt? What about you? Why don't you tell them THE DAY I SCREWED MY FIANCÉE'S BEST FRIEND?'

Richard said nothing. What *could* he say?

'Or how about HOW I TURNED FROM A WOMANISING PRICK INTO A ONE MAN WOMAN?'

Caroline was angry now. God, she rarely lost her temper. Richard was the only man in the world who managed to annoy her to the point of insanity. She shouldn't have agreed to meet him. It was a waste of time. He'd always be a selfish prick. And to think she'd almost married him!

Richard slapped his leg suddenly. 'You're a genius Caroline,' he cried. 'You're a bloody genius.'

She sighed. Now, what was he talking about?

'That's a brilliant idea. Every woman's secret wish is to tame a bastard – I remember reading that somewhere. God, I can't believe I hadn't thought of it sooner.'

Caroline screwed up her face. 'I wasn't serious you know. I mean, is that the type of person you're going to try and portray? You don't honestly think that'll work, do you?'

Richard gave a throaty laugh. 'Want to bet?'

Chapter Fifty-Three

Dublin. Early morning. Too early. Back in the studios. TV land. A land of lies and a multitude of insecurities. Mikey Mark was interviewing the couples. His beady eyes were flashing. He was back for the kill. 'Well guys, what's the feedback been like so far? Any stalkers or anything ha, ha, ha?'

'We don't watch TV so we didn't see the first episode,' the Australian woman said roughly.

'That's right mate,' her partner backed her up. 'We were walking up in the Wicklow mountains and got a bit lost. When we got home, the show was all finished. Ah never mind.'

Mikey Mark moved on to the Cork couple who were anxiously waiting to be questioned. 'What about you?'

'Oh 'tis fantastic,' the woman said, delighted the camera was finally zoning in on her. 'Two record companies have given us a shout so far, so things are really looking up, aren't they Martin?'

Martin: 'Sure.'

'But you didn't come on to the show to pursue your musical career did you?'

'Oh no,' the woman went bright red, 'sure we didn't Martin?'

'No,' said Martin.

'We're the happiest couple in Ireland.'

'Right we are,' said Martin.

Mikey Mark moved onto the 'girls'.

'We celebrated with a good old snog,' said the more butch girl with an aggressive wink.

'What did your families think?'

'Our families have known about us for years. Don't get too excited – you're not getting an exclusive here or anything. Our families are happy for us 'cos they know we're the happiest couple in Ireland and you can't get much happier than that can you?'

Mikey Mark felt his eyes glazing over. What a painful pair of twits. He moved swiftly on.

Richard and Caroline were next.

'We cracked open a bottle of vintage wine and sipped it beside a log fire as we watched the first episode,' said Richard in smooth tones, revelling in the attention. 'We didn't particularly want to invite round all our neighbours and friends. I've done the whole partying thing. I've played the field more than a Man U player. But I've met my girl now, and I don't want to be with anyone but her.'

'That's right,' Caroline beamed up at him in an Oscar-deserving performance, 'We preferred to be alone during that special episode. We don't need lots of people around us. We're happiest when it's just us as a couple.'

Bo . . . ring, thought Mikey Mark and moved on to the divorcees.

Their story was a bit more interesting.

But only marginally.

They'd invited over all their children from previous marriages and had had a bit of knees-up and a magician.

Yeah, whatever, Mikey Mark thought before questioning Emily-Ann and Graham.

'Ah yeah,' Graham said, when questioned, 'I celebrated in The Front . . .'

'In the front room of his parents' house,' said Emily-Ann swiftly. 'All our friends were there because, unlike Caroline and Richard, we're very sociable and like to share our happiness with people we love.'

Richard snorted with laughter and Caroline gave him a hard look, prompting him to produce a tissue and pretend he had a bit of a cold.

'Now,' said Mikey Mark, 'Time for the quiz.'

What quiz? Caroline panicked. Nobody had said anything to her about a general knowledge exam. She never played Trivial Pursuit and very rarely watched *Who Wants to be a Millionaire?*

But apparently it wasn't a general quiz after all. You just had to answer a few questions about your partner. Ah well that should be simple enough, Caroline reckoned. She'd known Richard for years. There wasn't much about him she didn't know.

They were to be interviewed separately.

It wasn't too difficult.

Caroline was the first interviewee.

Mikey Mark grinned at her menacingly.

'On a scale of one to ten Caroline, how would you rate your love for Richard?'

Oh Christ.

Something in Mikey Mark's tone of voice made her shiver. Had he heard something?

'Eleven,' she said emphatically.

Mikey Mark seemed suitably impressed. Caroline breathed a short sigh of relief.

He moved on to Emily-Ann. 'Our love is too special to rate,' she said resolutely, running a handful of perfectly manicured fingers through her hair and giving Mikey Mark her most irresistible smile.

Mikey Mark smiled back a rare smile. But wasn't taken in. Nothing added up here. This girl was overly confident with a tremendous zest for life. What the hell was she doing with the poncy Graham? Something just didn't ring true with the pair of them.

No, something definitely did not ring true and Mikey Mark was determined to get to the bottom of it.

Chapter Fifty-Four

Holiday time!

Caroline was so, so excited about the trip to Marbella. She couldn't wait to go away. Even if it wasn't really sunny (and it probably wouldn't be too hot during the second week of November), it would still be very pleasant. Pleasant enough to walk about in short sleeves.

If only Richard didn't have to come too, she thought. Wouldn't it be great if something urgent popped up and he was forced to cancel his trip? Then she'd have been *genuinely* happy.

If only Ronan was coming instead.

But that was just wishful thinking.

It was so annoying having to pretend that Richard was the only man for her. It was killing her. Caroline had told Maggie and the other old ladies in the home about the trip. They were all praying for her.

Maggie had shown her a picture of her brother. On a beach. The brother who never ever visited.

'That was him,' Maggie said. 'In Spain. I've seen Spain on the television. It's magical.'

Caroline promised to bring her home a traditional Spanish doll with a flamenco dress.

The seven couples met at Dublin airport. At the Aer Lingus customer information desk. Within minutes a hoard of autograph collectors surrounded them. The TV cameras zoomed in and Mikey Mark was waving his microphone about. The place was buzzing. Ronan was lurking in the background, keeping well out of sight of the TV cameras. Observing everything. He'd come to see the group off. Caroline wished for the hundredth time that he was coming with them. He'd promised to look in on Chi-Chi every day while she was away and had told her he'd miss her. *Not as much as I'll miss you,* she'd thought.

Nina did a quick interview with a *Sunday Mirror* journalist. At the end of the interview she asked the journalist to write hello to everyone in Mullingar.

Richard told *The Star* that if he ever parted with Caroline his heart would break. The Australian couple asked an *Irish Independent* journalist if there was anyway of getting a copy of their interview so they could post it off to Oz.

Emily-Ann was looking around to see if any representatives from the glossy women's mags were about. She'd kill to do a shoot for *Glamour, Company, Marie Claire* or *VIP*.

Richard hoped the TV3 cameras were getting him at a good angle.

Donal wondered where he could get a packet of fags.

Nina tried to find out if you had to pay for the drinks on board the aircraft.

After a half hour signing autographs, giving interviews and pretending to be 'oh so happy', the small congregation was ushered along to the Gold Circle lounge.

'Wow, this is fabulous, I wonder where Donal's disappeared off to – I'd hate him to miss any of this.' Nina nudged Richard excitedly. 'Em . . .' she lowered her tone slightly, 'Do you know if we can just help ourselves to whatever we want?'

Richard looked at her distastefully, 'Of course you can, I've been in here before,' he added untruthfully, 'often.'

Nina looked around enthusiastically to see if she could see anyone she knew. Not personally. After all, she didn't think any of her Mullingar neighbours would be here. *They wished* . . . but famous people regularly bided their time in lounges just like this, didn't they? Maybe she'd spot one of them. Gabriel Byrne helping himself to a coffee perhaps . . . or Bono pouring himself a gin and tonic . . . well you never know. God it was so exciting. She wished she had her little disposable camera with her. Just in case. She might never get to come back here. It was highly probable. However, after much snooping around the lounge, she was a tad disappointed. Their own little group were the only 'celebrities' in the bar, and the few businessmen sitting in the lounge working on their laptops or reading *The Sunday*

Times, seemed none too excited about seeing them. The Australians were helping themselves to Jameson. You were allowed to pour it yourself. And there was nobody there to tell you you were taking too much. Imagine. Nina could hardly contain her excitement. The luxury of it all!

Malaga airport was surprisingly small, Emily-Ann thought. And there wasn't a member of the paparazzi to be seen. She stood with the other contestants near the carousel waiting for their luggage. Among other Irish people. Civilians. Ordinary paddies pretending not to take a blind bit of notice of the group. Even though some of them *must* have recognised the group. But Irish people were like that. They didn't encourage other people to think too highly of themselves.

Emily-Ann suddenly remembered a story the priest had once told in Mass when she was a kid.

'There was a German going up a ladder and all the Germans were pushing him up it,' he'd shouted from the altar. 'Then there was an English man going up a ladder and all the English people walked up and down the street and didn't take a bit of notice of him. 'And lastly, there was an Irish man going up a ladder and the whole town were half-way up the ladder trying to drag him back down again.'

Emily-Ann laughed at the memory. The story was a bit far-fetched maybe. Most Irish people were decent enough. But there were one or two that weren't, she thought remembering the incident with her 'so called' best friend Celine on Baggot Street.

Anyway Irish people who frequented the Costa, especially those who could afford homes down here, didn't see why they should make a fuss of anybody.

Eventually the group headed out to the car park. A bus was waiting. Not a big luxury bus with a telly and built-in toilet. No, just an ordinary tourist bus. A standard bus. Suitable for package tours. It was a bit of a let-down really. Emily-Ann removed her sunglasses and stared at the interior. She was far from impressed. The sun was going down. But it was warm. T-shirt weather. The bus left the airport and soon they were speeding past Torremolinos.

The bus driver pointed it out.

'Oh is that Torremolinos? My sister went there on her honeymoon last year,' Nina squealed happily at the group. She'd had quite a few drinks on the plane and was now talking fairly loudly. 'She says it's great value. You can get a glass of wine in some of the bars for a euro.'

Nobody answered her. Not that she seemed to notice. 'It doesn't look much from here though, does it?' she asked nobody in particular as she stared out the left-hand side of the bus. 'It looks a bit like Ballymun in the sun, doesn't it?' she added, her eyes slitted against the sunlight.

Rows and rows of gaudy looking high-rise flats

stared back at her in the distance. They were hor-rifyingly ugly. 'God, I think I'd prefer Mullingar,' she said.

Donal was saying nothing. Her boyfriend never seemed to say much, Emily-Ann thought to herself. He was very quiet and thoughtful. Not a bit like Nina who rambled on and on about nothing. Half the time he looked as if he'd forgotten why he was here. Emily-Ann wondered how close the couple actually were. Were any of these couples really hopelessly in love?

Or were they all like herself and Graham.

Living one big lie?

Jack, the cameraman, was sitting up at the front of the bus talking to the driver. Ronan hadn't come on the trip. Emily-Ann wasn't sure why. He'd begun to disassociate himself from the contestants recently.

Graham was beside her, listening to his walkman. Emily-Ann could make out Christina Aguilera sing-ing *Dirrty*. She wished he'd lower the sound a bit. It was annoyingly tinny.

Graham also reeked of aftershave. A nauseating headache-inducing smell. But he wasn't as bad as Nina who positively stank after testing every single perfume back at the airport shop.

In a way, Emily-Ann was glad they were only going to be in Marbella for two nights. Ideally she'd like to stay two months. But only if she was going to be with a decent group of people.

Two nights with these head bangers was going to be nothing short of a nightmare!

She closed her eyes and started to drift off but was sharply awoken by the Australians who'd started up an annoying singsong at the back of the bus. Emily-Ann groaned and closed her eyes. This was worse than a school trip. Graham had his walkman off now and was fidgeting with his mobile phone. He was probably texting Barney. Barney was an English barman working temporarily in Temple Bar. Emily-Ann had warned him not to mention Barney's name over the next couple of days.

'And if you do,' she'd threatened him in no uncertain terms, 'I'll fucking kill you.'

The bus sped along with everybody looking out the dusty windows enjoying the view and the sunshine. Suddenly Nina let out a screech making everybody jump.

'Look!' she cried, 'Look it's Dunnes Stores. Imagine, a Dunnes Stores in Spain. Where are we now? Oh Fuengirola. Well then, imagine a Dunnes Stores in Fuengirola. It reminds me of being at home.'

'Why would you want to be reminded of home?' Richard snapped uncharitably, 'When you've only just got off the plane?'

Emily-Ann couldn't help smirking to herself. This weekend would be telling. She wondered how Richard would mix with everyone on the trip. Although he was a handsome guy, he had a tendency to act as if was superior to everyone else. Talking about big houses and people worth knowing and places worth going to. Emily-Ann had known plenty of people like Richard growing up. Because she'd lived in a big house. People like Richard were so *obvious*.

His arrogance was sexy in a way though. Emily-Ann didn't like men who were obvious pushovers. But she didn't care for the way he acted like he was so bored with the whole Marbella thing either. He'd been here three times this year already, he claimed. And knew all the right bars to hang out in, the best restaurants to dine in, the best courses to play golf on. So he said. Wasn't it a wonder he wasn't an official spokesman for the area? She wondered where he got all the money to fund his trips to the Costa del Sol? Somebody had told her that he'd inherited money. And that explained a lot. Because a job as a TV researcher wouldn't give you a weekend away in Athlone, never mind anywhere exotic.

The bus sped along. Occasionally a glimpse of the blue sea could be caught between the high-rise apartment buildings. Emily-Ann was beginning to feel excited. She couldn't *wait* for the following morning to stick her face in the direction of some sun. She'd heard so much about Puerto Banus, with its suntanned 'beautiful people' strolling along the glitzy marina, pausing to admire the state-of-the-art yachts, posing in designer sunglasses and matching designer gear. Wonderful!

It wasn't the type of place where you ran around in towelling shorts bouncing a beach ball. No. And that suited Emily-Ann just fine. She wanted a glimpse of the high life, happening nightclubs, cocktails, celebrities, meeting rich scrumptious London bankers who were over enjoying golfing weekends. The fortnight package in Salou was not for her, where common young girls drank from naggins of vodka and fell out of seedy Irish bars. No. Not for Emily-Ann. Not now. Not ever.

The bus was approaching Calahonda. 'Are we there yet?' Emily-Ann called out to Richard.

'About 20 minutes now Emily-Ann,' he replied.

'It's not as nice as Oz,' Emily-Ann heard the Australians comment from the back of the bus. 'It's a bit too commercial.'

The couple from Cork agreed. They'd been to Queensland on their honeymoon. Nothing could beat the vastness and the idyllic beauty of the Northern Territories, they insisted. In Australia, it wasn't unusual to walk for miles and miles on stunning deserted beaches without coming across anything other than a couple of crocodiles.

Richard sighed loudly and looked at his watch. Caroline sipped from her can of Diet Coke saying nothing. The two lesbians were listening to Celine Dion on the same walkman, sharing ear plugs, pretending to be closer than close. But Emily-Ann wasn't taken in by them. She'd heard them bickering over a certain song earlier on.

Not so romantic.

Emily-Ann was keeping well away anyway. She didn't want either of them to start thinking they might have a chance with her.

Instead she wondered if she'd be able to get some serious shopping done in Marbella. She wanted to buy something spectacular for her twenty-first, which was in a few months time. Her heart was set on spending hours browsing in some of the exclusive shops. She'd heard that Emporio Armani, Versace and Moschino were all in Puerto Banus. God, would they ever get there?

'Has anybody got a mobile phone?' Nina enquired. 'I'd love to ring Mam and Dad and tell them how I'm getting on.'

'Richard has,' said Caroline, trying not to smirk, 'He won't mind you using it, will you Richard?'

Richard reluctantly handed his phone to Nina.

She took it excitedly and dialled Mullingar.

'Hello Mam? Yeah, we're grand. We're all brilliant. There's a Dunnes Stores here and all. And you know Richard, well he's been here before so he'll probably show us around – point out all the hot spots – he's really trendy. From Dublin ... yeah Dublin. He speaks like the people on the news. Oh Donal's fine ... yeah I agree ... he's more handsome than all the other contestants. Mam you're hilarious. Ha? Speak up Mam ... we're nearly there, yeah. By the way, did you bring back the jumper Granny brought me for my birthday? If you bring it back to the shop they'll give a full refund and you can put the money in my bank account. And Mam guess what? You didn't have to pay for the drinks on the plane and you could choose anything you liked. No, I didn't get a free eye mask and ear plugs – I think you only get that if you're going to America. Ha? No, it's not my phone don't worry it belongs to Richard. Anyway I'd better go. See you now. I'll ring later.'

'Thanks a million Ritchie,' she handed the phone back to Richard. 'You don't mind me calling you Ritchie, do you?'

'Well nobody else calls me that,' he said coolly.

'What about Dick then?'

'How about we just leave it at Richard?'

'Oh look there's the big Marbella sign, we're here!' one of the lesbians shouted excitedly.

Emily-Ann looked out the window at the imposing white sign. At long bloody last. They'd finally arrived. The bus ride had already taken about 45 minutes. She was dying to get out now and stretch her legs. Get a bit of exercise. She hoped someone wouldn't suggest going for a meal or anything. If she were to fit into her skimpy bikini tomorrow, she couldn't possibly eat another morsel this evening.

After a while, the driver pointed out a small road veering to the left. 'That's the harbour down there,' he explained, 'Puerto Banus. You can't drive down there without a security pass.'

Emily-Ann craned her neck for a view. She couldn't wait to go down there.

She wanted to get out.

This minute.

Out of this claustrophobic bus.

The driver kept driving, and moments later took a turn to the right. He kept driving. And driving.

'Jesus, it's half way up the feckin' mountains,' Emily-Ann moaned. 'We'll have to be getting taxis up and down all the time.'

'I suppose if you lived down here, you'd have to buy a car,' Donal said.

'Or you could walk,' Nina suggested, 'Or get yourself a bike.'

Graham's eyes widened dramatically and he spoke for the first time since they'd sat in the bus. 'A bike? Daaaaarling, you couldn't be cycling down to the port and parking your bike outside one of the bars. That would be just too funny.'

The looming wooden gates were closed. The driver jumped out.

Everybody waited anxiously for the gates to open. The driver jumped back into the bus and continued to drive.

The group was reduced to silence as the stunningly beautiful whitewash villa came into view.

It was typically Spanish looking, its shuttered

windows were surrounded by creeping bougainvillaea. The round-shaped pool twinkled under a spotlight. If you stood at the front door you could see the Mediterranean in the distance. To the left stretched the beautiful, breathtaking, barren Andalusian mountains.

The driver led the way, followed by the group. Jack the cameraman was videoing everything.

Caroline's face fell when she saw the big double bed that herself and Richard were supposed to be sharing.

'What's the problem?' Richard didn't seem to mind in the slightest. 'You didn't think they were going to provide us with twin beds, did you? God Caroline, you can be very naïve sometimes.'

'Well if you don't mind, I'm going to opt not to share the bed with you, I'll take the sofa.'

Richard shrugged. 'Whatever.'

'Oh my God! We got the room with the jacuzzi babes, we got the jacuzzi,' Graham was jumping up and down with delight.

Emily-Ann followed him into the bathroom. Her face broke into a smile at the sight of the deep ceramic tub. On either side were two glass holders. Perfect for holding the champers. It was just like something you'd see in a five star hotel. On one of those travel shows. She could get used to this. In fact she would get used to it. Once she'd started jetting around the world to the catwalk shows.

'This is very romantic,' Donal wrapped his arms around Nina's waist and nuzzled at her neck.

'Yes,' Nina said stiffly, 'but I'm not that keen on the double bed, you know?'

'I think it's fine,' Donal said.

'I've got kind of used to sleeping in my own bed . . . alone like you know.'

'Oh I know,' Donal sighed. 'But sure we'll see what happens.'

'Yes, we'll see,' she agreed rather reluctantly.

Oh God!

Chapter Fifty-Five

As Richard checked out the pool, Caroline wandered into the kitchen. It was small compared to the rest of the house but pristine clean with all the basics. A large glass-topped dining table presided in the middle.

Perfect for a candle-lit dinner. A picture of a tanned Ronan in a white towelling robe, sitting at the table raising a champagne flute, sprung into her thoughts. *Go away Ronan.* God, she was going to have to stop fantasising about him during this trip. Else she'd go mad.

She looked around the kitchen. Somebody had lit the fire because a cold wind had started to howl outside. The place was probably at its best in the summer when you could sit outside and enjoy a barbecue. It was typically Spanish looking with its dark terracotta tiles and a tiny fireplace tucked into the corner. Who cared if the kitchen was fairly small? Caroline thought. If she won the house she wouldn't be cooking all day anyway.

'Did you see the note?' Mr Australia grinned at

her from the balcony, where he was sipping a bottled beer and staring out towards the dark ocean. The sea seemed a million miles away and you couldn't see much. Only the twinkling faraway lights of the sea-front. Miss Australia must've been outside. Playing hide and seek with Richard maybe. The divorced couple, Annie and Roger, had gone for a walk.

'What note?'

'Apparently we're not allowed to leave the house.'

'You're joking, aren't you?' Caroline frowned. He must be joking. It wasn't fair to lock them all up together, like caged monkeys.

One of the lesbians appeared. 'Oh we can go out if we want,' she was happy to explain, 'we're just not allowed socialise outside the house. For tonight anyway. Jack has to film us in the house having fun.'

'Well, hopefully tomorrow we'll be able to do our own thing,' Caroline said.

'We're all so happy though, we wouldn't want to be with anyone else though, would we?' said Lipsy. That was the lesbian's name. Lipsy. Caroline wondered was it was a made up name.

'Yeah, yeah,' she answered, not very enthusiastically. 'But what are we supposed to do for food and drink?'

'They've laid out a spread downstairs in the disco room.' Mr Australia said. He seemed to be a mine of information.

'The disco room? What are you talking about?'

'Haven't you seen it? It's down in the basement. Man, go down and check it out, it's amazing. Emily-Ann and Graham are already down there dancing for Jack. And Nina has started tucking into the champagne.'

'And there's a karaoke machine too,' sang Martin from Cork. 'We might have a go later on.'

Caroline's eyes widened. Were they serious? Caroline had always dreamed of having her own little private nightclub at home. Her cousins had one in their house in Carlingford, just outside Dundalk. A room with black walls and a disco ball hanging from the ceiling. A deadly bar in the corner, a tiny dance floor in the middle and massive loud speakers in all four corners.

She just had to see this for herself.

She skipped downstairs to the basement where Graham was already impersonating John Travolta on the dance floor. Emily-Ann was sprawled on a black leather sofa, munching on olives and watching with amusement. A sumptuous banquet had been laid on and Nina was digging in like there was no tomorrow. Caroline's eyes widened. Gosh, this really *was* like a mini nightclub. What fun!

'Here try some of this,' Nina poured her a glass of champagne, 'It's real champagne I swear, not just sparkling wine. I can't remember the last time I tasted champagne. I think it was at my cousin's wedding.'

Caroline accepted a glass.

And sipped slowly, letting the bubbles swim into her bloodstream.

'Cheers,' she said to nobody in particular.

Before long Richard arrived down and made a bee-line for the champagne. He looked less than happy at having to endure a get-to-know-the-other-contestants evening. He accepted a top-up from Nina who had taken it upon herself to be the hostess for the night. The Australian missus was down next. She was wondering if Graham wouldn't mind sticking on a bit of Kylie.

Graham didn't mind at all.

He'd dance to anything.

Except heavy metal.

The divorcees were next to join the party.

Followed by the lesbians.

After the third bottle of champagne was cracked open, some of the other contestants joined Graham on the dance floor. Not that he seemed to notice. He was too busy concentrating on himself in front of one of the darkened full-length mirrors beside the dance floor.

Donal was reluctant to join in the dancing. And wasn't too keen on the champagne either. Instead he joined the Australians who were knocking back Heineken. The food was incredible; light canapés and massive helpings of fresh colourful salads. Emily-Ann heaped her plate with shredded lettuce, leeks, tomatoes, pickled baby dill cucumber and water-cress.

'Have a bread roll, go on, this one's buttered,' Nina tried thrusting a chunk of bread in her face.

Emily-Ann gave her a withered look. *Not you too!*

The lesbians had started arguing with Graham. Lipsy wanted to play KD Lang but Graham was having none of it. He wanted George Michael's *Freek*.

'I'll give you *Freek*,' Lipsy threatened him with an empty Carlsberg bottle until he succumbed.

Emily-Ann rummaged behind the bar to see if she could find some Schwepps slimline tonic for her vodka.

'This is so much fun, isn't it?' Nina accosted her at the bar.

'Yeah, it's great,' Emily-Ann said. *Jesus. Would she ever go away and annoy someone else?*

Ah ha! Her eyes clapped on the bottle of slimline tonic. Oh Brilliant. There really *was* a God.

'Where would you normally go out when you're in Dublin?'

'Em,' Emily-Ann poured the tonic water on top of her splash of vodka. She wasn't really listening to Nina. The drink was beginning to go to her head. She was feeling merry. An incredible feeling. Wouldn't it be brilliant to be able to get merry and stay merry all night? Instead of having to go from merry to manky drunk, inevitably making a fool of yourself?

'Would you go to different places or would you just be say a regular in one particular club?'

Emily-Ann just looked at her. What was she talking about now? Nina was always babbling on about something useless.

'I find I don't go out to many clubs,' Nina carried on, not seeming to realise she was having a conversation with herself. 'I mean I don't have that many friends up in Dublin because I'm from the country. That's why I think it's brilliant meeting all of ye. When we go home we can meet up for reunions. You can get me into all the good clubs. I don't think I'd get into places like Lillies and Renard's by myself.'

'I'm sure you would,' Emily-Ann said flatly, swilling her vodka with a straw. How was she going to get rid of Nina without being obviously rude?

'So tell us,' Nina poured herself another glass of champagne. 'How long've you been seeing Graham? He's really good-looking isn't he? He's a great dancer and I love the way all his clothes match. Do you help him pick them out?'

'Excuse me a minute,' Emily-Ann bent down and rubbed her foot.

'Are you okay?' Nina looked terribly concerned.

'Um, I think I must have bumped my ankle off something earlier on,' said Emily-Ann, 'I think I'll just sit down for a while.'

She hobbled off.

Nina took another gulp of champagne. Mmm,

it was delicious. This really was the life, wasn't it? Her vision was becoming slightly hazy. She hoped the champagne wasn't going to her head. Anyway once Jack the cameraman left the villa, she could really let her hair down. Richard was sitting on one of the stools. All alone. Poor thing. Nina didn't like to see anyone looking left out. She'd better go and join him.

Failing to notice Richard's distinct look of dissatisfaction as she pulled up a stool, she tried to start a conversation. 'So tell us then,' she said trying not to slur her words. 'What's it like working in television? Have you met Gay Byrne?'

'Sure, I have.' It was obvious that Richard did not want to get roped into a conversation about Gay Byrne.

Well . . . obvious to everyone except Nina.

'And Terry Wogan? Have you met him? He seems nice.'

'I must say I like Terry Wogan,' Ms Divorcee chimed in.

'Who's Terry Wogan?' the Australians asked.

Jack the cameraman yawned, then said his goodbyes. He was looking forward to getting to his hotel. A few quiet whiskies by himself. And a bit of peace. He'd had enough.

Ah well, he couldn't say he hadn't been warned.

'Rather you than me,' Mikey Mark had said to him over and over again, 'Best of luck to you pal.'

When he'd gone Graham turned up the music. 'Now, let's get this party really started,' he shrieked.

'Have you met Pat Kenny?' Nina seemed determined to get some TV gossip out of Richard.

'Yeah, yeah.'

'Is he nice?'

'What exactly do you do in television?' Donal asked. He reckoned working in TV must be cool. Better than working in a garage with his da anyway. You never got to meet anyone interesting working in a garage. And his customers were mostly blokes.

'What's the similarity between Pat Kenny and Santa?' Nina asked with a giggle.

'Dunno, tell us,' Leanna said.

Everyone turned to look at her. So she did have a voice, they thought simultaneously. Before this, all she'd ever done was nod when her partner Lipsy spoke.

Her face reddened visibly.

She wasn't used to being the centre of attention.

'They've both got long white beards,' Nina gave a funny kind of a snort. ' 'Cept Pat Kenny ha, ha, get it?'

Nobody did.

'What did the bus driver say to the man with no arms and no legs?' Richard decided to tell his own joke.

Nobody knew.

'Howya, how are you getting on?'

A couple of people laughed politely.

Caroline groaned. She'd heard that joke so many

times. It was time Richard got himself a new one. One that was actually funny.

'Who else do you know in RTÉ?' Nina pressed.

Richard snapped. He'd had enough. 'I don't know anyone right? I'm a fucking cleaner in the damn place, ok?'

Donal stood up. And folded his arms. 'Have you something to say about cleaners?'

Richard barely looked up. 'Why? What's it to you? Are you a cleaner or something?' he sneered.

'No,' Donal said in a steely voice, 'No, I'm not but my mother happens to be.'

The atmosphere froze. Suddenly everybody stared into their drinks.

Except Donal.

He kept staring.

At Richard.

'Sorry man . . .' Richard began.

'No, I'm the one who's sorry,' Donal interrupted. 'I'm sorry that we have to share our weekend with a jerk like you. Who do you think you are insulting everybody left, right and centre? I've had enough of you and your bullshit. And I'm sick of your condescending attitude to my girlfriend. She's only trying to be friendly and you just keep ridiculing her. What are you looking for? A cheap laugh at someone else's expense?'

Richard apologised again.

'Don't say sorry to me. It's Nina here who deserves the apology.'

Richard turned to her sulkily, 'Sorry,' he mumbled.

'S'okay,' she muttered, looking like she wanted the ground to open.

The divorcees decided to call it a night.

Martin from Cork looked at his wife. 'Will we head on up too?'

She agreed. Sure there was no point doing the karaoke when the cameraman wasn't about.

Leanna stood up to go too.

'See you later darling,' Lipsy blew her a kiss.

'Aren't you going to join her?' Nina asked nervously.

'What do you think we are? Joined at the hip or something? Lipsy barked. 'Get a life would you?'

Nina was mortified. She stared at the ground. She didn't want to get into arguments with people like Richard and Lipsy. Especially Lipsy. She looked like one of those women you saw on late night TV programmes. The ones about women's prisons. Where they beat each other senseless. Over nothing. Nina was afraid of her.

But Donal obviously wasn't.

'Listen here,' he said to Lipsy, 'there's no need to be coming down hard on Nina. She didn't mean to offend you.'

'I agree mate,' Mr Australia cut in. 'We've all got to try and get along here.'

'Sorry,' Lipsy took a climb down, 'I do get a bit sensitive at times. I just hate the way everyone expects us to be all lovey dovey all the time. We're just like any other couple you know? I hate people thinking we're just some novelty freak show, know what I mean?'

Nina said nothing. She didn't know what Lipsy meant. Any of the time. Lipsy was aggressive and not friendly at all. Not that Nina wanted to be forming opinions about her. In case she came across as racist or whatever the word was.

But the truth was, Nina just didn't think she was a nice person.

Not like Graham who was fun even though he didn't say too much and was a bit fidgety.

Emily-Ann was okay too but a bit stand-offish. And Richard did sometimes come across as obnoxious. But everyone else was fine.

However there was no doubt in her mind that Donal was the nicest person here. And he had stood up for her too. Although she thought he might have overreacted a bit to Richard. She rested her head against his shoulder. He smelled nice. Why had she ever broken up with him? she wondered foggily. Mmm . . . why indeed?

Emily-Ann felt sorry for Donal as he carted a very tired and emotional Nina up the stairs. Graham was still dancing. Lipsy had now joined him on the dance floor. Caroline and Richard were sitting side by side saying nothing.

Emily-Ann wondered about those two. She'd love to know what was going on there.

She wondered if their relationship was a farce.

Because they were the most loved down couple she'd ever laid eyes on.

Caroline yawned. She wasn't enjoying this any more. Richard was being his usually grumpy self. He didn't see the point in being friendly or looking happy when the cameraman wasn't there. And he seemed very pissed off that Donal had confronted him in public.

She decided she wanted to go to bed now. Or sofa. She wanted to be asleep by the time Richard came up. She certainly wouldn't feel comfortable undressing in front of him. Not after all that had happened. She stood up, said her goodbyes and excused herself.

Graham had stuck on Celine Dion's *The Power of Love*. He was now over at the bar concocting a Sex on the Beach for himself.

'I don't know how you keep up with him.' Richard moved in closer to Emily-Ann when everybody had gone.

'I don't,' she said matter-of-factly.

Was she imagining it or was Richard staring at her very intensely indeed?

She fluttered her eyes at him with increased interest. And why wouldn't she? He wasn't bad looking. And it was boring in here. Cooped up with all these tedious people. Pretending to have a good time. Richard was definitely handsome. The problem was he knew it. Perhaps he was a tad too old for her ... but it wasn't like he was bald or anything. Or fat. Like a lot of older men were.

Everybody else had gone to bed.

Except for Graham.

And he didn't count.

'Would you like to dance?' Richard's hand brushed against hers. He seemed to be reading her mind.

She stood up. And moved towards the dance floor.

He followed.

Graham sat down with his Sex on the Beach.

Watching them.

With a glazed look in his eye.

'How can we get rid of him?' Richard murmured in her ear.

'Don't worry,' Emily-Ann grinned. 'He'll conk out in a few minutes.' She wrapped her arms around him. 'He always does that.'

She was drunk.

Hammered in fact.

And besides she hadn't snogged anyone for ages.

So, why not?

Suddenly a crash was heard.

Sure enough, Graham had fallen to the floor.

Emily-Ann took Richard's hand and led him upstairs.

Chapter Fifty-Six

Caroline woke staring at an unfamiliar ceiling.

With a crick in her neck.

Where was she?

She rubbed her eyes, then recognised the red-velvet fabric of the sofa.

A bloody uncomfortable sofa it was too.

She lifted her head to ask Richard the time.

It was hard to tell if it was early or late. It was still fairly dark. She didn't want to be wandering down to the kitchen with no make-up, only to bump into the cameraman.

But the sight of the huge, neatly made up, four-poster pine bed gave her a shock.

Good God.

Where was he?

Caroline knew Richard too well.

And knew there wasn't a chance in hell he'd woken up early and decided to make the bed.

She sat up and shivered. The room was chilly. She pulled on a jumper and walked barefoot to the window and looked outside. Wow. What an

extraordinary view. The sun was just rising. The pool
was the deepest shade of blue. It would be a Godsend
in the summer months when temperatures in the
south of Spain rose to over a hundred degrees.

Now, where was Richard?

This was weird.

She crept downstairs to the kitchen anxious not
to be waking anyone up. The kitchen clock said
7:45. Good God. That meant it was about 6:45
back home. No wonder she was the only person
awake.

Caroline opened the fridge and helped herself to
a can of Sprite. Her head was throbbing a bit from
last night's champagne. She sat down at the kitchen
table, trying to remember who'd remained in the
disco room when she'd gone to bed. Only Emily-Ann
and Graham as far as she could remember.

Emily-Ann. Hmmm. She wondered if . . . if . . .

A cold shiver ran down her spine. Right, she
was going to get to the bottom of this. She didn't
care who Richard shagged at this stage but she
wasn't about to let him jeopardise her chances of
winning the house. She tried to remember which
room Emily-Ann and Graham were supposed to
be in. But couldn't. She paused in the corridor,
wondering what to do next. She couldn't exactly
go peeping into all the bedrooms now, could she?

Just in case . . . in case . . . people were . . . you
know . . . God, they'd think she was some kind of
pervert.

Instead she made her way down to the disco room to see if she could spot any sign of life.

A small bundle curled up on the black leather sofa turned out to be Graham.

Aha.

Everything was making sense now.

'Graham?' she gave him a little prod.

He didn't budge.

'Graham?' she tried again

'Barney, oh Barney,' he mumbled.

Barney? Caroline stood up straight. Who the hell was Barney? God, this was bizarre. All these people were mad.

She went back upstairs. Ciara, the Cork woman was making herself a cup of tea. 'Oh would you like a cup?' she asked Caroline as soon as she saw her. 'I made sure to bring a few Barry's tea bags with us. I wasn't going to chance coming to Spain without tea bags.'

'Oh, that'd be great,' said Caroline and sat down. 'Poor Graham is out for the count in the basement.'

'Graham?' Ciara looked puzzled. 'Are you sure?'

'Absolutely.'

'It's just that . . . oh maybe I'm imagining it but . . .'

'. . . But what?'

'Well, to tell you the truth, Martin and I barely got a wink of sleep last night with all the shenanigans going on in the room next door.'

Caroline's ears pricked up. What room was she

in? 'Are you next door to Graham and Emily-Ann then?'

'Unfortunately,' Ciara said grimly. 'There's only two rooms at the top of the house. Theirs and ours.'

'Well you poor thing,' Caroline said. Then added mischievously, 'But Graham is still downstairs. In yesterday's clothes. It's baffling isn't it?'

'Baffling,' Ciara agreed, shaking her head in wonder.

Emily-Ann woke with a pounding head and a big hairy armpit in her face.

What the f . . . ?

She came to her senses very fast as last night's antics came flooding back.

'Richard?' she pushed him off her. 'Richard! Get out of here. Do you hear? Oh Jesus there's going to be war over this.'

Richard groaned.

'What time is it?'

'Time you got out of here. God almighty, what do you think you're playing at? Caroline will kill you.'

Richard made a face. 'What about Graham? Will he kill you?' he muttered sarcastically.

But Emily-Ann wasn't wasting time arguing. She wanted him out of there. Now.

The cameraman arrived at the villa just as Nina was heating up extra croissants. There was no limit on what you could or eat and drink so why not make the most of it?

She was feeling more than a little peckish after all last night's champagne. But there was more from where that had come from and she was looking forward to going on the razz again tonight. She'd woken up wrapped in Donal's arms this morning. It had been a nice feeling. It was too long since Nina had woken up to anything besides her cold hot-water bottle.

Of course she hadn't gone all the way. No. It was too soon for that now. And besides the lesbians were next door and she didn't want them to hear her any more than she wanted to hear them.

'Sleep well?' Caroline enquired scathingly as Richard emerged from the ensuite bathroom.

'Nah,' he said wiping his dark head of hair with a hand towel. 'I fell asleep down in the basement.'

'Did you?' Was he for real? Where did he get off telling lies?

He didn't even look the slightest bit guilty.

'I found Graham down there on his own earlier.'

'Oh right,' Richard said like lightning. 'Well I went out for a walk.'

'Yeah? And since when did you become the out-doors type.'

Richard looked annoyed. 'Listen Caroline,' he said gruffly. 'I'm not standing here being interrogated by you. You're not my wife and you're not my girlfriend.'

'Thank God for that,' Caroline stood up and flounced out of the room

Slamming the door behind her.

Thank God for that.

Chapter Fifty-Seven

The bus driver was outside. He said he was under strict instruction to take the group on a tour of the Costa del Sol and then drive them up to Micas where they could get a panoramic view of the coast. Jack was to film them all looking happy on their holidays and some tour company who'd invested a lot of money in the show, was insisting that all the touristy spots were covered. Emily-Ann was thoroughly pissed off. She wanted to go shopping in Puerto Banus. Not taking photos of views and smiling in front of a bloody camera all the time. They said there was no such a thing as a free lunch. Well that obviously applied to holidays too.

She didn't fancy being carted around with this lot for hours with Jack's camera lenses in her face. As if they were a bunch of stupid tourists. This was supposed to be a wild weekend away for God's sake. Not a bloody OAP day out.

'Don't worry,' the divorcees were more than cheerful about it. 'It should be fun. And the driver said we could stop off at a café for a little break whenever we feel like it.'

'In the meantime though,' Nina beamed at the other contestants, 'I have packed a load of sandwiches so there's no chance of us going hungry.'

Martin from Cork had brought his guitar. He'd learned how to play a typical Spanish tune and was looking forward to putting his skills to the test.

Graham had no intention of being subjected to such torture however. And had his earphones plugged firmly in his ears.

The driver did a head count. It was just like a school tour, Emily-Ann thought. Nobody was allowed to stay behind and God forbid, have fun.

Herself and Graham were sitting on the back seat. Far away from Richard and Caroline.

Emily-Ann had no intention of talking to Richard at all. It would only make things worse. Besides she'd only snogged him because she was drunk. And there'd been no one else around. But the experience would not be repeated tonight. She looked around the bus. There wasn't much else on offer. Unless she decided to become a lesbian, ha, ha. There was Donal, she supposed. He wasn't bad looking. Maybe a bit too rough for her liking. However, for some strange reason he genuinely seemed to be attracted to Nina. She'd no idea why. Okay, Nina was naturally pretty, but that was about it. Men always said 'It's the personality that counts.'

But Nina was absolute proof that you needed zero personality to get a man.

The bus took off and soon they were heading in the direction of Estepona. It was a glorious day with the sun straining to get through the dusty bus windows. The weather was fabulous, so much better than Dublin, Emily-Ann thought as she washed down a Disprin with her bottle of mineral water.

Graham was texting Barney again. Trying to find out where he was, what he was doing. God, he was so possessive!

Emily-Ann looked out the window as the bus whizzed through Estepona. This was a truly gorgeous resort. With a long promenade and nice beaches. Emily-Ann wouldn't mind living in a place like this. Not at all. It was very up-market, she thought, without the riff-raff that you might bump into in Torremolinos or Benalmadena.

She wondered aloud if it would be expensive to buy a place around here. Maybe she could get her dad to invest. Her parents had a place in Portugal, which was great in the summer but boring as hell in the winter.

'I'd say you're talking about quite a bit of money, you know?' said Martin from Cork.

'I wonder how much our villa is,' Nina said her ears pricking up.

'It's at least a million euro,' said Ciara.

'That's not that much though,' Emily-Ann said, 'when you consider what you'd get for that in

Dublin.' God, she thought, why would anyone want to live in Dublin when you could live here with all year round sunshine?

'Do you want to stop here?' shouted the driver. 'Or keep driving 'til we get to Sotogrande?'

'Oh keep driving,' said Richard. He'd heard a lot about Sotogrande. It was the second biggest port on the Costa after Puerto Banus and apparently Prince Charles's son Harry had came down last year to play polo. And Fergie was also spotted on the beach last summer with her two daughters. What was good enough for the Royal family was good enough for Richard.

Besides, he wouldn't mind getting a look at the Valderama golf course, which had hosted the Ryder Cup a few years back.

The bus sped on.

Everybody was talking.

Except Graham.

And Caroline. She wasn't saying much either. Emily-Ann wondered what she was thinking. Did she suspect anything? Was she pissed off? Then again, why should she be pissed off? Emily-Ann couldn't figure her out at all. According to Richard, their relationship was as good as dead. But maybe Caroline was one of those women who wanted all their exes to stay single like forever. Well tough, Emily-Ann thought. It was about time she started living in the real world.

The couple from Cork were discussing the evening

plans. The Happy Television company had invited them to party in Puerto Banus, all expenses paid. Martin and Ciara didn't fancy it much. 'We much prefer to sit in,' Martin explained.

'Oh God, I hope I never get married,' Emily-Ann said loudly. 'I would hate to sit in the whole time. It'd drive me mad.'

Ciara from Cork seemed to take offence. 'Aren't you and Graham going to get married some day?'

'You MUST be joking,' Emily-Ann was adamant. 'I couldn't think of anything worse. I think once you get married, that's the end of the dream isn't it? I mean, until then you never know what's going to happen. Every night out is an adventure, not knowing what's around the next corner.'

'But that's exactly why I wanted to get married,' said Ciara, 'I was tired of not knowing what was waiting for me around the corner. I found it very unsettling.'

'You mean you didn't get married for love?' Emily-Ann pretended to look shocked. She was beginning to enjoy this. She didn't care. Martin and Ciara were the most annoying couple she'd ever met.

She looked out the window. The sea was to her left, sparkling like a hundred thousand diamonds. It made her want to ask the bus driver to take a detour so she could get out and jump into the ocean. But the reality was it was probably freezing. After all, this was November.

After a while the bus reached Sotogrande. The

driver let his passengers off just before the port entrance and said he'd be back in an hour. You couldn't just drive into Sotogrande and park any old where. No. It just wasn't that type of place. Privately, Emily-Ann reckoned you wouldn't be able to park unless you owned a Porsche or a Lexus either. The group took seats outside a café on the corner, while Jack filmed them all looking as happy as could be. The huge white yachts were moored just a few metres away. A young Filipino girl was setting a table on the deck of one. She was wearing long white gloves.

'How pretentious,' said Emily-Ann, peering through her designer sunglasses.

'Yes indeed. I wouldn't like to be her,' agreed Nina. 'Working for people who made me wear gloves.'

'I wonder would the owners let us have a snoop around?' Graham wondered.

'I doubt it,' Richard said. 'It's not a tourist attraction.'

'But we could tell them we're Irish,' Graham pointed out. 'People always love it when you tell them you're Irish.'

'I bet they're not happy though,' Ciara said. 'The people who own the yacht.'

'I'd be happy if I owned it,' said Richard.

The waiter interrupted with their orders. Nina had ordered cake with her cup of coffee but the others had asked for mostly beers and glasses of wine. Jack kept his camera on them and then spent a bit of time filming the yachts to make everything seem more glamorous.

'I tend to agree with Ciara,' Caroline said. 'I worked as an au pair for a French couple who had a yacht. The man was so busy working though he didn't have time to use it. So it was harboured in Nice for most of the year. He used to pay someone to sail it to say, Monaco for the Grand Prix and he would then fly down for the night to stay in the yacht.'

'What about the wife? Couldn't she have used it?' somebody asked.

'Absolutely not,' Caroline shook her head firmly. 'He didn't trust her a bit.'

The villa was enveloped in darkness when they got back.

Richard was in a bad mood because he hadn't got to see Valderama. He'd heard so much about it and yet again he'd been down to the Costa and hadn't got to visit. But the others had been anxious to get back. Most anxious. They hadn't wanted to stop off at a golf course just for the sake of it. No. They wanted to get back to the villa, shower and change before heading out to Puerto Banus.

They were going to go for a meal first and then on to a nightclub. That was the plan. Somewhere cheap and cheerful with lots of people and lots of atmosphere. Richard was sulking because he didn't want to be going out just anywhere. Last time he'd been in Marbella he'd gone to the world famous Olivia's nightclub. He'd once seen Naomi Campbell drinking there. With a few of her buddies. And if it was good enough for supermodels, it was good enough for him.

Emily-Ann wouldn't have minded going to Olivia's to see if she could spot anyone interesting. But wasn't too keen to go just with Richard. No. That wouldn't have been too much fun. She wanted to stick with the others. But was panicking at the thought of going out for a meal though. She really couldn't afford to put on an extra few pounds – it would kill her. She said as much to Nina.

Nina looked at her in amazement. 'But you have to come out with us for a meal Emily-Ann. It's on the house.'

Emily-Ann looked at her with total disdain. 'That has nothing to do with it,' she said quite definitely. 'That has nothing to do with it at all.'

Eventually the group set off. The driver was to drop them off just before the turning into Puerto Banus.

But they were to make their own way home, he'd warned them.

Nina was a bit worried about that. 'We must all stick together,' she said.

'You must be joking,' Graham laughed. 'How can 14 people stick together?'

They went to Café Tomato, a cheerful Italian restaurant looking out on to the port. Emily-Ann ordered a tossed salad and spent most of the evening tossing it with her fork. She didn't want to be seen eating on camera. At least that's what she told the others. Bottle after bottle of wine was ordered. It was going down a treat.

The best thing about a place like this was being able to watch the people walking up and down the sea front. The beautiful people. All here to see and be seen.

It wasn't the type of place where you'd run along the street flying a kite or stagger about drinking your own cans of beer. God no. You had to strut along with your head held high.

Mind you it wasn't exactly beach weather either. It was like being out in Dublin at night in February or March.

Not very warm.

Cold actually.

Freezing.

People watching. It was fascinating. Of course here in Puerto Banus it was even more so. If you had a dog on a lead, it was just supposed to trot along obediently. Without growling. Without barking. And quite definitely without cocking its leg.

Caroline was amazed by it all. This parade of super human beings walking about, after midnight, pausing to look at the yachts, or the latest sports cars.

People with dogs on leashes. And children in prams.

Good children.

Children who didn't cry or yell.

They weren't like the toddlers back home in Dundalk. Yelling for ice cream. No. These were children straight out of Wonderland.

They could be seen and not heard.

Magical children.

Could you buy them somewhere around here?

Nina was happy. So deliriously happy. She'd never been in such a fun place before. All these people. Fun people. Walking around aimlessly. Looking into bars. To see if they could spot anyone. Interesting. And people in bars looking out. To see if they could spot anyone. More interesting.

Why did anyone ever leave a place like this? she wondered. How could you just leave it all and go home? To dreariness. If this was Puerto Banus in the winter, just think about what it'd be like in the summer! Walking around in a tank top eating ice cream. She wondered what Donal thought of all of this. She wondered what he was making of their weekend. He didn't seem to be getting too excited about anything on this trip. It was extraordinary. 'It's not real,' he'd said earlier on, 'This is not real life.'

'But it could be real life,' Nina had pointed out, 'If we won the house.'

'Nah,' Donal had kind of shook his head, more or less indicating that this whole thing wasn't really his cup of tea. 'I'd miss Ma and Da and the gang,' he said. 'And anyway there'd be nothing to do for them around here.'

'But that's ridiculous,' Nina had argued, 'They could come down for holidays. And play golf or something.'

'They wouldn't like it down here,' Donal had said firmly, 'All this posing and having to dress up all the time. It's not them. And they don't play golf. They'd rather be in Courtown having the craic in the pub with people they know. Not down here, you know, posing with people they don't know.'

Nina thought about it. Donal was very set in his ways. Wasn't it funny that he didn't want to 'better himself'?

Nina looked up at him. Her mother had always told her it was better if a man liked you a little bit more than you liked him. That made for a relatively stress-free life.

Donal liked her more than she liked him. Although she did like him an awful lot too. He said nice things to her. He said he saw a vulnerability in her that nobody else ever noticed. He said he liked the fact that she was honest and said whatever came into her head and loved the way that she was so unpretentious.

Nina wasn't sure if she agreed with all that he said. But at least he seemed to genuinely like her and that was much better than her having to chase a man around who wasn't at all interested. Or was carrying on with someone else behind your back.

But he didn't seem very keen to get married yet or anything. And that suited Nina. She was only twenty-six. She wouldn't be getting married for at least four years. She looked over at Donal whose cheeks had gone slightly red from drinking beer. Maybe he'd prefer to be in Torremolinos right now. That place they'd passed by in the bus, with all the high-rise buildings, where her sister had gone on her honeymoon and had the best fun ever. Herself and her husband Johnny had got drunk every night in the Irish pubs. Where people just off the plane sang 'The Wild Irish Rover' and 'The Green Green Grass of Home'. Every night. Where small family-owned Yorkshire pubs served cheap English beer and ran pub quizzes and had signs on doors saying 'Doris and Denis from Dorset extend a warm welcome'. Where live matches were shown after re-runs of *You've been Framed*. And tea and crumpets were a speciality.

Nina wondered if Donal would prefer to be in a place like that.

With 'the gang'.

After dessert, the group left the restaurant and split up.

The divorcees were heading home to ring their beloved children.

Leanna decided to share their taxi home with them as did Mrs Oz.

Emily-Ann decided she wanted to pop into Emporio Armani and also check out the Moschino shop at the end of the street too.

The rest of the group decided to wander about
with all the other beautiful people and see if they
could get a few drinks somewhere. Jack called it a
night. Said he'd enough footage now to keep the
producers happy. Richard said Emily-Ann could
meet them later in Café Banus.

Caroline followed the others as they headed around
the corner. Richard was anxious to take a look at the
biggest yachts on the harbour. They were moored up
near the massive Benabola complex. She wondered
if she'd imagined everything from the night before.
The goings on between Richard and Emily-Ann.
Emily-Ann seemed to have zero interest in Richard
and had been quite content to go off shopping by
herself.

   They walked along the pier. It was bitterly cold
now. Every now and again the crowd of strollers
had to part to make way for some gaudy sports car
with a big cigar-puffing sugar daddy sighing behind
the wheel. Caroline thought it was hilarious. Some
of the sugar daddys would be shouting into their
mobiles even though it was nearly 11:00. Who were
they talking to? And why, if they were in a hurry,
did they decide to drive into a crowd of leisurely
strollers, instead of just sticking to the main road?
Ah . . . men and their toys.

   They reached the end of the port. And stared at the
huge fuck-off three-storey boat with its helicopter
pad. It was like a small hotel. Two men wearing

sunglasses stood on the top deck. Looking down. At the on-lookers. Looking up.

A huge German flag flapped in the slight breeze. In fact, Caroline noted, many of the boats bore German flags or British flags. There were no Irish flags. It made her feel sad. If she ever won the lottery she thought, she'd get a boat just like this, with a massive green, white and orange flag. And moor it here.

They sat in Café Banus because it was too cold to stand outside. Richard said that in the summer months everyone usually drank on the street outside. Caroline thought that must be great 'cos you'd get to talk to a lot more people that way. When you were in a pub you kind of got stuck talking to the same crowd of people. And that kind of defeated the purpose of 'going out' didn't it?

She looked around the pub. There were a lot of Scandinavian types here and older people too. Well-dressed people. No lager louts. 'If you go to the street behind,' Richard pointed out, 'you have 'Linekars' and there's some Irish pub there too. You get more crowds of young lads there but it's not my scene.'

Caroline hoped they'd go to a few more places before heading home. This place was very nice but she didn't fancy sitting in the same seat all night. It was never as much fun just sitting down.

Suddenly Emily-Ann burst into the bar, laden with shopping bags.

'That was quick,' Nina said, surprised.

'Yeah,' Emily-Ann beamed, her eyes shining, 'that's the best thing about boutiques. You see exactly what you want and don't have to be messing around trying loads of stuff on.'

Nina looked at her incredulously. God, what was the point of shopping if you couldn't try everything on? Sure you'd only be cheating yourself out of hours of entertainment!

She was dying for a look at Emily-Ann's purchases all the same. Emily-Ann was only too happy to oblige. 'If you don't mind me asking,' Nina quizzed her, 'How much did you pay for all that.'

'Oh it wasn't too bad,' Emily-Ann smiled. 'Just under €2,000.'

Nina nearly dropped her Bacardi and Coke with shock. €2,000. Good holy mother of God! How could she justify it? Sure that would pay for groceries for a year. She unsuccessfully scanned Emily-Ann's face for signs of guilt. Emily-Ann was thrilled with her purchases though and wasn't about to let anybody pop her balloon. Nina felt ill at the thought of spending all that money. She remembered the day her father, a labourer, had come home with nothing in his pocket, having failed to find anyone willing to pay him for a day's work. You never forgot things like that . . .

'That wasn't too bad, I suppose,' Graham agreed with Emily-Ann. 'I mean the stuff is gorgeous. At home, you'd pay that for a coat in BTs.'

Nina's head was reeling. Good God, did these

people have no idea how hard it was to earn money? She wouldn't spend that kind of money on a car! Why did people spend that kind of money on clothes? It was outrageous. Sure you could get the exact same clothes in the chain stores for a fraction of the price and nobody would know the difference. She peered at a delicate red jumper Emily-Ann had purchased in Emporio Armani. Yes, it was lovely, but nobody would even know that you'd bought it in Emporio Armani. If Nina bought a jumper there, she'd at least want ARMANI printed in big bold letters across the front.

'I don't know how you can be so extravagant,' she said to Emily-Ann, 'When there's people starving all over the world.'

'People starving?' Emily-Ann's eyes flashed indignantly at her. 'What on earth are you talking about you silly girl?'

Nina reddened slightly. 'I just think it's too much money to spend, that's all.'

'I object to those kind of accusations,' Emily-Ann said firmly. 'I don't spend much at all but I do buy quality. This stuff,' she motioned to the bags, 'will last me ages. It's better than buying a cheap nasty top every week that disintegrates in the wash. I've seen people in shops buying new things every week. They never get out of the poverty trap. I, on the other hand, only buy things I need.'

'And do you really need all those things?' Donal asked quietly.

'Yes,' she replied. 'I do. I need to look well dressed if I want to get on in life. People judge you by the way you look. It's not a rule I made-up. I'm not saying whether it's right or wrong. It's just the way it is.'

'But you seem so privileged,' Nina said.

'Yes, well I get to drive my mum's car when she's not using it and I have a lovely bedroom in my parents' house. But I have no house of my own and I usually get the bus everywhere. So please,' she looked around the small group, 'do not make judgement on me by what you see or by what I buy because none of you really know me at all.'

God, I think I've died and gone to heaven,' Graham said, chewing his straw with a wounded look on his face.

'Hey, I saw him first,' Emily-Ann slammed her drink down on the table. A god had just made his way into the bar. Tall, blond, with turquoise eyes, wearing blue jeans, a well-cut navy blazer and a crisp-white shirt, he looked like he'd just stepped off a Calvin Klein catalogue. Nina craned her neck for a look. 'Which one are you talking about?'

'He's not that fantastic,' said the Australian.

The Cork couple agreed. As did Richard. Richard didn't think anyone was great. Except himself. And he didn't like the way Emily-Ann was eyeing up every man in the place. Had last night meant nothing?

*   *   *

Emily-Ann let Richard sulk. He wasn't the most exciting person in the world. And was too old for her anyway. Her eyes scoured the room to see where the blond guy had disappeared. He seemed to be looking for a stool. Emily-Ann grabbed her chance. She motioned to the stool next to her. 'This one's free,' she winked at him.

'That's Lipsy's stool,' Nina reminded her. 'She'll be furious when she gets back.'

'Lipsy's gone *home*,' Emily-Ann snapped. 'Did you not even notice?'

The couple from Cork were fading fast. Too much excitement for one day, they said. Richard and the Aussie were anxious to check out a few more bars. Donal was yawning. He wanted to go back to the villa and get some kip.

Nina hummed and hawed. She didn't want to be stuck here alone with Graham and Caroline. Emily-Ann had left the bar at frightening speed with the blond guy. And nobody expected to see her again before dawn. Nina didn't particularly want to be gallivanting around Puerto Banus with the lads. She wondered what she should do.

Donal made up her mind for her. 'Stay on,' he urged her. 'I'm just whacked, but why shouldn't you stay on and have fun?'

'Right ok,' Nina said doubtfully. *Was he trying to get rid of her?*

Richard brought them to a club around the

corner. They mounted the steps and entered the club. There was no door charge, Nina noted with a sigh of relief. Richard bought the drinks and kept the receipt for the TV show.

The Aussie was next to head off. 'Are you tired?' Nina asked him sympathetically.

'Tired?' he looked amazed. 'Not me mate, I'm off to find some action.'

He was gone.

Graham had disappeared too.

'I'm worried about him,' Nina confided to Richard who was goggle-eyed at this stage.

'Worried about Graham?' Richard snorted with laughter. 'Who do you think you are Nina? Mary Bloody Poppins?'

'Don't mind him,' Caroline said kindly. She was yawning herself now. 'I'm sure Graham knows exactly what he's doing.'

'And Emily-Ann?'

'Likewise.'

Caroline decided to leave with Donal.

That left just Richard and Nina.

'Come on,' Richard grabbed her hand playfully once the others had gone. 'Let's get down to some serious partying now.'

They met Mr Oz on the street. He'd hooked up with some fellow Aussies and was going to a beach party with them. Nina thought he mentioned something about grass. It was probably a picnic or something. A midnight picnic! What fun!

Richard dragged her away. God, these country girls hadn't a clue.

He brought her to a pub/disco with wooden floors and wooden beams and a throng of people dancing (not very well) to the pounding music. Emily-Ann was there. She introduced her new 'friend' Ollie. He spoke with an accent you could cut glass with. Nina reckoned he must be very posh altogether. Maybe he even had a title. Lord somebody. Like in the pictures at the back of *Tatler* magazine.

Richard wasn't very friendly towards Ollie. But Emily-Ann didn't seem to even notice. She whisked Ollie away after wishing the others good-night. Richard got a couple of vodkas and Red Bull at the bar. 'Get this into you,' he handed Nina hers.

'Thanks,' she muttered and took a sip. God it was strong. Very strong. She was beginning to feel shamefully drunk and her head was beginning to spin. She hoped she wasn't going to do something stupid. Like fall over.

She was enjoying herself. Really enjoying herself. She hadn't had this much fun in ages. She just wanted to keep drinking and dancing forever. What a happy place this was. Everyone was having fun. It was like an ongoing party. She never wanted to go home.

Ever.

Richard was dancing. Nina took a seat and watched him, laughing to herself. At first she'd thought he was a real prick but now she'd almost begun to like him. He was a real party animal. All that energy. And he was good-looking. Caroline didn't really deserve him, did she? She never laughed at his jokes or showed him any kind of affection off camera. Nina just couldn't see why they were together at all. Richard was twirling some girl around on the dance floor. Nina didn't really like the look of her. She was wearing one of those belly tops best reserved for seventeen year olds with smooth stomachs. This girl's belly was hanging over her hipsters in a most unbecoming way. She was wiggling her hips in a most provocative manner. Shaking her long curly-blonde hair and shoving her breasts in Richard's face. Nina was shocked. Had she no shame? Carrying on in front of a stranger like that?

She saw Richard excuse himself and wander over in the direction of the gents. She knocked back her vodka and Red Bull. Her vision was a bit funny now. She felt like she was wearing someone else's glasses.

That's why she didn't really take much notice when the girl in the belly top and hipsters came marching towards her.

The girl put her hands on her hips. 'What is the story between you and that bloke?' she demanded. God, she was scarier than Scary Spice.

Nina swallowed. 'Richard?'

'That's the one, yeah. He's not your boyfriend is he?'

Nina shook her head vehemently.

'Then HANDS OFF, d'ya hear me?'

'Now listen here,' Nina said crossly. 'I am not interested in Richard. He is just a friend.'

'Well if he's just a friend, why don't you be a friend and sod off?'

Richard was back. The belly-buttoned monster from hell suddenly broke into a huge smile. 'I was just introducing myself to your friend Richard.'

Nina looked at her in amazement. The cheeky tart! The nightclub was closing up and the gruesome twosome were insisting on getting kebabs at the little kebab shop at the end of the steps. Nina followed them down the steps, feeling like a complete tool. She didn't know what Richard was playing at. She hoped he wasn't going to invite this common little hussy back to the villa. Why didn't he just tell her to get lost?

Richard and herself took a stool as the belly-pierced one queued for kebabs. Nina could feel her eyes closing. She wasn't feeling so happy anymore. This was no longer any fun. She yearned to be back in the villa now tucked up in bed.

'If this was summer now, we could go for a swim,' Richard told her lighting a cigarette. 'Last summer I remember going for a swim at around 8:00 in the morning. Straight from the nightclub into the sea. At one stage I looked up and people were having breakfast on their balconies. Looking so civilised. It made me think I was really insane splashing around in the water, not having gone home to bed.'

Nina was too tired to answer or even care about

Richard's so called mad adventures. She closed her eyes and wished the girl would hurry up with Richard's kebab so they could get going.

'€30 for a blow job? Fuck off.'

Nina swung around in shock, wide awake now. Beside her was a 20 stone tattoed Englishman wearing a tight orange T-shirt and a gold hoop in his left ear. He was wolfing into a kebab, spilling ketchup and mayonnaise onto his fingers. A young black girl seemed to be haggling with him. Nina was stunned. God . . . was she . . . was she a . . . ?

'Did you hear that?' She whispered to Richard.

'Hear what?' Richard said in a loud voice.

Nina was mortified. She didn't want to be drawing attention to herself. Like she'd been listening in on somebody's conversation or anything.

She repeated what she'd heard very quietly.

Richard looked at her very oddly. 'Nina, I always thought you were naïve but now you're taking the piss. Of course she's a bloody prostitute. Puerto Banus is swarming with them.'

'Wh . . . at?'

'Ah Nina, come off it. What did you think this place was? Happy ever after land?'

'But . . .' Nina was almost too stunned to speak.

Richard's new 'friend' was back with the kebab.

'But I don't understand,' Donal shook his head. 'I mean what did you do? Did you just sit there watching them?'

'Of course I didn't watch them,' Nina sounded hurt. 'What do you think I am?'

'So you just waited until they were finished snogging?'

'Yeah,' Nina's head was pounding. She felt such a fool for staying out so late, depriving herself of a decent night's sleep. The last thing she needed now was 20 annoying questions.

'I don't get it,' Donal continued to shake his head. 'Why didn't you just get a taxi back?'

'I wasn't sure of the right address,' Nina sighed. 'Now will you please just drop it? And anyway, they were just snogging and not even for very long. It's not like they were having full blown sex in the street or anything.'

'So what are you going to tell Caroline?'

Nina shrugged. 'It's not up to me to tell her anything.'

Graham was soaking in the jacuzzi. Ah yes, this was really was the life. He was just going to enjoy one last glass of champers before getting ready to leave for the airport. It was sad in a way to be leaving this place. He'd never win the villa. He was realistic about that. There was no way in hell the public was going to fall for himself and Emily-Ann. And anyway, even if they won and people found out afterwards, they'd surely be disqualified. Ah well, he thought resting his head against the side of the bubble-filled bath, it had been worth it for the holiday alone. Definitely.

A knock on the door startled him. 'It's Emily-Ann, can I come in?'

'Sure baby,' Graham called.

Emily-Ann walked in looking like she'd just stepped off the cover of *Vogue*. *Bitch*.

'How do you do it?' Graham cried accusingly. 'That's two nights without sleep. How do you do it? It's so unfair.'

'Listen, I don't have time to fill you in,' said Emily-Ann, 'I'm taking a taxi to El Corte Ingles to get a few bits and bobs so if I'm a little late back just tell the driver not to be panicking ok?'

She vanished.

Nobody was too pleased to see Jack get on the bus with his camera. Especially not Emily-Ann. 'Get that thing away from me,' she threatened covering her face with her many shopping bags. She was fit to collapse. But it had been so worth it. Everything. Meeting Ollie. Shopping in El Corte Ingles where she'd bought up half the Burberry section. So what if Nina thought she was extravagant? It was her money and she had earned it. She was sorry to be leaving this place and going back home. She'd miss it. The sun. Everything. This holiday had been the best ever. And she was determined to come back again. The sooner the better.

Chapter Fifty-Eight

Back in Ireland.

Voting time.

The worst time.

In Caroline's life.

Ever.

She so badly wanted the house now.

Didn't want to feel that this had all been for nothing. The humiliation of putting up with Richard. And him disgracing her in Puerto Banus like that. It had been terrible. What with all the other couples whispering behind her back and feeling sorry for her.

She'd thought it couldn't have got any worse.

But it had. And now she hated Richard more than ever.

He had no respect for any living thing.

She felt nauseous. They (all the couples) had to sit in a room while the votes were being counted. Richard seemed very confident of not being voted out. He'd been busy getting everyone he knew to vote for himself and Caroline. Even Caroline's own mother had been practically out canvassing on people's doorsteps. The politicians had nothing on her.

And her brother John had posted VOTE CARO-LINE AND RICHARD posters in all the local pubs in Co. Louth.

The temperature in the studio 'waiting room' was steadily dropping. Nervous hostile glances were being exchanged, short stiff snippets of conversation overheard.

This was torture.

Even more painful was the fact that the cameras were on them. All the time. Waiting for the contestants to slip up. Richard's arm weighed a ton around Caroline's shivering shoulder. This was worse than waiting for the results of your Leaving Cert or an operation.

Ronan dropped in every now and then to make sure his protégées were okay. Every time he did, Caroline felt like running to him and burying her head in his chest. Maybe it was because she was feeling so unloved at the moment. Her morale had hit rock bottom.

But Ronan showed neither affection nor favouritism. Sometimes though, she did feel his eyes on her. And it was the most wonderful feeling when sometimes they exchanged secretive looks.

It made her feel safe.

And desired.

But behind Caroline's carefully put together image,

was a less confident woman. Being on camera and going home to watch yourself on screen in the evenings was like being naked most of the time. There didn't seem to be a place to hide. Never again, she promised herself quietly, would she ever do anything like this again.

Finally it was time for the dreaded eviction. The couples were escorted out of the waiting room and had to form a long panel. The cameras scrutinised their faces for signs of fear. Caroline refused to succumb. Her smile might as well have been glued to her face. She wondered if this was the way Oscar nominees felt when the spotlight was on them. The whole world watching . . . to see their reactions . . . when they lost.

Their dreams shattered.

Mikey Mark stepped forward with his little envelope. He was enjoying every moment of this. Caroline was sitting beside Emily-Ann and noticed her knuckles go white under the fake tan.

Mikey Mark scanned the panel; a slow seedy smile spread across his face. *Get on with it, would you?* Caroline urged silently.

'Annie and Roger, you are the unhappiest couple in Ireland. Goodbye.'

The two divorcees stood up and left the panel.

So Catholic Ireland isn't dead and gone, thought Caroline, breathing a short sigh of relief.

Chapter Fifty-Nine

Sandra sat in her bedroom watching the TV alone.

The show, although still in its early stages, was already a massive hit with the Irish public. Richard and Caroline had done interviews with most of the Sunday newspapers and magazines. The *Dublin Daily* wanted them to grace their cover. *Ireland AM* had also called them in for a brief chat. Nobody could have predicted such a frenzy.

Least of all Sandra.

'It's getting out of hand,' she told herself as she sipped on a glass of wine. The editor of yet another well-known woman's magazine had phoned looking for an 'exclusive' with Ireland's sexiest man. Sandra had told her she'd got the wrong number.

How long more was she going to put up with this? Why should she be the one sitting in like a bloody recluse while Richard and Caroline were carrying on like superstars? She wasn't the one lying to people. It wasn't right. No. It wasn't at all right. She ran a sweaty hand through her hair. What would happen when the media found out? It was bound to happen. Sooner or later.

Deirdre rang in the morning with the news.

'It's on the front page of *The Irish Sun*,' she screeched. 'A huge picture of Caroline and Richard. Go out and buy it, I swear they've got the entire front page!'

'What's the headline?' Sandra asked faintly, clutching her mobile. She felt ill.

'THE HAPPIEST LOVE OF ALL' it says in huge writing, 'I think this is a disgrace Sandra. What happens when everybody finds out you're pregnant? You've got to tell people sooner or later. Do your parents know? I've a good mind to ring up the radio stations as an anonymous caller and tell them the truth.'

'Don't you bloody dare,' Sandra warned her friend. 'These things have a habit of getting out of hand. The last thing I need is photographers hanging about in the hedges. Yeah, my parents know. Of course they do. I'm bloody huge now. And yes, before you ask, they're devastated. The last thing I need is to upset them even more.'

'But what are you going to do? The whole damn country is talking about that pair. I still can't believe you agreed for them to do it.'

'Excuse me, I *never* agreed to any of this. How do you think this whole mess makes me feel?'

'But someone's going to ask you about it any day now. You do know that don't you? It's inevitable.'

'Yeah but it was a pre-recorded show and there was nothing I could do about it.'

'There's only so long you can keep that story up San, the Christmas episodes will be aired soon. It'll be obvious then.'

'I know, I know,' Sandra said irritably, 'Don't worry about me though. I've got a plan.'

'What kind of plan?'

'I can't tell you now . . . but it involves an old photo I came across recently.'

'I hope for your sake that it's a good one,' said Deirdre.

It is a good one, Sandra thought putting down the phone. *Oh, it's a good one all right.*

Chapter Sixty

Good press coverage is often followed by not so good. And so it was something of a tumbling blow when Graham's real partner Barney sold out to *The News on Sunday*. Emily-Ann was devastated, crying buckets as she realised it was all over.

Her dream was now shattered.

And the Marbella house, with its pool, sauna, jacuzzi and spectacular views of the Mediterranean was now just a distant dream.

Unbelievably though, herself and Graham were not the next couple voted out.

Graham had amassed a huge army of fans at this stage.

Young male fans.

And they kept the phone lines hopping.

Plenty of the young and indeed not so young Irish male population, and teeny boppers of each sex, continued to vote to keep Graham in the show. His shiny-bronzed torso was proving to be quite an audience puller.

Every day the ratings rose. And the couples had to

take part in everything from line-dancing to reading each other romantic poetry on air. To say the show was tacky was an understatement. Yes it was tacky; tacky but addictive.

The viewers, sick to the teeth of Mrs Cork's endless opera crooning, voted herself and Mr Cork off.

The following day the lesbians were given the red card. And were immediately signed up to present a controversial *Late night loving with Lipsy and Leanne* show.

The Australians, Emily-Ann and Graham, Nina and Donal and Richard and Caroline made it to the final round.

And then things really began to hot up.

Public debate raged. From fitness centres to factories, pubs to playgroups. Keep 'em in or out? What's your opinion?

Offers were rolling in.

Caroline secured a part in a television detergent ad for an undisclosed sum. Richard was offered a year's supply of goods from a major DIY store. Emily-Ann was to be the new 'face' of a footwear range and a boyband manager was very anxious to get in touch with Graham.

The Australians had been offered to front a different kind of travel show, entailing trips to nudist beaches all around the world.

But nobody had got the house yet.

Tele-Fone workers were accosted by the paparazzi

coming out of work. What kind of a girl was Caroline in the work place? Could they dish anything on her?

'She's an attention seeker,' Mad Maureen was pictured with a sour face.

'She doesn't really mix,' said Lazy Luke.

Not with you I don't, thought Caroline indignantly as she flicked through the tabloids.

Emily-Ann's friend Celine, said she was a 'vain' girl at times but they were the best of friends anyway.

'*Like hell we are*,' Emily-Ann growled.

Great Gardeners of Ireland said she was their 'spokeswoman' and released countless photos, keen to cash in on all the free publicity.

And then the shit really hit the fan.

Apparently the Australian police were looking for the Australian couple. Nothing too serious. But an unpaid debt and a string of forgotten court appearances Down Under had emerged.

The couple were forced to quit the show.

Under a dark cloud.

Some said they should never have been in the show anyway because they weren't Irish and the show was supposed to be about the happiest couple in Ireland. Others said it was supposed to be about the happiest couple living in Ireland and not necessarily the happiest Irish couple. Others then argued, that if that were the case, the show would be full of Chinese students as they were the only ones who walked about holding hands all day.

By and large, everybody had an opinion. From taxi drivers to cleaners, school kids to office clerks, the whole country was talking about them.

That just left Caroline and Richard, Emily-Ann and Graham, Nina and Donal.

Everybody said it was a no-contest win.

Emily-Ann and Graham were just eye candy for the show anyway.

It was obvious.

And the viewers were getting heartily sick of Nina.

Donal was popular enough.

But Richard and Caroline were going to walk the prize.

Everyone said so.

It was now only two days before the final vote.

Chapter Sixty-One

Caroline looked at her watch. It was nearly 7:00. She was supposed to be going out to the opening of a new office block. Her new-founded celebrity status meant she got invited to a ton of things these days. Some construction company were paying her a ridiculous amount just to cut a piece of ribbon. This whole celebrity business was becoming crazy. Sure just earlier this afternoon, she'd popped out to the post box and a group of school kids had started chanting 'Go Caroline' and clapping. Why?

She thought she'd stop at the nursing home and say hello to Maggie, who was suffering from the 'flu. And no wonder, the place was so bloody damp. The nuns were forever turning off the heating.

She walked down the dark dreary corridor to Maggie's room.

Pushing the door open, she popped her head around. 'How ya Maggie?' she smiled.

'How's the film star?' Maggie smiled. She didn't look well. The women living in this home never got a decent blast of fresh air. It was a crying shame. Caroline asked her how she was feeling.

'I'm grand, not a bother,' Maggie said weakly. 'Did you have a nice time in Spain? I saw you on the telly, so I did.'

'I had a nice time,' Caroline said untruthfully, 'but it wasn't very relaxing. I'll tell you about it again properly. I've to go now, but I'll pop in again in a few days to see how you're getting on.'

God love Maggie, Caroline thought as she blow-dried her hair later on. She wished there was something she could do for that woman. And all the other women in the home. People who'd never got a fair crack at life. Caroline felt almost guilty about going out schmoozing with people while poor old Maggie just lay in a dark room staring at the ceiling.

She looked in the mirror. Now, all she had to do was put on her party dress and paint a fake smile on her lips. At half past seven she gave herself a final nod of approval. She liked the long dark-green chiffon dress she'd chosen to wear for tonight.

There was a slight knock on the front door. It was so slight, Caroline wondered if it was the telly. She walked to the door, humming lightly, and gently opened it. But as she opened the door fully, the humming died to silence.

Sandra was standing there.

Like a ghost from her past.

Caroline was speechless. She just stood and stared at her ex-best friend. At the woman who had tried to ruin her life. At least change it anyway . . . forever. What in God's name was she doing here? How had she the nerve to show her face?

Then suddenly everything seemed to fall into place.

She was here to get Richard back.

That was it.

She was here to warn Caroline off.

Of course she was.

What came around, went around.

Wasn't it funny?

Well Sandra could have him back now for all she cared.

'What do you want?' Caroline spoke first.

'To talk,' Sandra said and Caroline noticed she was trembling.

'I've nothing to say to you and I'm late for a function.'

'You look very nice,' Sandra told her nervously. 'Listen, this will only take five minutes.'

'It'd better not take a minute more than that,' Caroline said and stepped aside to let her ex-best friend inside.

Sandra sat down awkwardly on Caroline's sofa. 'Has Richard really proposed? I read it in the papers,' she asked bluntly.

Caroline folded her arms. 'He might have,' she said cagily.

'And he's decided you're the one after all?'

'He says he made a mistake. But don't worry. I wouldn't want him back.'

'I don't blame you,' Sandra looked at her hands. 'I left him Caroline.'

'Did you?'

'He was unfaithful to me,' Sandra continued. 'At least twice.'

'Go on.'

'I didn't want to believe it but . . .'

'Is that all you want to say?' Caroline interrupted looking at her watch, 'Because as I said, I'm on my way out.'

'That's all.' Sandra stood up. 'I just thought I should let you know. I take absolutely no pleasure in telling you. It wasn't easy for me to come here this evening you know.'

Sandra moved towards the door. Then stopped. 'I'm extremely sorry about everything,' she said. She looked like she was on the verge of tears. 'I often think I must be the world's most horrible hateful person.'

'Well, what's done is done,' Caroline said without emotion. 'And if you ever meet anyone else, I hope for your sake that some girl doesn't go after him like you went after my man.'

'I'm desperately sorry,' Sandra repeated. 'I really am but I've learned my lesson now. I'm on my own now. I'm going to set up my own business to support myself – a children's clothes shop.'

'What about the kid?' Caroline asked though it nearly killed her to mention it.

'The baby will be fine.' Sandra said slowly, 'It has a mummy who will love it and hopefully a daddy that can be mature about all of this . . . well I'll be off then. I hope one day the two of us can be friends again.'

'Thank you Sandra,' Caroline said, 'But I don't really think that's going to happen. I do appreciate you calling around though. And thanks for the tip-off about Richard. It makes a lot of sense.'

Sandra paused on the doorstep. 'So you're not going to go back with him?'

Caroline shook her head. 'I wouldn't go back to that prick if he was the last man alive. He was my Mr Wrong if ever I had one.'

Chapter Sixty-Two

She poured herself a vodka, a double. Good God, for one who never sought drama, Caroline certainly ended up with more than her fair share of it. Sandra must have felt very strongly about the whole thing to show up here this evening. The girl had looked like she was on the verge of a nervous breakdown!

And now she had to go to this damn office-opening and face members of the press and public. It was almost more than she could bear. If only Ronan was going along with her it wouldn't be half as unbearable. But there was no sign of him anywhere. No sign of him at all. She wondered where he was. She couldn't wait for this whole TV show to be over with. The press intrusion was getting to her. At this stage she cared less and less about getting the damn house.

She decided to give Ronan's mobile a ring.

The sound of his voice might at least manage to cheer her up.

A strange female voice answered straight away. 'Ronan Dexter's phone?'

Caroline hung up. What the hell . . . ?

A key sounded in the door, making Caroline jump.

Verda appeared.

'Oh hello celebrity,' she said, looking surprised to see Caroline. 'Are you going out?'

Caroline took another gulp of her vodka. 'Yeah I am,' she said quietly.

'You don't sound too excited.'

'Verda?' Caroline looked up. 'Have you seen Ronan recently?'

'Sure,' Verda said flippantly removing her fake-fur coat. 'He was here earlier on with some bird. Very pretty girl. About six months pregnant I reckon. He kept that very quiet eh?'

Ronan drove up to the entrance of the new office block. He was feeling uneasy about the whole publicity thing. It was beginning to get out of hand. He hoped Caroline could handle it. True, she was a well-poised articulate girl, but Ronan had been in this business a lot longer than her and knew only too well how the media could turn on you when you least expected.

Maybe he was worrying unnecessarily though.

Hopefully this was the case.

He didn't want Caroline to suffer any unnecessary stress. The last few days seemed to have taken its toll on her and she was beginning to look worn out.

He didn't trust Richard at all.

Bloody egomaniac.

He'd stop at nothing to get his hands on the house.

People like Richard sold their souls for publicity.

Ronan wandered in to the hall. Caroline wasn't too hard to spot. Surrounded by members of the media, she was smiling graciously, answering questions and shaking hands.

Ronan caught her eye but she seemed to blank him.

Or maybe he just imagined it.

'It's almost D-Day for yourself and Richard,' one hack said. 'Any nerves yet or is it already "in the bag" do you think?'

Caroline forced a smile. 'I don't think you should ever be too cocky in a game like this. Anything could still happen,' she said.

'Is there any advice you'd like to give to other couples?' asked another one. 'Couples say, that aren't as happy as yourself and Richard?'

Ronan stepped forward slightly protectively.

Questions like this were loaded.

'I think people should always be themselves,' Caroline said lightly. 'I mean, what works for some couples might not work for every couple you know? You have to work at a relationship. And you have to communicate.'

'Did you know from the start about Graham's sexuality?' One pushy female hack pushed a microphone into Caroline's face.

She cleared her throat and looked momentarily at ease. Suddenly Ronan felt an urge to take her hand and drag her away from all these people. She didn't need this. Not now.

'I judged Graham on his personality, not on anything else,' Caroline said firmly. 'Graham is a really lovely guy.'

She stepped down from the small 'specially erected' podium. 'Thank you very much,' she beamed at the small group of press.

'Just one last question,' somebody said. Ronan turned. Oh Jesus. How the hell did he get in here? Standing right next to him was one of the Sunday rags most cunning dirt-dishers.

'That's it, question time over,' Ronan made way for Caroline to escape. But too late. The guy's hand firmly grasped Caroline's wrist.

'One last question,' he repeated. 'How do you feel about Richard's impending love child?'

Caroline froze. The colour drained from her face. Horror became reality.

'No more questions,' Ronan insisted.

'Who the hell are you?'

Ronan grabbed Caroline's hand and pulled her away as the small crowd watched in astonishment.

They left the building.

At frightening speed.

Chapter Sixty-Three

'Oh God, that's it now, isn't it? It's all over Ronan isn't it?'

'Don't worry about it,' Ronan said gently as he squeezed her hand as they stopped at a set of traffic lights. 'You did fine in there.'

'I did fine?' Caroline was almost hysterical. 'I did fine? You are having me on aren't you? This time tomorrow I'll be the laughing-stock of the country and you're telling me everything will be fine?'

'Listen don't be thinking like that now.'

But Caroline was practically on the verge of tears. 'I'm not going back on the show tomorrow,' she was adamant, 'I swear to God, Ronan, this whole fiasco has been the worst thing that's ever happened to me.'

'Caroline, a lot of people must have known about Richard and Sandra anyway,' Ronan pointed out. 'Dublin's a small place.'

'But this is so different,' Caroline said quietly. 'From now on everywhere I go, people will be pointing and going "there's that clown from the telly, you know, the one who's fella was cheating on her".'

'Don't be so paranoid Caroline.'

'I've every right to be paranoid,' she said miserably. 'And you're right about Dublin being a small place. In fact it's smaller than you think. Verda told me you were round earlier with another woman.'

Ronan shook his head silently. Word really did travel fast in this town, didn't it?

'Did you want to introduce me to her?' Caroline said with a heavy heart. 'Is that why you called? After all I'm used to being let down aren't I? You probably thought I'd be able to cope with your good news.'

Ronan waited for her to calm down. He slowed down the car and pulled into the side of the road. 'Listen to me Caroline, that was Amy.'

'Lovely. And if it's a girl are you going to name it after Amy?'

Ronan grimaced. 'Amy is the girl I went out with in the States. I told you all about her Caroline. I've never kept anything from you.'

Suddenly Caroline's mobile rang. Richard's number was flashing. 'Hello?'

'Caroline, listen I'm at my parents' house at the moment. They're away on holidays, thank God. Listen I really need to talk to you. We've got to meet.'

'Right okay,' Caroline sighed. She turned towards Ronan. 'Can you drive me to Richard's parents' house?' she asked him wearily.

Ronan reluctantly did as he was told. But it seemed that the press had got there first. Photographers were hanging around the gate, lenses at the ready. Ronan did a swift U-turn. Caroline rang Richard as they sped away.

'Jesus Caroline, this is fucking insane,' he said, 'They're camping out here. I can't move. What did you tell them?'

'I didn't tell them anything,' she protested, 'What kind of person do you take me for?'

'Where are you going now?'

'I'm going home,' she told him, 'I can't go any-where else.'

'To Dundalk?'

'No, to Sandymount.'

'Remember you're vulnerable tonight Caro,' Richard said in a much gentler tone of voice. 'Don't let anybody take advantage of that.'

'Richard,' Caroline told him. 'The only person who has ever taken advantage of me, is you. Now, for ONCE in your life, would you ever PISS off?'

'So what did he have to say?' asked Ronan once they got inside.

Caroline told him the truth.

Ronan almost laughed when he heard. 'People taking advantage of you? That's rich coming from him. Anyway, it's really none of his business what you do.'

Caroline let it go. It was late. And besides she was

too drained to have a normal conversation. 'I'd like to go to bed,' she said.

'Okay,' he smiled, 'I'll see you in the morning.'

'Right,' she said. And stood up. Her heart was somewhere around her ankles.

Ronan stood in the doorway. 'Is there anything else I can do?'

'Yes,' she said unhappily, 'You can tell me why Amy was in this house this afternoon.'

Ronan looked hurt by her accusing tone of voice. 'Listen Caroline, the reason Amy was here is because she owns this house too. We bought it together. We were going to live here. But now we're going to sell it.'

Caroline's head was spinning. She felt awful for jumping to conclusions but the strain of the show was getting to her.

Ronan reached out to her. 'Come on now, this will all blow over. Here, let me give you a big hug. Everything's going to be okay.'

But Caroline shook her head.

She didn't need a hug.

Not now.

Her heart was snapping.

Her emotions were running riot.

She didn't need sympathy at all.

She needed love.

Not sympathy.

She wanted to be kissed passionately.

Not hugged like a teddy bear.

Failing that she wanted to be left alone.
That would be nice
Yes, that would be very nice.

Chapter Sixty-Four

In the morning, Caroline wandered into the kitchen, wearing a T-shirt to her knees. She was feeling bad. There'd been no need to snap at Ronan the way she had done. It wasn't his all fault. None of this was. This was all Richard's fault. A living nightmare that just never seemed to end.

Caroline was surprised to see a tall dark man, probably in his early thirties, making himself a cup of tea in the corner.

'Hello,' she said with an air of confusion.

'Hello,' he answered back hesitantly.

She wondered what he was doing here.

'Hi, I'm Mike,' he took a step towards her and proffered a handshake, 'I'm a huge fan of the show by the way.'

'Right,' she said warily. Who on earth was this guy?

'I'm a friend of Josie's,' he said, sensing her confusion.

'Indeed?'

'Listen I hate to bother you and everything but is there anyway you'd sign this for me?' He thrust a newspaper cutting in front of her.

Josie appeared from nowhere. 'Mike, would you stop that and leave the poor girl alone.'

Mike looked crestfallen. 'But it's not for me, it's for Ellie.'

He turned towards Caroline. 'My little sister's in hospital. She's been glued to the telly. She absolutely loves you.'

'Well thank you, that's a compliment.' Caroline smiled at him. She took the photo and wrote *Hope you get better Ellie, love Caroline*.

She smiled at Josie who looked mortified. 'Listen relax you,' she said kindly, 'I'm not Nelson Mandela or the Pope. Honestly it's very flattering.'

'I was listening to the radio this morning. Sorry to hear about your bad luck,' Mike said awkwardly.

'On the radio?' Caroline groaned. 'Oh God, I don't believe it, I really don't believe it.'

'Ah well these things happen. Listen everybody in County Clare will vote for you. I'll make sure of that. Tea?'

'Oh yes please,' Caroline nodded gratefully. 'And make it strong, won't you?'

He was a nice fella, Caroline thought. She wondered how he'd hooked up with Josie. Was he the man she was always rushing home to visit? She'd ask her about him later. At the moment her head was reeling. It was hard to think straight.

Mike left fairly promptly after finishing his tea. 'We'll definitely vote for you,' he said again before leaving.

'Thanks,' Caroline gave him a little wave.

Ronan called at lunchtime, looking immensely strained. Caroline wanted to throw her arms around him and beg forgiveness, but for some reason just sat there saying nothing.

'Okay,' he said solemnly, 'the good news or the bad?'

'Both,' Caroline sighed, 'Not that I honestly believe any good can come out of all of this.'

'The good news is that the rights to the show have been sold to Japan and New Zealand.'

'Well, that's good for you maybe, but I don't see how it can be good for me,' Caroline was candid.

'The show is prepared to offer the contestants €10,000 each to go back to Spain and appear on the show live until the last person leaves the house.'

'10,000! Jesus. But hang on a minute, what are you saying? Are you telling me I'd have to live in the house in Marbella with those crackpots? 'Cos I wouldn't do that for a million euro.'

'Wouldn't you?'

Caroline laughed. 'Well maybe for a million . . .'

'Will you do it for €10,000?'

Caroline looked at him, captivated by his steady gaze. If only he wasn't so damn handsome and impossible to refuse. 'What's in all of this for you Ronan Dexter?' she asked him quietly.

''Cos I know you're not persuading me out of the goodness of your heart. And anyway, why have the show's rules changed so suddenly?'

Ronan sat down and eyed her steadily. 'That's what this morning's emergency meeting was all about,' he explained. 'We all know that the happiest couple thing isn't working any more. But the public are hooked. They want to know more and more about you guys. The advertisers are prepared to pay over the odds. The show's got to go on.'

'Who gets the house?'

'Last one out.' Ronan said.

'Good God. What has Richard said?'

'He's agreed. Come on, he can't like living back with his folks so he kind of needs a place to stay anyway.'

'And the others? Donal and Nina?'

'They were the first to agree.'

'Even Emily-Ann?'

'Uh huh.'

'So everything depends on me, does it?' Caroline teased him with a slow smile.

'That's right,' Ronan pushed the hair from her face and gave her a slow stolen kiss on the lips. Her heart soared. 'I thought we weren't allowed to kiss,' she smiled.

'Well I made up that rule so I can break it,' he nuzzled her ear. 'It's just so hard to wait for this damn show to be over with. I can't stand you holding Richard's hand in front of the cameras all day long.'

'You're telling me. I just can't wait for it all to be over,' Caroline sighed. 'But tell me, what are the rules from now on? Do the public vote us out one by one or what?'

'No,' Ronan explained. 'The last to leave the house voluntarily, wins.'

'Ah Jesus,' Caroline exclaimed, 'That's madness. Richard could stick it out for the next two years! You've no idea what he's like.'

'Don't I?' Ronan sounded surprised. 'I've a fair idea.'

'Do you know something I don't know?'

'Well, I believe your ex-fiancé is already in talks with our producers about hosting an Irish version of *Blind Date* and I hear from a very good source that he's agreed to a behind the scenes 'tell all' to a certain paper for a substantial sum.'

'Christ.'

'You don't know the half of it Caroline. You're well shot of him.'

'Yeah, well, I guess I just always fall for the wrong ones, don't I?'

Ronan fiddled with his hands, 'Well, I'm not too bad,' he said quietly before looking up expectantly, 'Am I?'

Caroline stared straight into his eyes. 'Who says I've fallen for you?'

'Haven't you?'

Caroline refused to answer. She just didn't trust herself. She simply smiled and he returned the smile. Awkwardly.

He knew.

Chapter Sixty-Five

Richard, Caroline, Graham, Emily-Ann, Nina and Donal flew first class to Malaga. Again. Ronan was with them this time. Although he wasn't staying in the house. Unfortunately. Caroline would have given anything to spend a bit more time with him. Their feelings were obvious now, to both of them. She couldn't wait to touch him, kiss him, throw her arms around him, lose herself in him. The separation was torture.

Ronan, Mikey Mark and Jack were staying at the luxurious Puente Romana hotel about not too far from Puerto Banus. It would be hard to resist the temptation to escape and try and sneak into his hotel.

Media attention was escalating at an enormous rate. The fans were even in Marbella this time. A couple of hopefuls hung around the gates with autograph books, desperate for a glimpse of their favourite 'star'.

'This is crazy,' Nina commented to Ronan as they peered out through the windows at the autograph collectors. It's worse than *You're a Star*.'

'No, he said with a wink, 'It's a lot better.'

Inside the house, the mood was fragile. The cameras were only going to be switched on for 12 hours a day. The producers had agreed that 24-hour coverage would be too tedious with only six housemates. Thank God for that anyway, Caroline thought. Things were bad enough as they were. Graham was jittery, Emily-Ann cautious, Richard on edge and Caroline fraught with tension. She just knew that every day in this godforsaken house was going to feel like a year.

Richard no longer felt compelled to drape his arm around Caroline's shoulder as before.

There was no point. Now that everybody knew the truth. The producers had allowed virtually no means of entertainment. The contestants were not allowed to leave the villa this time.

But at least, they had their own rooms. Well, except for Nina and Donal . . . they were delighted to have bagged the ensuite jacuzzi.

Each contestant was worried.

How would they cope being cooped up like this?

It was worse than a chamber of horrors.

Emily-Ann longed to get out and give her credit card a bit of exercise.

Richard yearned for a game of golf.

Caroline sat in her room trying to read a book.

But the words only blurred in front of her eyes.

All she could think about was Ronan.

Nina tried to get a few conversations started but failed miserably.

Apart from Graham's entertaining dance routines, there was virtually no entertainment at all. The rain bucketed down outside and the pool was too cold to swim in anyway. Caroline wondered what they were supposed to do in order to amuse each other or themselves. Now the Australians had disappeared, there wasn't even the possibility of anyone conveniently dropping a towel to whet the public's appetite.

And you had to be thankful for that.

And there would be no hanky panky.

Obviously.

Unless Nina and Donal got it together.

Not the most entertaining thought.

The show's production team were more than a little uneasy.

They were facing a crisis.

The viewers would switch off without a bit of scandal.

Something had to be thought of.

And fast.

Then somebody came up with the novel idea.

How about a phone-in?

Live from the house.

Where viewers could pose questions.

And receive answers.

It sounded good.

Worth a try anyway.

The phone in was all set for 9:45 the following evening.

Emily-Ann's caller was first. A guy from Co. Offaly. He thought she was the most beautiful woman in the world.

'Thank you,' Emily-Ann preened into the cameras, 'that's very sweet of you.'

Teeth gritted.

The next call was also for Emily-Ann. It was Joe her 'model' agent.

Emily-Ann frowned for a minute.

Then remembered who he was.

'Like hell you are,' Emily-Ann spluttered into the camera. 'I'm not with you or with Sandy's model agency so I wish you'd stop pretending I am. I represent myself so thank you and good-bye.'

Click.

Next call.

For Graham.

'Hi Graham, it's Timmy, remember me Sweetie?'

Graham didn't.

Click.

A call for Caroline.

'It's your mam.'

Cheering heard in background.

'We're so proud.'

'Thanks Mam.'

Mikey Mark stepped in.

'Looks like you've your own private fan club there Caroline. Next caller please.'

'Hang on,' Caroline objected loudly, 'You can't just cut off my family like that.'

But they did.

'And now we have a call for Richard,' Mikey Mark said with a menacing leer. This should be interesting to say the least. The caller had been talking to the show's researcher for at least 20 minutes!

'Richard?' the soft fragile female voice came down the line.

Richard swallowed. Who the hell was this?

'It's Wendy.'

Richard stared at the cameras blankly.

No recollection.

There must be some kind of mistake.

But apparently not.

'It's Wendy, Richard,' the voice persisted. 'Remember me from that night in Temple Bar? I didn't ever think I'd get to see you again. I couldn't believe it when I saw you on the telly.'

Richard swallowed again, more uncomfortably this time.

'I don't know who you are.'

'Gosh Richard, that's disappointing,' said the voice, which was turning out to be not so fragile anymore, 'Don't you remember telling me I was the sexiest woman in the world?'

Richard shook his head. This was a wind up.

It had to be. Maybe one of Sandra's friends was taking the mickey. It wasn't very funny anyway.

'Do you want me to go on Richard? Would you like me to fill you in?'

Jack the cameraman, was trying to stifle his laughter. Caroline, Graham and Emily-Ann looked at Richard expectantly. His brow was accumulating hundreds of beads of sweat. Emily-Ann considerately offered him a tissue.

'I've no comment to make,' Richard shuffled in his seat uncomfortably. 'You must be mistaking me for someone else.'

'Ah yes,' the woman called Wendy, 'funny that you should mention that; I thought I was mistaken too ha, ha, when I saw you posing as one of the happiest couples in Ireland.'

Richard looked frantically across the room but nobody would catch his eye. Why wasn't anybody doing anything? Why wasn't this woman being cut off? This was outrageous!

'Then of course I heard that another woman was pregnant by you and I thought "Ah yes that sounds more like my Richard".'

Richard was speechless. Everybody watched him intently. Waiting for some kind of reaction.

'Well don't you have any response to that?' Mikey Mark honed in. 'What about this other pregnant bird then?'

Richard squirmed visibly.

'She's my ex-best friend,' Caroline piped up suddenly.

Even Mikey Mark was taken aback. What was Caroline talking about? What was all this about a best friend? Why had nobody told him anything?

'This is blasphemy,' Richard announced in a rage. 'I'm not putting up with this.'

'Anyone is welcome to leave at any time,' Mikey Mark said gleefully. He'd give anything for Richard's departure. He'd never met such an obnoxious bastard in his entire career in TV and boy had he met some right pricks in his time.

Richard didn't look like he was going anywhere though.

'I've no comment to make.'

'I'll bet you don't,' Mikey Mark muttered before taking the next call.

It was for Emily-Ann.

'Hi Emily-Ann,' the fake-happy tone could be heard clearly on air. 'It's your best friend Celine. I haven't seen you in ages, I'm looking forward to hooking up with you on a brilliant girls' night out once you're out of there.'

Emily-Ann just stared into the camera.

'Actually Celine, I have seen you recently,' she said in a decided voice, 'at a set of traffic lights. Only you didn't recognise me. And for your info, I am not looking forward to seeing you again. Ever.'

Click.

Caroline and the others gazed at Emily-Ann in amazement. What was that all about?

Mikey Mark was keen to keep the momentum going.

A call for Donal.

'Donal, it's your da, you're to bleeding come home right now and stop the messing, d'ya hear? I can't handle the January car sales by meself. The showrooms are being mobbed. So get back here now this minute and remember folks, Nelligan & Son Motors, open for business, seven days a . . .'

'Cut him off,' Ronan ordered.

Another call for Richard.

He groaned inwardly. Would they ever just get off his back?

'It's Jane,' the female voice could be heard clearly. 'I was just wondering Richard if you were going to keep your promise?'

'What promise?' he asked alarmed, his face reddening at an unbelievable rate.

'Remember?' she prodded, 'You told me if I kept quiet, the house would be ours . . . so I did . . . keep quiet that is . . . until now . . . it seems that I am not indeed the only woman that you had in mind for the house . . . and it would seem also that Caroline and Sandra are not really the needy idiots you made them out to be, are they now?'

Mikey Mark nearly shouted for joy. He hadn't really thought the PR people could pull this one out of the hat. It was unfucking believable.

Caroline herself was smiling. She couldn't help it. Despite everything, this was one of the funniest things she'd ever experienced. Especially when she saw that Richard was pulling his microphone off in a temper. She tried not to laugh out loud as he threw it to the ground.

Ronan quickly called for an ad break.

Richard stormed out of the house, ranting and raving about defamation and about all the influential people he knew back in Dublin who would get to the bottom of this.

Caroline looked after him in shock. God, what kind of person was he anyway? Had he really promised some other girl the dream home? He was mad in the head. Definitely. He needed professional help. Where did he get off messing people about? Ah well, it looked like he had certainly got his come-uppance now. Good riddance, she thought as he disappeared. As long as she never had to lay eyes on him again . . .

Chapter Sixty-Six

'RICHARD THE RAT'.

That's what *The News on Sunday* dubbed him.

And somebody had donated a picture of Richard's arse to another tabloid.

BUTT OUT, was the headline.

Caroline could hardly control her laughter. She knew exactly where that photo had come from.

Sandra had taken it at a party years ago.

The revenged woman eh?

Hell hath no fury and all of that.

Emily-Ann, Nina and Caroline lay sprawled on the floor of the dream house, listening to music, surrounded by the tabloids.

Graham hadn't got out of bed yet.

Or maybe he had and was now blowing bubbles in the jacuzzi.

Donal was nowhere to be seen either.

'Richard really is a nasty piece of work,' said Emily-Ann. 'You are so well shot of him. See here, he calls Caroline and myself the greedy duo in this so-called "exclusive". Imagine that. How dare he! There's nothing greedy about me.'

'He calls me a penny-pincher,' Nina said, 'and that's not true either.'

Emily-Ann and Caroline exchanged glances but said nothing.

'I'm beginning to feel exhausted,' Caroline said quietly, 'I just want to forget the whole thing. Coming on this show has really changed my perspective on things.'

'Me too,' Emily-Ann admitted, 'I've just realised how shallow people can be. God, when I think of that Celine one ringing the show pretending to be my best friend . . .'

'Was she ever a friend of yours?'

Emily-Ann told her about the 'modelling' incident.

At Baggot Street traffic lights.

Caroline was intrigued.

'You see, that's why I so badly wanted to win. I thought the show would open doors to the modelling world and I think it will now.'

'Maybe so,' Caroline agreed, 'Richard wanted publicity too . . . and he's certainly got that for himself,' she added with a chuckle.

'Who do you think will win the place?' Emily-Ann asked.

'Dunno,' Caroline said resignedly, 'to be honest my heart isn't in it any more. I don't want the media hassling my family now or people ringing up ex-boyfriends looking for topless photos.'

'Would they do that?' Nina looked horrified.

'Well you saw the photo of Richard's bum gracing a front page, didn't you?'

Emily-Ann and Nina stared at the photo sombrely. Suddenly it didn't seem quite so funny anymore. Neither of them wanted to draw that kind of attention on to themselves or drag up any more unwanted publicity.

'I can't wait to get out of here,' Caroline said suddenly. 'I mean, don't get me wrong, the house is to die for but I don't like the way we're cooped up in here and not allowed to go out. It's worse than prison.'

Emily-Ann stood up. 'Let's go and haul Graham out of bed, let's see what he thinks.'

They wandered into Graham's room.

Graham's bed was empty.

No sign of him.

He wasn't in the jacuzzi either.

No.

He was nowhere to be found.

Baffling!

Eventually Caroline found a note, propped up on his pillow. She gave a little scream, 'Jesus, he's deserted us,' she laughed.

'Read it,' Emily-Ann urged.

COULDN'T BEAR TO SPEND ANOTHER NIGHT WITHOUT BARNEY. ENJOY LIVING IN THE HOUSE.

'He must have escaped out the window,' Emily-Ann

noted. She gave a little sigh. 'God, it's so romantic. I'd love someone to love me enough to give all this up for me. One day I'm going to meet someone whose going to love me more than anything else on the planet and I don't care how long it takes. I'm not settling for anything less.'

Donal appeared in the doorway. Nobody took any notice. Until Nina spotted his suitcase. 'Where the hell are *you* going?'

'I've to go back. I'm feeling guilty as hell leaving Da at home to run the business. He says he's got hacks in all the time looking for me baby photos and what not.'

'Can't your mother deal with them?' Emily-Ann asked.

'Me mam's ill. Very ill.'

Nina stared at him, silenced. She felt dreadful. Why had he never said anything before this? The poor lad. No wonder he felt guilty about being out here.

'I'm very sorry,' Caroline was the first to speak.

'I'm sorry too,' Emily-Ann echoed her.

Nina stood up, went over to him and gave him a hug. 'You should have told me,' she said quietly.

'Ah you know, I didn't really want to talk about it, you know, burdening other people with my problems. I dunno, maybe that's not a good thing. But I'd better be going, I've a taxi booked. Keep in touch girls yeah?'

'If I win the house, you'll still get half,' Nina insisted.

'Don't be worrying about me now, sure I've got me €10,000. I rang Ronan's hotel room this morning to tell him. Well I'll be off then. See you soon Nina.'

He was gone.

'Poor guy,' Caroline said.

'I'm still in shock,' Nina said.

Emily-Ann looked at her oddly. 'I can't believe you didn't know . . . I mean . . . you two being so close and all that.'

Nina blushed. 'We weren't that close,' she admitted. 'In fact we only kind of got back together 'cos of the show.'

'Get away.'

'No, it's true, I'm pathetic aren't I?'

Caroline shook her head, 'That would make three of us.'

'The funny thing is though . . .' Nina said quietly. 'The funny thing is . . . I really think I love him now. More than ever.'

She stared at the closed door. It was true though. She did love him. She had the kind of love for Donal that Emily-Ann was talking about. And yet she was sitting here, letting that love walk away from her. It didn't make any sense, did it?

She got to her feet.

She didn't have much time to lose. She had to go after him. It wasn't as if the house was going to be hers anyway. Caroline was the favourite and

Emily-Ann, Ireland's answer to Cindy Crawford, had a zillion fans. But Donal was a wonderful person and Nina knew she was never going to ever meet anyone more down to earth. Forget the doctors and the dentists and all the 'good' catches. How somebody treated you was more important than what they did for a living.

Far more important.

She walked towards the door.

'Donal,' she called. 'Wait for me.'

Ronan arrived at the villa. This was an emergency and he had an announcement to make.

It was time to take a general vote from the public.

To decide the winner of the house.

Sexual tension, he insisted, was the main reason people tuned into this kind of show. Without it, viewers would switch off. His decision was greeted by immense relief from both girls. Neither of them had particularly wanted to battle it out.

So this was it.

The party was over.

It was time to go home.

Chapter Sixty-Seven

The doors of the villa were flung open to the media. Extra photographers and cameramen had flown in from Ireland and were now pushing their way into the disco room.

The girls were sitting behind a long table with nothing but two glasses of water in front of them.

A chilled bottle of Dom Perignon was on stand-by.

For the winner.

The girls were incredibly nervous.

Under the scrutiny of the camera.

The viewers had already voted.

Mikey Mark was about to deliver the verdict.

'Girls,' he crooned into his enormous microphone, 'it's a sad state of affairs to see two such beauuuuuuutiful women up here without a man in sight. Now, what does that say about our society at all at all at all?'

Nobody said anything.

The silence was insufferable.

Camera bulbs flashed.

Would he ever just get on with it?

'Of course,' Mikey Mark continued in menacing tones, 'Graham, Richard, Donal and Nina send their love and are sorry they can't be here with you tonight.'

Some members of the press tittered as the girls shifted uncomfortably in their seats. Caroline took a gulp of water.

The verdict was ready to be given.

The phone lines had closed.

You could hear a pin drop.

Mikey Mark waved the envelope in front of the girls' faces. He was clearly loving every minute of this.

The sound of a drum rolled.

Caroline bit her lip anxiously.

Emily-Ann wondered if her make-up looked okay. It was pretty hot in here. She hoped she wasn't going to start sweating.

'And the winner is . . .' Mikey Mark's voice boomed across the room.

Caroline closed her eyes. Her mouth felt dry. The silence was deafening. God, would they ever just get on with it?

'CAROLINE. Hip, Hip, HURRRRRRAAAAAH-HHHH.'

Caroline opened her eyes, shocked to the core. Had she heard right? Had they really called out her name? Oh God, OH GOD!

Emily-Ann's heart sank to the bottom of her Prada
heels. 'Well done Caroline,' she said throwing heavy
arms around her rival contestant. She'd watched
enough Miss Worlds to know that this was what
you were supposed to do. Whatever you felt, no
matter how devastated or angry, you had to pretend
you were happy.

Happiness.

There was so much emphasis on that bloody
word.

Wasn't there?

She tried to fight back the tears.

After all, this was only a game.

All of it.

And the whole world was playing.

Pretending to be happy.

But there were cheats playing this game too.

Ruining it for everybody else.

And that's why Emily-Ann didn't mind losing
this round. Too much. Her turn would come. Yes,
it would. Because there were no everlasting winners
in this game.

The happiest couple in Ireland?

No such thing.

The show had proved it.

She stepped down from the table. To hell with the
house – it wasn't the end of the world. Once she was
a supermodel she'd have homes all over the world;
maybe one day a yacht in Puerto Banus where she
could sit on deck sipping champers. It was worth

working for, worth fighting for, worth giving up nights in front of the TV for, and long wasteful hours in pubs talking about nothing.

They said money didn't make you happy. And that was partly true. But only partly. Because of course, nothing made you happy forever. Only a fool would think otherwise. Happiness was only ever short term.

But then again having money was better than having none. Emily-Ann believed that firmly. Because how many people, if they won the lottery, would give all their money away? How many people when offered a pay rise would go 'Ah no thanks, I'm grand with what I have'?

Wasn't it funny the way people who said 'Money doesn't make you happy' were the type of people who were probably never going to make any money anyway?

Emily-Ann liked to think of herself as realistic. She wanted to be wealthy for the power it would give her. So that she'd never be in a job she hated – because she couldn't afford to leave. So that she'd never be a penniless spouse asking her husband for the price of a new pair of tights. Never again have to stand on a street corner in a catsuit giving freebies to rude car drivers, nor put up with the ignorance of other rich people snubbing her, not thinking she was good enough. Like her old friend Celine, who had insulted her at a time when she'd been feeling most vulnerable.

She wanted money, not to make other people feel inferior or to make herself feel superior, but for the freedom it would give her. So that if someone desperately needed her help, she wouldn't have to hesitate. She could just write a cheque. Like her dad had done when she'd told him about the old women in the home Caroline worked in. And how they had no money to travel to Marbella for a week's holiday. He hadn't had to sit down with a pen and paper, to figure out if he could afford to write the cheque without having to sell the family fridge. No, he'd just asked Emily-Ann what amount would be needed. And signed.

And that was a kind of happiness, wasn't it?

To able to do stuff like that.

Wasn't that happiness . . . in a sense?

Well at least Emily-Ann hadn't won the house, Nina thought to herself as she wiped a lone tear from her eye. She was sitting in Beaumount Hospital watching the TV with Donal's arm around her. His mother was going to be okay, thank God. She'd got the 'all clear' just minutes beforehand. But Nina didn't have any regrets about coming home early. Donal would have done the exact same for her. And that kind of loyalty was priceless.

But at least Caroline had won the house. If Emily-Ann had won, it would have been just too hard to stomach. Still, Nina thought, she'd done very well getting to the final three. Nina from nowhere who'd never even gone to college. Now everyone in the country would know who she was. And maybe the attention wouldn't be too bad at all. And she might find herself inundated with all kinds of requests now. To turn up to things. Celebrities sometimes got a couple of grand just to show up at events.

She'd read that somewhere.

A grand just to turn up and say a few words.

Or say nothing.

And failing that, at least Tele-Fone would be delighted with all the coverage she'd granted them throughout all her interviews. So maybe they'd promote her when she got back.

And think of all the parties she'd get invited to. Sure remember that one Narinder from *Big Brother*? Every time Nina borrowed a magazine, she saw Narinder at something or another with a glass of wine in her hand.

It wasn't all over yet. No. The hype wouldn't go away for a long time. And there *had* been offers. It's just . . . it's just . . . she wasn't sure if they were the right offers. It was very hard to know, wasn't it? One newspaper editor had got hold of her number and had been keen to offer her a column.

Nina had nearly dropped the phone in shock. Her own column – imagine that! Excitedly she'd asked him what kind of column it was. Just in case. She didn't want to do a Dear Nina . . . kind of thing where people wrote in about sexual fantasies.

The editor had explained that it was a kind of

financial column. Nina had frowned. A financial column? How bizarre. It wasn't like she was an economist or anything. How on earth did he think she'd be qualified to write something like that? Maybe the editor was mistaking her for someone else.

'Are you sure you're looking for me?' Nina asked in a small voice. 'After all, I've no experience doing that sort of stuff.'

'No experience?' the editor had laughed. 'You must be joking. You're exactly what our readers need. Most of our readers are in debt but with a bit of advice from you, they'll be back in the clear in no time.'

'How's that?' Nina wasn't sure if she liked where this conversation was going.

'Our readers don't identify with men in grey suits peering out at them with money advice. But they know your face from *The Happiest Couple in Ireland* and they love you. Everyone knows that you wouldn't spend Christmas but they love you anyway, do you know what I mean?'

Nina had been too shocked to answer. Her ears were smarting, her heartbeat was thunderous. What on earth was he saying to her? Did the nation think she was stingy? Good God, she wasn't tight. Absolutely not! She was 'careful' all right, but that was different. You had to be careful in this day and age with people trying to rip you off left, right and centre. But she wasn't mean. No way. It was out of the question. She wasn't mean at all. They'd all got it wrong.

'Can I ring you back about this please?' she'd asked him before putting down the phone and waiting until her breathing returned to its normal state.

She discussed the job offer with Donal. She asked him outright if he thought she was mean. He hadn't said no straight away and Nina had been shocked. She remembered what her own cousin Sheena had said. And she remembered a couple of comments Emily-Ann had made on the holiday. Good God, maybe people did think she was mean. How terrible.

Donal told her not too worry too much about what other people said. Donal said he didn't think she was mean but he did think she was frugal which was apparently a different matter altogether. Donal said it didn't bother him though because his last girlfriend had had a gambling problem and it had wrecked their relationship. He said he found Nina's attitude to money quite refreshing. The last girl had sold his computer without telling him and bet the money on horses.

Nina had been horrified. She couldn't understand how anybody could gamble money like that. Donal said it was an illness. Just a very sad illness.

Nina thought about the job offer carefully. And in the end decided to turn it down. It just wasn't for her, she thought. She wanted to do something else. Get more out of life. She didn't want to be known as the person who simply gave advice on cutting out coupons and making two cups of tea from the one tea-bag. And anyway, now that she'd be getting a bit of money from various things off the back of the show, she didn't want to be thinking of millions of ways to save anymore. That had been all right in the days when she'd had no money. The days when she'd been afraid to spend for fear of going cold or hungry. Just like she'd done as a child. Back in Mullingar when her da had been on the dole with seven mouths to feed. It was time to move on now. Time to buy herself a few nice things. Bring her mother on a well-deserved holiday or something. She was never going to be poor again. She knew that now. So let that editor get someone else to do his column.

Chapter Sixty-Eight

'I'm not planning on living in Marbella full-time. Not yet anyway,' Caroline smiled at the flock of reporters. A small press conference had been organised for Caroline in the Holiday Inn.

'You said, Caroline,' one reporter thrust his mike in her face, 'that the other contestants were more than welcome to go down anytime for a holiday. That's very generous of you. Does that invitation extend to Richard?'

Caroline felt her body tense up. *Take a deep breath*, she told herself, *and relax. It's nearly all over now*. 'No,' she said politely but firmly, 'No it does not.'

'I believe Nina was offered a travel programme called *Around Ireland on a budget*,' interjected another reporter.

'Was she? I hadn't heard. Well I'm delighted for her.'

'What about you? Any film offers? I believe your dream is to be an actor.'

'Well we'll see,' Caroline said diplomatically, 'I'm

a realist and I'll audition like everybody else but yes, I'd like to give it a go.'

'Do you think Emily-Ann is Ireland's answer to Cindy Crawford?'

'I think,' Caroline smiled, 'that Emily-Ann is a beautiful girl in her own right. She doesn't need to be compared with anybody.'

'And finally Caroline, now that Richard is out of your life is there anybody else you might consider entertaining in your new villa?'

Caroline paused. Her eyes found Ronan's gazing at her from among the crowd, gazing at her in that way that he did. A way that made her feel that nothing in the world was as important as the way she felt about him. 'Yes,' she said quietly, 'yes there is.'

'Would you care to give us a name?'

God this was a bit embarrassing, wasn't it? Caroline thought, as the bright camera lights nearly blinded her. It was like the end scene in *Notting Hill*, wasn't it?

Only it wasn't.

Not really.

Not at all in fact.

Because this was real life.

Real life, where people let you down and unreciprocated love was more common than any other kind.

Where people that seemed happiest of all, weren't really happy. And Ronan wasn't putting up his hand the way Hugh Grant did. No. Because this wasn't a big Hollywood movie, was it? And she wasn't Julia Roberts playing a leading role. No. She was just

Caroline. Caroline on reality TV. Reality. She hated that word. It was so dreary. Reality. Ugh. Bring back escapism. Bring back Hollywood.

'Well, I'm not really sure where I stand with him at the moment,' Caroline answered eventually, 'but if anything happens, you'll all be the first to know.'

'Finally, there's a rumour going around that you plan to open the doors of the villa to elderly Irish women for a period every summer. How true are these rumours? Would you care to elaborate?'

'I don't want to go on about it too much but yes that is part of my plan for the villa. It's very easy for us to close our eyes to what has, and in a way still is, going on in Ireland. The economy in Ireland is pretty good now and most people can go on at least two foreign holidays a year.'

She paused and took a deep breath.

'But I happen to know of some people who have never set foot outside Ireland and never will, unless they get help in some way. I don't want to name these people. Everybody has their pride. But I'd like to thank all the companies who have donated so kindly to the show and sponsored the contestants. I have had a cheque from one anonymous donor to help fund the travel arrangements for the elderly to go over to the villa.'

'So you're not planning on throwing any wild parties down there yourself?'

'Wild parties? Me? In Puerto Banus? In a villa with

a private bar, a dance floor and a jacuzzi upstairs? What do you think? I'm not a nun you know.'

The crowd laughed. The press conference was over. Caroline breathed a happy sigh of relief. She felt she could go to bed now and sleep for a week.

One by one they disappeared until finally Ronan and Caroline were left facing each other.

'Well done,' Ronan kissed her. 'I'm so proud of you. I know the show has been far from easy. Are you sure this is what you want?' he enquired gently.

'Absolutely,' Caroline insisted. 'It's my own idea. I want something good to come out of this. Else it will all have been for nothing. I didn't work for any of this you know. I just got lucky.'

She rested her head against his chest.

And closed her eyes momentarily.

She felt safe in his arms. And happy. Yes, happy.

'Of course I'm not sure where I go from here,' she said slowly, 'after all I can hardly go back to the nursing home now or back to Tele-Fone, can I?'

'You don't have to go back,' Ronan assured her. 'In fact a couple of casting agents have tried to get in touch with you since the airing of the show.'

Caroline took a step back and eyed him quizzically. 'What are you talking about?'

'Actually, there's been more than a few requests for you,' he smiled.

'Really? Why didn't you tell me before?'

'I didn't want to distract you from the show. I couldn't, the show was my first priority, and besides

I was terrified that the media might pick up on, you know . . . us.'

'Us?' Caroline could feel herself blushing furiously and then stared at the ground.

But Ronan persisted. 'I saw you catch my eye back then. I'm the guy you were talking about back there, right?'

Caroline felt herself go scarlet.

'I should have put my hand up back there, shouldn't I? But I couldn't – it's just not my personality. I'm just shy really.'

'You're shy? Get away.'

'Caroline, I've liked you since day one. Actually "like" doesn't even come close to the way I feel about you. Ever since the night I bumped into you after that party I've been hooked. But I genuinely didn't want to jeopardise your chances in the show. Dating the producer would have been a disastrous move.'

Caroline broke into a smile. She just couldn't win with him.

'Hey, look at me Caro, I have to go back to America next week. More meetings with producers over there. If they end up buying the US rights to the show, there'll be no end to your popularity.'

'Well, I'll miss you,' she said hesitantly. She really would. She didn't care about being massively popular or about people running up to her looking for autographs. She just hated the fact that Ronan was about to disappear on her yet again.

'Miss me?' Ronan raised an eyebrow. 'I'm not going to give you the chance to miss me Caroline Kreevan.'

'Huh?'

'I've bought you an open ticket. Come with me. If you don't like it over there you can always come home early.'

Caroline wasn't sure what to say. Her mind was racing.

'And Caroline? I've been thinking, we might not ever be happy enough to win *The Happiest Couple in Ireland*,' he said with a grin, 'but there's no harm giving it a bash.'

'What do you mean?' she stepped back from him. 'What are you talking about?'

'Well I hear that next summer *The Happiest Couple in Ireland 2* will be made. How about it? I reckon we might win. We've as much of a chance as anybody.'

'Are you serious?' Caroline said, beginning to laugh. 'What's the prize?'

'A dream house,' he said in a deadpan voice. 'On the moon.'

'God, you're an awful messer,' she pretended to hit him.

'Hey, stop that,' he caught her arm, drew her into him, and kissed her.

The game was over.

She'd won.

Won the house, the man.

By God, she'd even managed to win back her pride.

And now she was ready to take on the world.

Maggie was just sitting there. Alone. Staring out the window. At the trees. Delicate rosary beads entwined in her rough course hands.

Her grey eyes lit up as she recognised Caroline coming along the corridor.

'You're not coming back, are you?'

'No Maggie,' Caroline sat down, shaking her head. 'But I'll be back to visit. Often.'

'You're a star now, on the telly.'

'But I'm not a star, not really, just ordinary Caroline enjoying her 15 minutes of fame.'

'I loved the house in Spain. Fit for a queen so it was. Was it as nice as on the telly?'

'Nicer Maggie, but you'll see for yourself soon enough. We're taking you down there for at least a week.'

'I don't know if the nuns will let me.'

'Of course they will, I've already spoken to Sr Breege about it. And Emily-Ann, one of the contestants, said she knew a man who was willing to pay for the flights. So everything's sorted.'

'I love Spain.' Maggie took the dog-eared faded photo from her cardigan pocket.

Of her brother.

Caroline stared at the photo of the young man standing in the sea. He was slim, tanned and happy-go-lucky with wavy dark-blond hair. He didn't really look like Maggie. No. Not at all. She couldn't see any resemblance. 'He's very good-looking.'

'I wasn't bad looking either,' Maggie said as if reading Caroline's thoughts. 'But he was the best,' her eyes filled with tears. 'He was a heartbreaker.'

She stared into space.

'I love children, I do. I love them,' she said sadly.

Suddenly everything fell into place. Good God. Caroline felt a shiver shoot along her spine. It was all so clear. The man in the photo. That man. Of course. He wasn't her brother at all, was he?

That was it! He was the reason why Maggie waited in the hallway every Sunday. Waiting for him.

The man who would never call.

Caroline looked into Maggie's eyes and took her hand.

'When did you last see him?'

'1945.'

Caroline felt a big lump getting caught in her throat. She was determined not to get over emotional in front of the old woman. But it all made sense now. Everything did.

They'd taken her baby.

But she hadn't let them take away the photo.

It was all she had left.

A photograph.

'What happened Maggie?' Caroline took the photo

and gently held it up to the light. 'What happened to the man in the photo?'

'He married Eileen,' Maggie fiddled with her rosary beads. 'I knew her well. A quiet girl. Her da owned the pub and the grocery shop. They couldn't have children though. Our da had no money. I love these rosary beads, aren't they lovely?' she whispered. 'They were blessed by a priest.'

Caroline said nothing. She just sat there, thinking.

In the distance a police siren could be heard.

Nothing else.

Caroline sat in silence. It was best; best to say nothing at all.

'Some people said . . .' Maggie fingered the beads and looked up suddenly, 'some people said . . . they were the happiest couple in Ireland.'

Caroline looked into her faded-grey eyes.

But Maggie was far away.

From St Bridget's.

From the bleak damp corridors.

With their ghastly smell of detergent.

And cold stone floors.

'And were they?' Caroline asked, almost whispering.

She thought she saw a slight flicker of a smile dance on the old woman's lined lips.

But maybe she imagined it.

'I don't think anyone will ever know the answer to that Caroline,' Maggie spoke eventually.

In a voice so quiet it was barely audible.

THE END.